Praise for *Beneath the Surface*

"This vivid start of Blackburn's Dive Team Investigations series [is] a real page-turner."

Booklist

"Fans of Dani Pettrey's Alaskan Courage thrillers will enjoy this nail-biter of a series opener."

Library Journal

"Award-winning author Lynn H. Blackburn grabs readers by the throat and doesn't let go until the final heart-pounding page."

Fresh Fiction

"Lynn H. Blackburn is an amazing new voice in romantic suspense—don't miss her!"

Lynette Eason, bestselling and award-winning author of the Hidden Identity series

"[Blackburn's] exceptional storytelling skills shine as she weaves an intricate plot, populated with characters we care deeply about. Another up-all-night-because-I-can't-put-down-the-book read."

Edie Melson, award-winning author, blogger, and director of the Blue Ridge Mountains Christian Writers Conference

"*Beneath the Surface* is a swoon-worthy romantic suspense that packs a punch from page one. The nonstop action will keep you guessing until the end."

Rachel Dylan, author of the Atlanta Justice series

"Just when you think you can relax, Blackburn brings you back to the edge of your seat in this riveting, high-tension suspense story."

Patricia Bradley, author of *Justice Delayed*

IN TOO
DEEP

Books by Lynn H. Blackburn

DIVE TEAM INVESTIGATIONS

Beneath the Surface
In Too Deep

IN TOO DEEP

LYNN H. BLACKBURN

Revell

a division of Baker Publishing Group
Grand Rapids, Michigan

Published by Revell
a division of Baker Publishing Group
PO Box 6287, Grand Rapids, MI 49516-6287
www.revellbooks.com

Printed in the United States of America

Library of Congress Cataloging-in-Publication Data
Names: Blackburn, Lynn Huggins, author.
Title: In too deep / Lynn H. Blackburn.
Description: Grand Rapids, MI : Published by Revell, a division of Baker Publishing
     Group, [2018] | Series: Dive team investigations ; [2]
Identifiers: LCCN 2018020579 | ISBN 9780800729295 (paper : alk. paper)
Subjects: | GSAFD: Mystery fiction. | Suspense fiction. | Christian fiction.
Classification: LCC PS3602.L325285 I56 2018 | DDC 813/.6—dc23
LC record available at https://lccn.loc.gov/2018020579

18   19   20   21   22   23   24   7 6 5 4 3 2 1

To Drew—my favorite blue-eyed boy. My warrior child. You've had me wrapped around your little finger from day one. You're fierce and tender, serious and silly, and I'm amazed that God allowed me to be your mom. I know God has big plans for you, and while I'm in no hurry for you to grow up, I'm excited to see what he has in store for you. I love you!

Acknowledgments

Writing a series requires a long-term commitment from the author as well as from the men and women who've volunteered to help the author. There is no way I could write these stories without the input of a host of experts and the support of family and friends.

Continued gratitude to . . .

Josh Moulin, cybersecurity expert (https://JoshMoulin.com)—for answering long, disjointed emails and patiently explaining everything from hard drives to the dark web. Your willingness to answer my questions was vital to keeping this story on track. All mistakes and misrepresentations of the field are on me.

Mike Berry, Master Underwater Criminal Investigator (UCIDiver.com)—for reading my diving scenes and giving me direction on everything from safely removing a vehicle to how to find a briefcase and detailing which type of search pattern works best. Any mistakes in diving and underwater criminal investigation procedures are mine.

Jonathan Parker, director of city involvement at Fellowship Greenville—your insights into the labor trafficking in my own city and on the streets where I shop and work were crucial to the storyline and have had a permanent impact on the way I see the world I'm living in. Our conversation left me heartbroken, and my prayer is that eyes will be opened and these precious souls will be seen and freed.

Investigator Tim Martin—for explaining the world of white-collar criminal investigations to me and for helping me bring Adam to life in a realistic way.

Sergeant Chris Hammett—for your insights into the life of a homicide investigator and your gracious explanations of police procedures. Thank you for continuing to answer my emails!

Jennifer Huggins Bayne—my sister and favorite nurse practitioner for once again replying to countless texts about hospital procedures and setting me straight about CTs and MRIs and how fast you can get out of the ED. Your patients are blessed to have you advocating for them. And I'm eternally grateful to have you as my sister and my friend.

Mecina Hapthey and Angelina Zimmer—thank you for your insights into Yapese culture and the life of a missionary family. Anissa's character wouldn't exist without you.

Angel Glover—for sharing your experiences and helping me find a layer of complexity that Leigh was missing before your input.

My critique group—for helping me brainstorm this series. The storylines and characters are all richer because of you.

My sisters of The Light Brigade—you've been there for me from the beginning. Your prayers, love, and support are never more than a Facebook message away and I am eternally grateful for you.

Lynette Eason—for believing in me and giving the Carrington dive team such a fun case in one of your books!

Tamela Hancock Murray—my amazing agent. Thank you for your enthusiastic support and continued encouragement.

Andrea Doering—for saying yes to this series and to the crossover idea.

Amy Ballor—for editing this manuscript with an attention to detail that is both terrifying and thrilling.

Sandra Blackburn—for being the most supportive mother-in-law a girl could have and for being willing to do anything to help.

Ken and Susan Huggins—for being the kind of parents who taught me to work hard and love books and for still being there for me whenever I need you. Which is all the time!

Emma, James, and Drew—for still being excited about every new book and for continuing to keep my real world far more interesting than any I could make up.

Brian—without you there would be no stories with my name on them. My imagination never would have taken flight without your encouragement and your continual support and love.

My Savior—the Ultimate Storyteller—for allowing me to write stories for you.

Let the words of my mouth and the meditation of my heart be acceptable in your sight, O LORD, my rock and my redeemer.

~ Psalm 19:14

1

The shrill ping of his cell phone earned white-collar crimes investigator Adam Campbell a vicious glare from his aunt Margaret. His cousins all dropped their gazes to their plates, several of them failing to suppress snickers, as Adam stood. He glanced around the table at the assembled family members before focusing on the matriarch of the family. "Excuse me, Grandmother. Everyone. I'm on call."

Grandmother sniffed. "Very well."

Conversation resumed as Adam made his way around the perimeter of the oval dining room. He refused to look down or run like a frightened schoolboy. He maintained a measured pace and made eye contact with anyone who bothered to look in his direction. He had nothing to be ashamed of.

His parents were in Italy until Thursday, or his mother would have given him an encouraging smile. Oh well.

No one glared at his brother when he was on call. Grandmother never batted an eye when Alexander needed to miss Sunday lunch because he was in surgery. But heaven forbid Adam miss the monthly meal. Keeping the citizens of Carrington, North Carolina, safe was a perfectly good job as far as Grandmother was concerned. But not for a Campbell.

Grandfather Campbell caught his eye.

And winked.

Adam didn't bother trying to hide his smile as he left the room. His grandfather was a rock. They met for breakfast at least once a week at the Pancake Hut, and Adam regaled him with stories from the sheriff's office.

The restaurant was a favorite with the law enforcement and medical communities in Carrington, and Adam's standing breakfast date with his grandfather had gotten a lot of attention when he first joined the force.

The Pancake Hut wasn't the kind of place the Campbell family usually frequented.

As Charles Campbell made it a point to get to know Adam's co-workers by name, Adam's fellow deputies soon realized he might be worth several billion dollars, but he was no snob.

It was a poorly kept secret that Charles Campbell was in the habit of picking up the tab for every law enforcement officer in the Pancake Hut whenever he was there—whether or not he was with Adam.

Grandmother wasn't exactly aware of that arrangement.

Before long, deputies and investigators started coming by Adam's desk and saying, "Yo, Campbell, I've got one for your grandfather. He'll get a kick out of this." Or they'd stop by their booth and share something that had happened while they were on patrol.

Grandfather ate it up.

Over the last few years, Grandfather had managed to fund several scholarships for law enforcement officers, and he'd fallen completely under the spell of homicide investigator Anissa Bell, captain of the Carrington County Sheriff's Office dive team. All Anissa had to do was hint that she'd been eyeing some new piece of equipment for the team and Grandfather made it happen.

Grandmother wasn't exactly aware of that arrangement either. Adam paused in the hallway and looked again at the text that had saved him from another hour of family politics.

Uh-oh. He walked briskly as he maneuvered his way through the library and music room and then hit the marble floor of the large foyer.

"Everything okay, Mr. Adam?" The concerned words from the family's longtime butler slowed his steps.

"Not really, Marcel. A car ran off the highway and over the embankment at the double bridges. Probably last night. A boater found the car this morning."

The double bridges spanned Lake Porter and connected the tourist side of the lake to the city of Carrington. The car would have gone close to a hundred yards over bumpy terrain next to the bridge approach before plunging into the water.

Failed brakes?

Road rage?

Suicide?

It had happened before.

"Was someone in the car?" Marcel asked the question in a low voice.

When Adam nodded in the affirmative, Marcel shook his head in dismay.

Adam's family, and Marcel was family, had come unglued when a car accident took Adam's younger brother, Aaron, at the far-too-young age of ten. None of them had ever completely gotten over it.

"You going to have to get in? It's cold." Marcel handed Adam his coat.

"We have dry suits," Adam said. "We'll be okay."

"Be careful, sir." Marcel opened the door, and Adam broke into a jog. "Thanks, Marcel. Hold the fort."

Marcel's low chuckle reached his ears as he slid behind the wheel and took the turns of the lengthy driveway at a speed that would

15

have gotten him on Grandmother's bad list, if he hadn't already been there.

It took fifteen minutes to reach the double bridges. The bridges had a formal name—after a local politician from the thirties—but no one used it.

He slowed as he approached the roadblock, then pulled in behind fellow dive team member and homicide investigator Gabe Chavez. Gabe climbed out first and met him at the door, giving a low whistle as he looked the Audi over. "When you gonna let me drive this baby?"

This was why he tried not to drive his personal vehicle to crime scenes, but sometimes he didn't have a choice. Grandmother had given him the car for his college graduation—even though he had told her he didn't need it—and she didn't approve of him arriving for Sunday lunch in the unmarked sedan he drove for work.

He held the keys out to Gabe. "Any time."

Gabe eyed the keys, longing evident on his face. "One of these days I'm going to take you up on it."

Adam pulled his bag out of the back, locked the car, and pocketed the keys. He glanced at the line of cars on the side of the road. "Who else is here?"

"Ryan is hiking in the mountains with Leigh," Gabe said. Homicide investigator Ryan Parker was the second-in-command on the dive team. His girlfriend, Leigh Weston, had survived an attack by a serial killer last spring.

"Hiking? Or proposing?"

Gabe grinned. "I guess we'll find out when they get back. He got the text about this, but Anissa told him to disregard it."

"You've talked to Anissa?" Gabe and Anissa hadn't gotten along well since she'd kicked him off the dive team a few years ago when his undercover work had repeatedly kept him from making it to training dives. But since he'd come back to Homicide, and since two of their divers had left the team—one for medical reasons and another for retirement—she'd been encouraged to allow him back. Their relationship remained strained, but since the serial-killer case involving Leigh last spring, the tension between them had eased.

Slightly.

"Yeah. I talked to her. She bit my head off for being on the wrong side of town and told me to hurry up because she and Lane were already on the scene."

"She didn't call me," Adam said.

Gabe smirked. "Man, it's the second Sunday of the month. We all knew where *you* were."

Adam bit back a retort. He loved his family. He really did. Some of them were awesome. Some of them weren't. Same as most families, he imagined. And a sight better than a lot of the families he'd seen while working in the uniformed division. Even Grandmother's disapproval, which irked him to no end, was part of her way of showing love.

At least Grandfather said it was. He said she worried over her grandson far more than her frosty demeanor indicated.

Gabe punched his arm. "Don't worry about it, man. This is an evidence-recovery situation. Nothing we could have done for the victim even if we'd been sitting in the water waiting on the car."

"How do you know?"

"The guy who found her said he was out here around lunchtime and saw the car. Dove in and pulled the body out. Probably destroyed a ton of evidence. He said she was limp in her seatbelt, but he thought maybe she was just unconscious. After he got her to shore, his take on it was that her neck was broken."

Adam fought the image Gabe's words created in his mind. He was sorry for the victim. Horrified at the manner of death, whether it had been a dreadful accident or a successful suicide attempt. But he wasn't sorry he wouldn't have to be the one to pull her body from the water.

He scrambled down the incline to the waterline. There would be no need for any of their fancy sonar equipment on this case.

He could see the car from the edge of the lake. Dive team captain and homicide investigator Anissa Bell and Deputy Lane Edwards were in dry suits, checking tanks and gauges.

"'Bout time," Anissa said. "We're shorthanded. Chavez, sketch the scene. Campbell, get suited up for backup, but you're on topside evidence. Get the path of the car, etcetera. I want all of it documented before we pull the car out and contaminate the scene." Anissa pointed to a makeshift changing area—a couple of tarps tied up between a few trees. "And be quick. We don't want to run out of daylight."

"Yes, ma'am," Adam said.

Gabe glared at Anissa for a second before grabbing a sketch pad and getting to work. "She thinks she's being mean, but I didn't want to get wet today anyway."

Adam didn't bother responding to Gabe's mutterings. Partly because he wasn't so sure Anissa had been trying to be mean. As far as he was concerned, she'd given the worst job to him. It took him fifteen minutes to change out of his clothes, get into the dry suit, and prep his own tanks and gauges so he had everything ready if Anissa or Lane required assistance.

He tried to ignore the shrouded body near the water's edge. They couldn't do anything about the evidence destroyed by the man who'd jumped in the lake and tried to save the victim. Even after he was sure she was dead, he'd gone down repeatedly until he freed her and pulled her body to the surface.

Adam focused on the work Anissa and Lane were doing in the water, prepping the car to be retrieved. The car was in water shallow enough that they didn't need lift bags to float it to the surface. They would be able to tow it out of the water with a wrecker.

Anissa was using this as an opportunity for Lane to be the rigger—he would wrap a chain around the car's axle a few times and then stretch the chain to the shore, where it would be hooked to a tow truck. Anissa was acting as the safety, observing everything and ready to assist if Lane needed it.

18

"Adam." Anissa's voice came through the earpiece he was wearing. "You might as well go ahead and call Sabrina."

Dr. Sabrina Fleming was a local professor of cybersecurity and computer forensics.

"What did you find?" Adam asked.

"A laptop."

The Carrington County Sheriff's Office had a wonderful forensics team, and they did great work, but Sabrina had a lab filled with all the latest equipment as well as everything that would be needed to attempt to pull any information from the waterlogged computer.

"I'll send her a text now." Adam retrieved his phone from his bag. He didn't need to look her up in his contacts. He had her number memorized.

She responded immediately.

"Anissa," Adam said, "she can come now. How long will it be before you bring it up?" Underwater criminal investigators never removed anything from the water. The laptop would need to be placed in a special box filled with lake water. Recovering anything from the hard drive was actually harder if it dried out improperly.

"Tell her to come on," Anissa said. "We'll have it ready."

Adam fought the grin that tried to cross his lips. This wasn't the time for it. Someone had died. But at least he'd get to see Sabrina this afternoon.

A shower of gravel drew his attention to the steep incline surrounding him. He gave Dr. Sharon Oliver, medical examiner, a nod as she inched her way down the embankment to the body. "Weren't you on call last weekend?" he asked her.

She let out a huff as she set her bag down beside the body. "I was. And I will be on call for the next two weeks while Dr. Sherman enjoys his thirty-fifth anniversary by traipsing all over Europe."

Adam laughed. She sounded put out, but he knew she wasn't. "You're just jealous."

She flashed him a wicked grin. "You got that right."

"All right, honey," she said, addressing the victim. "Let's see what you can tell me, and then let's get you away from prying eyes."

Gabe approached the body and snapped pictures as Dr. Oliver examined it. "I assume you're talking about our hovering friends?" He glared at the heavens, where a news helicopter was circling.

"Indeed," she said.

Adam studied the surface of the water, thankful he had an excuse to look away from the body.

But Gabe's low whistle was hard to disregard.

"Um, Campbell?"

Adam tried to ignore Gabe, but he didn't want to be unprofessional. "What?" He didn't turn.

"You may want to see this."

Jerk. Gabe knew how he felt about dead bodies. Everyone knew. He couldn't look at one without seeing Aaron. "I'm watching Anissa and—"

"Adam." Gabe's tone was . . . off. What was going on?

He kept his eyes on the water but backed toward the body. "What is it?"

Gabe clapped a hand on his back. "I'll watch the water. You need to talk to the doc."

"Wha—"

Gabe shook his head and then nodded toward the body.

Adam made eye contact with the doctor. She pointed to the victim. Why were they so insistent that he look at a dead body?

Fine.

Lord, help me.

He glanced at the victim.

Then stared.

There, written in permanent marker on the victim's abdomen, were six words.

They killed me. Ask Adam Campbell.

Sabrina slowed her MINI Cooper as she neared the police barricade at the double bridges over Lake Porter. A young deputy, hand raised, approached her car.

"I'm sorry, ma'am. You'll need to follow the detour signs and go around."

She handed him a business card. "Investigator Campbell called me," she said. Where was Adam? He was always so courteous. She couldn't remember a time when he hadn't met her at the police barricade and escorted her through.

Technically, she didn't need to collect the evidence. This dive team knew what they were doing. She'd never received evidence from them that hadn't been properly handled. No laptops in plastic bags. No flash drives in Styrofoam. No one ever took a hair dryer and tried to dry out a cell phone before sending it her way.

She could trust them. She did trust them.

She also liked them.

A lot.

Some more than others.

Her friend list was short. When she added people to it, she made it a point to try to keep them there. And it was always a good idea to help out your friends. That's why she'd jumped at the chance to pick up the laptop. At least, that was her story and she was sticking to it.

The deputy smiled. "Give me a minute, ma'am." He ducked under the police tape and signaled to someone. A few moments later Gabe Chavez appeared on the other side of the tape and waved for her to come through.

She fought the disappointment that Adam didn't greet her, pasted on a smile, and nodded.

The deputy returned and showed her where to park her car, then he escorted her to where Gabe stood, arms crossed.

"Hi, Doc. Sorry to bother you on a Sunday." Gabe gave her a tight smile.

"It's no problem." She couldn't stop her eyes from scanning the scene below. Where was Adam? Was he under the water?

"You want to scramble down there? Or would you rather me bring the box up to you? I don't mind," Gabe said.

"I'll come down if that's okay," she said.

"Sure thing. Be careful. It's steep."

She eased her way down the side of the hill.

"At least you're dressed for it," Gabe said as they made their descent. "Nice shirt. I haven't seen that one. Is it new?"

This was one of the things she liked about the dive team. They didn't give her grief about her standard uniform—superhero T-shirts with skinny jeans and Converse tennis shoes. "Old. I've had it about ten years," she said.

"Cool. Pretty boy showed up dressed for church. Probably ruined his expensive shoes."

Sabrina ignored the pretty boy comment. She hadn't been too sure about Gabe when she first met him earlier this year. She'd bristled each time he'd made a snide remark about one of his co-workers. It had taken a while, but she'd finally realized many of his comments were meant as jokes and had no malice behind them. Adam liked Gabe and enjoyed working with him, so that was good enough for her.

"Sunday lunch with the family?" Sabrina asked.

"Yep."

Poor Adam. He had a love-hate relationship with those lunches. Loved the people. Hated the drama.

"Is he in the water?" She tried to keep the question light. It wasn't unreasonable for her to ask, especially since Adam had called her.

"Um, no."

At Gabe's words, she stopped watching her feet and looked at him. She should have picked up on it before now. Gabe was not his usual jovial self. For Gabe, he was almost . . . serious.

22

"Is he okay?" Again, she tried to keep the question professional in tone. But based on the way Gabe's eyebrows shot up, she must not have succeeded.

"Depends on your definition of okay," he said. "Physically, he's fine. Hasn't even been in the water."

They'd reached the bottom of the incline, and Sabrina paused to take it all in. The medical examiner hovered over a body to her left. The dive team van was parked near the shore—they must have driven down here on the service road the utility companies used. Two divers bobbed around the car.

But still no Adam.

Gabe tilted his head to the left and she looked beyond the body. There he was.

Adam paced along the edge of the lake in the direction of the double bridges.

Nothing about this made any sense.

"Dare I ask?" This time her words were a mere whisper.

"I'm the lead investigator on the homicide, and under normal circumstances there wouldn't be much I could say. But there's been a development I'm going to need to share with you because you need to know what you're dealing with when you start working on that laptop."

Gabe motioned for her to follow him toward the medical examiner.

This was getting weirder by the second.

They stopped a few feet away from the body. "Dr. Oliver, have you met Dr. Fleming?" Gabe's formal introduction caught Sabrina by surprise.

Dr. Oliver stood. "I'd shake your hand, but—" She indicated her gloved hands. "I don't know if we've met in an official capacity or not, but I've heard wonderful things about you, Dr. Fleming. I'm Sharon."

"Likewise. And I'm Sabrina."

"I'd like Sabrina to see what you showed us a little while ago,"

Gabe said to Dr. Oliver. "She'll be the one trying to recover any-thing we can get off the laptop, and while we intend to keep this little piece of evidence out of the press, I think it's important for her to be aware of it. I trust her implicitly."

Sharon regarded Sabrina with a speculative look. "Have you ever seen a dead body?"

Why on earth did they want her to look at this poor victim? Sabrina swallowed hard. "I have," she said.

"You won't pass out?" Sharon pressed.

"I will not." Sabrina wasn't offended by the question. Sharon Oliver had no idea the kinds of things Sabrina had seen. She got no pleasure from viewing this poor victim's body, but there was no way it would replace the stuff of her nightmares.

Sharon pulled the sheet away from the body. A woman. Prob-ably in her late forties to early fifties. Pixie-cut hair. Something about her looked familiar.

Why was she lifting the woman's shirt?

As the words written on the victim's abdomen came into focus, Sabrina blinked a couple of times and then knelt closer. She didn't say anything. She didn't want to risk anyone overhearing, although no one stood within twenty feet of them.

She straightened and tried to process it.

They killed me. Ask Adam Campbell.

She took a closer look at the victim's face.

No. It couldn't be. "Do you have a name yet?" she asked Gabe.

"Yeah," he said. "Her name is Lisa Palmer. She's an—"

"Accountant," Sabrina said.

"Do you know her?" Gabe asked.

"Only by reputation." Who had killed her? Why? And what did Adam know about it?

"What can you tell me about her?" Gabe asked.

"Not much," Sabrina answered. "She was my father's accoun-tant. I saw her leaving the house once. I never met her."

"*Was* your father's accountant?" Gabe frowned. "Did he fire her?"

"No. He died."

A deputy called Gabe's name and waved for him to come up to the road.

Gabe pointed at her. "We're not done."

Awesome. Her mind spiraled through the possible ramifications. All her family's secrets part of the public record. Adam would find out . . .

"I'll be back to get your statement."

"Fine." She pointed to Adam. "Can I go talk to him while I'm waiting?"

"You can try. As soon as I took his statement, he changed back into clothes and said he wanted to be alone, but my guess is you might be the exception to that request."

"I don't know. If he wants to be alone . . ."

"Go on. He needs to talk to someone. Maybe he'll talk to you."

She refocused on Adam. He'd stopped walking and now sat on a fallen log near the water's edge. He might have been staring at the water. Might have been praying. She couldn't tell.

Gabe gave her an encouraging nod and took off in the direction of the road.

This was so not her area of expertise. She worked best in a world where the facts reigned supreme. Emotions always left her fumbling for words.

And saying the wrong thing.

But even from this distance, Adam's misery was so evident it made her chest hurt. Her feet started moving toward him before her brain registered what she was doing.

Lord, I'm going to need a lot of help here.

2

It took her a couple of minutes to reach Adam, and while she was almost certain he knew she was approaching, he didn't acknowledge her.

Not typical Adam. Not at all. Even on his busiest days, his chivalry quotient was off the charts.

"Hi," she said.

He nodded but didn't speak.

"Mind if I join you?"

A shrug.

Wow. This was going . . . great. No greeting. No hello.

She'd seen him frustrated. Overwhelmed. Even despairing when they thought they'd lost Leigh last spring. But she'd never seen Adam so dispirited.

She sat beside him, and he scooted over a few inches to give her a little more room, but her left leg still brushed against his right thigh. She couldn't decide what to do with her hands, so she clasped them in front of her and leaned forward with her elbows on her knees.

Lord, that help we talked about? Anytime you'd like to get started, that would be awesome. I'm out of ideas.

She had a bad feeling she was handling this all wrong, but since she couldn't think of anything to say, she just sat with Adam.

If he wasn't so miserable, and if there wasn't a dead body fifty yards away, she could have enjoyed this.

Adam kept her at a professional distance most of the time. The last time she'd been this close to him was last spring when they got the call that Leigh was safe. She'd been sobbing with relief when his arms wrapped around her. He held her and whispered to her that she'd done a great job. And at one point, she'd thought he might have kissed the top of her head.

But since then, things had been . . . off.

Movement to her right pulled her attention back to the present. Dr. Oliver was overseeing the removal of the body.

"I don't know her." Adam's gruff voice startled her. "But I think she's dead because of me."

"You had nothing to do with her death."

"Just because I didn't send her car over the embankment doesn't mean I—"

"Don't go there. There's nothing logical about that statement, Adam." Sabrina tapped his knee with her fist.

Adam pulled his knee away from her. "I'm not in the mood for logic, Sabrina." The anguished way he spoke the words took some of the edge off them. Some. Not all.

I'm messing this up, Lord. I don't know how to take the logic out of anything.

"Sorry." She didn't know what else to say. She did know this wasn't the right time to bring up the fact that the victim had probably known more about her dad than she did.

"Her name is . . . was . . . Lisa Palmer," Adam said. "Gabe was able to get the identification from her car. She came to the office last week. Said she wanted to meet with me, but I wasn't in. One of the other investigators tried to help her, but she said she only wanted to talk to me. He looked at my calendar and set up a time for her to meet with me on Monday. Told me about it when I came back to the office. And that's the last I thought about it until I saw my name on her stomach."

He dropped his face into his hands. "If I'd had any idea she was in danger, I could have met with her on Saturday."

"But you didn't know." She tried to say the words in a comforting way. He didn't throw her logic in her face this time, so maybe she was making a little progress.

"Where were you last week?" she asked.

"What?" He mumbled the word through his hands, still not looking at her.

"Why were you out of the office last week?"

He sat up. "I was in court."

"What kind of case?"

His face contorted in sorrow. "Elder abuse."

Sabrina placed a tentative hand on his arm. "Was it bad?"

He groaned. "An adult child siphoned off the parents' life savings. Years of hard work and tucking money aside, and their own son deceived them. They can't afford food or medicine, and they didn't deserve it. And it's a no-win situation. They know what happened to their money, but now their son will be in prison and they have no one to help them."

"How awful," she said. "Were you in court all week?"

"The case closed just before lunch on Friday. The evidence was overwhelming. The jury had him convicted by three. He wanted to take a plea, but the DA wasn't offering." He looked at her. "I know what you're doing."

She tried to look innocent. "What?"

"You're trying to make me see that I wasn't in the office because I was doing my job, and I was helping bring justice to a horrible situation."

"I think you've made a good point."

28

"But a woman died. She's not poor. She's not sad. She's dead. And I could have—"

"Adam." She couldn't take it anymore. "You're hurting for her, and you feel guilty because she's dead and you want to believe you could have prevented it. But that's the biggest fallacy of all. I know you don't want to be logical about this right now, and I'm not trying to make you unfeel the very real emotions you're experiencing, but you need to remember that you're one piece of an elaborate puzzle."

He didn't argue, so she kept going. "If that message said, 'Ask Sabrina Fleming,' I would feel the same way. But you aren't in control of the world. And where human understanding fails us, we have to trust that God isn't surprised by this."

"I don't know if I've ever heard you talk about God before," he said.

That stung. Had he really never heard her mention her faith? "Unfortunately, many of my colleagues believe science and faith are at odds with each other instead of seeing how they are, in fact, beautifully interwoven. Over the years, my faith has become more and more private. Which isn't something I'm proud of, by the way."

He rested one hand on her knee and squeezed. "I get it. I don't talk about my faith with my family much. The general feeling is that it's okay for everyone to attend services at a respectable place of worship as long as their faith doesn't start interfering with their social life or as long as no one gets too fanatical about it."

Sabrina could imagine Margaret Campbell Lawson saying that.

"I'm not proud of it either," Adam said. "I'm still finding my way. But I'm not sure what I think about why God couldn't have let me get justice and be in the office to prevent this." He waved a hand toward the area where the body had been moments ago.

"You may never know," she said. "For now, you have to trust that you were doing the job God gave you to do last week, and it didn't include meeting with Lisa Palmer. But this week God has given you the job of finding out why she wanted to meet with you and getting justice for her. And I hate to go all drill sergeant on you, but you aren't going to find out what happened if you sit here all night."

He squeezed her knee again. "You're right. As usual."

He twisted toward her on the log, and she had to move her arm to stop herself from falling to the ground.

He reached for both of her arms with his hands and steadied her. "I'm sorry," he said.

"No harm, no foul," Sabrina said.

"I don't mean about bumping you off the log," he said. "I mean about what I said before—about logic."

"It's no big deal. I stink at comforting people. And at emotions. Or talking about emotions. Or pretty much anything that can't be explained with a spreadsheet or a diagram."

Adam laughed. "You're amazing."

The look on his face was one she'd seen from time to time but didn't know what to make of. She'd seen that look on others. Ryan looked at Leigh that way a lot. The best word she could come up with to describe it was *adoration*. But she didn't know what to make of that either. She must not have been reading it correctly.

A shout from the shoreline saved her from having to say anything. She would have been sure to say something wrong anyway. Gabe waved at them. She couldn't catch his exact words, but his meaning was clear. It was time to go.

Adam stood and pulled her up with him. "Thank you."

She didn't know how to reply, so she didn't. She took two steps away from the log and rolled her ankle on a rock. "Ouch!" She caught her balance and sighed. Dumb feet. She had never been particularly graceful.

Adam didn't point out her clumsiness, but he did offer her his arm. "Walk with me?"

Funny how this man managed to make her feel protected while never making her feel like she needed to be protected. He walked beside her until they got to the base of the hill, then stayed close as they made their way up the rocky slope.

"The laptop is up here," Gabe said to Sabrina. "I'll need you to sign for it. Forensics has already started working at the victim's house, and I need to get over there. But you and I are talking tomorrow."

Something to look forward to. "Okay. I'll take it to the lab and get started on it."

When everything had been signed off, Gabe tapped the pen on the clipboard he'd been using. "You're going to your lab now?"

"Yes," she said. "It will take a while for it to dry out."

"It's Sunday night."

Sabrina had no idea where Gabe was going with this. "Technically, it's late afternoon, but it's almost dark, so—"

"Afternoon. Night. Whatever. That's not the point. It's going to be dark by the time you get to the university. Will there be anyone there?"

"I'll go with her," Adam said from behind them. Gabe's face and posture relaxed at the words.

"I spend plenty of time in my lab alone." She looked at Adam. "I'll be fine."

She turned back to Gabe in time to see him shaking his head at Adam. She wasn't any good at verbal nuance and had a bad habit of misreading body language cues, but even she could tell something was up with these two. "What am I missing?"

Adam shuffled his feet a little. He didn't want to scare Sabrina, but she needed to understand how serious this was. "Someone killed this woman. They may or may not have known she had the laptop in her car. They may or may not have known she had written

31

a message on her stomach. We have no idea what or who we're dealing with."

He glanced around the darkening surroundings. Gabe did as well.

"There were news helicopters out today." Gabe's hatred of news helicopters clearly hadn't abated in the years since a reporter used one to blow his cover on a high-profile drug bust. "I think it's safest for us to assume the bad guys know you're here. For all we know, you could be followed as you leave. I don't think it's wise for you to have possession of the laptop without having someone around to provide some protection."

Adam tried to hide his relief. "I can go with her tonight," he said. "Her lab is secure. Once we get it there, I think she'll be fine."

"Okay." Gabe pointed at Sabrina. "I won't be surprised if we wind up with more items requiring your assistance. I've already talked to the captain, and he's given me the approval to send everything straight to you. And Adam, you're officially on this case as well. Clearly, whatever she wanted to talk to you about is at the heart of this, so my guess is we'll need to solve the white-collar-crime angle for us to find her killer."

Excellent. Adam fought a smile. Now he wouldn't have to fight to be kept in the loop. Sabrina's pep talk must have worked better than he'd realized. An hour ago he had dreaded the thought of digging into this case. Now, he was chomping at the bit to solve it—to bring justice to the woman he hadn't had the opportunity to help while she was alive.

"I'll be with the ME in the morning for the autopsy," Gabe said. "She said she was going to start around nine." Gabe's expression changed. "Adam."

Uh-oh. Why didn't he like his tone?

"Since you'll be hanging out with Sabrina this evening, maybe you could go ahead and get her statement about the victim. That would be one less thing I have to do later."

"Statement? What statement?"

Sabrina studied her shoes and didn't make eye contact.

"She didn't tell you?" Gabe asked.

"It didn't come up." Sabrina's words were low, but there was a defensiveness to them Adam couldn't make sense of.

"Well, it's up now," Gabe said. "Our victim was Sabrina's late-father's accountant. I have no idea if it makes any difference to our case, but please get a statement before you call it an evening."

Sabrina gave Gabe a curt nod.

Adam's mind swirled. He'd known Sabrina's dad had needed continuous care. Early onset dementia had taken his mind several years ago. But when had he died? How could Sabrina not have mentioned it?

And the victim had been his accountant? What was that all about?

Based on the mutinous expression on Sabrina's face, she didn't want to talk about it.

Gabe appeared to be oblivious to Sabrina's displeasure. "Want to plan to meet me for lunch tomorrow and we'll see where we are?"

"Sure," Adam answered.

Sabrina regarded him with an expression he couldn't decipher, but something was wrong.

"I don't need a babysitter," she said.

"I'm not babysitting you. I'm the protective detail for the evening."

Her expression darkened.

"Come on, Sabrina." Gabe's voice had done that thing it did when he was flirting. It went all soft with a bit more of a Spanish accent than he usually had. "I know it stinks to have to hang out with pretty boy, but it will make things much easier if you can take one for the team. Just for tonight. I promise I'll get some burly deputies to hound your every step for the next few days at the lab."

She glared at Gabe. "I don't know how long this will take tonight. Adam's going to need to get some sleep."

Whoa. Did she think he was that fragile? "What am I, a three-year-old? None of us will get much sleep for the next forty-eight hours."

Gabe shifted his feet in a way that put him between Adam and Sabrina. "Adam's right. I probably won't sleep until Monday night. If I'm lucky. Too much time-sensitive stuff to do. You can make him sit outside your lab if you want. Just take a picture and send it to me so I can post it on the bulletin board in the office." Gabe chuckled at his own joke, but Sabrina's expression hadn't softened.

"Do you think I can't defend myself?"

That brought Gabe's chuckle to an abrupt halt. "I think you shouldn't have to."

Sabrina blinked a few times at that and the set of her mouth relaxed a fraction. Adam eased closer to Sabrina, forcing Gabe to step back. "Please," he said. "If you don't give me permission, I'm going to be sitting outside the lab anyway."

"Fine."

"Thank you." Gabe handed her the box containing the laptop. "I'll be able to focus on my work knowing you're in good hands." Gabe winked at Adam. "I'll be in touch."

When he was several yards away, Sabrina muttered, "I still think this is ridiculous. You're an investigator. Not a nanny."

"I'm glad we're clear on that. I had several nannies growing up. They were awful." He shuddered for effect.

Sabrina didn't laugh at his attempt at humor. Okay. It was a lame attempt, but she could give him a few points for effort.

She paused at the door of her car. "I had a wonderful nanny." She had a faraway look about her, and even in the twilight he could see an ocean of pain in her eyes. "She sacrificed too much for me. I never want anyone to have to do that again."

Before Adam could form a coherent response, she stepped to the back of the car, opened her tiny hatchback, and settled the evidence box inside. She slammed the lid of the hatch with a bit more force than necessary and all but ran to the driver's-side door. "I'll see you at my lab." With a grim nod, she climbed in and pulled away even before she had her seat belt fastened.

What had just happened?

Adam jogged to his car and jumped in. It took him a minute to catch up to her on the highway, and once he settled in behind her, he attempted to make sense of their conversation.

He'd known Sabrina for two years. She'd contacted the sheriff and formed a partnership that would allow the sheriff's office to benefit from the lab and high-tech equipment in the new forensics department at the local university. The sheriff had asked him to help set up the procedures and operational guidelines, and over time he and Sabrina had developed a friendship.

He couldn't deny he was attracted to her. Had been from day one. She was unlike anyone he'd ever known.

His family pushed women toward him all the time. Women he had zero interest in. They were always beautiful and usually intelligent. But too often they worried too much about how long it had been since their last pedicure and what zip code they lived in. All they wanted to talk about was the latest social event or where they wanted to vacation. And while there wasn't anything wrong with those things, he couldn't make himself care.

But Sabrina was different. She worried about things that mattered. Her work ethic blew him away. She didn't care about clothes or hair or how many square feet the pool house had.

He'd rather sit in her lab with her, her hair pulled up in a messy bun and glasses sliding down her nose while she pulled data from a hard drive than sit in the fanciest restaurant in Carrington with any of the elegant women who populated the social circle he'd grown up in.

Gabe and Ryan teased him about her, and he tried to downplay it, mostly to keep them from doing it more.

But he had it bad for Sabrina Fleming. And he couldn't have her.

The day after he'd decided to ask her out, he saw her at dinner. With his cousin Darren.

He wouldn't mess with anyone's relationship. Especially not Darren's. Darren was all right, and he couldn't blame Sabrina for being interested in him.

So he tried to be content with a friendship that meant the world to him, although she kept a tight lid on her past. But tonight a window into the mysterious inner world of Sabrina Fleming had opened.

He couldn't help but wonder if Darren knew about Sabrina's father. Or about the self-sacrificing nanny.

Somehow he doubted it.

Fifteen minutes later he pulled into a parking space beside her and met her at the back of her car. Gabe had been right. It was completely dark outside of the glow from the streetlight Sabrina had parked under.

He should send an email to campus security about the lighting out here. There were way too many dark corners and shadows. He scanned the area around them as Sabrina lifted the evidence box from the car. He stepped closer, every sense attuned to the sounds around him.

"Paranoid much?"

He heard Sabrina's snide whisper but didn't respond. They could chat when they were in her lab. And the doors were locked.

He didn't offer to take the box from her. She probably wouldn't let him, and she didn't need him to carry it. But the main reason was he wanted to be free to respond to any threats without worrying about the evidence.

Grateful for the excuse to walk close to her, he put one hand on the small of her back as they walked inside.

The building was locked up for the weekend, so she punched in security codes for the exterior door and then the elevator before they reached the door to the forensics lab. This time she entered a code and then leaned forward for an iris scan before the door lock released.

Adam didn't allow himself to relax until the outer door had latched behind them and the motion-sensitive lights flickered on, illuminating the entire room.

Sabrina nudged him with her elbow before stepping away and placing the evidence box on a long row of tables. "Thank you for your service, Investigator Campbell." Sarcasm dripped from her words.

He laughed. "Are you hassling me?"

"I'm trying to. Is it working?"

"Yes, it is."

"Good," she said with a self-satisfied smirk.

Adam pointed to a chair near the door. "Will I be in the way there?"

"Not at all," she said. "Mi lab es su lab." She pointed to a big, shiny silver machine. "Except for that. Don't touch that."

"Yes, ma'am," he said.

None of his cases last summer had required her assistance, so it had been a while since he'd been in her lab.

It was a rectangular room. One computer station after another filled the perimeter, each with multiple oversized monitors and keyboards. Locked cabinets filled the walls above each station. In the middle of the room were several taller stations, also with massive monitors. He knew from past experience that Sabrina preferred to work standing up.

Her personal office could be reached through a door at the far end of the lab. He liked her office—it reflected her quirky personality, and had a comfortable, rather than a formal, feel.

But she didn't head for her office.

Sabrina tapped away at a few keyboards and then took the evidence box over to a low desk beside a wall that looked more like something you'd see in a medical lab than a computer lab. Boxes of gloves, tiny vials, and random stickers were on small shelves on the wall, along with compressed air and more typical office items like staplers and pens.

She opened the cabinet above the table and removed a bowl and a massive bag of rice. She donned the latex gloves, poured the rice into the bowl, and only then did she turn her attention back to the laptop.

"Let's see what we have here," she said.

"What do we need this to be?" Adam asked.

"Well," she said around a small screwdriver she was holding in her mouth, "unless she made some crazy modifications to this machine, we should have a nice solid-state hard drive."

"Right." She'd told him about this before. "Solid state is better for recovering data. Remind me again why that is?"

She kept working, taking the laptop apart with the care of a heart surgeon. "Solid-state hard drives don't have any spinning platters inside. Those babies are quick to corrode and much harder to retrieve evidence from once they get wet. But a solid-state hard drive is just sticks of memory on a circuit board."

"Have you ever gotten data off the spinning-platter kind?"

Her little smile answered his question before she did. "Yes. But it's challenging."

"But you're the best."

She snorted. "Hardly. I'm very good. But sometimes it's serendipity over skill. You can't recover what's not there anymore."

She continued working for another five minutes before she lifted the hard drive out and settled it in the bowl of rice.

She took the components of the laptop and placed them in a separate container before putting all of them in an evidence storage locker in a large closet. From the outside it looked like a large broom cupboard—or it would if a broom closet required an iris scan to open it.

"I'll be done in a few minutes," she said as she tidied the workstation. "Don't you need to take a statement or something?"

3

S abrina glanced at Adam in time to see the surprise on his face before he pulled it back to a more professional demeanor.

Maybe if she didn't look at Adam it wouldn't be so bad.

Can I tell him? Everything? Can I trust him?

She forced herself to analyze her emotions. Why did she care? Shame for the things her family did without her consent? Yes, that was part of it. A big part of it.

But . . . that wasn't all of it. She hated to admit it, even to herself, but part of it was because she wasn't sure how Adam would respond. Or how his family would respond if . . .

Oh, who was she kidding? It wasn't going to happen. Guys like Adam Campbell might fight it for a while, but eventually they married someone the family approved of.

And she would never be that someone.

She risked a glance at Adam. He leaned against one of her tall desks. A notepad and pen he must have snagged from one of the workstations sat in front of him. When they made eye contact, he gave her a sad smile.

"We don't have to do this," he said. "Gabe can handle it if

you don't want to talk to me. I can tell you don't want to tell me anything about this."

"Adam," she said, "I never wanted to tell anyone about this."

He didn't say anything. He waited without a hint of impatience, like there was nowhere else he'd rather be.

He tapped the desk. "Would it help if we walked as we talked?"

"Yes, it would. But how will you take notes?"

"I have a pretty good memory," he said. "I'll type it up later. You can read it before I send it to Gabe to be sure I've captured everything accurately."

"Are you sure it's safe? To be outside?"

He quirked an eyebrow. "Are you saying you don't think I can protect you?"

"Of course not. I . . . I . . ."

Adam laughed. "I'm just messing with you, Bri. The main concern for your safety was that someone might try to attack you to get the laptop before you could analyze it. I think we need to be cautious, but if I really thought someone was going to come after you, I'd insist you go into protective custody tonight."

"Oh."

He put the pad and paper back and waited for her by the door. "I can't imagine what's so hard for you to talk about, but I promise to treat anything you say with the utmost confidence and respect."

"Thanks." Sabrina glanced around the lab. Everything had been returned to its previous pristine condition. And unless you opened the evidence locker, there was nothing to indicate anyone had been in the lab over the weekend.

"All done?" he asked.

She answered by grabbing her jacket and following Adam out of the lab, pausing to be sure everything had locked. Satisfied the lab was secure, she joined Adam, who was waiting a few steps away. He extended his arm and she rested her hand in the bend.

Adam led them outside and deeper into the heart of campus. "Where are we headed?" she asked.

"I thought a stroll around the pond would be nice."

"The roar from the fountain will make it hard for anyone to overhear us, and the lighting is excellent," Sabrina said.

Adam grinned. "Yes. That's why it's so nice."

"I thought you said I wasn't in any danger."

"I don't think you are, but I'm not taking any chances."

They continued in silence until the walkway around the pond came into view. Adam didn't pressure her to speak, and they made it halfway around before she managed to force out a few words.

"I don't know where to start," she said.

"Try the beginning."

"I'm not sure where that is," she said. She wasn't sure of anything.

He placed his left hand over hers. "It's okay if you ramble. This isn't a lecture. It's a conversation. It doesn't have to follow a timeline. Although now that I think about it, maybe you'd prefer a spreadsheet. Or a PowerPoint presentation?"

She fought a smile. "You know me well."

Adam didn't respond.

"Although I guess right now you're probably thinking you don't know me as well as you thought you did."

He patted her hand. "I'm thinking I wish you would trust me enough to know that no matter what you say, it isn't going to change—"

He cleared his throat.

"Change what?"

"Anything," he said.

Somehow she didn't think that's what he'd been planning to say, but she didn't have the mental energy to try to figure it out right now.

Father, help me.

Maybe if she got the worst of it out, it would be easier. Like ripping off a bandage.

"I have absolutely no proof, but I have a very strong suspicion my nanny was a slave."

Adam never broke stride, and although she'd been prepared for him to distance himself, he instead pulled her closer to him. She didn't fight it. Somehow leaning against him gave her the courage to keep talking.

"My parents were both workaholics," she said. "My father was a professor of physics on tenure track. Very much a publish-or-perish kind of job. He worked all kinds of crazy hours. My mother, well, she was busy climbing the corporate ladder."

"What did she do?" Adam asked.

"She's the CEO of YTT Healthcare."

"Present tense? As in right now?"

"Yes. I doubt she'll ever retire. I thoroughly expect her to drop dead at her desk." She could hear the bitterness in her voice. "Imagine if your aunt Margaret was in the business world."

Adam shuddered.

"Exactly."

"I guess she was gone a lot when you were a kid," he said.

"Oh yeah. Sometimes she'd be gone for two weeks at a time. My father was working constantly. My nanny raised me. Her name was Rosita." Her eyes burned with tears, and she blinked them away. "Both of my parents are from wealthy families, and both of them were incredibly driven to be successful. One of my mother's sisters is a federal court judge. One is a concert pianist. Her brother is a senator."

"What a bunch of underachievers," Adam said.

"I know you're joking, but my grandfather would have agreed with you," she said. "None of them ever did anything fast enough or well enough to suit him."

"He sounds delightful."

Sabrina couldn't stop the chuckle that bubbled out. "You're terrible."

He squeezed her hand and laughed with her. "Sorry."

"No, you aren't," she said. "And that's just it. He was delightful in public but a nightmare in private. And my dad's family was no better. His father was a surgeon. My dad was an only child, but his mom came from a family that made their money in newspapers—back when that was a profitable venture. While my mother's family expected her to be successful and wealthy, my father's family expected him to make a significant contribution to the world. They pounded it into him that it would be a crime to be blessed with his intelligence and not use it for the greater good."

"That's a lot of pressure," Adam said.

"It is. But it's no excuse for what I'm afraid my parents did."

"What made you suspicious?" Adam asked the question with such tenderness that the tears threatened again. She looked toward the pond so he wouldn't see.

"Not long after I became a Christian, I got involved with an anti–human trafficking organization in Virginia. It's what first whetted my appetite for computer forensics. I helped one of my professors pull photographs off a hard drive the perpetrator had tried to destroy. The photographs led us to a sex-trafficking ring. Those photographs . . . I'm a very visual person, and while I don't have a photographic memory, I have excellent recall. I can never unsee those pictures."

"I get that," Adam said.

"But as awful as it was, and is, I realized if I was that traumatized by a few photographs, then the women and children in those pictures who had actually lived that life were in desperate need of help—help I could provide. How could I not do everything in my power to aid them?"

"It takes deep compassion to step into someone's anguish rather than run away from it," Adam said. "Most people would run."

"I don't know about that," she said. "I think most people choose not to see it in the first place."

"Good point."

"Anyway, at first I thought all human trafficking was sex trafficking. I didn't realize modern-day slavery existed in the US. I thought that was something that happened overseas. And that the only slaves anywhere near me were being sold for sex."

They moved to the far right of the path to allow a jogger to pass them.

"But then I learned about labor trafficking and realized anyone could be a victim. The man bussing my table in the restaurant. The woman changing the sheets in the hotel." She blew out a hard breath. "The nanny who tucked me in every night."

"You recognized the signs of labor trafficking in your own home?"

"I don't know for sure," she said. "I was young and the specifics are fuzzy. But with what I know now? It's very possible. Labor trafficking is insidious. Men and women are often prevented from learning English because their captors want to make it impossible for them to develop outside relationships. They may be in private homes or working in public places, but people don't realize they aren't being paid a livable wage. They may be forced to work eighty hours a week or more, and even though they're walking down the sidewalk, they aren't really free. Someone has their passports and has threatened to deport their children if they don't keep their mouths shut and work. They live in fear, and they're everywhere and no one sees them."

"You see them," Adam said. "You're making a difference."

"Maybe, but I wish I'd understood earlier."

Adam squeezed her arm. "What happened to Rosita?"

"Rosita was everything to me, and when I turned ten, she disappeared. No goodbye. No address. No way to keep in touch. I came home from school one day and she was gone."

Sabrina brushed away the rogue tear that had escaped down her cheek. "At the time I was devastated. Then I was angry. My parents told me she'd quit. They said they were angry with her. They told me they were sorry. And I'm almost certain it was all a lie."

Adam's phone buzzed. He ignored it.

"You can get that." She'd be grateful for the break.

"It can wait," Adam said. But it buzzed again. "Or maybe it can't. I'm sorry." He pulled the phone from his pocket. "It's Gabe." He tapped the phone. "What's up?"

He listened, his eyes narrowing and his brow furrowing. Something must have been wrong.

He shook his head a few times. "Okay. I was talking to Sabrina, but I guess we can finish up tomorrow . . ."

She nodded. Yes. Please. Tomorrow.

"Okay. I'll be there as soon as I can."

A pause.

"I don't know. Maybe thirty minutes? I'll walk Sabrina to her car and follow her home, and then I'll head your way."

He heaved a massive sigh and put the phone in his pocket. "I am . . . this is awful," he said. He took her hands in his. "Gabe is convinced I need to come see the victim's home. Tonight. Now. He thinks whatever you have to contribute to the investigation can wait until tomorrow. He wouldn't go into any further detail."

"Gabe's a good guy," she said. "I'm sure it's important."

"So is this. I don't want to brush over how hard this is for you."

He had no idea. He couldn't possibly know. His family was made up of the most upstanding citizens in the community. Hers was full of modern-day slave traders. But he was listening with compassion and without judgment. It was more than she could have hoped for.

She fought the urge to lean in to him. If she did, what would he do? Would he wrap his arms around her? Would he rest his head on hers?

45

He tucked her arm in his again and turned so they were walking back toward the parking lot. "I have one more question for tonight."

"Okay."

"When did your dad die?"

This she could answer. "He died in his sleep last June. It wasn't unexpected. He'd been failing for months. He had a plot purchased here and the funeral home took care of everything. There wasn't really a service. He'd made it very clear he didn't want one. And I'm his only remaining family, so . . ."

"Still, I wish you would have told me. I . . . you . . . I'm sorry you had to go through that alone."

How could she explain to him that going through things alone was what she did? That it was the only way she knew to do it? She didn't know what to say, so she just shrugged.

He must have accepted that as enough because he said, "Why don't we talk about something else for now, and we'll come back to the family stuff tomorrow?"

Yes. Tomorrow would be much better. She'd gladly change the subject.

"How was lunch today?" Sabrina asked.

Adam could hear the relief in her voice as the conversation moved to something lighter. The Campbell family dinners were a regular topic of conversation with Sabrina. "Fine. Mom and Dad are in Italy, and Alexander is on call."

"So you had to deal with the craziness on your own."

"Pretty much."

"Were you still eating when you were called in?"

"Yep."

"I'm going to need you to give me the play-by-play of that." Sabrina didn't even try to hide her enjoyment of the story. "I bet your aunt Margaret gave you some grief."

"Nonverbal grief. Yes."

"She's good at that," Sabrina said.

Had Aunt Margaret been unkind to Sabrina? Why would Darren allow that? Darren's own mother had passed away from breast cancer when he was twelve. Aunt Margaret had stepped in as the mother figure in Darren's life. Poor guy.

"I don't know how Darren deals with that all the time," Adam said. What would Darren think if he saw him walking with Sabrina like this? He should pull away from her, but after everything she'd shared, he didn't want her to think he was trying to distance himself in any way.

He could feel the shrug of her arm against his. "Who knows? I haven't talked to Darren in three months."

Adam's feet froze in place, and he jerked Sabrina to a stop.

She turned to him. "Are you okay?"

Way to play it cool, Campbell. "I'm fine." He scrambled to come up with some excuse. "Sometimes I forget how to walk and talk at the same time."

Wow. That was lame.

Sabrina's mouth twisted into a wry smile. "Happens to me all the time."

She tucked her hand back in the crook of his arm and they kept walking, but the conversation didn't resume. How could he get her talking again? Preferably without being too obvious.

"Where were we before I tripped over my own two feet?" He didn't give her a chance to respond. "Oh yeah. We were talking about Darren. I haven't talked to him in four months. I guess you would still know more than I would."

If Gabe or Ryan had heard that, they never would let him hear the end of it. He was usually quite good at making conversation, but he experienced these kinds of social interaction disasters frequently when he was with Sabrina.

But she didn't seem to notice.

"You aren't close?" She sounded surprised by this.

Had she and Darren ever talked about family at all?

"I'm not particularly close to any of my cousins. We see each other at Sunday lunch each month. But my career choices haven't exactly endeared me to most of the family."

"Ah."

He waited, but she didn't say anything else.

"I like Darren fine though. He certainly appreciated the work you did." Sabrina had been able to prove Darren wasn't behind an embezzlement scheme one of his business partners had set up. "In fact, Grandmother keeps hinting that she wants to meet you."

Sabrina's entire body went rigid.

"I'm guessing you're not interested in meeting her."

"She terrifies me."

"I wish I could tell you she's harmless, but . . ."

Sabrina relaxed against him but didn't say anything else. He debated about trying to restart the conversation, but he'd learned when Sabrina was quiet, she was thinking. Which happened a lot. And he didn't want to interrupt her thoughts.

When they reached her car, she turned to face him. "You didn't ask me why I haven't talked to Darren."

Oh boy. "Was I supposed to? I was trying not to pry."

"You don't already know? I thought he might have said something to you and that's why you didn't ask."

"I have no idea why you haven't talked to him." He refused to say "broke up with" because that would imply a relationship he didn't want to acknowledge.

Then a horrible thought flew through his mind. "Did he—did he hurt you?" He didn't care that Darren was family. If he'd hurt her, he would pay.

"No. Of course not. Not at all." She pulled off her glasses and rubbed her eyes. "He said I'd led him on. Which I still don't understand. I made it very clear to him that we were just friends." Her expression clouded. "Or I thought I did. I'm horrible at that kind of stuff. I probably botched it."

Friends. Adam had never heard a more beautiful word.

"But then he kissed me."

Adam saw red.

"And he was shocked when I told him to stop. He said he thought I was playing hard to get."

He clamped his teeth together in an attempt to keep from saying the kinds of words he'd given up saying.

"I don't know why I told you all that. I shouldn't have. But I wondered if he'd said anything to you. I'm not the kind of girl who plays hard to get. I don't know how to be that kind of girl. The only reason I went out with him in the first place was because he only asked me to go to things related to fundraising for the university. I was going to have to go anyway, so I didn't see the harm in saying yes to going with a friend. And I thought I'd made myself clear." She frowned. "You're sure he hasn't said anything to you about it?"

"I'm sure," Adam said. Although he was going to have plenty to say to Darren about it.

"Huh."

"Why did you think he would have told me?"

She swallowed. "I don't know. You've been more like yourself tonight, but overall you've been a little distant lately. I thought maybe you were mad at me. I'm not good at reading people. But I knew something had changed, and that's the only thing I could think of. If it wasn't that, then what was it?"

Now she'd done it.

Adam's face glowed red in the light they were parked under.

"I knew it. There is something, isn't there?"

He swallowed hard a couple of times. "I am not now, nor have

I ever been, upset or frustrated with you. I apologize for causing you any distress, because that is the last thing I would ever want to do. Ever."

"That isn't an answer," she said. "That's a deflection. I didn't mean to imply any malice on your part, but if I'm missing something, you're going to have to tell me what it is. Because if you're waiting on me to figure it out, then you don't know me very well at all."

His mouth opened and closed a couple of times, like he couldn't force the words out of his mouth.

"Oh, good grief, Adam. What is it? Spit it out."

"I—"

Flashing lights and the blip of a siren cut off his words. A campus security car pulled up beside them and a security officer stepped out of the car. "Everything okay, Dr. Fleming?"

"Fine. Thank you."

"You sure?" His concerned expression turned into a glare when he looked at Adam. Then his gaze dropped to Adam's waist, where his badge and gun were in full view.

Adam stuck out his hand. "Good evening. Adam Campbell."

The security officer didn't speak.

"I'm with the Carrington County Sheriff's Office. And you are?" Adam prompted.

"Tyler Vance, campus security." Tyler finally shook Adam's hand.

"Nice to meet you." Adam's southern charm was on full display. "I appreciate the way you checked on Dr. Fleming."

"Just doing my job," Tyler said.

"And doing it well. Thank you."

Tyler looked back at Sabrina. "If you need anything at all, Dr. Fleming, just holler."

"I will."

Tyler returned to his car, but instead of driving away, he started talking into his radio.

Adam rolled his eyes. "He's going to stall until we leave."

"Why?"

Adam chuckled. "Tyler has a crush on you."

What? She glanced at Tyler. How could he have a crush on her? She'd never spoken to him before tonight. "I think you're mistaken."

"Trust me."

Tyler continued to have a conversation with someone and made no move to leave.

"What makes you so sure?"

"Did you not see the way he was looking at you? The desire to rip me limb from limb simmering behind his eyes? The delayed, then overly firm, handshake? He was trying very hard to stake a claim."

"I don't even know him!"

"He's probably been waiting for a chance to make a good impression."

"This makes no sense. If he wanted to talk to me, why not say hello? What's hard about that? And men say women are complicated."

Adam opened her car door for her and she settled into the driver's seat. "He hasn't talked to you because he's scared of rejection. He probably thinks very highly of you and isn't sure you'd be interested. And if he told you how he feels and you didn't reciprocate those feelings, then things would be awkward between you."

"Like they aren't awkward now?"

She couldn't make any sense of the look he gave her. Was he agreeing with her? Disagreeing? He was kind of smiling but kind of looked sad at the same time. "I'm following you home." He closed her door gently, and from the rearview mirror she saw him give Tyler a jaunty salute before climbing behind the wheel.

She was pulling out of the parking lot before it occurred to her that maybe Adam hadn't been talking about Tyler at all.

51

4

The ringtone Sabrina had assigned to Adam broke into her thoughts.

"Hey," she said.

"I got another call from Gabe."

Uh-oh.

"I'm going to head over to the victim's house. He has a deputy on the way. Once he intercepts us, he'll follow you home."

"What happened?" The silence on the other end of the line told her it was bad. "Adam?"

"Gabe didn't give me a lot of details. But it turns out Lisa Palmer was the accountant for several prominent businessmen in town."

"Let me guess. Someone's been up to no good."

"It's unclear. We're going to need a forensic accountant to go through everything. She left a note, but Gabe thinks it's fake." He let out a frustrated groan. "It's too soon to know anything. We don't even have an exact cause or time of death. But it's unlikely her death was a suicide, and it's more likely she knew something— something dark enough that someone killed her for it. And I'm guessing it's what she wanted to talk to me about last week."

Sabrina took a moment to process his words. "But we already suspected that. Why does Gabe need you to come tonight?"

"He wants me to see the place. He thinks someone's been through everything."

"Someone tossed her house?"

"No. They didn't. On the surface, nothing obvious is missing. But Gabe is convinced someone's been looking for something. Carefully and methodically. Probably most of last night. He wants another set of eyes."

Sabrina pulled to a stop at a red light. A marked police car flashed its lights to her right. "I'm guessing that's my escort?"

"It is," Adam said. "I'm sorry to have to rush off. Pete will take good care of you."

"It's not a problem. I'll see you tomorrow."

She disconnected the call. The police car followed her, and in her rearview mirror she saw Adam turn left.

She reached the driveway to her house ten minutes later and punched in the access code on the keypad. The gates swung open and the deputy pulled in close behind her. When she parked, he hopped out of his car and jogged to her door, motioning for her to roll the window down.

"Yes?"

"Hi, Dr. Fleming. I'm Pete. Adam wants me to check everything out before you go inside. He insisted."

Adam did have a chivalrous streak. It was unnecessary, but she knew him well enough to know he couldn't help it. It was part of his DNA.

And the truth was, she rather liked it.

"No problem." She handed the keys to Pete.

"Do you mind staying in the car?" he asked.

"Sure."

He was back in three minutes. "Cute house, Dr. Fleming. I've seen these tiny houses on TV, but I've never been inside one. Doesn't take long to check out, that's for sure. But everything looks good."

"Thank you."

Pete opened her car door and waited as she grabbed her bag. He handed her a card. "That has my direct number on it. I'm going to be in the area tonight. If you need anything, let me know."

"I appreciate it, Pete. That's very kind of you."

"Um . . . Adam asked me to wait until you put my number into your phone."

Oh, good grief. "I'll do him one better." She punched in the number and Pete's phone rang. "There. Now it's in my phone and it's my most recently dialed number."

Pete grinned. "Thanks, Dr. Fleming."

"It's Sabrina." She extended her hand and he shook it.

"Thanks, Sabrina. I'll stay until you're inside."

"Did he tell you he's going overboard with this? That I'm in no danger at all? The laptop is in my lab, not here."

Pete shrugged. "Your house is in my patrol area, ma'am. I don't know that it's overboard to want you to have a quick way to reach me. You live out here all alone. Might be nice to have my number handy."

"Okay. I get it. You're as bad as he is. But that's okay. I appreciate it. Have a good night, Pete."

"Thank you. I hope you do too." Pete leaned against his patrol car and watched her until she entered the door. As she turned the deadbolt, she heard his car door close.

She glanced around her small space. Nothing obvious was out of place. She opened her tiny fridge and selected last night's leftover pad Thai. While it spun in the microwave, she pulled her laptop from her bag and ran a quick search on the victim. She'd start with the basics—social media and regular internet searches. But there was so much more information available online than most people realized. Of course, it helped if you knew where to look. And she did.

"Lisa Palmer, what have you been up to?"

An hour later she still had questions, but she also had a lot of answers. Lisa Palmer was forty-three years old even though she looked a decade older. Single. Never married. Not a local. She'd graduated from the University of Georgia and worked as a CPA in Atlanta for ten years before moving to Carrington to start her own business. Her largest client was Zinzer Hospitality Group. They provided contract services for the hospitality industry all over the Southeast. They offered housekeeping, janitorial, groundskeeping, and facility maintenance services. She'd worked out of their offices for five years before she cut ties with them. It wasn't clear why. At that point her clientele became even more elite. Fewer businesses and more wealthy individuals. At some point after that she began working with Sabrina's father.

How had her dad found this woman? Had she had any idea what kind of man he was? Or what he had done? Sabrina had never been able to get an answer from her dad. Well, not an answer she could make sense of.

Sabrina chewed on her lip. On paper, everything looked legitimate, but something felt off. *Stop it. You've spent too much time looking for the bad guys and now you see them everywhere.* Lisa Palmer may very well have been innocent and gotten caught up in something she didn't understand.

Sabrina kept digging. Lisa Palmer had a dog until about five years ago, when he died of an accidental poisoning. Her parents still lived in Georgia, her sister in Tennessee. She had two nieces who smiled toothy grins in every picture.

She dropped her head. *Oh, Father, be with them.* So much pain was headed into their world.

Her phone rang. A different ringtone. Sabrina glanced at her clock—9:28 p.m. A bit late for Martine to be calling. "Hello," she said.

"Hi, Sabrina. You doing okay tonight?"

"I'm good, Martine, thanks." Martine Roberts ran a local anti–human trafficking group that Sabrina volunteered for called FreedomForAll.

"Great. Listen, I was wondering if you might be available to help with the Campbell Christmas Charity Gala this year. Since they have so graciously made us the primary beneficiary of the gala, we've volunteered to help make reminder calls to the guests and then be there a little early to welcome people as they come in."

Sabrina set her glasses on the table and rubbed her eyes. "I'm sorry, Martine. Galas aren't my area of expertise. And I'm afraid I'm in the middle of a big project right now and it's taking most of my time. I'm not going to be able to—"

"Oh, it wouldn't take much time," Martine said. "The gala committee has everything lined up. It would just be a few phone calls and then helping on the day of."

Sabrina fought the annoyance spreading through her mind like a virus. Martine was passionate about ending modern-day slavery, and Sabrina appreciated that about her.

"I'm afraid that won't be possible," she said in her firmest professorial tone. "I can't take on anything else right now."

"Well, I'll pencil you in as a maybe," Martine said. "If you finish up your project, you can let me know, okay?"

This woman would be the death of her.

"Martine, I'm going to have to go. I'll talk to you later."

"Okay. Thank you!"

Sabrina set the phone on the table and put her head in her hands. She'd specifically said no and somehow Martine decided it was okay to pencil her in? Really?

Sabrina pushed the aggravation from her mind and focused on typing her notes about Lisa Palmer. When she was finished, she emailed the file to her secure email account and to Adam's. Maybe the digging she'd done tonight would save him some time tomorrow.

She ran another search. This time for Rosita Garcia. It was the same basic search she ran every night. And again, the results were the same.

A big fat zero.

Sabrina needed to find Rosita. She needed to know for sure what had happened. Lives weren't like hard drives. She could never wipe the slate clean. But if it was as bad as she feared, she needed to do everything she could to make reparations for the things her dad had done.

Her phone rang again. This time she cringed when she recognized the ringtone. "Hello, Mother." She tried to keep her tone respectful.

"Hello. I only have a few moments. I'm meeting a client for dinner and then catching a red-eye from Seattle to Dulles."

"Okay."

"I was wondering if you've given any more thought to selling the house."

Her mom was never one to beat around the bush.

"I told you I talked to my lawyer. It makes sense to wait until I'm thirty. Everything will be much easier then. We don't need the money. It isn't hurting anything. I check on it every week."

"I don't understand why you don't move into the house if you won't sell it. It makes no sense to live like a pauper in a tin can on the property."

Sabrina didn't bother responding.

"You could at least stay in the guesthouse."

The guesthouse was two thousand square feet. "I don't need that kind of space, Mother."

"Everyone needs that kind of space," her mother said. "I have never understood you."

The feeling was mutual.

Her mother made a sound of displeasure. "My car is early. Why can't people show up when they say they will? Anyway, there's a chance I'll be in your area sometime in the next week or two, but nothing is definite yet. I'll let you know."

"Okay."

The only response was dead air.

At 6:00 a.m. Sabrina's alarm jolted her to awareness. Her dreams had been troubled. Nothing specific, but everything was dark and angry. That's what she got for digging up the past.

She guzzled a glass of water, dressed, chose some music, and slid her phone into the zipper pocket on the leg of her jogging pants. She stepped outside and secured a wireless earbud in each ear. With sunrise still an hour away, stars twinkled and the moon shone brightly as she jogged down the long driveway toward her father's house. She'd turned the corner by the pond when her earbuds died. Awesome. Now she'd be stuck with nothing but her thoughts for the rest of her run.

She eyed the large home visible in the distance past the pond. She'd never lived in it. Never wanted to live in it. Never understood why he'd bought the monstrosity in the first place.

But he'd been adamant that he would not go to any sort of assisted living facility. Said he didn't want anyone's sympathy. Lined up all his own caregivers before his mind completely deserted him.

She stretched out her legs and tried to lose herself in the feeling of her feet hitting the pavement, the crisp air stinging her ears and nose, the air whooshing in and out of her lungs.

But the memories came anyway.

It was one afternoon while she was sitting with her father that he'd said the words that had turned everything on edge. "Rosita, where have you been? I've been looking everywhere for you. I'm sorry."

Over the next few months, he mentioned Rosita from time to time and called her Rosita more than once.

She'd tried to make sense of the rambling, but—

She slammed into a large mass. One earbud fell from her ear as she crashed to the ground on her right hip.

Her leg throbbed as she tried to scramble to her feet, but something hard shoved her back to the ground. The other earbud fell and she heard heavy breathing. A dark shape rose in front of her.

She rolled to her right, mind racing. She pushed back the panic rising in her. She had to think. Fight back or run?

She was fast, but not faster than a bullet. But it was dark enough that she wouldn't be an easy target. If she could get this guy on his back, she could make a dash for the trees. She'd never lived in the house, but she'd spent hours exploring the grounds around it. If she could get away, she might stand a chance.

Desperation clawed through her mind as he moved toward her. It was now or never.

She made a swipe for the legs she could barely make out in the fading moonlight. The bulky form stumbled back a step but then recovered and lunged at her.

Pain splintered through her head.

And everything went dark.

Monday morning came way too early. Adam parked his unmarked sedan in the sheriff's office parking lot before seven. He checked his phone as he climbed out—no messages from Sabrina. Pete was going to make a final pass near her house before his shift ended in a few minutes.

A brief blast from a horn startled him. He glanced around until he found the culprit. Ryan Parker laughed as he got out of the car and started walking toward him. "Gotcha."

Adam didn't bother to respond.

"Wow. You're cheery this morning," Ryan said as they entered the building.

Even Ryan's sarcasm was upbeat. It took longer than it should have to register why that might be. "Wait a minute," Adam said. "Did you propose to Leigh?"

A Texas-wide grin spread across Ryan's face. "Yep."

"That's awesome." He clapped Ryan on the back. "Congratulations." They entered the elevator that would take them to their offices on the third floor.

"Thanks, man, but you're assuming she said yes."

"That was a foregone conclusion. And even if I had a smidgen of doubt, your excessive happiness would have made it pretty clear how things went."

The elevator doors opened.

"I'm not excessively happy."

Gabe glared at the two of them from the coffee station. "Yes, you are. Congratulations."

He stalked toward the homicide offices without a backward glance. "Campbell. I have information for you when you're ready."

"This is going to be a fun day." Ryan didn't sound convinced of his own words.

Gabe poked his head out the door. "Ryan, you come too. I want to bounce a few things off you." He disappeared, then reemerged a few moments later. "I don't suppose Leigh made cookies or anything?"

Ryan held up a lunchbox. "Two dozen."

The elevator doors opened again and Anissa Bell stepped out.

"I love her," Gabe said.

"Who?" Anissa looked around the room.

"Leigh," Gabe said. "Who else?"

"You love Leigh?" Anissa's brow furrowed. "Um . . ." She glanced at Ryan. Then Adam.

"She made cookies." Ryan patted the lunchbox. "Apparently Gabe's love can be purchased with baked goods."

"Not true," Gabe said. "But it doesn't hurt."

Anissa's face relaxed and she focused on Ryan. "So . . ."

That same goofy grin lit Ryan's face. "She said yes."

Anissa hugged Ryan. "I knew it. Congratulations. Have you set a date?"

"Maybe spring? Leigh doesn't want anything big. She just wants her brother and a few friends from the hospital to come. And all of you, of course." He turned to Adam. "And Sabrina."

Sabrina would be so excited for Leigh. And Ryan.

"Look, none of us are surprised by this, so can y'all get your coffee and get in here? We have a murder to solve," Gabe said.

Adam braced himself for whatever was coming. Gabe's bad mood didn't give him much hope that the evening had gone any better after he left the victim's house.

Anissa and Ryan went to their desks. Adam pulled a chair out from one of the vacant desks and waited for Gabe to fortify himself with three cookies. Gabe pointed to Adam. "Want to start with what we know from last night?"

"Our victim, Lisa Palmer, went over the embankment at the twin bridges around 2:24 a.m. That's Saturday night/Sunday morning. There was no indication of braking—no skid marks—to indicate she was forced off the road. And while there are a few cameras on the bridge in that area, the video footage we have doesn't show any other cars either."

"She could have fallen asleep," Anissa said.

"Possible. But if she'd fallen asleep, we would have expected to see some evidence on the video of her trying to maneuver the car as she went down the hill. A few good bumps and she should have been awake and panicked. But there was nothing. The video quality is poor, but from what we can see it appears the car bounced down the embankment and into the lake. It took a few minutes to sink. It doesn't appear that it hit the water that hard or fast. Unless she hit her head and got knocked out somehow, we would have expected her to try to get out of the car, but if our not-so-Good Samaritan can be believed, she was still in her seat belt."

"I thought somebody said her neck was broken," Ryan observed.

Gabe rolled his eyes. "Yeah, turns out that is also an observation from the moron who dragged her body out of the lake. Dr. Oliver said she couldn't say just by looking at her if it was broken or not."

"Well, she went down a pretty steep hill and hit the water. The broken neck thing seems reasonable." Adam took a bite of his cookie.

"You'd think," Gabe said, "but Dr. Oliver says it's not a foregone conclusion. She says plenty of people survive a trip down a hill like that, and the entry into the lake is at a gentle enough angle that, based on what she saw, she wouldn't assume Lisa broke her neck on the way down."

"Wait a minute. So we're saying she was either unconscious or already dead—and managed to drive herself into the lake? How is that possible?" Ryan asked.

"No idea," Gabe said.

"So, let me get this straight." Ryan took a sip of coffee. "She definitely was in the driver's seat when she ran off the road?"

"What are you thinking?" Gabe asked.

"Could she have been in the passenger seat and someone slid her over into the driver's side and then swam away?"

Adam tried to suppress a shudder from the mental image of Ryan's words.

"That is actually possible," Anissa said. "Our no-Good Samaritan claimed both driver- and passenger-side windows were down. If he had left the body alone, we might have been able to tell if anyone else was in the car with her, but the scene was too contaminated."

"The guy free dove down and got her out of the car?" Ryan asked. "Couldn't he tell she was already dead?"

Anissa shrugged. "He was drunk."

Ryan choked on his coffee. "What?"

"Oh yeah. We couldn't even interview him properly until he'd dried out. He told the first responders on the scene that he'd been fishing and saw the car, so he dove in to help the lady. He said he had to dive down several times and eventually he was able to drag her out. He claims he didn't realize she was dead until after he got her to shore."

"Great." Ryan set his mug on his desk. "So it's possible someone drove the car over the embankment and into the lake, then put her in the driver's seat, maybe while the car was sinking, and then once it was underwater they swam away?"

"Theoretically." Gabe snorted. "I'll know more by lunchtime. Dr. Oliver is going to do the autopsy this morning. I don't know that there's much sense in speculating about the manner of death until we get everything from her."

Ryan held up his hands in a sign of surrender. "It's your case. It's just weird."

"Oh, it's about to get weirder, bro." Gabe pulled four sheets of paper off his desk. "There's a suicide note."

"What's weird about that?"

"Read it."

I don't know how long it will be before you find my body. I can't live with myself anymore. I've done horrible things and hurt so many innocent people that there's nothing I can do in this lifetime to redeem myself. I can only pray God will be merciful to me.

"That doesn't seem weird to me," Anissa said.

"What makes it weird is that, from what we've been able to determine, the woman was a saint. She volunteered at her church with the teenage girls. Sang in the choir. Went on mission trips every year. Took care of the neighbor's dogs when he traveled. Looked in on the elderly neighbors across the street. As far as the people in her neighborhood were concerned, she was a wonderful person."

"Everyone has secrets," Anissa said in a grim voice.

"No doubt." Gabe agreed with a nod toward Anissa. "But if that's true, she had a lot of people fooled."

"I agree," Adam said. "Sabrina did some kind of search last night and wasn't able to find anything out of the ordinary. She emailed me everything she has uncovered so far. Said she was going to do a deep dive on her today while she's waiting on the hard drive to dry out. I'm going to go through Lisa Palmer's financial records, phone records, and then whatever Sabrina can pull off the laptop. I'll let you know if I find anything suspicious."

Gabe pointed at Adam. "Forensics found three flash drives and an iPad in her bedroom. Sabrina's going to look at all of them for us, so we'll see if there's anything that would indicate Lisa was hiding some deep, dark secret. Can you get them to her?"

"Happy to," Adam said.

Ryan snickered.

Gabe rolled his eyes.

Even Anissa was fighting a smile.

"What's so funny?" Adam asked.

"Nothing," Anissa said.

"You are," Gabe said at the same time.

Ryan laughed. "Do you really think you have us fooled? You've been carrying a torch for Sabrina for at least a year."

"Longer." Gabe coughed the word into his hand.

"I'm not . . . we're not . . ."

"And why is that?" Anissa asked.

The three investigators stared at him. "What is this?" Adam countered. "Are we solving a murder or analyzing my love life?"

"I don't think we said anything about a love life," Gabe said. "Did you mention love?" He pointed at Ryan. Then Anissa. "Did you?"

They both shook their heads no.

"You're the only one talking about love, bro," Gabe said.

"Don't you have an autopsy to go to?" Adam asked.

Gabe tapped his watch. "Not for another hour."

"Just give me the stuff you want me to take to Sabrina." Adam held out his hand.

"We're only asking because we want you to be happy," Anissa said.

"I'm perfectly happy."

It wasn't until all three of them roared with laughter that Adam realized he'd growled the words. He took the box from Gabe, signed off on the forms giving him custody of the evidence, and walked away without another word.

They followed him out of the office, but he ignored them. He turned to the elevator and they went to the coffee station. He had to wait for the elevator to reach their floor and overheard Ryan ask, "Do you think we made him mad?"

"Nah," Gabe said. "He's aggravated because he knows we're right."

"I wonder if Sabrina even realizes how much he cares about her," Anissa said. "It's obvious to the rest of us, but she doesn't always pick up on things."

The elevator doors opened and four officers stepped out. Their chatter drowned out the rest of the conversation, but Adam couldn't get their words out of his mind as he rode to the ground floor.

Father, do I risk our friendship to see what else we might have?

His phone buzzed.

"Hey, Pete," he said.

"Adam, go to the hospital right now." Pete's usual easygoing manner had been replaced by an intensity Adam hadn't known the young officer possessed.

"What—"

"I don't have time to explain. I'll meet you there."

The phone disconnected.

This had to have something to do with Sabrina. Adam ran for his car, praying the whole way.

5

Adam's phone rang again as he pulled into the Carrington Memorial Hospital parking lot. This time it was Gabe. He didn't bother saying hello. "What?"

"Leigh called Ryan. She's with Sabrina."

Terror warred with gratitude. He was relieved Leigh was taking care of Sabrina. But the uncertainty of what had happened to her was killing him. "Did she say what happened?" He parked his car in a spot reserved for law enforcement and jogged inside.

"Still don't know. They're taking her back for a CT scan. Leigh didn't give us any details. Just said Pete had come in with her and . . ."

Adam's chest tightened. "And what?"

"Leigh said Sabrina had been hit on the head and knocked out."

A primordial rage bubbled in Adam's limbs.

"Ryan's talking to Pete right now. We're on our way to Sabrina's house. Keep us informed about her condition."

"Okay."

The automatic doors opened, and the antiseptic air of the emergency department waiting area assaulted Adam's senses. He went straight to the front desk.

The security guard looked him over. "Are you Investigator Campbell?"

"Yes."

He pushed a button and then waved Adam through. "Pete told me you were headed this way. I'd recommend you check with Miss Edna before you go wandering around."

"Thanks," he said.

Everyone—nurses, doctors, housekeeping staff—everyone deferred to Miss Edna. She ran the emergency department, and no one dared tell her otherwise.

Miss Edna had also taught Adam's Sunday school class when he was in fifth grade. She was simultaneously the meanest and kindest person he'd ever known.

He approached her desk and paused.

She didn't even look up from the paperwork she was searching through. "I see you standing there, Adam Campbell," she said. "Pete's waiting on you in room 4. Down the hall to the right."

"Thank you."

"Don't you worry, baby," she called after him. "She's going to be okay."

He stopped and returned to the desk. Miss Edna gazed at him over her reading glasses. He reached a hand across the desk and she squeezed it.

"Thank you, Miss Edna."

She sandwiched his hand between both of hers and gave him a nod. "Be nice to that boy. He's a wreck."

She must have been referring to Pete.

"I will, Miss Edna."

"Now, go on."

She released his hand and he fought the desire to run down the hall. Room 4 was only a few steps away. When he walked inside, Pete jumped to his feet.

"Adam, I'm sorry. I didn't know she was going to go for a run, and I—"

"Pete," Adam said, "did you hit her on the head?"

Shock crossed Pete's face. "Of course not. I would never—"

"Then this isn't your fault. You can't take the blame for something you didn't do." Pete's shoulders slumped. "Now slow down and take me through it from the beginning."

Pete blew out a long breath. "I did what you asked. I stopped by every half hour. I even walked around her little house each time. Never saw a thing. Then my phone rang, and it was Sabrina. Except when I answered it, all I could hear was a scuffling sound. I called her name, but she didn't respond."

He paced around the small room. "I was two minutes away, so I hit the siren and raced over there. I banged on the door. She didn't answer, so I . . . I tried the door. It wasn't locked, so I let myself in." Pete's eyes pled for understanding.

"Good," Adam said. "Exactly what I would have done."

"But she wasn't there. Her car was still there, but she was gone. I had no idea where she might be. I called for backup and took off down the driveway toward the big house. And that's when I saw her. About half a mile down."

Pete ran his hands over his shaved head. "She was on the ground. I ran to her. There was blood. I thought it was a lot, but Leigh says head wounds bleed a lot and it's not as bad as it looked. I called for an ambulance. Checked to be sure she was breathing. But I was afraid to move her. I felt like a jerk leaving her on the ground, but the ambulance was only three minutes out, so I covered her with my jacket."

He pulled a notebook from his pocket. "I looked for footprints or any sign of someone being there. The driveway is paved, but I took pictures of some muddy prints, pretty big. I'm guessing a man, size eleven or twelve. The footprints disappeared into the woods. I took pictures of everything and sent them to Gabe. He's getting forensics out there."

He glanced at his notes again. "I didn't see anything that could have been used to hit Sabrina," he said. "I don't know if they used a stick or a rock or a . . . a fist."

Adam tried not to picture any of those options.

"Anyway." Pete flipped his notebook closed. "The ambulance arrived, and the paramedics did the whole neck brace thing. When they started moving her around, she woke up. She was confused but not anything I wouldn't expect after what had happened. She was answering questions and stuff. The backup I'd called for had gotten there by then. I told them to secure the scene, and I followed the ambulance here."

He leaned against the wall. "By the time I got inside, Leigh was with her. She told me she was going to stay with Sabrina every second. I think Leigh may technically be off work now, but she went with Sabrina for the CT scan. Before they went to radiology, she came by and said Sabrina was awake and talking and I could wait in here."

Pete closed his eyes. "I seriously thought she was dead. When I saw her on the ground . . . I don't know if I could have lived with myself."

Adam clapped him on the shoulder. "I'll tell you what Sabrina told me yesterday."

Pete looked at him with interest.

"You can't hold yourself responsible for what happened when you weren't around. You did a great job."

"Thanks. I still haven't figured out how she called me though. She didn't have her phone, although her little wireless earbuds were lying on the ground near her."

"We'll figure it out," Adam said. "You can hang around if you want, but if you're ready to head back and get things written up so you can get some sleep, that's fine with me. I'll keep you informed."

Pete blinked hard a few times. "Leigh said it wouldn't be long. I think I'll wait a few more minutes, if that's okay."

"Absolutely," Adam said.

His phone rang. "It's Ryan," he said to Pete, then swiped the screen. "Hello."

"Hey," Ryan said. "What's the story on this house out here at Sabrina's place?"

"It belonged to her dad," Adam said. "Technically it belongs to her now, I guess. Why?"

"I want to go through the house and look for any signs that someone's been in there. It would have been a great place to hide if the attacker was trapped inside the gate," Ryan said.

"I'm sure she'd be fine with that," Adam said.

"Fine with what?"

Adam whipped around. Sabrina smiled at him from a wheelchair. He forced himself not to run to her as a transporter pushed her into the room, then she and Leigh helped Sabrina onto the bed.

Adam held back until she was settled. Then he reached for her hand. "Hi," he said.

"Hi." She frowned. "Don't look at me like that."

"Like what?"

"Like I have a terminal disease. It's just a mild concussion."

Adam bit back the things he wanted to say. There was no need to point out how much danger she'd been in and probably still was.

"Excuse me, Dr. Fleming." Leigh's tone carried a mixture of exasperation, annoyance, and worry. "You took a serious blow to the head this morning. You passed out. You can't take this lightly. No, you don't have a terminal disease, but the people who care about you have been worried sick, and while we're relieved you're okay, we're still very concerned for your safety. You're going to have to deal with us hovering for a while because that's what friends do. Got it?"

Sabrina's mouth had fallen open as Leigh spoke.

Pete studied the latex glove boxes on the wall like they were the most fascinating things he'd ever seen. His red face was the only indication he'd heard Leigh's speech.

For his part, Adam couldn't win by disagreeing with Leigh or antagonizing Sabrina, so he chose the safest path. He squeezed

Sabrina's hand. "I can't argue with you or with Leigh. You aren't dying, so we don't need to be ridiculous about this. But you came awfully close to it this morning, so you're going to have to give us room to be worrywarts for a while. Okay?"

"Fair enough." Reluctance laced her words. "What happens now?"

Adam deferred to Leigh.

"As soon as Dr. Sloan gives you the okay, you'll be free to go home, although I think it's safe to say no one will want you staying by yourself for a while."

Sabrina's brow furrowed. "Can I go back to work? I have a lot to do on this case."

Leigh scrunched up her entire face and glared at Sabrina. There was no real heat behind it, but Sabrina looked worried.

Leigh pointed to her own face. "You see this? This is my 'You're killing me' look. Memorize it. It means I don't like what you're suggesting, but I know you're going to do it anyway. It doesn't mean I don't like you, so don't look at me like I'm being mean to you."

Sabrina's expression cleared as Leigh spoke. "So I can go to work?"

"I'll talk to Dr. Sloan," Leigh said. "No promises."

Adam's phone rang. He ignored it. It rang again. "Oh no," he said as he grabbed it. "Sorry, Ryan. I forgot you were there."

Ryan laughed. "No problem. Can you ask Sabrina about getting into the house?"

"Let me put you on speaker," Adam said. "Go ahead."

"Hey, everyone," Ryan called out.

Everyone gathered in the small room replied, "Hey."

"Sabrina?" Ryan said.

"Yes," she said.

"Is there any chance we could get into the house? We need to check for any signs of intruders."

Sabrina's face paled. "Of course. There's a set of keys to both the main house and the guest house behind it. They're on the key ring in my house. I assume you've already been in there."

"We have," Ryan said. "Nothing looks out of place to me, but you'll have to check it carefully to be sure. There's no rush on that, of course."

"Oh, she thinks she's ready to go back to work," Leigh said. There were chuckles all around.

"I'll leave that to the medical professionals," Ryan said. "Is there a security system at the house, Sabrina?"

"There is," she said. "A really good one. My dad was at high risk for wandering. The gates, fences, doors, everything is all monitored. I can't figure out how anyone could have gotten in without setting it off."

"All the more reason for us to check it out," Ryan said.

Sabrina gave him the code, and before he disconnected the call, Ryan promised to keep her informed.

"Pete," Sabrina said. "You have to quit looking at me that way. I'm fine. But I have to ask . . . how did you know to come looking for me?"

Pete gave Sabrina a halfhearted smile. She could see how much effort it took for him to do it. "You called me," he said.

"I did what? When?" She hadn't called Pete. Not on purpose, anyway.

He pulled his phone from his pocket and scrolled through. "The call came in at 6:23 a.m. I answered the phone, but all I could hear was a rustling sound and what I thought was you grunting. I called your name several times, and when you didn't answer, I was afraid something was wrong. I was hoping you'd butt-dialed me and it was no big deal, but I didn't want to risk it."

Sabrina processed Pete's version of the events. How had she called him?

"Sabrina?" Concern saturated Adam's voice. "Can you tell us what you remember?"

She started at the beginning. Top down. Just like a computer program. It would help if her head didn't feel like someone was taking a jackhammer to it, but she could figure this out. "I got up and got ready to go for a run."

Adam raised his hand and she nodded at him. "Do you run every morning?"

"Weather permitting," she said. "I don't care to run in the rain."

Adam raised his hand again. Pete snickered. "Do you carry your phone, or is it in your pocket?"

Her pocket . . . She patted her right thigh. "My phone's gone. He took my phone."

Pete's eyes widened.

"Let's go back a little." Adam spoke through clenched teeth. "I'm assuming by the way you're patting your leg that you put your phone in your pocket before you ran?"

Sabrina focused on retracing her steps. "Yes. I got up. Got dressed. Picked a playlist. Put the phone in my pocket. Put in my wireless earbuds. Left the house. Went down the driveway. My earbuds died about five minutes into my run, but I didn't bother taking them out."

How much farther had she run? Where had the guy come from that she didn't see him?

"They were on the ground near you," Pete said. "I assumed they fell out when you—"

"It was a man," she said. "I don't know where he came from. He was just there. I thought I'd run into him. But now I'm not sure. Maybe he ran into me."

Adam tilted his head as if he was considering her comment. "If he'd been waiting for you, he could have popped up right as you ran by him."

"I guess." Sabrina leaned back against the pillows. "Ugh. I wasn't paying attention. I should have been more on guard."

"You were out for a jog on gated private property," Pete said. "Hardly a reason to expect someone to attack you."

Sabrina wasn't sure she believed him, but it was nice of him to say that. "Thanks, Pete."

"Are you sure it was a man?" Leigh asked.

Sabrina considered her question. "Yes," she said. "When I ran into him, I grabbed his arms. He was hairy. And his arms were thick, but not like fat thick. He was solid muscle. He was at least a foot taller than me. His hands were . . . huge."

"We won't completely rule out a woman." Adam nodded toward Leigh. "But it's more likely the attacker was a man."

"Agreed," Leigh said.

"Now, where were we?" Adam ticked off items on his fingers. "You ran into the attacker . . ."

"Yes. It was like hitting a wall. I reached out with my hands, to catch myself." Sabrina stretched out her arms. "But when I grabbed his arms, he threw me to the ground. I wasn't sure if I could outrun him, but I thought if I could get him on the ground I'd have a better chance. I tried to get up . . ."

Why was it hard to remember the details? "I'm not sure what happened. I think I tried to kick his legs? Maybe? Or grab them? I think I pushed him away from me, but that's the last thing I can remember."

"It's okay," Leigh said. "Your brain is protecting itself. Don't fight it. You might remember more details over the next few days. Or you might not. It's okay either way."

"No, it isn't." Sabrina closed her eyes. None of this was okay. The phrase "pounding headache" had never made more sense to her than it did in this moment. Her right leg . . . "Oh."

She sat up fast. Too fast. Searing pain scorched its way through her skull and she caught her breath at the intensity of it.

Adam's hand on her back and arm sent a shiver through her. "Are you okay?" His words came low, right at her ear.

"What is it?" Leigh asked.

"My leg. My phone. That's how I called Pete."

Leigh, Adam, and Pete all made eye contact with one another, but not with her. What wasn't clear about this?

"My leg is killing me," she said. She pulled the hospital gown away from her right thigh, revealing a rectangular-shaped bruise already forming. "I fell on my phone. I'd put Pete's number in last night, and when I fell I must have leg-dialed him. With my earbuds dead, the Bluetooth would have been off, so Pete would have been able to hear, but it would have been through the material of my pants, so it would have been muffled."

Now they all nodded in understanding. "Makes sense," Pete said.

"And if you were only two minutes out, in the cool morning air, the sound of the siren would have reached the attacker in advance of you," Adam said to Pete. "You may have saved her life."

Pete's face flushed. "I would have liked to have saved her a headache." His words were gruff, but his smile was more natural now. "So the attacker hears the siren, takes Sabrina's phone, and rabbits," Pete said. "The property is fenced. How did he disappear?"

"My guess is however he got in. When we check the perimeter, we'll find out how he did it." Adam narrowed his eyes at Sabrina. "But until then, I don't think you should stay in your house alone."

He said it nicely, but there was an undercurrent she didn't recognize in Adam's voice. Either he was mad, which she didn't think was accurate, or he was not going to be easily dissuaded. But was he suggesting what she thought he was suggesting? "Well, my house isn't big enough for two people, and I'm not staying in my father's house by myself or with anybody else," Sabrina said.

"I'm not suggesting you should." Adam's tone was conciliatory. "But—"

"I can go to a hotel. Or I can sleep at my lab. It's secure. I have a sofa in my office."

"You can't sleep in your office. Come stay with me!" Leigh's excitement was impossible to miss. "It will be awesome. Like old times. You guys can all come over tonight, and I'll cook. You'll solve the case."

A sleepover at Leigh's? Sabrina couldn't quite picture it, but it did sound better than a hotel. And it was way better than sleeping in her lab. That sofa was awful.

"What do you think?" Adam looked so hopeful that she wasn't sure she could have said no to anything he asked her to do.

"Sure. Why not? But I need to go to my house and pack."

"I'll come with you," Adam said.

"Excellent," Leigh said. "Now that we've got it all figured out, I think Pete here needs to crash." Her mouth stretched into a huge yawn. "For that matter, so do I."

Heat flooded through Sabrina's entire system. "Oh no! You've both been up all night and I'm yammering. Pete, I appreciate everything you've done for me, but I think you should go get some sleep."

He nodded. "I will, but I'm going to call you later to check on you."

"Sounds good."

Adam shook Pete's hand. "I can't thank you enough." Adam's voice sounded a little funny and Pete didn't say anything. He just nodded. It was like he and Adam were having some conversation without words.

When they were done, Pete stepped to the side of her bed and gave her hand an awkward pat. "Don't do anything crazy today," he said.

Leigh followed him to the door. "I'm going to go spring you," she said to Sabrina. "Be back in a sec."

Sabrina watched the door close, then she turned to Adam. "Leigh's been so wonderful. I'm so glad she was here. The ED was deserted when I came in, but I'm sure Leigh helped move things along. The doctor was in my room within a few minutes and then they whisked me off to radiology. She said I was lucky to be in here on a Monday morning and not a Saturday morning."

Adam gave her a weak grin. She got the feeling he wouldn't have minded if things had gone a little slower.

"What can I do to help today? Besides taking you home. Are you supposed to drive? Should I take you to your lab?"

Sabrina studied Adam's face, looking for any clue that he was joking. "You aren't going to give me grief about going to work?"

He sat on the edge of the bed. "Would it do any good?"

"No. But I'm surprised you aren't trying."

"I know you too well." He laughed. "You aren't going to go home or go to Leigh's and take a nap. It's not in your nature. Not only are you itching to start working on the evidence we recovered from Lisa Palmer's house, but my guess is your brain is already working overtime on who attacked you, how they got in, what they wanted, and why they took your phone."

He was good. And somehow the idea of being known so well wasn't terrifying as long as it was Adam who was doing the knowing.

"Well, in that case . . ."

Juan was an idiot.

Sabrina Fleming was still alive.

How could that blockhead have messed this up? He outweighed her by at least a hundred pounds. She was alone. It was dark.

The plan had been foolproof.

Until the fool proved him wrong.

And then Juan took her phone. Why?

He didn't need her phone! He needed her dead.

At least the oaf had called him immediately rather than driving straight back with the phone on and searchable.

That would have been a disaster.

As it was, the phone had been disposed of. And if by some fluke of fate it was discovered? Well, that wouldn't be such a bad thing.

He sipped his espresso and considered his options. He'd had to talk fast to convince Juan that trying again today would be a mistake. They would wait. Watch. An opportunity would present itself and when it did, Juan would be free to get the vengeance he craved.

He had time. Not a lot, but enough. This was but one piece of the intricate puzzle he'd been putting together for the past three years.

The phone rang.

Ah. Another piece.

"Hello, dearest. How was your flight?"

6

By 10:30 a.m. Sabrina regretted the decision to go to work with every fiber of her being. She refused to slump against the seat of the car and instead held her back and neck straight as Adam parked in front of her lab. She needed to get some more ibuprofen into her system. Soon.

But more than anything, she wanted to get someplace where she felt safe. She hadn't been prepared to feel so exposed, so vulnerable, but from the moment she'd stepped out of the emergency department doors she'd been unable to shake the sense that someone was watching. That at any moment a red dot would appear on her chest, or worse, Adam's.

"Bri."

She turned to Adam, but he wasn't looking in her direction with the earnest, concerned expression she'd been expecting. He sat in the driver's seat, leaning forward at a slight acute angle. He clenched the steering wheel. His throat worked and his mouth moved, but he didn't speak. He shook his head a couple of times, then blew out a long breath. "Sit tight." He climbed from the car.

What had just happened?

He opened the trunk, closed it, and opened her door seconds

later. "Don't stand up too fast." He had a box tucked under his arm and extended his hand toward her. "Or that headache you're pretending you don't have will set you on your rear."

"Excuse me?" How did he—?

He took her right hand, and she twisted toward him. She put her left hand on the door and swung her feet to the ground. Instead of pulling her, he waited. He studied her the way she studied computer code, like he could read everything she wasn't saying just by watching her face.

And maybe he could. Because the moment she thought she could stand, he pulled her toward him. He didn't start walking, just took one step back and steadied her.

"Ready?"

She nodded. Ouch. That was a mistake.

He offered her his arm as he had last night and set a slow pace toward the lab.

She focused on putting one foot in front of the other. To think that earlier this morning she'd been running, feeling the air in her lungs, the breeze on her skin. Now she wanted to run but couldn't. All she could do was pray she could stay on her feet long enough to get to her lab and sit down in the safety of those four walls.

"Almost there." Adam's lips brushed against her hair.

Did he know how scared she was? Or how much she was hurting? Or both?

They rode the elevator in silence. He stayed close until they reached her door. He stepped back, his body angled between her and the open hallway. She leaned forward for the iris scan. The motion sent pain splintering through her head, and she sucked in a sharp breath.

Adam's hand tightened on her elbow. "Are you okay?"

She didn't dare nod. "Yes." The door clicked, and he opened it for her. She stepped inside and leaned against the wall. Maybe the room would stop spinning if she closed her eyes.

She heard the door close. Heard him set the box on a desk.

Then she sensed more than heard Adam move toward her. "Bri." He pulled her against him, his arms tightening until her face was pressed against his chest.

Her arms wrapped around him without her conscious permission.

"I . . . I thought I'd lost you this morning," he said. "When they told me . . ."

He pressed his forehead against the top of hers and for the first time in several hours, she relaxed. They had stood like that for what could have been a couple of minutes but was probably only a few seconds, when his entire body tensed.

He pulled away, his neck and face flushed. "Sorry about that."

Why was he sorry? She wasn't complaining. She'd take a blow to the head once a week if it generated that kind of response from him.

Well, maybe not every week. That probably wouldn't be good for her brain cells.

Still . . .

Adam cleared his throat. "Let me get you a chair. You need to sit. Where do you want to sit? Over here?"

Adam Campbell was rambling? Adam Campbell didn't ramble. "I can walk."

He grabbed a chair and placed it beside her at the workstation she'd paused by. "Sit. Please."

"I'm fine." She eased into the chair. It would be easier to make him believe her if she didn't feel like someone was shoving an ice pick through the top of her head.

He pulled a small bottle from his pocket and handed it to her. "Leigh gave me this before we left." The little cylinder contained pain relievers. "She said you're going to need something stronger but to take this to get you by until you're done working."

She opened the bottle and poured a couple of tablets into her palm.

"How badly are you hurting?" he asked.

"Honestly?"

"That would be preferable," he said with overdone nonchalance. "Saves time, but you can keep lying if it makes you feel better."

He knew anyway, so why was she compelled to keep up a front? If she couldn't be honest with Adam, was there anyone she could be truthful with? "I'm not sure anything can help me feel better," she said.

"Sleep would help." Adam flashed a cherubic smile.

"You won't let me go home yet."

"Leigh said you could go to her house."

"I'll think about it. But for now, let's see what we're dealing with."

Adam frowned at her, but he retrieved the box he'd carried in and placed it on the desk in front of her.

She pulled three flash drives and a tablet from the box. "This is it? This is all you found at the victim's house?"

Adam nodded. "I was there last night. The flash drives were in a little bowl on her dresser. The tablet was on her bedside table. If she had anything else, we haven't found it yet."

"Hmm."

"What's bothering you about this?"

"Is forensics going to look everywhere?"

"I should hope so." Adam tapped the desk. "That's what they do."

"I'm not talking about desk drawers, or even under the mattress. I'm talking about inside cereal boxes, food in the fridge, bottles of lotion that may or may not contain lotion."

"You think she hid something in a bottle of lotion?"

"I don't know. But this is a small digital footprint for someone who made her living on a computer. One laptop, a tablet, and a handful of flash drives?"

"You think we're missing something?"

"I know we are." So many things. "To start with, where's her phone?"

"We don't know. It wasn't in her purse, and it wasn't in the car. We got the search warrant for everything last night, and I ran a search for her phone. The last place it pinged was a tower in the vicinity of her home. But that doesn't mean she didn't turn it off. Anissa and Ryan are going to search the lake for it today. We didn't find it yesterday, but we didn't finish the search grid either. We ran out of manpower when Gabe and I both had to focus our attention elsewhere."

"They aren't going to find it in the lake."

"What makes you say that? The guy who went down there and pulled her out could have dislodged it."

"Do you really think her phone floated away?" she asked. "The car was submerged overnight. Given the nature of the trip down the embankment and into the water, it's unlikely the phone would have remained on the seat. And even if it did, phones don't float. If her phone was anywhere in the car when it entered the lake, it would have settled on the floorboards."

"I think we would be foolish not to look for it, regardless of whether or not I think that's what happened." Adam paced around the desk. "We can't make assumptions at this point in the case. It would be irresponsible not to finish searching the grid we laid out. We might find something we weren't expecting. You never know what might break a case open."

He had a point. "Fine. I'll agree with that. But where are the external hard drives? There's no way she didn't have some."

"We didn't find any. Maybe she used the cloud."

"I'm sure she did, but there's no way she didn't have some hard—"

"Not everyone is as tech savvy as you are," Adam said. "Lots of people are walking around without any kind of backup for their computers, phones, photos."

"I don't understand people like that."

Adam laughed. "I know."

"Does she have a safe deposit box?" Sabrina asked.

"No record of one. But that doesn't mean we won't find something later."

"What about an office?"

"She's worked from home for five years."

This didn't make sense.

"Sabrina, what are you thinking?"

"What?"

"You have this frustrated look on your face." Adam's smile was gentle, not teasing. He did tease her from time to time, but he was very careful about it. "Please tell me what's bothering you."

"It's this," she said. "Three flash drives and an iPad? Even if she used cloud storage, she should have more than this. I bet your grandmother has more than this, and she's not an accountant. There should be a desktop. Multiple monitors. The laptop you found was a nice enough machine, but it's too small to do a lot of work on."

"Maybe whoever killed her took it," Adam said. "Although Gabe was right. The house didn't appear to have been tossed. It was more a feeling. Like something was off, but since we'd never seen it before, we didn't know what we were looking for."

"Maybe they knew what they wanted and didn't bother with anything else."

Sabrina tried to slow her swirling mind. Many possibilities floated before her, but now wasn't the time to explore them. They didn't have enough information. She needed to focus on what she could do in this moment and leave the loose ends alone until she could do something with them. And until she wasn't muddled by pain.

"One more question. And I promise I'm not complaining or trying to be difficult, but why is Gabe insisting that I look at this?" She palmed one of the flash drives. "Forensics can handle it."

"The captain thought it was a good idea for the sake of continuity. And forensics is backed up, so it might be a week before they get to it."

Sabrina was itching to get to work. Maybe focusing on digging through the files would take her mind off her pain and fear. "Fair enough. Are you headed back to the office?"

"Not a chance."

"That blow to your head must have shaken a few extra screws loose if you think I'm leaving you alone," Adam said. He blinked away the mental image burned in his brain after Pete's recounting of the morning's events. The very idea of Sabrina lying on the cold ground in a pool of blood . . .

"I'm perfectly safe in this room."

She couldn't possibly know how adorable she was when she got all stubborn and stuck her chin out. "Assuming you don't pass out," he said.

"You have work to do."

She had him on a technicality there. Although . . .

"Your systems are secure here." He should know. Making sure the sheriff's office and her office could communicate securely was the way he'd gotten to spend a lot of time with Sabrina in the months after they first met. He'd always been thankful he'd been the one chosen to be the liaison. "For what I need to do this morning, I can log on and work in that corner. You won't even know I'm here." He didn't wait for her to agree or disagree. He settled himself into a chair in the corner and logged in.

Something about the look she gave him made him think he hadn't fooled her, but she didn't put up a fuss. "I'm going to my office," she said. "I think better there. And before you ask, no, I do not need any help."

She stood with care and eased to the glass door separating her office from the main lab. She left the door open, and he watched her until she was settled behind the bank of monitors. When he heard the tip-tap of her fingers on the keyboard, he relaxed.

A little.

They worked in silence—except for the omnipresent clicking of keys—for half an hour.

"When will your students be here?" Adam asked.

"I'm not expecting anyone today. It's exam week. My grad students are proctoring exams, and none of my undergrads have exams with me this semester."

"You must be their favorite professor," he said.

Her laugh floated to him through the door. "This semester was all lab work. They gave a final presentation last week and then were done. Next semester will be an entirely different experience."

"Your gleeful tone makes me think you might be looking forward to it a bit—"

"What in the—?" A furious pounding of keys accompanied Sabrina's outburst. "Adam, you need to come in here."

He was already through the door.

"When will Gabe be done?" Sabrina's fingers never stopped moving. Her eyes never left the screen.

"They delayed the autopsy this morning, but I would think they would be done by one. Maybe two. He's supposed to call—"

"Can you call him now? Will he answer?"

"Um, probably. Why?"

"I want to speak to Dr. Oliver."

Adam had no idea what was going on in Sabrina's brain. He'd have to find out when Dr. Oliver and Gabe did. He called Gabe. As soon as it rang, he put it on speakerphone.

Gabe answered after the second ring. "Sabrina okay?"

"I'm fine, Gabe."

"She's hurting," Adam said at the same time.

"Okay." Gabe drew out the word. "I'm going to let you two sort that out. What's up?"

"Gabe, are you still with Dr. Oliver?" Sabrina asked.

"I am."

"Could you ask her if she's checked for broken bones? Not from the crash, but previous breaks that have healed?"

"I'm putting you on speaker," Gabe said. "Dr. Oliver, I have Dr. Fleming on the phone. She has a question for you about our victim."

"Hi, Dr. Fleming, how are you?"

"It's Sabrina, and I apologize in advance for asking you this before you've finished your investigation. That kind of thing always drives me crazy, but I think it might be relevant."

"It's no problem, and it's Sharon."

"I'll be quick, Sharon. Have you found any evidence of abuse or torture? Specifically broken fingers?"

Even through the phone's speaker Adam heard Sharon's quick intake of breath. It mirrored his own. "I can't say if her injuries were the result of torture or not, but yes, the X-rays indicate five of her fingers had been broken. Badly. And probably at the same time. How did you know?" Sharon Oliver's tone was full of nothing but respect.

"It was a hunch. Would you say this happened five years ago? Can you tell something like that?"

"I think five years is a very reasonable time frame for this," Dr. Oliver said. "How did you know?"

The expressions flashing across Sabrina's face intrigued Adam. She didn't seem surprised to be right, but he got the impression she wished she'd been wrong.

"I found evidence of a dictation software that was in heavy use five years ago."

"You got broken fingers from dictation software?" Gabe asked.

"Not exactly. It's hard to explain. The file setup from five years ago is all wonky. Her files are extremely organized. What I would expect to see from the stereotypical ideas we all have about accountants. Orderly, logical, systematic."

"I feel a huge *but* coming," Gabe said.

"This flash drive contains a group of very specific files that go back seven years. Around the five-year mark, nothing is where it's supposed to be. It's a mishmash of folders, files, directories. It screamed anomaly, so I opened a few files. The number portions of the spreadsheets are probably correct, but the descriptions, labels—anything with words—are a mess. Totally unprofessional."

"I still don't see how you got broken fingers from that," Dr. Oliver said. "She could have broken her arms or her wrists or had shoulder surgery."

"Oh, sorry. Yes. I found finger strengthening exercises and a log sheet where she'd kept up with what she did, how often, even her pain level. That kind of thing."

"Okay," Gabe said. "Just so we're all on the same page, you started surfing through the flash drive, found a set of files from five years ago that looked off, and when you opened them you realized our victim had been using a dictation software to populate them. And then you made the leap from the finger exercises that she'd broken her fingers. Right so far?"

"Yes," Sabrina said.

"I still don't get it," Gabe said.

"Me either," Sharon said.

"Don't get what?" Sabrina's crestfallen expression lampooned Adam's heart. She shook her head in bewilderment. "You think I'm wrong?"

"No!" All the voices filled the air.

"Then what?" Sabrina put her head in her hands.

"If I may?" Adam asked.

"Go for it," Gabe said.

"We're in agreement with what you've said, and we can see how you made those connections, but what's baffling to us, or to me at least, is why would you assume she was tortured or abused? Why not assume she got her hands slammed in a car trunk or fell off a horse?"

"Adam's right, Sabrina," Sharon said. "There are myriad ways to break fingers. Why are you sure she was tortured?"

Sabrina lifted her head, eyes clear of their earlier frustration. "I'll admit it was a leap, albeit I believe a reasonable one given what we know."

"And what is it that we know?" Gabe asked.

"She was laundering money. Millions of dollars, by the looks of it." She pointed at Adam. "Your forensic accountants are going to have their hands full, but when we find the files, you'll see."

"Um, sorry?" Gabe said.

"Money laundering," Sabrina said. "Not her money, obviously. But you don't deal with this much money unless you are up to your neck in it with some very bad people. Probably drugs or human traffickers. Someone who has way more money than their legal businesses can account for. I've actually seen this tactic before. My guess is she went to work for someone legitimately and learned of their illegal side ventures, and they decided to let her live as long as she continued to work for them. They probably threatened her parents. Oh, Gabe, you should check with her parents. See if they had some sort of accident or trauma about five years ago."

"Okay, but what files do we need to find?" Gabe asked.

Adam bit back a smile. Keeping up with Sabrina's mental gymnastics was always a workout. Gabe was a smart guy. Smarter than he generally let on. But Sabrina was . . . well, she was on another planet when it came to this kind of stuff.

"Right. Sorry. I only have hints of files here. The real files must be somewhere else. They may be on the laptop, although I doubt it. My guess is they're on an external hard drive we haven't located yet."

"Awesome. You're sure she was laundering money, but we can't prove it until we find the files." Fatigue and frustration laced Gabe's words.

"Exactly." Sabrina's voice, however, held an edge of excitement. He'd seen her like this before. She did enjoy the thrill of the hunt. "One more question, Dr. Oliver, and then I'll let you go. I realize this was very rude of me, but I got excited."

"Don't apologize," Sharon said. "I've found it quite fascinating."

Sabrina either ignored or didn't catch the compliment. "Is it too soon for you to know if there is any form of disease present in the victim?"

"What?" This time Sharon sounded like she was choking on a frog.

"I'm wondering if there could have been something . . . possibly colon cancer?"

"How . . . ?" This time Sharon sounded a little winded.

"Is that a yes?" Gabe asked. "Did she have colon cancer?"

"Yes," Sharon said. "Quite advanced."

"Untreated?" Sabrina pressed.

"As far as I can tell."

"Thank you, Dr. Oliver. I mean, Sharon," Sabrina said. "And again, I apologize for asking for information while you're still gathering your data. But this has been most helpful."

"You're welcome."

"Adam, you still there?" Gabe asked.

"Yes."

"I'm coming to the lab when I finish here."

Adam wasn't surprised. Gabe's head was probably whirling. For that matter, so was his. "We'll be here. Text me when you head this way. I'll order lunch."

"Fine."

Adam ended the call and slid the phone into his pocket.

"I shouldn't have done that." Sabrina's self-chastisement sliced through the air. "It was unprofessional. I came across . . . weird. Didn't I?"

"You came across as a genius," Adam said. "You're going to have to show me how you came up with those conclusions, because right now I'm pretty sure Sharon Oliver and Gabe are convinced you're a mind reader."

7

How could she explain something when she didn't know how she'd done it?

"It's hard to explain," Sabrina said.

"Let's start with what you've been doing over here." Adam waved a hand at the monitors.

"I've been looking," she said. "The hard drive from the laptop isn't ready for me to try to get anything off it yet, so I duplicated all these flash drives and the information from this tablet, and I'm looking for anything that might give us a clue."

"I would tell you this isn't the best use of your time," Adam said. "But given that you just accurately predicted the results of an autopsy, I'm going to go with the idea that you can do whatever you want right now."

"I do think it's the best use of my time. These files were encrypted. You wouldn't have seen them if you'd looked at this. No offense."

"None taken."

Adam knew his way around a computer better than most, but he wouldn't have been able to follow the file paths she'd followed.

"But your expertise is in the computer itself—the act of getting the files off the hardware. No one expects you to analyze the data."

"True, but I have a very analytical mind. I would never presume to tackle the forensic accounting required to sort through everything. Or for that matter, to claim I've found everything there is to find. I have a colleague who I'm going to have look at this. I won't be surprised if he finds another layer of encryption and files I'm not even seeing."

Adam didn't look pleased at the idea of her bringing in a colleague.

"Mike's great," she said. "I trust him. He's incredibly skilled and has been thoroughly vetted by the department."

"I trust your judgment," he said.

"You look unhappy."

He quirked an eyebrow at her.

"Am I wrong?"

He shifted his weight from one foot to the other. What was he trying to hide from her? "Adam?"

"It's nothing," he said.

"I don't believe you."

"Oh, good grief, Bri. Are you going to make me spell it out for you?"

"Spell what out?" This man. Most of the time she thought she understood him—got him—better than anyone else. But he was making no sense. "Somebody conked me on the head this morning, Adam. I'm not known for my ability to read emotions and nuance on my best days, so you'll have to forgive me if I'm not following you. I'm not trying to be dense, I'm just—"

"I'm jealous, okay? I'm jealous of Mike." Adam's face and neck burned bright cherry and he swallowed hard, but he didn't drop his eyes. They bored into hers.

Jealous?

"I've heard you talk about Mike before. He's a genius. You

respect him professionally. You like him a lot. I'm sure he's more than capable of doing this. I'm sure he's trustworthy. I'm sure he's a great guy."

"But?"

"But I don't like him."

"You haven't even met him." Adam was usually so rational. "Why don't you like him?"

"Because you do."

"You're jealous of Mike because I respect him?"

Adam shook his head and turned to walk out of her office. "When you put it that way it sounds ridiculous. Don't worry about it, Bri. I'll let you get back to work."

She should say something. Something about how Adam didn't need to be jealous of anyone. Ever. Or maybe she could mention Mike's wife and three kids. Or that even if Mike hadn't been married, he wasn't her type.

She hadn't realized she had a type until she met Adam.

Tall. Lean. Strong, but not bulky. Light brown hair with a bit of a wave to it. His face was perfectly proportional. She'd run it through a program just for fun one day and the percentages were amazing. His eyes, nose, mouth, cheeks—everything was exactly where it should be.

What did it mean, that he was jealous? Did it mean he liked her? More than as a friend or a colleague?

She'd always thought they had a very unique bond. A relationship that was more than professional and more than friendship, but she hadn't been able to find the word to describe it.

Leigh told her it was called *infatuation*, but Sabrina had dismissed that. She'd looked the word up, and infatuation implied that someone had taken leave of their senses.

Her senses were firing on all cylinders.

But there were other words in the same family. Words like *adoration, devotion, warmth, passion.*

Jealousy was a passionate emotion.

She peeked around the corner of her monitor. Adam had returned to his seat, but his hands weren't on the keyboard.

They were laced behind his neck. Every few seconds he would shake his head with a look that was either disgust or anger. Or maybe sadness. Those emotions were too close to each other for her to distinguish easily.

Her phone chimed. Leigh had sent a text.

How's your head?

> Killing me, but I'm fine.

Ok. Take some ibuprofen. How's Adam? Is he hovering over you?

> Not exactly.

Really? I'm surprised.

> He said he was jealous.

He said that?!?! Who is he jealous of? Should he be jealous? I thought you liked him?

Sabrina stared at the text string. Leigh didn't seem surprised that Adam was jealous. She did seem surprised that he'd told her he was jealous.

> Maybe we should talk tonight.

Three little dots blinked back at her for a while. Was Leigh writing a book?

Okay, but don't be afraid to talk to Adam. He's

got it bad for you. I'm not sure how it's possible
that you're the only one who doesn't know that.

He had it bad for her? And everyone knew it? Sabrina tried to
think about it objectively. Rationally.

Adam did seem to enjoy her company. Prefer it, even. And he
was quite protective. He was chivalrous to a fault with everyone,
but she had to admit that he took it to an entirely different level
with her.

Her heart pounded in her chest. She couldn't let herself think
like that. There was too much of a chance she was wrong. She
read things wrong all the time.

But Leigh didn't.

Leigh read between the lines in ways that left Sabrina dumb-
founded. Leigh could read people the way Sabrina read code.

And Leigh thought—

Adam appeared in the doorway. "Gabe's getting ready to leave.
I was going to order lunch. Any preferences?"

He didn't seem flustered anymore. If anything, he was almost
cool. Or tough. Like nothing you could throw at him would hurt
him.

Had she hurt him?

The last thing she would ever want to do was hurt him.

He was by her side so fast she barely registered that he'd moved.
"Are you okay?" His eyes roved over her face.

"I'm fine."

"Are you sure? You kind of spaced out there for a second."

Now it was her turn to flush scarlet. "Sorry. I, um, no. I'm fine.
Anything is fine."

Adam's worried expression didn't lighten, but he didn't press
her further. "How about soup and sandwiches?"

"That would be perfect," she said.

"Maybe you should lie down for a little while." He pointed to the sofa in her office. "Gabe's going to pick up the food. He'll be at least thirty minutes."

"I'm good," she said. "But thank you."

He frowned. "Okay." He muttered something that sounded like "stubborn" as he returned to his desk. He placed an order that had her mouth watering, then sent a text. Probably to Gabe. He set his phone on the desk and looked over his shoulder.

And totally caught her staring at him.

He didn't look away.

Neither did she.

Was it possible? Could Adam Campbell care for her?

Could he possibly not know how much she cared about him?

His hands rested on the arms of his chair and he pushed himself upward, never breaking eye contact. He'd gotten two steps toward her when a series of chirps filled the air.

Someone was trying to access the lab.

Someone who didn't have permission to be there.

Adam rushed to Sabrina's side. He had to get his head in the game. It was clear if he waited for Sabrina to figure out how much he cared about her, they would both grow old alone. He was going to have to quit trying to be subtle and just spell it out for her. It might not be romantic, but it would be effective. Or he might just kiss her and see what happened.

He'd been leaning toward the kiss option when they were interrupted. It was probably for the best, although . . . the way she'd been looking at him . . .

Enough, dude. There would be plenty of time for him to come up with a PowerPoint presentation expressing his ardent devotion to one Dr. Sabrina Fleming—after they'd finished this case.

For now, he needed to keep her safe.

She didn't speak as he slid behind her desk, but she did point to the monitor on her right. She'd already pulled up a video feed from the hallway.

"Darren?" Sabrina's shock was nothing compared to Adam's frustration.

Darren Campbell. Seriously? He was standing outside the lab, bearing a ginormous bouquet of red roses. Every few seconds he tried the door again, which kept the warning chirps going through the lab. He was saying something, but he wasn't looking at the right camera, and Adam couldn't read his lips.

"Can you tell what he's saying?"

"Just a second. I keep it on mute to avoid hallway noises." Sabrina tapped a few keys. The high-tech equipment that protected the lab included full-color cameras and microphones in the hallway outside that she had access to from her computer as well as several stations in the main lab. Only a handful of people could access the lab from the outside using the iris scanner. Everyone else had to be buzzed in, and anyone who tried to open the door too early was greeted with a recorded "Access denied" message.

Darren's saccharine words oozed through the speakers. "I know you're in there, Dr. Fleming. I was out this morning and saw these and my thoughts flew to you. As they often do."

"Ugh," Sabrina said.

At least they were on the same page.

"Ignore him," Adam said.

"Adam." The rebuke lost all sting when she started laughing. "What am I going to do? I haven't talked to him in months and he shows up with flowers? At my lab?"

Darren continued speaking into the wrong camera. "I know we haven't talked much lately, what with your work schedule and my travel. I want to make it up to you. I don't think you realize how much you mean to me. And I don't care who knows it."

"I think I just threw up a little," Adam said.

"You and me both." Sabrina stood. "I'll let him in."

"Where do you want me to go?"

"I don't want you to go anywhere. I want you to stay right here. I don't have time for this nonsense, and maybe he'll be a bit less, er, amorous if you're here." She cringed as if the thought of an amorous Darren Campbell was disgusting to her.

Hallelujah. "I'm here for you." He followed her out of her office and paused by the desk he'd claimed as his own.

Sabrina pushed the entry button from the wall farthest away from the door, and he heard the click as it unlatched. Darren walked all the way into the lab with a confident smile on his face.

"Sabrina. Darling. These are for you." He extended the flowers, but Sabrina didn't reach for them. Everything about her body language screamed "Go away."

"Darren, I hope you'll understand that I can't accept such an extravagant show of affection. It would be inappropriate and might give the wrong impression."

Adam gave a silent cheer.

Darren extended the flowers again. "Nonsense." Darren still hadn't noticed Adam.

Sabrina backed up farther. Adam dug his fingers into the edge of the desk. He didn't want Sabrina to get the idea that he thought she couldn't handle herself, but she'd been attacked this morning and Darren was coming way too close to overstepping the bounds of propriety.

Grandmother would be livid.

Darren paused. The overdone earnestness of his expression faltered for a moment, and a calculating look took its place. Almost as soon as it appeared, it was replaced with one of excessive concern. "Sabrina, what on earth happened to you?" He stretched his hand toward her head, and she stepped back again. This time she bumped into the desk.

He had quite literally backed her into a corner.

Jerk.

Darren took one more step and stretched his hand toward Sabrina's head.

Adam had had enough. "If you touch her, I will break your fingers."

Darren froze. Sabrina took the opportunity to slide around the desk so it was now between her and Darren.

Darren turned toward him. "Hello there, cousin. I didn't realize I was interrupting official police business."

"Who said you were?"

"Why else would you be here?" Darren looked around the room. "In this empty lab. With Dr. Fleming. Alone." The words were spoken with false sincerity. The insinuation rang through the room.

"Why do you not understand that Sabrina doesn't wish to accept those flowers? Nor does she want you to touch her. This is the part where a *gentleman* retreats with grace."

Darren returned his gaze to Sabrina. "Have you lost the ability to speak, my dear? Is Adam harassing you? Should I call security? Or perhaps the sheriff?"

Adam could only hope Sabrina wouldn't be concerned by Darren's bluff and bluster.

"Darren, let me be clear," she said. "I have never dated you, nor do I intend to date you in the future. If you misconstrued my agreement to attend a few fundraisers with you—despite the fact that I made myself quite clear on those occasions as well—then let there be no possible mistaking my words or intention now. I don't want the flowers, the attention, the phone calls, or the gifts. They aren't endearing you to me. Have I made myself clear?"

His lips flattened into a thin line. "Crystal."

He turned on his heel and stalked from the room. When he reached the door, he turned back. "Watch out for that one," he said with a vicious glare in Adam's direction. "He's not known as the family heartbreaker for nothing."

He placed the flowers on the nearest desk and walked out the door.

Sabrina held herself straight, her mouth set as he left, but the second the door sealed behind him, she sagged against the desk.

"Bri." Adam was by her side in seconds. He pulled her against him and her arms wrapped around him.

Oh, how he could get used to this. He would give anything to be able to hold her when things were good instead of only daring to when things were falling apart.

Still . . .

"I'm sorry," she said.

"For what? You were amazing."

"I never should have said yes the first time."

"You cannot be serious." He leaned away from her and tilted her chin so she had to look at him. "He's scum. I'm sorry I'm related to him. I thought he was all right, but clearly he's not. There's a predatory streak in him that I had no idea was there."

Sabrina's eyes closed, and she rested her head against his chest. "You can't help who you're related to. Trust me."

"I didn't mean—"

"I know you didn't," she said.

A bitter laugh floated toward him. "What's funny?"

"I don't even like red roses."

"What do you have against roses?"

"Nothing," she said. "I love them. But red roses are for love. Totally inappropriate. Yellow roses or even pink or peach would have at least made sense."

What was she talking about? "You lost me."

"It's nothing." Her words were muffled against his chest. "Flowers have meanings, that's all."

He would have stood there for an eternity, but that wasn't the best idea for her. "Do you want to sit down? Lie down?"

"No," she said.

Was it possible she'd stepped even closer to him? He dared reach one hand to her hair. She had great hair. Straight and falling down to her mid-back, brown with some lighter streaks that he suspected were natural because Sabrina wasn't the hair-salon type. When it was down, it often had a bit of an unkempt look—like she'd run her hands through it a lot—which she did and was why he supposed she kept it up in a messy bun most of the time.

But this morning's hospital adventure had led to it being down all day. He let it slide gently through his fingers. It was as soft and silky as he'd imagined it would—

The door buzzed. Appropriately this time. No weird chimes or warning signals accompanied this request for entry.

"That must be Gabe," Sabrina said against his chest.

"Probably," he said.

"We should let him in." Sabrina made no effort to move.

"Do we have to?" He risked squeezing her closer, and her acquiescence left him in a state of stunned bliss. He'd seen the way she had stood up to Darren. This wasn't a woman who couldn't make herself—or her desires—known. If she didn't want to be there, in his arms, she wouldn't be.

"Gabe who?"

Oh man. He was a goner.

The door buzzed again.

"I don't think he's going to go away," she said.

"No."

"He'll probably call the police if we don't open the door."

"I am the police."

Sabrina laughed and pushed herself away from him. He released her by inches and saw the moment the realization touched her eyes. She knew he wanted her.

At least, he thought she did.

She hit the buzzer and Gabe walked in with two huge bags and set them on the counter. "Hey," he said.

"Hey," Adam and Sabrina replied in unison.

Gabe pulled containers from one bag. "Well, don't rush to thank me for bringing the food or anything."

"Thank you, Gabe," Sabrina said. She joined him at the counter. "You're a lifesaver."

He looked at Adam. "See. That's what I'm talking about." He turned back to Sabrina. "We have tomato soup with cheese curds, vegetable beef, and chicken and dumplings. Name your poison."

"I'll have the tomato, please." She flashed a brilliant smile at Gabe, and Adam didn't even bother to deny the swell of annoyance that filled him at the sight of it. She was just being nice.

"If you'll excuse me for a moment, I'm going to wash my hands." She disappeared down the short hall to the secure restroom.

As soon as she was out of sight, Gabe was in Adam's face. "What on earth, dude? You can't bust a move on the girl when she has a concussion."

"I wasn't . . ." The denial died in his throat. She did have a concussion. He shouldn't take advantage of that.

Gabe doubled over in laughter. "I'm only joking, man, but apparently you have something to feel a wee bit guilty about."

"I didn't . . ."

Gabe pulled three sandwiches from the bag. "Seriously, man, I'm kidding. It's about time, buddy."

Sabrina reappeared, and to Adam's shock, Gabe dropped the subject. No teasing. No snide remarks.

Gabe pulled a chair out and ushered her into it. "Girlfriend, you need to take a nap. Let's eat and talk fast so you can lock things up and go home. Well, not *home* exactly. Maybe to Leigh's?"

"She's insisting," Sabrina said with a groan.

"What's wrong with Leigh's?" Gabe put a bowl of soup, a spoon, and a grilled cheese sandwich in front of her. "She has great food. Plenty of room. Gorgeous views. If you sleep in the guest room, get the one on the right side of the bathroom downstairs. It has the best mattress. Trust me."

Sabrina smiled. "She's texted me a couple of times. She's excited for me to come. She doesn't work tonight, so I guess that's what I'll do." She shifted toward Adam. "But I'll need to go back to my place to get my things."

"Of course. We should have gone there first," Adam said.

"No." She took a bite of soup. "I wanted to get to work. I don't need anything until tonight, so it's no big deal."

Adam sat down across the desk from her, a steaming bowl in front of him. The vegetable beef was his favorite.

"So, Dr. Fleming"—Gabe leaned against a file cabinet—"Dr. Oliver is now convinced you have some sort of crime-solving super-powers." He took a drink of soup straight from the container.

Sabrina dipped her head in obvious embarrassment. "I do not. I have excellent observational skills, and I'm able to apply previous experience to current situations in a way that often leads to conclusions others miss." She made the statement without the slightest hint of arrogance. For her, this wasn't bragging. It was a statement of fact.

"Well, Dr. Oliver asked me to give you this." He pulled out a small card from his back pocket. "It has her contact information on it. She'd love to have lunch sometime."

"Why?"

Adam bit down on the inside of his lip to keep from laughing at Sabrina's horrified expression. Gabe made no such effort. "She wants to get to know you. Be friends. This is what girls do apparently. They have lunch."

Sabrina wasn't convinced. "What do guys do?"

"Dive," Gabe said.

"Even with all your fancy equipment, you can't have a meaningful conversation while you're diving," she said.

"Exactly. Less bother."

"That makes no sense."

Gabe took another swig of soup. "If I can't respect a guy in the water, then I'm not going to want to hang out with him anywhere else. If he's sloppy. If he's lazy. If he takes unnecessary risks, then I don't need to get to know him any further. I'm not saying he's a terrible person, but I already know he's not someone I'm going to want to be friends with. You may not know this about me, but I don't have many friends."

"I can't imagine why," Adam said under his breath.

Sabrina didn't hear him.

Gabe did. "I don't need many friends. I'm not trying to win a prize for the most people who will show up for my funeral. I just need a few people who will have my back and who I might enjoy watching a ball game with from time to time."

Sabrina took a dainty sip of her tomato soup. "I feel the same way."

"Oh really?" Gabe threw a satisfied smirk in Adam's direction.

"Yes," she said. "I don't make friends easily. I'm too blunt. I'm not trying to be rude, but I often say what I think before I think about what I'm saying."

Adam couldn't argue that point, and Gabe couldn't either.

"I do enjoy being around people, but I'm never going to be any good at having a large group of friends or maintaining some vast social network of teas and"—she waved Sharon's business card—"lunches."

Gabe patted her hand. "You're brilliant, but sometimes you overthink things. Sharon's interested in getting to know you. There are no strings. Just two super-smart women having lunch. You'll probably wind up talking about dead bodies and computers. It will be terrifying to anyone close enough to overhear."

"Fine." Sabrina slid the card into her pocket. "I'll consider it. But I don't believe you came over here just to tell me you think I should have lunch with Dr. Oliver."

"No, I didn't. I want to know everything you can tell me about Lisa Palmer."

8

'm happy to help," Sabrina said. "But I'm not ready yet."

"You're killing me," Gabe said.

"I'm sorry, but right now I have a crazy amount of information swirling in my brain and it wouldn't make any sense." How could she get him to understand when she was still figuring it out herself?

"Can you give me a synopsis? Something? Anything?"

"I can give you a little bit," Adam said.

Bless him.

"Fine," Gabe said. "Her stuff is better than yours, but I'll take what I can get."

Adam stood, grilled cheese sandwich in one hand. "First, Lisa Palmer was a very good accountant."

"Fascinating," Gabe said, clearly not fascinated.

"No, I don't think you appreciate how good she was," Adam said. "She worked in a specialized division that handled some of the most delicate accounts her firm managed. When she left to start her own business, forty huge clients went with her. Ten of them, including Zinzer Hospitality, got together and paid off the firm when they tried to come after her for violating her non-compete clause."

"That's . . . unusual."

"It is."

"What was so awesome about her?"

"Well, I've been doing some of my own digging today and I don't have proof yet, just some hints, but I think what made Lisa Palmer so good was she kept a lot of secrets."

"This is supposed to be helpful? That she kept secrets doesn't tell me much. Any secrets she kept died with her." Gabe bit into his sandwich.

Adam didn't back down. "Why were you so good as an undercover cop?"

Sabrina didn't make eye contact with either man. She'd never heard Gabe talk about his undercover work. She wasn't sure if she was going to now. She risked a glance and found him in a staring contest with Adam.

"Fine," he said. "People trusted me. I'm very good at getting people to confide in me."

Adam didn't say anything. He just let Gabe's words sit there. Adam took two bites of his sandwich before Gabe spoke again.

"Once someone has shared their deepest secrets with you, there are only a couple of options. Either they want to keep you close or . . ."

"Exactly," Adam said.

Sabrina couldn't take it anymore. "Exactly what?"

"They'll either keep you close or get rid of you," Gabe said. "There aren't any other options."

"So you think Lisa Palmer was an accountant for a lot of nefarious individuals and one of them decided to have her killed?" she asked.

"I think it's an angle worth pursuing."

"Let me guess," Gabe said. "A lot will depend on what Sabrina can get off the laptop."

"Maybe," Adam said. "But if Sabrina's conclusions are accurate, it's unlikely this woman would have been driving around with a laptop full of incriminating evidence."

"What if the killer put it in the car with her, hoping to destroy it?" Gabe asked.

"I think the killer put it in there to get us looking in the wrong direction," Adam said.

"And what's the right direction?" Gabe wasn't really asking her or Adam, and neither of them tried to answer.

Poor Gabe. He looked so frustrated. "Gabe. I need another day or two. My head is pounding. I hurt pretty much everywhere. And I need to let this information marinate as I keep digging. I'm not trying to be evasive. We have evidence of two very different Lisa Palmers. On the one hand, we have the choir-singing, good-neighbor, nice lady who may have been clueless about the people she was working for. At least for a while. The torture might have been inflicted by the people she worked for to guarantee her continued cooperation after she did find out."

Sabrina took a sip of her soup. "On the other hand, all of her so-called good behavior might have been a front to disguise her own evil. She may have been up to her eyeballs in dirty money long before she left Atlanta and came to Carrington. She may have known exactly what was going on and only recently decided to come clean."

"Why do you say that?" Gabe asked.

She chose her words with care. "Sometimes people who know their time is short will try to make amends, or confess to criminal or immoral activity."

Adam gave her an encouraging smile.

"True," Gabe said. "So you're thinking she might have been getting ready to confess or turn over evidence to Adam?"

"Possibly," she said. "We'll have to do some checking, but I won't be surprised if we find she refused treatment for her cancer. She may have seen it as some sort of just retribution."

"Like she was getting what she deserved?" Adam asked.

"Something like that."

"And they found out." Gabe wadded a napkin into a tight ball and lobbed it toward a trash can.

"I suspect so."

"Come on, Sabrina. What did you find that makes you think that?" Gabe asked.

She had to give him something. "The internet history on the tablet," she said. "She researched colon cancer. And not general colon cancer. A very specific type. And then she researched life expectancy with and without a specific type of treatment. From what I can see, she actually had a good chance of surviving and living a long time if she'd pursued treatment."

"But Sharon said the cancer was advanced."

"These searches go back a year. This is all speculation, Gabe. But my guess is the reason we haven't found the files we need is because she hid them. She's probably been building a case—possibly many cases—and I wouldn't be surprised if she knew she didn't have long to live and was going to bring it all to Adam and then disappear with the hope the cancer would get her before the bad guys did."

Gabe shuddered.

Adam slumped.

"How do we know if you're right or wrong?" Gabe asked.

"I'm not sure," Sabrina said. "We're going to need to catch a break. Maybe something in her house will give us a clue. Can I look at the crime-scene photos?"

"You can do one better," Gabe said. "You can come look for yourself."

Adam straightened. "She has a concussion. She needs to be in bed."

"I'm not saying she has to go right now." A mischievous grin spread across his face. "But you know she wants to."

Adam looked from Gabe to her.

She was hurting, but she was going to be hurting wherever she was. And she did feel a compulsion to find out more about Lisa Palmer. "It might be helpful," she said.

"Yes!" Gabe didn't bother to hide his glee. "Finish eating. We have a crime scene to visit."

This was a bad idea.

Adam pulled in behind Gabe on the street in front of Lisa Palmer's house. Sabrina moaned as she straightened in the seat beside him.

"Did I fall asleep?"

"For about five minutes," he said. "You need to rest."

"I know," she said. "But I feel like this is important. Don't you?"

He wanted to disagree, but he couldn't. "Yes. I'm worried if we don't move fast we're going to miss something big, but I'm concerned you're overdoing it."

"I'm tough."

"I know."

"Let's go." She reached for the door.

"Wait," he said. He hopped out and rushed to her door. He opened it and offered her his hand.

"Always the gentleman," she said as she placed her hand in his.

"Do you mind?"

"It's who you are, Adam. I love it." She blinked a few times, and Adam got the impression she'd been unintentionally honest.

"Good." He helped her from the car and closed the door behind her. She tucked her hand into the bend of his arm, even before he'd had a chance to offer it to her. Like it belonged there.

Which was fine with him.

"Can we walk around the outside first?" Sabrina was in full investigatory mode while he was mooning over where she'd put her hand. He needed to get a grip.

109

"Sure."

He stayed with her as she meandered around the small bungalow.

"Cute house," Sabrina said.

"You think?" It was a house. He wasn't sure if *cute* was the appropriate description.

"I do," she said. "If I were to upsize, I wouldn't mind something like this. It has great curb appeal, a nice color palette, blends into the area. Well, it would if it wasn't wrapped in crime-scene tape."

"I don't know." He tapped the tape. "It adds a certain panache."

She laughed. "You're terrible."

"You're laughing."

"I'm terrible too. This woman died. I realize she may have done some horrible things—or helped people do horrible things—but that doesn't mean someone had the right to kill her."

"Agreed." If she was going to insist on being professional, he would be too. "Do you see anything about the exterior of her house that gives you any insights?"

"No. I'm not even sure what I'm looking for."

"You'll know it when you see it."

Gabe called to them from the porch. "Where do you want to start? Upstairs? Downstairs?"

"Wherever she worked," Sabrina said.

Gabe nodded and held the door for them to go inside. "Right this way."

They stepped into the tiny entryway and Gabe opened the French doors into what had probably been intended to be a formal living room but Lisa Palmer had used as an office. Sabrina released Adam's arm and wandered through the space. Gabe leaned against the door frame and watched Sabrina. "Can I sit in her chair?" she asked.

Gabe nodded.

Sabrina sat down and swiveled the chair from left to right.

"You're sure there was no computer when the forensics team got here?"

"No. But I can't imagine that she didn't have one."

"Two," she said.

"Why do you say that?" There was no rancor in Gabe's voice.

"The desk is faded. In two identical places. One is a little lighter than the other, which makes sense with the way the sun comes in."

"Which means someone took them."

"Unless she destroyed them herself," Adam said.

"Why would she do that?" Gabe asked. "If Sabrina's supposition is correct and Lisa Palmer was planning to hand over all the evidence to you anyway, wouldn't it have made more sense for her to leave them?"

"Maybe she knew what people like Sabrina can do. That they can find files that were supposedly deleted."

"Okay. I like it. Or maybe she wanted to control the narrative," Gabe said. "She gives you files, but they're the files she chooses to give. And to avoid risking us uncovering anything she doesn't want us to know, she destroys the computers the files were created on."

Another very real possibility.

"Or the murderers took them and melted them down in acid, and that was that," Sabrina said. "It's all conjecture. Not one shred of evidence."

"We have to start somewhere," Gabe said. "If you were living in this house, where would you hide a hard drive?"

Sabrina grinned. "Oh, Gabe, there are so many places."

"I'll make a list. We'll have forensics search every one of them," Gabe said.

Adam had to give Gabe credit. He wasn't taking anything lightly.

For the next hour, Sabrina walked through the house. Every now and then she'd make a suggestion. By the time she was done, Gabe's list had everything from the more obvious places, like false

111

bottoms in desk drawers and cushions, to the not-so-obvious possibilities, like the soles of boots and eye shadow containers.

"Seriously? Eye shadow?" Gabe had asked.

"Do you know how small a microSD card is?" Sabrina didn't give Gabe a chance to answer. "You're looking for something the size of a fingernail. It could be hidden beneath any kind of pressed makeup, like eye shadow or blush, or it could be in a lipstick tube. The problem with the micro cards is that they could be almost anywhere."

They entered Lisa Palmer's upstairs bedroom. Gabe went first, followed by Sabrina. Adam was bringing up the rear, but he rushed forward when Sabrina groaned.

"Are you okay?" Adam asked. "Do you need to sit down?"

"No," she said. "Look at this room."

"Oh." Now he understood. One entire wall was a bookshelf filled with books. On the other wall was a large shelf with a display of Japanese puzzle boxes.

Adam shook his head. "This could take days—"

"Weeks—" Gabe said.

"Months." Somehow Sabrina's pronouncement of the situation made it much more dire. "Of course, it's probably not in here at all."

Gabe threw his hands in the air. "What? This is the most logical place to hide something small and flat."

"Which makes it the least logical place."

"Unless," Adam said, "she figured people would assume it was the least logical place, thereby making it the most logical place."

Gabe and Sabrina glared at him.

"What?" He wasn't wrong. They were just mad because he was right.

"Forensics is going to hate me," Gabe said.

"They already do." Adam tried to keep his expression serious.

"Not helping, Campbell."

Sabrina had already moved on. She examined the bathroom, the picture frames in the short hallway, and then spent twenty minutes in the kitchen looking at everything from salt and pepper shakers to trivets to cabinet pulls.

"You seriously think she hid a memory card in a cabinet pull?" Gabe pretended to pound his head against the wall.

"No, but I think you have to check. Forensics should already know this, but make sure they take all the outlet and light switch covers off. They're going to have to literally take this entire place apart to be sure we aren't missing something."

"We already know we're missing something. Like the entire computer system. Why are you sure there are other things to find?" The way Gabe asked the question made Adam think he didn't disagree with Sabrina, but that he was looking for more reasons he could use when he contacted the forensics team and told them what he needed.

"If she was planning to turn over evidence on someone, she would have needed to have the information stored on a small, portable, easily concealable device. It's obvious she thought they were on to her." Sabrina picked up a set of candlesticks and examined them.

"Why do you say that?" Gabe opened a cabinet door, and three spice jars fell onto the counter.

"Add the spice cabinet to your list," she said. "And I say that because that message she wrote on her body was her final insurance policy. She knew they suspected her, and she hoped if they killed her, they wouldn't notice she'd left a message from beyond the grave."

"They must not have noticed," Adam said. "Or they wouldn't have left her body to be found at all."

Gabe shrugged. "Actually, if it hadn't been for that message, just based on the evidence we have—her note, no skid marks to indicate that she tried to stop herself from going off the road, no

obvious car issues like a cut brake line—we might have been leaning toward suicide as the cause of her death."

"You're kidding."

"Sharon says she drowned."

"What?" Sabrina grasped the edge of the kitchen table, and
Adam moved to stand beside her.

"Sorry," Gabe said. "I guess I forgot to mention it before."

Sabrina's hands trembled on the table. She had to be past the
point of exhaustion.

"I say we discuss this later." Adam made eye contact with Gabe
and then cut his eyes in Sabrina's direction.

Gabe got the message. "I agree," he said.

"But—" Sabrina wasn't going to let it go.

"I need to get forensics over here," Gabe said. "You go with
Adam to get your stuff from your place, and let me see if I can pull
all my thoughts together on this. We'll check in with Ryan and
Anissa to see if they found anything in the lake today."

"That sounds great," Adam said. "Leigh has already invited
everyone over for dinner. Let's plan to hash it out then."

Sabrina frowned but tucked her hand in the bend of Adam's
arm and walked with him to the front door. Gabe noticed, but
other than a quick smirk he kept his comments to himself.

Although Adam wasn't sure Sabrina would have noticed if Gabe
had said anything anyway. She was lost in thought, eyes unfocused,
as they stepped onto the small front porch.

"She okay?" Gabe mouthed to Adam.

Adam didn't know. Maybe the stress of the day had caught up
to her? Maybe her brilliant mind was solving the case? Who knew?

The window to his right shattered. Were they being shot at?
His first thought was to throw himself on Sabrina and cover her
from bullets.

But then he saw it.

A streak of smoke snaking through the yard.

114

"Run!" Adam pulled his arm away from Sabrina and wrapped it around her waist. It took half a second for her to fall into step with him. He hated to force her to move like this. It had to be excruciating, but—

The force of the explosion threw him to the ground. He covered Sabrina as debris fell all around them and the air filled with smoke and dust.

A second explosion shook the ground, and the air around them warmed in an instant.

Then something heavy landed across his back.

And he couldn't move.

9

Everything hurt.

Her head throbbed with every pulsing beat of her heart.

Her face, hands, and knees stung. How far had they skidded on the sidewalk before coming to a stop after the explosion threw them off their feet?

Her chest burned with each intake of breath. Bruised ribs, probably from where Adam had landed on her.

She would never tell him that. Ever.

It had all been a blur. She lay frozen beneath Adam as the ground shook and everything around them seemed to be breaking apart and burning.

Until, finally, the chaos stilled.

Adam's chest was draped across her back. His left arm was over her head like he'd landed on her sideways. His face was turned away from her.

"Adam?" She coughed into the dust-filled air and pain sliced through her. "Adam?"

Why wasn't he answering her?

"Adam? Sabrina? Oh no!" Gabe's anguished cry terrified her more than anything that had happened in the last twenty-four hours.

"Gabe!"

"Sabrina! Thank God! I, um . . . Oh, Father, help me."

Was Gabe praying?

"What's wrong with Adam?" She gasped the words. He was so heavy. She never would have expected him to be as heavy as he felt at that moment.

"Sabrina, I'm going to need you to stay calm."

"I'm trying, but I'm having some trouble"—she sucked in a breath—"breathing."

"Adam's not conscious," he said. "And there's a huge piece of the roof on the two of you. I'm afraid to move him. It isn't burning, thank heaven."

The roof? No wonder she couldn't breathe. But then . . .

"Is he breathing?"

God, please let him be breathing.

"He is," Gabe said. "But if you can hold on, I'll see if I can shift—"

"Don't!" The effort to yell the word cost her precious oxygen, but she didn't care. "Wait."

"You're sure? He'll kill me if I don't get you out from under him," Gabe said.

"I'll kill you if you move him," she said.

Gabe knelt beside her. She could barely see him through the space between Adam's arm and the ground. "I have no doubt you would," he said. His eyes were red.

Sirens rent the air and Gabe's relief was palpable. He got to his feet. "I won't try to move the roof off completely, but I'm going to try to lift it up a little so you can breathe."

She heard his grunt and the pressure on her rib cage eased. Not much, but enough for her to get a slightly deeper breath.

"He saved our lives," Gabe said.

"What was it?" Part of her didn't care. Part of her knew this was her brain's way of protecting itself from the things she didn't want to think about. If she could focus on the facts, she didn't have to focus on the emotions that lay heavy across her heart.

"An RPG, I think."

"A what?"

"A rocket-propelled grenade. Must have been on a timer. Or maybe it didn't go off the way it was supposed to. Either way, it was lucky for us. Those things usually blow on impact."

"How do you know that's what it was?" Whispering was easier than trying to project her voice, but he heard her.

"You can spot the smoke trail. Adam saw it first. I just ran when he said to run. I didn't see it until we were already jumping off the porch. I'm guessing the explosion from the RPG hit some of the gas lines and caused them to blow. It's a wonder there's anything left of the house."

She peered under Adam's arm, but everything was blurry. Where were her glasses? Probably in a thousand pieces somewhere.

From what little she knew about RPGs, mostly from news reports from the Middle East, she was fairly certain they didn't have a long range. Whoever had fired it had been close enough to know they were on the porch.

Close enough to see them now.

Doors slammed and footsteps pounded. "Gabe!"

Was that Anissa? Why was she here?

"Gabe!" That was definitely Ryan.

"Are you okay?" Anissa asked.

What was Anissa seeing that had her so worried for Gabe? How badly was he injured?

"I'm fine, but—"

A muted conversation took place above her. She heard whispers but couldn't make out what was being said.

"Sabrina!" Anissa knelt beside her. "Hang in there, hon."

"I'm fine," Sabrina whispered. "Adam?"

"He's breathing." Anissa's voice trembled. "We'll get that stuff off him in a sec."

The squawk of the sirens pierced her tender ears and then cut off. More running steps. More yelling.

And then a new sound reached her ears. *Thump, thump, thump.* A helicopter.

"Well, that's great." Gabe's annoyance filtered through the chaos.

"Ignore it." Anissa wasn't being bossy. She didn't sound annoyed with Gabe either. She sounded . . . compassionate. Anissa and Gabe had been getting along a lot better than they used to, but if she was being compassionate toward Gabe, then something must be wrong.

Gabe must be hurt far worse than anyone was letting on.

Father, please. Don't let my friends die. And Adam, oh, God, please. I can't . . .

"Let's see what we have here." A new voice. Deeper. Calmer. "My name is Clark. What's yours?"

"Sabrina." She tried to answer him, but she wasn't sure if he understood.

Gabe spoke. "Dr. Sabrina Fleming," he said, "and Investigator Adam Campbell is the guy pinned under the roof. I was afraid to move it completely, but we need to get her out from under there. She's having some trouble getting enough air."

"You did the right thing," Clark said.

Someone new knelt beside her and pushed Adam's arm away enough to slip a mask over her face. The flow of oxygen did help. Some.

"Dr. Fleming? A medical doctor?"

"No," Anissa said. "She's a PhD. Computer forensics and cyber-security."

"Nice." Clark sounded impressed.

Sabrina would be impressed if he were more focused on Adam.

"We're going to get a collar on Adam," he said, "and then we'll get this roof off of him and get him off of you."

"Okay," she whispered.

119

"When we move him, I need you to stay as still as possible," he said. "I know you're going to want to get up, or roll over, but please don't until we check you out."

More conversations happened above and around her. Adam's weight shifted. "It's okay," Anissa whispered. "They've almost got the collar on."

Another shift, this time of Adam's legs. Why were they moving his legs?

"Whoa," Clark said. "Calm down, Adam."

They weren't moving his legs. He was moving them!

"Bri?" Adam's raspy voice in her ear was the most beautiful sound she'd ever heard. "Bri!" The panic in it was not okay.

"I'm okay," she rushed to assure him, "but you have to be still." Her voice was muffled by the mask. She hoped he could hear her.

"Adam, listen to Dr. Fleming," Clark said. "You've been knocked unconscious and pinned down. We need to stabilize you before we move you, and the sooner we do that the sooner we can get you off of her so she can breathe."

"Okay."

Adam's hand squeezed her arm.

He could move his hands. *Thank you, God.*

"Okay," Clark said. "You're going to lift the roof and walk backward with it. As soon as they're clear, we'll get Adam on the board and off Dr. Fleming. On the count of three. Ready?"

Far more people responded yes than she'd been expecting.

"One. Two. Three. Lift."

Instantaneous relief.

Adam wasn't anywhere near as heavy as Adam plus a piece of the roof.

She heard the grunts of the people moving the roof. The ground shook as they dropped it.

And faster than she'd expected, Adam was gone. Cool air rushed over her as her lungs expanded fully.

"Lie still." Anissa squeezed Sabrina's now-exposed fingers.

"Sir, we need to take a look at that—"

"Later." Gabe's tone left no room for argument.

"Gabe." Anissa's reproach was tender. Her worry tangible. "She's right. You've lost a lot of blood."

"I'm fine."

"No, you're not," Ryan said.

Their conversation shifted out of earshot as they followed the group taking Adam to the ambulance.

Anissa stayed by her side, and for the next few minutes all Sabrina could do was answer questions and nod and move the parts of her body the paramedic, a young woman named Dorothy, asked her to move.

They settled Sabrina onto a stretcher and strapped her in. "You're going to be fine, Dr. Fleming," Dorothy said. "But it's protocol in a situation like this for you to go to the emergency department. They'll take great care of you."

"I know," she said. "I was there this morning."

"We have another ambulance ready." Dorothy pointed toward the road. "Just waiting for the first ambulance to leave."

Adam was in that ambulance. Why hadn't they left yet? He needed to be X-rayed, maybe have CT scans and MRIs. He might need oxygen. He could have burns. "What's taking them so long?"

"They're just being extra careful," Anissa said. "But he's talking, and I saw him moving his hands and legs. We'll get a full update as soon as we get to the hospital."

"Hey." Gabe handed Sabrina her glasses. "Thought you might want these. The frames are a little wonky, but I don't think the lenses are scratched."

"Thank you." She settled them on her face—wonky was an understatement—and looked around.

The house was a smoldering heap.

Gabe's head and arm were bleeding. His pants were shredded on one side. "You need to go to the hospital," she said.

"He will," Anissa said.

Gabe glared at Anissa but didn't argue.

"Then I guess I'll see you there," Sabrina said.

Ryan joined Gabe and Anissa by her stretcher. "I've already called Leigh," he said. "She'll probably beat you there."

"She doesn't have to be my personal nurse."

"She doesn't want you to be alone," Ryan said.

Wow. Sabrina's chin quivered and she clamped her jaws together to stop it. She would not fall apart. Not now.

When she thought she could speak without blubbering, she whispered, "Thanks." The ambulance pulled away and they all watched it go. "Has anyone contacted Adam's family?"

Ryan patted her arm. "The captain was going to call his parents, but—"

"His parents are in Italy," Sabrina said. Dorothy pushed her stretcher toward the waiting ambulance.

"I'll call his grandfather," Anissa said. "Then I'll be sure Gabe gets seen. We'll see you at the hospital."

Sabrina rested her head on the stretcher. Before the doors closed, she saw Anissa on the phone. Gabe had his head in his hands and Ryan had a hand on Gabe's back.

"Hey," she called out. Ryan and Gabe looked up. "Be careful."

They gave her a thumbs-up and the driver closed the doors.

"We'll be there in ten minutes," Dorothy said. "Try to relax."

Like that was going to happen.

So far today someone had attacked her, then left her to bleed on the ground, where she could have died, and then someone had blown up a house while she was still in it.

And . . . all the evidence.

The horror of it washed over her again. Gabe was hurt. She was hurt—again. The evidence was gone.

122

And Adam . . .

He'd sacrificed himself for her. He'd protected her from the first explosion and the second. If he hadn't been hovering over her, she might have been killed.

A tear escaped. Dorothy saw it.

"You're doing great," she said. "You've been through a lot."

This sweet girl had no idea.

"Your boyfriend is in the best hands," she went on. "If I was hurt, Clark's the one I'd want by my side."

"He isn't my boyfriend," Sabrina said.

Dorothy coughed a couple of times, but it sounded a lot like "yeah right" and then "liar."

"He isn't," Sabrina said.

Dorothy patted her hand. "Then you need to do whatever you have to do to change that. I've never had a man care enough about me to even open a door, much less shield my body with his own. You're a very lucky lady."

Despite everything that had happened today, somehow Sabrina thought Dorothy might be right.

"I need to see her," Adam said. Again. He'd been saying that for the past hour. No one had been able to give him any information. They'd sent him to radiology, and they'd cleaned and bandaged his back, which at the moment felt great thanks to the lidocaine they'd used. He didn't want to think about how it would feel later, but all in all they'd taken fabulous care of him physically. But did no one care that he was freaking out over here?

He understood the privacy laws they were bound by, but couldn't they give him something? If she was really okay, why hadn't she been in to see him?

A doctor—he assumed it was a doctor—leaned into Adam's field of vision. The collar they had around his neck prevented him from turning his head. "Mr. Campbell, I'm Dr. Sloan. I'm thrilled you're doing well enough to insist on seeing your girlfriend, but I'm afraid you're going to have to wait a little longer."

"She isn't my girlfriend. She's . . ." He couldn't bring himself to say "just a friend," because she was so much more.

Dr. Sloan smiled. "Boy, you've got it bad. And I promise I'll let her come in to see you as soon as possible."

"Is she okay? They wouldn't tell me anything in the ambulance."

"Yes," he said. "She's fine."

The doctor sounded convincing, but he could be saying that to calm Adam down. "How do you know?"

Dr. Sloan winked at him. What was that supposed to mean?

The doctor called out a few orders—it sounded like Adam might be able to get out of the neck brace soon—but then the doctor's tone changed. "Have any of you ever met Dr. Fleming?"

"No," a female voice replied.

"She's the patient visiting us in room 4 for the second time today. If she keeps this up, we're going to have to name it after her," he said. "She's a professor at the university. Her specialty is computer forensics."

"Cool," another voice chimed in.

Adam appreciated what Dr. Sloan was doing. He was simultaneously letting him know that he really had seen Sabrina, and she was okay, without violating any privacy laws or revealing anything about her physical condition.

"It is cool," he said. "I'm going to see if the school will have her come in and do a cybersecurity class for my kid's middle-school class. I think it would be quite informative for them. She said she'd be happy to."

"Was that before or after you stitched up her head? Again."

Adam knew that voice. "Leigh?"

"Hey." Someone—he assumed it was Leigh—squeezed his hand.

"Let me guess," Dr. Sloan said, "you've been sent by Dr. Fleming to ascertain the status of Mr. Campbell."

"I have," Leigh said. She leaned over Adam. "She's fine, Adam. Completely fine."

"Does she have a head injury? She already had a concussion from this morning."

"Um, no. A few bruised ribs. Some minor contusions." Leigh's eyes shone with honesty and the vice grip around his heart released.

"Did they check? Because she can't be trusted to tell the truth about how much pain she's in."

"Yes," Leigh said. "X-rays and scans and examinations—all done. A few stitches, thanks to Dr. Sloan, and she's being released."

"How bad is she hurting?"

"Adam." Leigh gave him a kind but firm look. "She almost died today. Twice. A little pain? It's not such a bad thing."

He understood what Leigh was saying. And she was right. Pain beat the alternative. Except he didn't want her to hurt at all. Ever.

"Your CT looks good, so let's get you out of this," Dr. Sloan said.

In a few moments, his neck was free from the collar. He took in the room around him. "Thank you," he said.

Dr. Sloan frowned at him. "I'm going to tell you what I think you should do. I think you should go home. Take Dr. Fleming. Find a comfortable chair or couch and rest. Put your feet up. Watch a movie."

Adam didn't respond. He wouldn't lie to the man. And he would try to get Sabrina to agree to the doctor's recommendations.

But it wouldn't work.

Dr. Sloan's frown deepened. "But since I know you're going to ignore me, at least agree you will take it easy. That you will take the meds I prescribe. That neither of you will be alone tonight and someone will be around to check on you."

"I will," Leigh said. "They can stay with me."

Dr. Sloan didn't give Adam a chance to disagree. "Excellent." He turned to Leigh. "Take care of them."

"I will."

Dr. Sloan left the room muttering something about workaholics.

"How's Gabe?" Adam asked Leigh.

"Grouchy. He's already gone back to the house to see if there's anything salvageable. Ryan's with him. They said you would understand."

He did. And he was thankful they'd done that. Neither of them could help him by sitting in a hospital waiting room. They needed to find out who did this.

Now.

"Anissa's still here," Leigh said.

"Why?"

"She's with your grandfather in the waiting room."

"What?"

"Actually, I believe she's with both of your grandparents."

"Grandmother? Is here?"

"Yes. I think they want to see you. I've been holding them off, but you probably should . . ."

"Of course. Yeah. Okay."

Five minutes later he heard Anissa's voice outside the door. "He's in here." Grandmother entered first, followed by Grandfather.

"Oh my." Grandmother's whispered words stunned him. For Virginia Campbell, those two words were equivalent to a shout of horror.

Grandfather placed his arm around Grandmother's shoulders and squeezed. Grandmother leaned into him for a brief moment before straightening.

"I do not appreciate getting phone calls in the middle of my bridge club," she said. He might have been hurt by the severity of her remark if he hadn't noticed the way her hand shook as she brushed back her hair.

"Anissa shouldn't have called." He shot daggers at Anissa, who didn't look nearly sorry enough for putting him in this situation.

"She most certainly should have." Grandmother bestowed a smile on Anissa. "She clearly understands the way mothers and grandmothers worry. Besides, how would it look for a Campbell to be in the hospital and no one from the family present to advocate for him."

"Grandmother." He wanted to say he didn't need anyone to advocate for him. And he didn't care how it looked. But then he caught Grandfather's eye. "I'm sorry. Things got a little crazy for a while."

Anissa smirked, and she and Leigh slipped into the hallway.

"From what we heard, you saved Dr. Fleming's life today." Grandfather had a twinkle in his eye that didn't bode well. If Grandfather got the idea he had any sort of feelings for Sabrina . . .

"Well, of course he did," Grandmother said. "He's a Campbell." High praise from Grandmother. If he hadn't gotten the all clear from the doctor, he would have been worried there was something seriously wrong with him.

"How're you feeling? Investigator Bell told us you were nearly crushed by a large section of roof."

"I don't know about crushed—"

"And we ran into Investigator Chavez in the parking lot as we were coming in. He told us your quick thinking saved all of you," Grandfather added. "Said if you hadn't reacted when you did . . ."

Grandmother sucked in a quick breath. "We're proud of you, dear. When will they let you out of here?"

"Any minute now."

"Do your parents know about this? Or Alexander?" Adam's brother, Alexander, was an orthopedic surgeon in Chapel Hill.

"He knows, Grandmother. I talked to him for about thirty seconds before they did all the scans. He was going to call Mom and Dad as soon as they knew what we were dealing with. But with the time difference, I'm not sure they'll get the message until tomorrow."

Grandmother pinched her mouth into a tight line. "Good. I don't wish to be part of any form of deception. Parents need to know what's going on with their children."

"Yes, ma'am."

"What do you need, son? What can we do?" Grandfather patted Adam's leg.

"Nothing. It's just some bruises and lacerations. Nothing major. I'm fine." There was no way he needed his grandmother worrying over things that would heal. "Thank you both for coming."

Grandmother gave him a small smile. "Would you like me to send Marcel over tonight?"

She was offering to do without her butler for the evening? Good grief. He'd never heard of her doing that. Ever. Grandfather looked surprised by the gesture, but he supported it. "That's an excellent idea, Virginia."

"Thank you for that kind offer. Truly. But I'm fine. The doctor doesn't want either Dr. Fleming or me to be alone tonight, and our friend Leigh Weston has agreed to keep an eye on us. She's a nurse practitioner here in the emergency department, so she's eminently qualified."

"Judge Weston's daughter. Yes. I know who she is. She's quite respected in her field. An excellent choice. You'll give her our number," she said. "And tell her to call us if she has the slightest need." Grandmother didn't ask this—she stated all of it as an imperative.

"Yes, ma'am. I will."

"And you will call us tonight? Just a little check-in?" Grandfather did ask.

"Of course."

"Very well." Grandmother looked around the room. Grandfather must have taken that as a sign that it was time for them to leave. He patted Adam's leg, again. "Keep up the good work."

"Yes, sir."

But rather than walking to the door, Grandmother came closer, leaned over his bed, and planted a kiss on his cheek. "Be safe."

"Yes, ma'am."

Grandfather winked and they left the room.

Adam touched his face. He had no recollection of his grandmother kissing him. Ever.

He had no idea what had just happened. Was it possible Grandmother had finally decided to give him her blessing?

He didn't need it, of course.

But he couldn't deny that he rather liked it.

"You okay?" Leigh said from the door.

"I think so."

She came in, twirling a cream-colored card in her hand. "Your grandmother gave me her card. I'm to call if I need anything. She's quite worried about you."

"Yeah, I think she is."

Who'd have ever thought that would happen?

It took another thirty minutes for him to get released. When he was finally free, the nurse wanted to push him to the door in a wheelchair.

He declined.

He found Leigh in the lobby. "Where's Sabrina?"

"Right here."

Her voice came from his left. Her eyes were red. Her right cheek was scraped. She might wind up with a black eye based on the bruising he could see forming. Her wrist had a bandage on it. There were stitches at her hair line.

She was the most beautiful thing he'd ever seen.

"You're okay?" she asked.

"Come here." He pulled her to him and wrapped his arms around her. She held on to him like she might never let him go.

129

Which would be fine with him.

"We're okay." He kissed the top of her head, and he didn't care that Leigh was standing six feet away with a goofy grin on her face and a tear slipping down her cheek.

Sabrina's entire body trembled. Was she cold? Or maybe having some sort of delayed reaction to the day's events?

"Adam," Leigh said, "Sabrina has insisted that I take her to her lab. Would you care to join us?"

"The lab?" He tried to keep the "Are you crazy?" out of his voice.

"The hard drive," Sabrina said. "I need to see if I can get anything off it."

"Tonight?" he asked.

"You think we dare wait for tomorrow? We almost got blown up today. They've probably destroyed whatever evidence might have been in the house. We'll never know for sure. The hard drive's all we have left."

As much as he hated to admit it, she had a point.

A terrifying one. But a good one.

"Okay," he said. "Let's go."

10

How did Anissa and Ryan wind up at Lisa Palmer's house?" Adam asked as Leigh drove them back to Sabrina's lab. "They had been at the lake all morning, but they were headed back to the sheriff's office when they heard about the explosion. They drove straight to the house," Leigh said from the front seat of her car.

Sabrina had slid into the back beside Adam, and she'd not objected when he'd reached for her hand. Her fingers had laced through his almost before she'd realized what was happening. His thumb made tiny circles across hers.

Somehow, after everything that had happened today, it seemed like the most natural thing in the world.

"Did Ryan happen to say if they found anything in the lake?" Adam asked.

"A whole lot of nothing." Leigh drummed her fingers on the steering wheel. "They're with Gabe at Lisa Palmer's house now."

Sabrina studied her friend. There was something about Leigh's tone, her stiff shoulders, her busy hands that didn't feel right.

"How much burned?" Adam asked.

"My understanding is it's a total loss. What didn't burn was soaked by the time the fire department finished putting out the blaze."

The odds of them recovering anything from the house would be infinitesimally small.

"How's Gabe handling it?" Adam squeezed Sabrina's hand as he spoke, and when she looked up she found his eyes roving over her face. She must have looked rough.

Not that she cared.

Or she didn't usually care.

Why should she care now?

"He's . . ." Leigh's voice trailed off.

"Yeah," Adam said.

"She didn't say anything," Sabrina whispered to Adam.

Leigh chuckled. "Sorry, Sabrina," she said. "Adam was reading between the lines. Same as Ryan and Anissa have. That's why they're with him. Gabe's a wreck. He's worried about the case. He's worried about you and Adam. He's worried about finding who fired that RPG. He's worried about who is behind this and what they're capable of. And most of all, he's worried they—whoever they are—will find whatever it is they're looking for before he does."

"He told you all that?" She'd never imagined Gabe would be that forthcoming about his insecurities.

"No."

Then how did she—oh. "You got all that from his body language?"

"Pretty much. That and because the more time I spend with Ryan, the more I learn about how cops are and how they think. And Gabe is a very good cop. He's also a friend."

She made eye contact with Sabrina in the rearview mirror. "And he's dealing with a lot of rage right now. I wouldn't have been surprised to see steam coming from his ears. Anissa was the only one who could get him calmed down enough to stay still for the X-rays at the hospital."

"Anissa? Wow." Adam continued to speak to Leigh, but his eyes never left Sabrina's face.

"Yeah. Go figure," Leigh said. "They've come a long way. I'm not sure what happened, but there's been a noticeable thaw between them since y'all helped that friend of Gabe's with that boat that was sunk in Lake Porter."

"Miracles never cease," Adam said.

Was he still talking about Gabe? She wasn't sure anymore. He reached toward Sabrina's face with his free hand and tucked a stray hair behind her ear. His thumb traced her cheek as it passed by and the heat of that gentle caress startled her. She almost leaned into his palm but caught herself.

What was she doing?

This was a bad idea. A terrible idea. She'd had this conversation with herself before. Adam Campbell needed a certain type of woman.

She wasn't that type. She couldn't be that type. And if she cared about him, she needed to remove herself from consideration.

She straightened in the seat but couldn't bring herself to pull her hand away from his. She could enjoy this. For now. Right?

"Dr. Sloan got him out of there as fast as he could. I told Ryan to be sure he gets him back to the house tonight. I'll set up a mini-clinic and check out all three of you again. How long do you think you'll be at the lab?"

"I'm not sure. A couple of hours at least." Sabrina turned to Adam. "Do you need to go to your office?"

His hand tightened around hers. "I'm not going anywhere."

"But—"

"No."

If Gabe had been steaming earlier, Adam was practically vibrating. Probably the same causes. Rage. Frustration. Worry. Stress.

Regardless, there was no point in fighting it. Sabrina closed her eyes and tried to settle her own nerves.

The next thing she was aware of, Adam was rubbing her arm. "Bri?" He spoke her name with gentle reverence.

"Did I fall asleep?"

"Yes," he said. "Sorry to wake you."

"It's okay."

Leigh was looking at her phone. "Ryan says he's going to have a couple of deputies on the scene bring you your car. He said it was undamaged."

"Great." Adam released Sabrina's hand and climbed from the car. She waited. Seconds later, he opened her door. "Thank you," he said.

"For what?"

"For letting me be a gentleman."

She took the hand he extended. Wow. She was stiff. Between this morning's attack and this afternoon's explosion, her entire body ached. Her legs didn't want to work, and rather than stepping away from the car the way she'd intended, she tripped and stumbled. Right into Adam. He caught her with her face mere inches from his.

The air between them hummed.

"Thank you," she said.

"For what?"

"For being a gentleman."

He cleared his throat and steadied her, making sure she wasn't going to fall over before he released her. "I try."

"Are you two sure you're okay?" Leigh asked from behind the wheel. "I don't know about this."

"We're good," Adam said. "When we finish here, I'll take Sabrina to her place to pack a bag and we'll come stay with you."

"Okay. I expect you to work quickly," Leigh said. "You both have been through a lot of trauma today. At some point, your bodies are going to crash. You can only keep them going by sheer force of will for so long. You need to be in a place where you can let down your guard and get some rest when that happens."

"Yes, ma'am." Adam tried to keep a straight face but failed.

"I'm not kidding, Adam Campbell. I'm speaking as both a medical professional and someone with firsthand experience. You may be willing to test my theory, but I know you don't want Sabrina to."

Adam bit down on his lip. "You're right. We'll work as fast as we can."

"Excellent. Be careful."

"We will."

Adam closed the door and Leigh drove away. He slid an arm around Sabrina as they walked to the lab.

"Did Leigh seem a bit tense to you?" she asked.

"A bit?"

"That's a yes?"

Adam held the door for her. "Sorry for the sarcasm. She's more than a bit stressed."

"What's wrong?" Sabrina pushed the up arrow for the elevator.

"You're kidding, right?"

"No . . ."

He pointed to her bandaged wrist and the stitches in her forehead, then pointed to his own head.

"She's worried about us?" Sabrina stepped into the elevator and Adam followed.

"Very."

"What aren't you telling me? Or what am I missing that should be obvious?" There must be something.

Adam looked at the sides of the elevator. "Are you going to make me spell it out for you?"

"If you don't, I'm going to be wondering what's going on."

He didn't speak as they walked to the lab entrance, or as she leaned forward for the iris scan, or as they walked into the dark room. The motion-activated lights flickered on one by one, and she waited as he made a silent inspection of the lab and her office.

"Everything clear?" she asked.

"As far as I can tell."

"You still haven't answered my question."

"I'm still trying to figure out how to do it."

"I'm not sure what's so difficult about this." Sabrina unlocked the evidence closet. "You open your mouth. Words come out."

"Fine," he said. "We almost died at Lisa Palmer's house a few hours ago. We don't know who fired the RPG or where they might be hiding. While we may want to assume the attack was intended not to kill us but to destroy evidence, the reality is that the person who fired knew where we were and knew there was a good chance we would not be able to get away in time."

"I understand all of that," she said. None of this was new information.

"Ryan, Anissa, and Gabe are all there. Now."

The weight of Adam's observation settled over her and the walls suddenly seemed to close in. She reached for a chair and sat down. Hard.

"I'm sorry." Adam knelt in front of her. "I was trying not to scare you."

"What if he comes back? What if he kills them?"

Adam didn't shrug off her worries. He didn't even try to ease them. She wasn't imagining the risk.

"That's why she's stressed." Now it made sense.

"Yes."

"And that's why you're stressed."

"Yes."

"And why you've agreed to stay at Leigh's tonight."

"Yes." Adam rested his hands on her knees. "Let's get this taken care of so we can get over there."

He stood. It took him a lot longer than it should have. "Are you okay?" she asked.

He gave her a tight smile. "It's nothing that won't heal. Are you okay?"

Was she?

She'd almost died today. Twice. And she hadn't had time to think about it. Maybe she could talk to Leigh tonight. Leigh might be able to help her make some sense out of the jumble of emotions flooding through her.

Relief at being alive. Fear for her friends—and herself. Worry about what she was going to find on this hard drive and what implications it might have for her own family.

And then there was the way her heart ricocheted around in her chest whenever Adam touched her. The way chills raced across her skin and her breath caught in her chest.

If she kissed him, would he respond the way she shouldn't hope he would?

She looked at him, still waiting on her to respond to his question, and she knew.

He would.

"Bri?"

She was looking at him . . . no, she was looking . . . at his mouth? No. But?

No.

She shook her head like she was trying to clear it, then winced. If she felt anything like he did right now, she had to be hurting.

"I'm okay," she said. "Let me see if I can get anything off this drive."

He watched as she connected the drive to a write blocker. He'd learned all about them when they were setting up the procedures between her lab and the sheriff's office. The write blocker kept anything from accidentally being written onto the hard drive and prevented anything currently on the hard drive from being modified. Going through this step kept everything forensically sound and was critical if they ever needed to use anything she recovered from the hard drive as evidence in court.

He breathed a huge sigh of relief when she was able to power up the drive and successfully duplicate it. Once the original drive was safely tucked back into the evidence closet, her forensic software scanned all the recovered files, indexed them, and then marked them if they were damaged or encrypted.

And a lot of them were encrypted.

"Now we're getting somewhere." She gave him a gleeful smile. "I love cracking encryptions."

He loved to watch her work, but today he needed to stay focused. And it wasn't like he could do anything to help her. When she started talking about building custom dictionaries to use as an attack on the encrypted files, whatever that meant, he left her to it.

He returned to the computer he'd claimed and continued his own search into the life of Lisa Palmer. Where she'd come from, what she'd done, how she'd spent her money, where she'd liked to eat, play, shop, vacation.

Nothing was too small to consider.

He owed it to her.

No matter what she'd done, she'd come to him—or tried to come to him—for help. The least he could do was help her now.

But there wasn't much to work with.

Lisa Palmer had worked alone. She'd been a good neighbor and had a good relationship with her sister.

No romantic liaisons.

Gabe had people interviewing the rest of her neighbors, but Adam didn't expect much to come from that.

She had bank accounts at Carrington First and at a national bank. She had some retirement and investment accounts with national funds—but no local financial advisor.

No surprise there. She wouldn't have wanted anyone to have access to her financials.

He kept digging. Kept clicking. Until the words and numbers

started swimming on the screen. He checked the clock. Almost eight.

"Bri?" He hadn't heard anything more than the clicking of her keyboard in at least an hour. When she didn't respond, he stood.

Wow. His back was one solid sheet of agony. No way he'd be able to get comfortable enough to sleep tonight. He twisted, shifted, and rolled his shoulders and neck before stepping away from the desk. "Bri?"

She had earbuds in. Her eyes fixed on the screen in front of her. Hands flying.

Wow. She was beautiful.

Without warning, she tossed her hands in the air—and grimaced as she reached back to massage the base of her neck. A pained and tired—yet satisfied—grin stretched across her face. "Gotcha."

She caught him watching her and her face flushed. "It will take a while to get through all these files, but I've been able to crack 98 percent of them."

"Awesome."

"Yeah." Her grin faded.

"What is it?"

She pulled a flash drive from the computer. "I'm wondering what we're going to find. I have a bad feeling about this. Like it's not going to be good."

"Do you mean about your dad?"

"My dad. Yes. But also whoever she was working for that killed her. That tried to kill us. You don't go around blowing up people with an RPG over a few years of tax evasion."

"Well, we would hope not."

That remark earned him a flicker of a smile. He needed to get her out of there. Somewhere she could decompress.

"Bri?" She looked up. "Can we go home?"

Relief mixed with something he couldn't quite put a finger on crossed her face. "Yes."

It took her a while to back everything up, shut everything down, and get to her feet. She moved slowly. He knew she had to be in agony and didn't try to rush her. She winced as she retrieved her bag from the floor beside her desk. "Ready."

When they stepped into the hall, they were met by two uniformed officers standing on either side of the door. Both of whom looked like they'd just graduated high school and couldn't possibly be old enough to be on the force. He recognized one of them. Ben something. "Ben? What's going on?"

"Hey, Adam, Dr. Fleming," Ben said. "We're here to escort you wherever you wish to go."

"Seriously?" Sabrina looked at Adam. "*You* need a bodyguard?"

"Investigators Chavez, Parker, and Bell insisted, ma'am." The other officer nodded at Sabrina in a manner that was all too appreciative and not nearly deferential enough. "My name's Zac," he said. "I was standing there when they were talking to the captain. I don't know what you two are doing, but it must be crucial to the investigation."

"Dr. Fleming is a cybersecurity and computer forensics expert," Adam said. "At this point, she *is* the investigation."

Zac shared a look with Ben. "Yes, sir."

"They seemed to think you were pretty important as well, sir," Ben said.

So they sent baby cops to babysit them? Why didn't he feel safer?

"Fine," he said. "We're headed to Dr. Fleming's place so she can pack a bag. Then we're going to a friend's house for the night."

"Together?" Zac's implication was clear.

"Oh, no, I mean—" Sabrina started to explain.

"Yes." Adam placed a hand on Sabrina's back. They didn't owe this little punk an explanation, and when Sabrina wasn't present, he would be sure to point out to him how inappropriate that remark had been.

"Of course, sir. Sorry."

He would be. They didn't speak as they took the elevator down to the main floor. When the doors opened, Ben put his arm out. "Sir, if you don't mind . . ."

Adam leaned against the elevator wall. "Go ahead." Sabrina followed his lead and waited with him.

The officers stepped out and returned a few moments later. "We're clear."

Two minutes later they were in Adam's car, the young officers following them. "What was that about?" Sabrina asked. "You let that guy get the wrong impression. He thinks we're . . . well, you know."

Yeah. He knew. "He was already thinking that," Adam said. "His job is to do his job. Not to question you about your activities."

"I don't know about that." Sabrina looked out the window. "Seems like he was trying to understand the situation fully so he would know how best to act."

"He was trying to understand the situation fully so he would know if he could ask you out," Adam said.

Sabrina scoffed. "Unlikely."

"Absolute certainty."

"You're biased," she said.

"You got that right. Doesn't mean I'm wrong."

She laughed. "He's not my type anyway."

She had a type? He wanted to know what her type was, but what if she said she could only see herself with another academic? Like that Mike guy she was talking about earlier. Or maybe she preferred body builders. Or guys who were good with their hands— woodworkers or artists. Or musicians.

But she didn't elaborate. Maybe he could get her to say more. "Not your type?"

"Definitely not."

That wasn't helpful.

She closed her eyes and let out a deep sigh. "I'm not sure if I have ever been this tired," she said. "It's not that I'm sleepy. It's more like an all-encompassing fatigue. My body hurts. My mind won't shut down, even though it needs to."

He reached for her hand and she laced her fingers through his. They rode the rest of the way to her house in silence. The baby cops went inside her house first, gave them the all clear, then returned to their car. Adam followed Sabrina inside and then sat in her tiny living area while she packed. She said she only needed ten minutes.

He scanned the small space, intrigued by what it might tell him about this woman who had completely taken over his mind and heart.

There were a few magazines. Some fun figurines.

But only one picture, and it wasn't of her family.

A small four-by-six snapshot sat on the tiny corner table. A young Sabrina—she might have been eight or nine—smiled at a stunning Hispanic woman. The woman was probably in her twenties, and she was smiling at Sabrina with a level of adoration that pierced his heart.

This must be Rosita.

And at least in the moment this photograph captured, it was clear she'd adored Sabrina.

He needed to talk to Sabrina about her relationship with her family and what made her think Rosita had been a slave.

But the day had been so crazy that there hadn't been time.

Tomorrow they would make time.

11

Three hours later, Sabrina sat on the edge of Leigh's bed while Leigh listened to her breathing.

"Is this really necessary?"

Leigh held a finger up. Right. Talking would mess up whatever breath sounds Leigh was listening for.

She took six more deep breaths in and out before Leigh stepped back and removed the stethoscope from her ears.

"You sound fine," she said. "How much does it hurt?"

"What? Breathing? It's hard to say. It's blended in with all the other hurts."

Leigh put the stethoscope on the dresser. "You need to take the pain meds Dr. Sloan prescribed."

"I don't want them."

Leigh leaned against the dresser, arms crossed. "So you want to hurt all night, not sleep, and then not be able to do what you need to do tomorrow?"

"That's not what I said."

"That's what's going to happen."

"I'll think about it."

Leigh handed her the bottle of pills. "You think too much."

"I still need to talk to Adam," she said.

"It's almost midnight. And these will take about thirty minutes to kick in," Leigh said. "You aren't planning on keeping him up half the night, are you? Because he needs to rest as well. He's—"

"What's wrong with him that I don't know about? Are you keeping something from me?"

Leigh had set up a little rotating clinic twenty minutes earlier. Gabe had gone first. Then Adam. She was the last one.

"He got blown up today. Same as you. And while you get to add a concussion to it, he gets to add a chunk of the roof slamming into his back while he was protecting you from being squashed. The bottom line is that you're both a mess. I don't care what you need to talk about. I want you both in bed in thirty minutes. Take the medicine. Go talk to him. And then get in bed."

"I might need more than thirty minutes," she said.

"Then wait until tomorrow."

Could she wait until tomorrow? Would she be able to sleep if she didn't get it all off her chest now? Probably not. "Fine."

Leigh followed her down the stairs. She stuttered to a stop at the bottom and Leigh almost slammed into her. "What?" Leigh asked.

Sabrina pointed.

Adam was standing with his back to them. No shirt. Gabe, Ryan, and Anissa were all standing behind him. His entire back was red except for the large stripe across the middle that was bandaged.

"Oh. Yeah. It's going to look worse before it looks better," Leigh whispered in her ear.

"Dude," Gabe was saying. "I can't believe it didn't break your back. That thing weighed a ton."

"How are you even moving?" Anissa pointed to a place where blood had seeped through the bandage. "You are—"

"In bad shape." Ryan finished the thought.

"I'm fine," Adam said.

"All that red is going to turn some nasty colors and you're going to hurt worse tomorrow." Gabe said this with authority. Had he ever had an injury like this? None of them took issue with his pronouncement, so maybe he had.

"Better me than her," Adam said.

Ryan and Gabe both said, "True."

"Here." Ryan handed Adam his shirt.

"Thanks." He tried to put the shirt on, but the effort was clearly painful. Anissa took it from him and held it out so he could slide one arm in, then the other. Adam turned around to face them and there was no way for Sabrina to pretend she wasn't gawking at him.

He hurried to button his shirt. "Hey, Bri. You get the all clear from the medical authorities?" Ryan, Gabe, and Anissa scattered at his words, looking for all the world like three little kids who'd been caught with their hands in the cookie jar. Or in this case, like three grown adults who were supposed to be her friends who had been caught hiding from her how bad Adam's injuries were.

She turned on Leigh. "You said he was okay."

"He is." Leigh reached for her arm, but Sabrina pulled it away.

"There was nothing okay about that." Sabrina could hear the hysteria in her own voice, but she couldn't seem to find any way back to rational thought. "I thought you just checked him out. I saw blood."

"Bri." Adam's voice cut through her rant.

She turned back to him. "You told me you were fine," she said. "You've been sitting in the lab, and working, and—"

"So have you," he said.

"I'm not . . . I don't have . . ." She didn't even know how to describe Adam's back.

"No, you just have a concussion and stitches," Adam said.

"But that—"

"Looks worse than it feels." He spoke in a soothing tone, but it only annoyed her more.

"I don't believe you." She turned to fuss at Leigh, but she was gone. They were all gone. When had everyone else disappeared? Chickens. If they thought getting away from her would somehow spare them from her wrath, they didn't know her well at all.

"Are you sure you're okay? Because you're not being quite as logical as you usually are." Adam frowned as he studied her face.

"How am I supposed to be rational when it looks like—"

"Like a roof landed on my back today? From what I could see, it looks exactly like I would expect it to."

Was he . . . laughing? "This isn't funny."

"I don't know," he said. "I'm rather enjoying it."

"What do you mean you're enjoying it?"

"I'm not enjoying the way my back feels, but I'm intrigued by your reaction to it. Why are you upset?"

"How could I not be upset?"

"Leigh isn't upset. Neither is Anissa."

"They're used to this kind of stuff," she said.

"I don't think that's it." His hand slid around her waist. "I'm wondering if maybe you're upset for some other reason."

"Of course I am. You were protecting me. And now you're all battered. And everyone lied to me about it. And it's . . . it's my fault you're hurt."

"Oh baby." He glanced around. Maybe he'd realized no one was in the room. "Come with me."

She followed him, and they wound up on the covered, screened-in part of the back deck. Lake Porter glistened in the moonlight behind them. "We need to talk."

Oh no. Even with her limited experience, she knew those words were the kiss of death.

"Would you like to sit?" Adam pointed to an overstuffed chair.

"No. I want to talk."

"Fine," he said. "We've already covered this. It's not your fault."

"But you lied to me."

"I'm sorry."

"You're admitting it?"

"No. Yes. I don't know. I wasn't trying to be deceptive, but I'm very sorry you feel like I was. I knew you would shoulder a certain amount of responsibility for my injuries. Even though you shouldn't. And I wanted to downplay it as much as possible. But it was never my intention to keep the truth from you. Ever. I don't want there to be secrets between us. About anything."

No secrets? But there were so many secrets.

"Will you accept my apology?"

She nodded. "I'm sorry I lost it."

He smiled. "You've had an exceptionally trying day," he said. "You're allowed to be less than rational. Although I will admit it kind of scares me when that happens."

"Sorry."

"Don't be sorry." He took a step toward her. "I'm glad I can make you irrational."

He had no idea. No clue how much she wanted to let him make her irrational in more ways than one.

But that wasn't who she was.

She was a rational and logical woman who was in control of her emotions. Or at least who could choose when to act on them and when not to.

And now was not the time.

"I think we need to finish our conversation from yesterday." She glanced at her watch. "Or I guess it was technically two days ago."

Adam slowed his approach toward her. "You want to talk about your parents? Now? Tonight?"

"I think we should." She sat in one of the chairs and pointed to the one beside her.

He stared at her longer than she was comfortable with. "Okay." He leaned against the back of the chair. "You'll forgive me if I don't sit, I hope."

The formality in his tone suffocated her more than the combined weight of his body and the roof had this morning.

"Of course. Whatever you need."

"Thank you."

Thick silence wrapped around them. He didn't prompt her to start. In some ways he almost seemed like he didn't care if she started talking or not.

"I know you're going to have to tell the others this," she said. "And honestly, at this point, I don't even care. Some secrets are too heavy to carry. But I would appreciate it if you would ask them all to use this information with discretion."

"Of course."

Here goes nothing. "My parents divided all their assets when I was in my early twenties. Just like you would if you got a divorce. Except they never got the divorce. And then when Dad got sick, he got a new accountant, new lawyer, new financial advisor—new everything. There are even a few documents that are sealed until my thirtieth birthday. There's some sort of trust. I don't even know what all will be involved. And, of course, my mother was furious but is no help."

She'd never been any help.

"My parents' marriage was a sham. I didn't know that either." She shook her head. "I sometimes wonder if the extreme dysfunction of my family life is part of why I am so extraordinarily bad at picking up on social cues. The interactions modeled for me in my home were all . . . wrong. What I thought was love was manipulation. What I thought was acceptance was more often a power play. What I thought was true . . . was a lie."

The only way she knew Adam heard her was that he shifted his feet.

"Before Rosita left, my mom pretty much left me alone. She didn't get too worried about what clubs I joined in school or even what classes I was taking. I was smart. As long as I was bringing home straight A's, I don't think Mom cared one way or the other what I did. The only time she insisted on anything—at least that I can remember—was a dance and etiquette class. It was very important to her that I knew how to waltz and which fork to use."

Adam still didn't respond.

"But when Rosita left, my mother got . . . very interested." She shifted in the chair, but pain shot through her head. If Adam wasn't going to engage, then maybe she shouldn't either. She leaned back on the cushion and closed her eyes. This was better.

"Everything came under her microscope. And nothing was good enough. I was in the wrong clubs. Didn't have the right friends. Didn't wear the right clothes. Didn't have my hair styled the right way. My nails were a disgrace. My eyebrows, a train wreck."

Fifteen years later, she could still hear the words coming out of her mother's mouth. See the fury on her face.

"The summer between eighth and ninth grade, she launched into an 'improve Sabrina' project the way she would have tackled an assignment at work. I'd started school a year early and skipped a grade in elementary school, so I was only twelve at the time. I was already the youngest student headed to high school that fall. I would have been insecure enough without my mother's frequent reminders of how far I fell short."

She could still picture the outfit her mother picked out for her to wear the first day of high school. It had been cute, but Sabrina had hated it.

"Unfortunately for my mother, her efforts failed. You can put the geek into preppy clothes, but you can't make her fit in with the preppy kids. While my mother's friends had daughters who were worried about homecoming dances and running for student council, I was president of the computer club. Which sounds more impressive than it is. There were only three of us."

One of those guys had killed himself her junior year. The other one had gotten lost in a world of mind-altering drugs and disappeared after his freshman year of college.

She cleared her throat. "The point is that my mother fought me and my wiring for years. But at some point, the façade in my home began to slip. Or maybe it had never been there, and I just started seeing things more clearly. Regardless, I was sixteen when I realized my parents didn't just not love each other. They hated each other. And I began to suspect that while they didn't exactly hate me, they resented me. I assumed they had stayed together for my benefit. I now know they had stayed together for their own benefit. My needs would never have been enough for them to make that big of a sacrifice."

She didn't open her eyes, but she heard Adam move from behind the chair. Heard him move toward her.

"I left for college at sixteen," she said. "As soon as they drove away, I took everything out of my closet, loaded it into my car, and donated it to a thrift store that supported abused women. I bought jeans and T-shirts and Chuck Taylors. I went to a salon and got my hair cut the way I wanted it. I probably would have gone a little goth for extra spite, but that seemed like too much work. I decided I didn't care what anyone thought about me. That I wouldn't conform to anyone's definition of beauty or societal appropriateness. I didn't go home until Christmas. When I got out of the car, my father just shook his head. My mother was away on business and when she got home, she didn't get in a fight with me. She got in a fight with my dad. I'd never heard such venom. And they were spewing it at each other equally."

She blew out a breath. "From then on I spent as much time at school as I could. I don't even know what to say about my dad. He was so passive. He let Mom have her way most of the time. But after I turned eighteen, he started calling me on a regular basis to ask if he could take me to dinner. I always said no."

Light pressure on the chair told her Adam had rested his hand on the back of it. She needed to hurry and get through this.

"But then I met a grad student who invited me to church. My reaction to God and Jesus was understandably cynical, but this girl had a happiness about her—a joy I couldn't help but envy. It took a couple of years before my logical, rational search for truth led me to the One who is Truth."

Thank you for pursuing me, Father.

She knew Adam was hovering over her, but she still didn't open her eyes. "My dad never stopped calling. He called once a month to ask me to dinner. I ignored him for four years. But then we went through a study at church on forgiveness. It was convicting. So the next time he called, I said yes. It was awkward, but I felt compelled to at least be respectful of him as my father. We were just starting to figure out how to get along when he got sick."

So many emotions swirled through her. That stupid medicine Leigh had insisted she take was kicking in. Her entire body felt heavy and her eyes fought for permission to close permanently. But this conversation had to happen. Now. And then it would be over.

"He made all his own decisions. Bought the house. Lined up medical assistance. Didn't want my mom to see him. Made all his own arrangements. To be honest, I didn't expect to spend much time with him, but when the university here offered me a position, I felt like it was what God wanted me to do. So I moved here. I made it a point to visit him a couple of times a week. Eventually I bought my tiny house and put it on the edge of the property. It let me check on him every day without having to move in."

Moving in had not been an option.

"But then he started talking about Rosita. Sometimes he talked to me like I *was* Rosita. He told me he was sorry. Over and over again. One time he looked straight at me and said, 'Yvonne will kill us both if she ever finds out,' which has made me wonder if my mother had any idea what was going on. I have no idea if he had a consensual affair with Rosita or if he forced her . . ."

Adam's quick intake of breath came from far closer than she'd expected.

"And knowing what I know now about labor trafficking, I can't help but wonder if she was a slave. I don't know why she didn't run."

Adam's hand curled around hers, but she pulled her hand away. "I know you feel sorry for me," she said. "But don't. I'm fine. I'm just telling you all this so you'll understand." She had to say it. No matter how much it hurt. "You need to understand how messed up I am, Adam. I'm the most wrong person in the world for you. And I'll never be able to be the right one."

"Because your family was a hot mess?" Even though he whispered the words, she could hear the intensity in them. "Because your parents were horrible to you? Because you like skinny jeans and T-shirts?"

"No," she said. "Because I don't know how to be any different. I don't know how to pull off a dinner party. I don't even know how to maintain a regular friendship, much less know how to have a healthy relationship."

"You're a quick learner, Dr. Fleming."

She'd let this go on way too long. Now they were both going to hurt. A lot. But it was the only way. She had to do it. "I'm damaged goods. The only person who I think ever really loved me probably wasn't even free to leave the premises. Trust me on this. You'll be much better off without me."

Sabrina yawned.

She'd been slurring her words for the last couple of minutes. She still made sense, except for that part about how he would be better off without her.

That was ludicrous.

The brush-off she'd given him earlier had hurt his feelings, but now he had so much more insight into how she ticked.

And if it was possible, he was drawn to her more than he'd ever been. His family had its share of dysfunction, but nothing that compared to what she'd been through. His parents hadn't understood his choices. They'd tried to convince him to go to law school—even sweetening the pot with some lucrative offers most twenty-two-year-olds would have jumped at.

But never, not once, had he ever felt unloved. Unwanted. Unimportant.

He studied her face, her lashes that fluttered closed. He could hear the anguish in her voice. How was he going to handle this?

Did she care about him and just didn't think they could be a good match long term? Or maybe she was trying to let him down easy with the classic "It's not you, it's me" brush-off.

"We can talk about this tomorrow," he said. She gave a weak shake of her head. "Come on. Let's get you in bed."

She leaned on him as he walked her back inside. Leigh and Ryan were cuddling in an oversized chair by the fire. Leigh jumped up when she saw them.

"Is she okay?"

"I'm fine." Sabrina's mumbled response was less than encouraging. "Those pills."

"I'm glad you took them. They should have knocked you out cold twenty minutes ago." Leigh gave Adam a knowing look. She knew better than anyone how much pain he was in. "Do you want Ryan to help her up the stairs?"

"No. I've got her." Adam reached down and scooped Sabrina's legs into his arms. Her resistance was so weak it worried him. "What did you give her?"

"Pain medicine," Leigh said. "The same stuff I'm going to give you in about five minutes. And you're going to take it or Ryan has been instructed to handcuff you and force it down your throat."

"To look at you, no one would expect you to be such a violent little person," Adam said.

Leigh led the way up the stairs. "You think I'm kidding."

The only thing Leigh was ferocious about, besides Ryan, was her patients. "I *know* you are, but I'll do as you've requested. After she's settled."

Leigh turned right at the top of the stairs and opened the first door on the right. "In here. The girls are getting the upstairs. The guys get the basement." She must have gotten the room ready earlier, because the sheets were turned down and a small lamp cast a subtle glow over the room. Adam laid Sabrina on the bed and slid her glasses from her face. He placed them on the nightstand and stepped back to make room for Leigh, who adjusted Sabrina's head and legs, pulled the covers over her, and turned out the light.

"You're next," she said. "So it would be helpful if you put yourself in a bed before the meds kick in."

When Adam got downstairs, Gabe, Ryan, and Anissa were conversing at the bar in the kitchen. "Where did you come from?" he asked Anissa.

Anissa had on a pair of gym shorts and a T-shirt. And her hair was wet. "We're all staying at Hotel Weston tonight." She pointed at Leigh. "This one is very hard to argue with."

A grin stretched across Leigh's face. "I wish we could all hang out when we weren't worried about someone getting killed, but I'll take what I can get."

Leigh had a servant's heart and a gift for hospitality she didn't get to use nearly as often as she wanted. "I'll fix breakfast in the morning, but not before eight. I expect Gabe, Adam, and Sabrina to sleep at least that long."

She handed Gabe and Adam each a small capsule, then slid glasses of water toward them. "Bottoms up."

"You *are* very hard to argue with," Gabe said. But he took the medicine without further complaint. Adam followed suit.

"Now," Gabe said, "before we both lose our senses, what's the connection between Sabrina's dad and the accountant?"

When Adam finished retelling Sabrina's story, four sets of eyes stared back at him, their expressions ranging from horror to sorrow. Leigh got up and grabbed a box of tissues. "How could anyone be so . . . so . . . mean? To their own daughter?" She blew her nose.

Ryan squeezed Leigh close. "So based on Sabrina's suspicions about her father, you think the accountant was mixed up in some sort of human trafficking ring?"

"I think we'd be crazy not to consider that possibility. It fits what we know so far."

"This is going to get messy." Gabe rubbed his eyes. "I worked a couple of human trafficking cases when I was undercover. They're a special kind of awful."

"I guess we know why Sabrina is so passionate about her volunteer work." Anissa took a tissue for herself and handed the box back to Leigh. "I worked a case with that team she's on. Those people are amazing. So dedicated."

Sabrina was part of a team of self-proclaimed computer nerds—high-level nerds. Not a single one of them had less than a PhD. Most of them had several. They got together one weekend a month to give another set of highly trained eyes to the video and computer evidence that human trafficking investigators all over the Southeast compiled and sent to them.

Their success rate was off the charts.

"Is she going to be able to handle this if the investigation turns up solid proof against her parents?" Gabe poured himself some water. "Because even though they were horrible to her, they're still her parents. And her mom is still alive. And is a high-powered executive who probably wouldn't hesitate to sue for defamation of character."

Adam considered the question. "I think it will be harder than she expects, but she'll do it. She's been carrying this secret for a long time. She doesn't have any actual proof and no way to know if her mother knows anything or not. It's been a nagging suspicion for a long time. In some ways, it will be a relief to have solid answers."

He hoped.

"We need to pray for her. We need to pray for all of you," Leigh said. "This case has already been dangerous. I have a bad feeling it will get worse before it gets better."

She leaned into Ryan, who nodded at all of them. "I think she's right. Let's pray. I'll open."

All eyes flicked to Anissa. "Fine. I'll close," she said.

Five heads bowed. Ryan began and they went around the circle, praying for wisdom, insight, safety. Leigh focused on healing and protection. Then it got to Anissa.

"Oh, Father. We're tired. We're tired of fighting evil and watching it seem to win time and again. We're tired of hearing stories like the one we heard tonight of children being mistreated and humans—men and women made in your image—sold as property. We long for the day when you return and everything that has gone wrong gets made right. But until that day, we're your servants and we ask that you give us guidance as we do the work you've given us to do. We know that despite the evil these people are perpetrating, in a way that is both holy and merciful, you love all of us. You love the victims and you love the victimizers. We don't understand that, Lord. We don't know how you can do it. But we do know that in your love for these evil men and women, you will not allow them to continue in their sin indefinitely.

"We've seen how you've allowed tragedy into our lives to bring an evil person to justice, and we pray now that you will use the evil that has touched the life of our friend to help free the captives and restore homes and families.

"Abba, as she sleeps, help Sabrina remember that she isn't fatherless. That you adopted her into your family long ago and she is a beloved daughter in your house. Please heal the broken places and give her the grace she'll need to walk through the days ahead. Give her the courage to step into new relationships that are part of your plan for her and help all of us guard her from those who might use this information against her.

"Help us sleep safely in your peace tonight. We love you. You're the best. Amen."

12

Sabrina woke up in pain.

Why was she hurting?

Memories from the previous day assaulted her. The fear. The pain. The embarrassment. The emotional turmoil.

Monday had been a very bad day.

It took way more effort than it should have, but she managed to roll over onto her side. The clock on the bedside table said it was ten o'clock. The daylight told her it was morning.

But wait. How did she get in this bed? She'd been on the porch with Adam.

Fresh misery—a different kind of pain than the piercing headache she'd woken with—filled her heart. She'd told Adam. Everything.

And she'd broken up with him.

Hadn't she?

Not that they'd been together in the first place, but she'd slammed that door shut. Or she thought she had.

She forced herself to sit up. Whoa. A wave of dizziness threatened to knock her back. She rode it out and didn't vomit. A good sign.

She retrieved her glasses from the nightstand and took a better look around the room. The room was familiar, but only because Leigh had shown it to her last night. Her bag was on the chair by the door, where she'd left it.

But she could not remember coming in here.

She got to her feet and waited for the room to stop spinning before she shuffled to the bathroom. She thought about a shower, but she really wanted to know what had happened after the meds had kicked in.

Or maybe she didn't.

She ran a brush through her hair, going easy around the stitches and in the area where she'd been struck. She shouldn't have been surprised she still had a headache, but she'd hoped she'd wake up pain-free.

Instead, she hurt worse today than she had yesterday. Probably from lying still for ten hours in a drug-induced slumber.

Sabrina made her way down the hall and took the stairs one at a time. The comforting smell of coffee wafted toward her. And something else. A sweet scent. Leigh had probably baked something. From scratch.

Because that's what Leigh did. She fed the people she loved.

"Hey." Leigh appeared at the bottom of the stairs and didn't even try to hide the way she was examining her.

"You could pretend I don't look as bad as I feel," Sabrina said.

"You look fabulous as always. But you don't usually care. I wonder why you care now?" Leigh didn't wait for an answer but pointed toward the kitchen counter. "I have cinnamon rolls and coffee ready for you."

"Thanks."

Leigh grabbed her phone from the counter. "In case you're curious, I'm texting Adam."

"I wouldn't bother." Sabrina dropped her head. "I pretty much ended whatever that . . . whatever that was."

159

Leigh frowned. "What are you talking about?"

"Oh, come on." Sabrina unwound a cinnamon roll. "I know you know I have a crush on him. Apparently everyone knows. And maybe he has something he thinks is a crush on me, but it would never work, and I've been deluding myself to even hope it would."

Leigh continued texting. "What exactly did you say to Adam last night?"

"He didn't tell you? I assumed he would tell everyone about my family and our immoral and criminal activities."

Leigh patted her on the back. "He mentioned your parents' possible immoral and criminal activities. Somehow he failed to mention yours. Pretty sure that's because you haven't committed any such acts. So do us all a favor and don't lump yourself in with that. You're not responsible for what your parents have or haven't done. And I know you're far too logical and rational to argue with me on this point."

"Fine." Sabrina crammed a bigger bite of the cinnamon roll into her mouth. Maybe Leigh would get the hint that she didn't feel like talking. And the cinnamon roll was amazing.

"However, he didn't mention you'd broken up with him. And, frankly, he didn't seem all that upset, so if you think you somehow ended this relationship, well, you're going to have to do it again because it didn't stick."

"I can't do it again. I barely managed it the first time."

"Then, congratulations. You still have a boyfriend. And don't be surprised when he shows up in a few minutes to take you to the lab."

"I never had a boyfriend in the first place. Especially not Adam."

"Yeah, see, I think that might be where you two need a little bit of an intervention, because you've sure been acting like you're together."

"We're just friends."

"So did you break up with him, or did you tell him you didn't want to be friends? I'm confused. Because I know Adam and if you'd made it clear that you didn't want to see him again, he would honor your wishes, even if it killed him to do it."

"I told him I'm not the right girl for him."

"And you thought that was breaking up with him? Or ending your friendship? Or whatever you want to call it?"

"I'm all wrong for him."

"Why on earth would you think that?"

"He needs a woman who can interact with his family. Who can carry on conversations over dinner about . . . I don't know . . . restaurants or the opera. He needs someone who can be a Campbell."

Leigh spun her around on the barstool until she was facing her. "Listen to me. I've tried to stay out of this because I don't want to get in the middle of something between two friends. But you need to hear this. Adam Campbell doesn't need a woman who can be a Campbell. He needs a woman who loves him for who he is. He needs a woman who doesn't care if he's a Campbell or not. Do you have any idea how rare those are in his life? How many women have come after him because he's a Campbell and only because he's a Campbell?"

"No."

"Well, I do. I've known Adam since we were kids. It was already happening in middle school. Girls and boys both who wanted to buddy up to the Campbells. His older brother, Alexander, was a few years ahead of me and had the same issue. It's very difficult for them to know if people are trying to get to know them—or like them—because of who they are. Or if they want an invitation to a party or to be seen in public with them. And some of the Campbells are okay with that. They even seem to encourage it."

"Not Adam."

"No. He's been the opposite his entire life. Always had a heart for the underdogs and the marginalized. Always had a kind word for the kids no one else wanted to talk to. Always marched to his own drum. Always been on the tightrope between being respectful and honoring to his family and not letting them dictate his life."

Leigh put her hands on Sabrina's arms. "You're exactly the kind of woman Adam Campbell needs. But it sounds to me like you're going to have to decide if he's worth it or not."

"What? No! Of course Adam's worth it. This isn't about Adam. This is about me."

Leigh squeezed her arms and then released them. She walked around the counter and poured herself a cup of coffee. Was she going to respond?

"I don't want to hurt your feelings," she finally said. "But that is one of the most self-absorbed and arrogant ideas I've ever heard come out of your mouth."

How could Leigh get that impression? "I'm trying to protect him!"

"You're trying to decide what's best for him rather than letting him make that decision for himself. And at the same time, you're telling him that the aggravation of becoming a Campbell is more trouble than he's worth."

"I never . . ."

Leigh waited with an expectant smile on her face. "I'm going to run upstairs for a few minutes while you wrestle with that. If you're willing to consider it objectively, you'll see I'm right. And if you aren't? Well. Then you're about to make a mistake you'll regret for the rest of your life. It's your call."

She grabbed her coffee cup. "Adam will be here in five minutes. Maybe less. He has a key."

Leigh headed toward the stairs, then turned back. She wrapped a gentle arm around Sabrina and hugged her. "I love you, friend. I'm not trying to be harsh. I've been praying for you all morning,

162

and I feel like what you need right now isn't people who are trying to be nice but people who love you enough to be honest."

She left Sabrina sitting at the counter.

Three minutes later, Adam walked in.

He gave her a tight smile as he walked right to her. "I can't stay. But I brought you this." He placed a box in her hand.

A new phone. "Thank you."

"No problem. Listen, we need to talk."

"You said that last night."

"Yeah. We still need to talk about that, but right now we have to talk about the case."

Part of her was relieved. The other part of her wanted to find out what he wanted to say to her.

"What about the case?"

"The forensic accountants have been working on the flash drive files. The ones you pulled up before we went over to Lisa Palmer's house."

"And?"

"They've found some files they can't do anything with. They want to know if your friend Mike might be able to have more success with them."

"I'm sure he'll be willing to take a look."

"Great. I have to run, but there's an officer coming. His job is to stay with you all day. And I do mean with you—in your lab, not outside the doors—and then to escort you back here when you're done. If you check your email, you'll see the request from Gabe for Mike. It's probably best that you work directly with him. It will save time if I don't see your response."

He wasn't hanging out with her today. And he wanted her to talk directly to Gabe? He never wanted her to talk directly to Gabe. This was so wrong. All she could do was nod.

He was still himself, but he wasn't. He was polite and gracious and friendly. But something was . . . off.

"I'll see ya."

She finally made her mouth work. "Busy day?"

He paused. "I'm meeting Ryan and Anissa and the rest of the dive team, well, except for Gabe, at the double bridges."

"Why?"

"Good old-fashioned police work. We were able to track Lisa Palmer's activities the last few days of her life based on the GPS in her car. Noticed that she made a trip over the double bridges Friday evening after she came to see me."

"She would have had to drive over them to get to her house," Sabrina said.

"I agree, but it took her far longer than it should have. So I asked an officer to pull up the footage from the area around the double bridges and see what he could find."

"He found something?"

"Maybe. Maybe not. But someone dumped something off one of the bridges Friday afternoon."

"Lisa Palmer?"

"We're pretty sure it's a woman. It could be Lisa Palmer. I've emailed you the video file to see if you can enhance it with that software you guys have."

"I'll try."

"Regardless, we're going looking for it."

He'd be diving all afternoon. "Is that a good idea?"

"What do you mean?"

"I mean . . . you're injured. Maybe Anissa and Ryan should do the diving."

Adam got a glint in his eye that she didn't know what to make of. He stepped closer and whispered, "Are you worried about me, Dr. Fleming?"

"Of course I'm worried about you."

She thought he might give her a hug or reach for her hand the way he had done. But he didn't. "I'm a big boy," he said. "I can take care of myself."

"But they should know better," she said. "They shouldn't let you dive in your condition."

"I appreciate your concern. Really. I do. But I'll be fine." He walked away.

"Adam, wait."

"What?" She couldn't make sense of the way he was looking at her. Where was the Adam she'd come to know and, well, whatever it was she did?

Leigh must have been wrong. Adam must have gotten her message loud and clear. "Just be careful. And thank you for bringing the phone."

He gave her a little salute and walked out the door.

It wasn't until the door closed behind him that she realized he'd never asked her how she was feeling or about her headache or her sore wrist.

He'd been professional. Courteous. Respectful.

But not her Adam.

What had she done?

Adam stood on the other side of Leigh's door and forced air in and out of his lungs.

He would never be able to do this. Never be able to work with Sabrina again. Never be able to be just . . . friends. Or whatever it was they were.

All he wanted to do was go back in there and pull her off that barstool. He wanted to hold her, trace her face with his fingertips, drop kisses on her eyelids, her nose, her cheeks, and then taste her lips.

But she didn't want that from him.

At least, she said she didn't, and he would respect that decision. Leigh had said Sabrina would come around. To give her time. To remember she was under an enormous amount of stress and had a concussion. Plus the emotional turmoil of sharing the darkest secrets from her childhood. It all added up to a woman who might not be in any condition to make relationship decisions.

She'd said to pull back a little. Keep things friendly and light and avoid confusing her further.

But he didn't know how to do light and friendly. He'd seen the hurt and confusion in Sabrina's eyes just now. He'd had to run out the door to keep from begging her to reconsider. But in his efforts not to push her into a relationship she didn't want, he'd managed to hurt her feelings.

What did that mean?

If she really only wanted a friendship from him, why would it matter how he treated her?

Had he actually made things worse?

His phone buzzed and he shoved himself away from the door and toward his car. "Campbell."

"Did you get lost?" Ryan asked.

"I stopped by Leigh's. I'll be there in ten minutes."

"Everything okay?"

"Nope."

"Want to talk about it?"

"Nope."

"Okay. See you when you get here."

At ten thirty, Adam parked his car to the side of the bridge and walked to the middle, where Lane was waiting for him. "Is this the spot?"

"As far as we can tell," Lane said. "The video techs said the object looked heavy. Heavy enough to fall through the water and possibly land on the bottom."

"It's deep through here."

"It is," Lane said. "Anissa's had the team out all morning running the side-scan sonar. The problem is the bottom is a littered mess. People must throw all kinds of stuff over the bridge. We've got twenty items that had roughly the same dimensions as what they were looking for. Anissa wants you to set up the jackstay search. And she wants me to help."

"Okay." He enjoyed working with Lane. He was a good deputy and a good diver. And he was eager to learn. Jackstay searches weren't as complicated as some people thought, but the rigging ropes and buoys and weights required to set them up could be a bit overwhelming. A jackstay used weighted lines and buoys to ensure that no part of the area was missed in the search.

It was Anissa's preferred search pattern because it almost always worked. With two divers who knew how to work the pattern, they had a 99 percent chance of finding what they were looking for.

Adam and Lane took a few minutes to get down to the shore with the equipment. Anissa and Ryan were already suited up.

He shouldn't have let Sabrina worry about him getting into the water. It had been unkind to do that when he knew he wouldn't even be getting wet. He had the most experience setting up these kinds of searches and that was the only reason Anissa had even let him come out.

But the way Sabrina had responded—with the worry? He was almost certain she cared more than she realized. Or maybe she did realize it and it scared her.

But . . . she'd also told him that she had no idea how to make a relationship work. So which was it? That she didn't want a relationship with him? Or that she didn't want to try a relationship with him because she was afraid of things going south? Or maybe she just couldn't see herself spending a lifetime with a Campbell. Who knew?

His gut told him that she did care about him but was scared.

And that made sense. With her background, he could see how she would be afraid to put herself out there. Afraid of getting hurt.

But he could be wrong. She was smart, and he had seen her stand up to someone she didn't want around. It was the height of arrogance to presume he knew what she wanted or needed better than she did. How would that make him any better than Darren?

He and Lane set up the jackstay on the shore. Once the lines, buoys, and weights were set and coiled, they carried it back up to the bridge to set it.

"You ready?" Adam asked.

Lane nodded and they threw both sides of the jackstay at the same time. Lane dropped his straight down from the bridge while Adam threw his away from the bridge. The weighted lines dropped beneath the surface as the buoys bobbed on the top, pre-rigged for the maximum depth of the water, giving Anissa and Ryan a starting place for their search.

Adam and Lane returned to the shore. Lane suited up to be on hand if needed.

Cops were everywhere, keeping lake traffic and nosy onlookers at a safe distance as the team worked. They found computers, phones, a couple of books, and one leather jacket but left them in the water. Ryan suggested to Anissa that they use this spot to train the new dive team members. They'd have no shortage of items to practice their evidence recovery skills on.

Thirty minutes in, Ryan's voice came through the earbud Adam was wearing. "I've got something. This one feels like a briefcase." A briefcase would have the right dimensions based on what they had seen from the sonar. The distance from the bridge made sense too.

But the initial thrill of the find was replaced by disappointment. A briefcase wasn't waterproof. Whatever was in there . . .

"Adam, give Gabe a call," Anissa said. "He'll want to be here when we open this."

He placed the call as the team followed all the steps necessary to bring the briefcase to the surface. Ryan did everything he was supposed to do. He marked the briefcase with a buoy and took photographs underwater, and then the team on land took pictures of the buoy once it reached the surface.

Ryan and Anissa took their time ascending. They'd been down long enough that they had to make a five-minute safety stop when they got within ten feet of the surface. Nothing in that briefcase was worth getting decompression sickness over. When they got the briefcase to the shore, they handed it off to Adam.

Gabe arrived while Lane and Adam were setting up a secure area to open the briefcase away from prying eyes.

Once they had everything situated, Ryan and Anissa, still in their suits, stayed back as Gabe opened it. Water gushed out.

Great. This didn't bode well for the contents. The only way to recover wet documents was to let them dry completely. And they really didn't have that much time.

Gabe reached into the briefcase and removed something. It wasn't the glob of wet paper Adam had been expecting. It looked more like a stack of laminated photographs. "Adam, will you take a look at these?"

"Why me?"

"Some of these places look like pretty high-end establishments," Gabe said. "Some private homes. I'm hoping you'll recognize some of them."

Adam recognized all of them.

"Gabe, if you don't mind, the rest of us are going to go pack up," Anissa said.

"Oh, sorry," he said. "If I can keep Adam, then we're good. Thank you."

When the others had left, Gabe tapped the photos. "Okay. What am I looking at?"

"That's Senator Carson's house. That's Gus Johnson's boat.

That's the Van Storber spa." Adam flipped to another photo showing an image of a door. "That's The Back Door."

"No kidding," Gabe said. "The back door to what?"

"It's a restaurant." Adam handed him the photo. "It's called
The Back Door."

"Never heard of it." Gabe handed him another photo.

"They don't advertise."

"Why not?"

"Don't need to."

"I don't get that," Gabe said. "Restaurants need people talking
them up. They need to get their name out. They need people to be
able to tell where they are. Where is this place?"

"It's in a small building not far from the marina. And they have
plenty of people talking about them. Last time I checked, they're
booked about six months out."

"Have you eaten there?" Gabe asked.

"I have. Food's good. But their big draw is their exclusivity.
They have seating for fifty. You eat whatever the chef is serving.
There's no menu. It's a foodie's paradise. And the kind of place
movers and shakers like to take their clients . . . to show they can."

Adam pointed to the photographs spread in front of him. "I
can't figure out the connection. We have three restaurants. A couple
of private residences. A spa. A hotel. A boat . . ."

"Are any of them yours?"

"If by 'yours' you mean do any of them belong to a Campbell,
then the answer is no."

"Not even the hotel?"

"It's not one of ours."

"I thought your family owned all of them."

"No," Adam said. "This is The Porterhouse. It's been here for
seventy years or so. The Sullivan family owns it, but they've farmed
out the running of it to some company that specializes in boutique
hotels. I don't think they're even on-site anymore."

Gabe frowned at the photo. "I thought the Campbells owned everything."

Adam hated talking about the family business. To anyone. But this time he didn't have much choice. "Point of clarification—we do not own the entire town."

"Close enough," Gabe said.

"Look, my great-grandfather had four sons. He was a hard worker and did quite well for himself. All four of his sons stayed in the area. Two of them opened up their own businesses while he was still alive, and two of them took over the businesses he'd started. When he passed away, his sons had added to his already successful ventures, and their children and grandchildren are still operating most of those businesses to this day. But just because something has 'Campbell' on it doesn't mean I know much about it. There are a lot of Campbells in town, and I don't have Sunday lunch with my fourth cousins."

"Okay, but I thought it was your branch of the Campbells that had the hotels."

Gabe was going to keep asking until he spelled it out for him. He might as well do it now and save himself the trouble of having to do it later.

"My grandfather owned five different businesses at one time. He sold two of them decades ago to a couple of his nephews. The primary holding company—which my father runs—has three main divisions: finance, real estate, and hospitality. Within those divisions are everything from accounting firms to general contracting to hotels and restaurants."

"What about your dad's siblings? Why didn't they get any of the businesses?"

"My dad is the oldest of three. My uncle Stuart and my aunt Margaret and her husband, Derrick Lawson, own DOR. DOR was part of the hospitality division years ago before they split off on their own."

"Why all the splitting?"

Adam tried to keep his tone civil. Even though the implication irked him, he had to admit it was a fair question. "Would you like to work with your family every day? Or be fifty years old and have your fifty-two-year-old brother for your boss?"

"Ah."

"There were a couple of spectacular blowups during my grand-father's time. But my dad and his siblings kept things much more civil. No drama. Just a division of labor and assets that worked for everyone."

"So, back to these photographs. Why would she bring them to you and why would she have thrown them away?"

"No idea. But I'll go through them and try to figure out what the unifying theme is. Maybe when Sabrina has a chance to go through the files she found, we'll be able to come up with something."

"Can I ask you a question?" Something about Gabe's query set off warning bells in Adam's mind.

"I guess."

"Don't take this the wrong way, but . . . have you ever actually asked Sabrina out?"

"Whoa. Where is this coming from? And what does this have to do with the case?"

"Who said it had anything to do with the case? I thought we had covered everything case related and could move on to something more interesting. Like your love life. Or lack thereof."

"I really don't—"

"I know everyone thinks I don't have the ability to maintain a long-term relationship." Gabe shrugged. "And I don't disagree with them. But you know what I do know? I know women like to be asked out. They don't like some guy to assume they're an item without ever bothering to be sure they are."

Adam tried to come up with a crushing reply, but . . . he had nothing. Gabe had a point. A terrifyingly good point.

"You want Sabrina in your life, then quit goofing off. We all know the girl can barely tell when we're joking or serious. You've probably got her in knots about the signals you've been sending. If you ask me—"

"Which I didn't."

"But you should have." Gabe didn't miss a beat. "If you ask me, you need to woo her."

"Woo her?" Who used *woo* in a sentence these days?

"Friendship is a wonderful basis for a relationship, man. Probably the best there is. But if you want that girl in your life, you're going to have to man up and be bold about it. Quit dancing around it and tell her. Show her. Sweep her off her feet."

"I agree," Ryan said.

Where had he come from? He'd changed out of his dry suit and was back in dry clothes. "What is this? Some sort of relationship intervention?"

"No. Just friendly advice." Ryan ran his hands through his hair. "You need to ask her out."

"Like you did? Because I seem to recall that Leigh fell hard for you before your first date," Adam said.

"Well, the fact that someone was trying to kill her put a damper on the dating options, but she knew where we stood," Ryan said. "She knew how I felt. She wasn't having to guess."

Gabe snorted. "Adam, do yourself a favor and do not use Ryan as an example of how to get a girl to go out with you. But do listen to him. And to me. We can all see how crazy you are about her. And I'm pretty sure she's as into you as you are into her. But you're going to have to give her something to work with. Sabrina's not the kind of girl to come after you. You're going to have to go after her."

"I'm not sure she wants me to."

"Yeah, that's where the asking part comes in." Gabe spoke like he was trying to explain something to an eight-year-old. "You ask her out. She says yes or no. Then you know."

Adam didn't argue. He couldn't. But it burned him up that his friends had seen something he'd missed.

"I'll see you guys back at the office." He grabbed his phone. A plan was forming in his mind and if he called now, he might be able to put phase one into effect today.

It was time to see if Gabe and Ryan were right.

Or completely wrong.

13

The buzzer at the exterior door of the lab pulled Sabrina away from the monitor she'd been staring at for the past several hours. Her clock told her it was almost four.

"We've got company, Dr. Fleming." Dave, the officer who'd escorted her to the lab, smiled. "But it isn't unexpected. Let me go out and speak to him."

"Okay." It had taken her over an hour to get her new phone set up. She must have missed something. A phone call or a message maybe. Dave didn't seem concerned. She'd been so focused on the video surveillance and the files she'd sent to Mike, she hadn't even realized how late it had gotten.

A few clicks of the mouse and she had a view of what was going on in the hallway. Dave was standing outside the door chatting with a teenager holding a massive bouquet of . . . lavender roses.

No one but Adam would send her a bouquet like that.

She gripped the sides of the desk and pulled herself to her feet. She suspected the blast had pulled every single muscle in her body. She hurt in places she hadn't known it was possible to hurt.

She shuffled her way out of her office.

"Dr. Fleming, these came for you." Dave handed the flowers to her.

"Are you sure they're safe?" She was only half joking.

"Yes, ma'am. I checked them out."

Apparently, Dave wasn't joking. Okay then. "Thank you."

Sabrina carried the vase to her desk and positioned the flowers where she could see them regardless of which monitor she was using. She took several deep breaths, the fragrance soothing a place she hadn't realized was agitated until it calmed.

There was no card, but she didn't need one.

Adam had sent her flowers.

Flowers she actually liked, so unlike the garish red bouquet still sitting by the door where Darren had left it . . . had it been only yesterday?

Why would Adam send her flowers? He'd seemed very cold to her this morning. Not that she didn't deserve it. She folded her arms on her desk and dropped her head. She was incredibly tired. And confused.

Her office phone rang. Adam's number.

"Hey," she said.

"Hey."

"Thank you for the flowers."

"How do you know they're from me? I'm sure you have many ardent admirers."

"It was you. And they are . . . stunning. Perfect. I keep staring at them. And they smell amazing."

"I'm glad." The pause that followed hummed with a kind of anticipation that sent a shiver down her spine. "Listen, I hate to be all business, but Gabe is trying to see who can meet here at the office around four thirty to compare notes. We have a lot of moving parts and right now none of them make much sense."

Huh. Business hadn't been the direction she'd been expecting their conversation to go. "Sure. I assume Dave can escort me?"

"He can."

"Okay. I'll see you then." She should hang up and let it go, but she couldn't. "Wait. Adam . . . why did you send the flowers?"

Silence. Had he hung up and not heard her question? "Adam?"

"Hmm?"

"Did you hear me?"

"I'm trying to think of how to respond."

Adam Campbell at a loss for words? That didn't happen every day. "I'd go with honesty. But that's just me. We all know my filter's weird."

He laughed. "Your filter *is* weird. But okay. I'll tell you, but remember you asked."

That sounded . . . ominous.

"When we met a couple of years ago, our relationship was, by necessity, professional. But then . . . it wasn't. And along the way, I messed up."

"Oh." What had he messed up?

"I've been thinking a lot about what you said last night. And earlier today I was prepared to go quietly and leave you alone, even if it killed me to do it. You're an intelligent woman who knows her own mind and can make her own decisions."

In theory. Although at the moment she wasn't so sure about that.

"But I think it's important for you to have all the facts first. And the next time I see you, and when you aren't on pain medicine, I intend to revisit our conversation from last night."

"The facts?" She liked facts. "Such as?"

"Here's a fun fact. When my father met my mother, he sent her a bouquet of flowers the next day. And then the next time he saw her, he asked her out."

He'd sent flowers.

"That's an interesting fact. Very romantic."

"I've always thought so."

"So . . ."

"If I hadn't been too chicken to do it, I would have sent you flowers—these specific flowers—the day after we met."

A sound in the background filtered through the phone.

"Ugh." Adam's frustration was evident. "I'm sorry. I have to go. But I promise we'll talk—about the flowers—soon."

"Okay."

"I'll see you in a little while. Stick close to Dave. He's a good guy."

Sabrina hung up the phone and studied the flowers. Adam said he would have sent these specific flowers the day after they'd met. Lavender roses weren't cheap. This arrangement had two dozen roses in it and deep green leaves. The vase was crystal, not glass.

Purple was her favorite color, so it would be easy to assume he'd sent them because he knew that.

But he wouldn't have known that the day after they met.

Lavender roses were unique. They weren't apology flowers. They weren't "Let's be friends" flowers. Adam knew how much she enjoyed discovering the meaning behind different types of flowers and he would know lavender flowers went way beyond "I like you" or even "I'd like to see where this is going."

Lavender roses conveyed the idea of love at first sight.

That kind of instantaneous infatuation was an idea she'd never believed in, but somehow she had a feeling Adam wasn't kidding.

Was she okay with that?

Her mind said she shouldn't be.

But her heart . . . her heart was soaring.

Thirty minutes later, Dave escorted Sabrina into the sheriff's office. "You'll be okay from here?" he asked.

"Yes." She made her way upstairs to the large room where the investigative team worked. The homicide investigators had their own room off to one side, but most of the other investigators worked at desks arranged around the room by area. Adam wasn't at his desk. She skirted the edge of the room and peeked into the homicide office.

He stood staring at a wall covered in photos and random papers. No matter what her mind thought about the situation, she couldn't deny the way her pulse quickened at the sight of him.

A low groan escaped as he rolled his neck from one side to the other.

"Are you okay?"

Adam made a slow turn toward her. "Come on in."

"You didn't answer my question."

He grinned. "I have a new appreciation for how the Wicked Witch of the East must have felt when Dorothy's house landed on her. But at least I'm still walking around and no one stole my shoes. How are you?"

"I . . . don't know." Sabrina closed the door behind her.

She'd never been this confused in her life. She cared about Adam. More than she should. More than she'd realized she did until this morning when he'd been so . . . not her Adam. But the fact that she cared that much was exactly why she had to stay away from him. She had to, for his own sake.

But if she was determined to stay away, why was she walking toward him?

He didn't move as she approached. "Thank you for the flowers. They are . . . I don't even know how to describe them. It killed me to leave them in my office."

He swallowed hard and cleared his throat but still didn't move. "How's your head?"

"Better than yesterday. Is it soon yet?"

Adam's eyes widened. "Um . . . I'm pretty sure you still have a concussion."

"Yes, I do. Which is why it would be cruel to keep me waiting. The stress is making my headache worse."

He glanced around the room. They were alone, but that could

change at any moment. Still, she couldn't take it much longer. A man who sends lavender roses had better be prepared to back up a statement like that.

"Fine. But this could make things awkward later."

"I do awkward all the time. I'd rather have awkward than tense."

He smiled a little at that. He took one step toward her and reached for her hands. He was tentative and unsure. Not at all like he'd been yesterday. He'd definitely heard her last night, but he was still there. Still trying. Still fighting for them. And that made it so much harder for her to be rational.

Especially when her hands slid into his again like there was some sort of magnetic force pulling them together.

"I want you to know I heard you last night. I did. And I get that I'm probably more trouble than I'm worth. There's a lot of family stuff, and social stuff, and I get that those are huge negatives. But I want to be clear. I'm not looking for someone to throw dinner parties. I'm not interested in someone who can charm investors or make nice with my partners' wives. I'm not even looking for someone who pleases my family. Those things simply aren't important to me. And if they were important to you, honestly, that would be a problem for me."

She had no idea how to respond, so she nodded.

"If you truly don't want to be anything more than friends, I'll respect that. But before you decide, you need to know that I'd love to have the opportunity to show you that being with a Campbell isn't as bad as you seem to think it would be. It might even turn out to be so much fun you never want it to end."

He might be right about that.

"You don't have to answer me now. Or even this week. But I would very much like to take you out on a date. And then another and another. Until you have enough information to make an informed decision about me."

The smile he gave her was so tender and hopeful and nervous

that she couldn't answer him fast enough. "I'd love to go out with you. Thank you for asking me."

He squeezed her hands. "I should have asked you two years ago."

"Better late than never."

Her hands trembled in his. She was saying yes. And everything about her body language agreed with her words, but she was terrified. He didn't think she was afraid of him but maybe of what going out with him might mean.

He would have to be very careful. Take it slow. Not pressure her into anything. Let her set the pace and have time to get used to what her heart wanted.

Because he was pretty sure her heart and her mind were not in full agreement at the moment. His mission was to get them on the same page.

A sharp rap on the door shattered the moment. Sabrina jerked her hands away like they were on fire. Or like she was going to get in trouble if they got caught.

"Come in," he said.

"Adam!"

His mother rushed in and threw her arms around him. He couldn't quite stop the grunt of pain her ferocious hug generated. She released him immediately, but her hands moved to his face and she studied him the way she'd done for as long as he could remember.

Over her head, his father stood in the doorway beside the captain. Both of them wore bemused expressions. Sabrina had plastered herself to the wall. Her expression leaned more toward horrified.

"Thank you." His father shook the captain's hand.

"My pleasure." The captain nodded in Adam's direction. "You'll escort them out when they're ready?"

"Of course, sir." His mother had stopped examining him and now stood with one hand on his arm.

"Very good. I'm heading out." The captain caught sight of Sabrina. "Dr. Fleming. How are you?"

Sabrina peeled herself from the wall. "I'm fine, sir. Thank you."

The captain clucked his tongue. "I think you both should be home in bed, but I appreciate the dedication. Don't overdo it. That's an order."

"Yes, sir," Adam and Sabrina answered the captain and he left the room.

"Dr. Fleming?" Adam's mother rounded on Sabrina.

Oh no.

She approached Sabrina, arms outstretched. Awesome. Mom was going for the "we've never met but we're going to hug anyway" move. So much for his plan to ease Sabrina into Campbell life.

"Dear. How are you?" The hug she gave Sabrina was brief and gentle, and Sabrina looked more surprised than traumatized. "We've heard so much about you. It's a thrill to finally meet you."

"Thank you, Mrs. Campbell," Sabrina said. "It's lovely to meet you."

His father eased his mother to the side and extended his hand toward Sabrina. "Art Campbell. This is long overdue."

Thanks, Dad.

"It is. Thank you, Mr. Campbell."

"Enough of that," Adam's mom said. "It's Art and Abby. If you call either of us Arthur or Abigail, we'll refuse to answer. And anytime someone says Mrs. Campbell, I get a little twitchy."

"Ha-ha, Mom. Not that I'm not thrilled to see you, but what are you doing here? I didn't think you were coming home until the end of the week."

His dad pointed at his mom. "We changed our tickets as soon as

Alexander called. We drove straight here from the airport. Haven't even been home."

"I needed to see your face, dear." His mom's voice quavered. What?

"Imagine getting a phone call in the middle of the night that your baby boy has been blown up." His mom shuddered.

"I told you I was fine," Adam said.

"In a voice mail," she said. "Not good enough. I needed to see for myself. I know how you are. I wouldn't have been surprised if I'd gotten home and found you in traction."

She turned to Sabrina. "This one hates to make me worry. I never had to worry about him getting into real trouble. But I did have to worry about him downplaying his injuries."

"He's still doing that," Sabrina said in a conspiratorial whisper.

His mother ate it up. "You'll tell me the truth, won't you, Dr. Fleming? How is he really?"

"First, it's Sabrina. And second, a big chunk of the roof landed on his back because he was protecting me."

Was Sabrina getting choked up? His mom certainly thought so, because she patted Sabrina's arm.

Sabrina kept talking. "He's hurting more than he's letting on. His back has some bad lacerations and is probably starting to turn purple by now. But I've been assured it's nothing he won't fully recover from. And the more he moves, the better off he'll be. If he lies around, he'll get stiff and hurt even worse than he does now."

Leigh must have told her that. He owed Leigh big-time.

"Thank you, dear. I never would have gotten that information from him." His mom shook her head in overdone sadness. "And how are you?"

As if Sabrina's scraped-up face and almost-black eye didn't make her condition clear enough. "She has a concussion and lacerations and stitches in her head," Adam said.

His mom looked between him and Sabrina. "I think the captain was right. You shouldn't be working."

"It's a big case, Mom. And like she said, sometimes it's better to keep moving than it is to sit around."

"I guess." His mom had a look on her face that Adam recognized. And feared. "How late are you working tonight?"

Where was she going with this? "I don't know yet. We're having a meeting at four thirty. It will probably last a couple of hours. We may call it a night then."

"Excellent. You can come for a light supper at seven."

What? No. He tried to catch his dad's eye to get him to help, but his dad was eyeing the wall of photos and papers. "Mom—"

"You have to eat. It won't be formal. We'll have chicken salad and chat for thirty minutes and you can go home and crash. Sabrina, this includes you, dear."

Sabrina's mouth moved a few times before anything came out. But then an expression settled on her that he didn't recognize. "Abby, we'd be delighted. But there's no guarantee we won't wind up working late."

"I understand," his mom said. "You call around six thirty and let me know if you'll be able to make it?"

Sabrina nodded. "We will."

We'd be delighted? We will? Where did all this *we* business come from?

"Abby, if they have a meeting at four thirty, we probably need to have Adam walk us back to the car."

Oh, so *now* his dad stepped in. After his mom had invited them to supper.

"Oh, of course. You're working. We'll go. See you tonight, Sabrina."

Sabrina nodded and smiled. Adam ushered his parents out of the room. "Be right back," he said. Then he mouthed "I'm sorry" as he closed the door.

Sabrina stuck her tongue out at him.

He wasn't sure if that was good or bad.

His parents didn't say much as they wound through the office and to the elevator, but as soon as they got outside his mother turned to him.

"She is beautiful. Stunning. Even with her injuries. I can see why you're smitten with her, dear."

"Abby." His father's laughing reproach fell on deaf ears.

"I love her already."

"You don't know her, Mom. How can you love her?"

His mom shook her head. "Because you do, dear. That's enough for me. Always has been."

"Mom—"

"Best not to argue, son. Especially when you know she's right." His dad gave him a gentle hug. When he pulled back, he looked deep into Adam's eyes. "Are you sure you're all right?"

"Yes, sir."

"Abby Campbell? What are you doing here?" A woman Adam didn't recognize rushed up the steps toward his mom.

His dad pulled him to one side as his mother and the woman chatted.

"You scared us, but Mother says you were quite brave and you saved your friends' lives. I'm not sure if I've ever heard her be quite so demonstrative in her praise of you."

"She came to the hospital. She kissed my cheek. She even offered to send Marcel home with me."

His dad laughed. "She has her moments."

"That she does."

"Son, I know you're tired and you're hurting more than you're letting on. But try to come by tonight. It will do your mother good. She's actually holding it together quite well, but she was a wreck." He took a deep breath. "Truthfully, we both were."

"I'll come."

"Bring Sabrina."

"I'll try. I just got up the nerve to ask her out. I wasn't planning on subjecting her to a family dinner this soon."

"This will be family dinner lite. Think of it as a practice run."

"Great."

"Tonight." His mom rejoined them and took his dad's arm.

"Yes, sir."

As they walked down the steps, his mom turned back and gave him a soft smile, tears shimmering in her eyes. She would never make a scene. Especially not where he worked. But those tears . . .

"Mom. Wait."

She released his dad's arm and ran back to him. Her tears fell free. "I wouldn't know what to do if I lost you. I don't tell you that often enough," she said.

"I know. I'm sorry you were scared. But I'm fine. Really."

She squeezed him close again. "Okay, baby."

"I'll see you tonight."

She sniffled and patted his arm. "You'd better."

His dad gave him a nod. The kind that said "Good job" and "Thanks" all in one.

As soon as they disappeared from view, Adam headed—as fast as he could, which wasn't saying much at the moment—back to Sabrina.

Voices reached him before he got to the homicide office door. Gabe. Anissa. Ryan.

This was going to be awkward.

He opened the door. Everyone was seated around the conference room table except for Gabe, who stood by the wall. "Good. You're here. Let's get to work."

186

14

Poor Adam.

He looked . . . awful.

"Dude. Did someone run over your cat?" Gabe frowned at Adam.

So it wasn't her imagination.

"I'm fine." He eased into the seat beside her with a small grunt as he tried to find a comfortable position.

The three homicide investigators were staring at Adam. What were they looking for? And what did they see that made all three of them—Anissa first, then Gabe, then Ryan—return their attention to the wall where photos of the victim, crime scene, and evidence were lined up in rough chronological order?

What made them decide Adam was okay? Or was it that they decided he didn't want to talk about it? Whatever *it* was?

Sabrina still hadn't figured it out when Gabe dove in.

"I realize it's late, and three of us got blown up yesterday, and we're not feeling awesome today. So I'm going to hit this hard and fast. Once we have a strategy, we'll call it for the night and reconvene tomorrow."

Nods all around.

He began with the timeline of events. Lisa Palmer coming to the sheriff's office to see Adam. Dropping the briefcase of photos into the lake. Returning home or somewhere near it based on the GPS in her car and phone.

"The ME thinks the time of death is a few hours before Lisa Palmer went into the lake on Saturday night/Sunday morning," Gabe said.

"I thought you said she drowned," Anissa said.

"She did. But Dr. Oliver is certain it was earlier in the evening. She was already dead before her car went into the water. Sharon's running some tests on the water in Lisa Palmer's lungs, but unless we get a confession we'll probably never know exactly where she was drowned."

Adam leaned forward. "Just to be sure I'm following you, Lisa Palmer did drown, but not in the lake. And if she hadn't written that note on her abdomen . . ."

Gabe's nod was grim. "Dr. Oliver says we might never have realized it was anything other than an accident or a suicide. There would have been no evidentiary reason to suspect foul play."

Wow. This woman was actually helping them solve her murder from beyond the grave.

Sabrina wasn't sure if that was cool or creepy.

"There has to be something significant about the photographs. She had that briefcase with her when she came to the office to see Adam," Gabe said. "This is conjecture, of course, but it would make sense to me that she wouldn't have been comfortable driving around with incriminating evidence. She would have wanted something she could use to prove her point, but only if she was telling the story. If anyone else saw the contents of her briefcase, it would be meaningless to them."

Sabrina looked at the photographs again. "We need to find out what they have in common," she said. "It could be anything from a single employee who has worked at all of those places to a paper supplier or a loan officer."

"I agree," Gabe said.

"And I still think it would help if we could get a list of her clients and see who she's worked for," Adam said. "We need to be careful not to assume anything, but given that she was coming to see me, it makes sense that she was planning to report some type of economic crime."

"There's a team of forensic accountants going through the files I recovered from the hard drive," Sabrina said. "And Mike—Dr. Bledsoe—is looking to see if he can find another level of encryption or some backdoor stuff."

"Any idea when he'll be done?" Gabe asked.

"I talked to him this afternoon. He said Wednesday late. Maybe Thursday before he can get you anything. And your forensic accountants said it could be next week for the first round of information. It will take months for them to get through it all."

Gabe pretended to pound his head on the wall. "We don't have until next week, much less next month."

"I . . ." Sabrina turned to Adam. She needed some help here. "I don't think there's any way to get this sooner, Gabe. Mike's the best. And he's working hard on it."

"Gabe knows that, Bri. He's just tired. And frustrated. We all are. We have a lot of hunches and almost no hard facts. It's—"

"Awful," Gabe said.

They discussed every angle of the case for the next thirty minutes before Gabe threw up his hands. "I give up. We have a whole lot of nothing."

"We have the potential for a whole lot of something," Anissa said. "I'm still working through everything we found in and around the car as well as what we found under the bridge. You'll just have to be patient."

"I don't do patient."

"I've noticed."

Gabe ignored Anissa's comment. "Okay, tomorrow our number

189

one priority is figuring out the unifying factor behind these photographs. There has to be one. Let's meet around ten. And let's not forget these people have already tried to take Sabrina out twice. And almost got Adam and me as well in their quest to destroy evidence. They've been quiet today, but I'm afraid the closer we get to the truth, the more dangerous they'll be."

More nods. Chairs scraped as everyone stood.

"Leigh said you're all welcome for dinner." Ryan looked at Gabe and Anissa, both of whom nodded and said "I'm in" at the same time.

"Great." Ryan turned in her direction. "Sabrina? Adam?"

Adam looked like he'd swallowed an ice cube. Would he lie? Or maybe leave out a few key parts of the story?

"Can we get in on dessert later? My, um, my parents want us to come for dinner tonight."

"We? Us?" A grin flashed across Gabe's face.

"Sabrina and I."

"Wow. You move fast."

Adam gave Gabe a grin so fake even she could tell he didn't mean it. Did he not want her to go to his parents'? Or did he not want the others to know he'd asked her out?

An emotion she couldn't name flashed through her.

"Ignore them," Anissa said, waving between Gabe and Adam. "Gabe's being a smart aleck and Adam's trying to be polite when what he wants to do is tell Gabe off." She grinned at Sabrina. "The Campbells are lovely. I'm sure dinner will be fantastic. And I'll be sure we save some of whatever dessert Leigh makes."

"You're planning to stay at Leigh's, right?" Ryan asked.

"Yes," Adam said. "Like Gabe said, there's no way we can risk having Sabrina unprotected. Too many unknowns."

"Agreed. I'm going to be sure we have a couple of deputies at the house tonight." Ryan made it sound like it was perfectly normal to need a few deputies parked outside the house at night.

"Sounds good." Adam could have been agreeing about the weather. When had this all become commonplace?

After a chorus of "See you later," Adam's hand closed over her arm so gently it was more a caress than a hold. "I need to stop by my desk for a second," he said. "And then we can go. Are you okay with that plan?"

"Sure."

They walked to Adam's desk, and true to his word, he paused just long enough to grab a jacket and a notebook before returning to her side and directing them to the elevator.

It wasn't until they were outside that he turned to her. "Bri, I want you to know you don't have to do this. Taking you to my parents' for dinner was not even in the same galaxy as what I'd had in mind for a first date. My mom, she can't help herself. But she'll totally understand. I can tell her you were tired. Or needed to work."

She was pretty sure he was just trying to give her an out. She could guess, or she could just ask him to be sure. "Do you want me to come with you?"

He tilted his head toward hers. "Always."

For a three-second count, she forgot how to breathe.

"But," he continued, "that doesn't mean my mom gets to decide how we spend our evenings. You never have to do something, or go somewhere, just because she asked."

She found her lungs again and took a deep breath. She hoped she wouldn't regret this. "I want to come."

"Why?"

Could she tell him? Could she risk that kind of vulnerability? "Because you'll be there, and honestly, even though I think I'm horrible for you, I'd rather be with you than anywhere else."

Adam did that thing again where he tilted his head and leaned toward her. It wasn't something she'd ever seen him do with anyone else. Like he was giving her his full attention and also maybe like he might be thinking about kissing her.

"Okay." His voice had a huskiness that hadn't been there before. "Let's go."

Two hours later, Adam leaned back in a chair in the breakfast room.

Sabrina and his mom were chatting like long-lost friends. His dad was resting his elbows on the table—Grandmother would never approve—and laughing.

Was he having an out-of-body experience?

This . . . his parents and his . . . well, could he call her his girl-friend? Probably not. A bit presumptuous. His date? No.

His friend?

Yes, but . . . so much more.

Sabrina took a sip of her tea and made eye contact with Adam over the rim of her glass.

He was fairly confident she wasn't miserable, but he didn't want to press his luck any further. "Mom, Dad, this has been great, but—"

"Oh, goodness. Look at the time." His mom's face was a mask of worry. "You've had such a traumatic couple of days and here we are keeping you from your rest. Which you need."

His dad yawned on cue. "They need? We"—he waved his hands between them—"need."

"True," she said. "Sabrina, dear, if you'll come with me, I'll get your coat for you."

Uh-oh. This had the markings of sabotage.

As soon as they were out of earshot, his dad tapped the table. "I need to talk to you about something."

"Okay."

"Those photographs in the office today—"

"Dad, I can't talk to you about an ongoing investigation. You know that. Honestly, the captain never should have let you in there."

"But you do need to talk to me. More than you realize." His

dad rubbed his face with his hands and sighed. "I know what the connection is."

He did? "What?"

"Barclay Campbell." There was no equivocation in his dad's voice. He was as certain that his cousin was involved as he was that the sky was blue or that Grandmother would be wearing her pearls on Sunday.

But Adam couldn't stop himself from asking. "Are you sure?"

His dad nodded.

"I still don't see it."

Sabrina's voice carried down the hall. They were coming back.

"Look for it," his dad said. "You'll find it. And Adam?"

"Yes, sir?"

"Be very careful. And keep that girl close. He's always been mean. I wouldn't put anything past him."

The worried expression on his dad's face melted into a genuine smile when Sabrina reentered the room, her coat draped over her arm and his mom beaming at them.

"Adam, dear. I know you're both tired, but Vanessa left us a note. They finished the lights this afternoon. I'm sure it would be a lovely way to end your evening."

His mom was brilliant. He'd owe her forever.

They said their good nights, and his parents retired to their room. Instead of leading Sabrina to the front door, he directed her to the back.

"Where are we going?"

"You'll see."

It didn't take long to find the remotes. The staff had left everything lined up the way they did every year. He flipped a couple of switches and then took Sabrina's hand. "Come on."

They stepped out onto the back patio and Sabrina gasped. "What is this?" She spun in a circle, her mouth in a perfect little O as she took in the glittering scene.

"Most people have backyards," he said, "but not Campbells. We have gardens."

Sabrina laughed.

"Every year at Christmas, Mom and Dad would take us to see the lights at the park by the lake. We'd drive through and ooh and ahh at all the displays. It was a tradition we all loved. But one year . . . I'm not exactly sure how old I was. Six? Seven? Anyway, I got chicken pox. We couldn't go anywhere. I was miserable. I gave it to Alexander. We were covered in spots, and the fact that we were missing our Christmas festivities made it even worse. This was before Aaron came along."

"Anyway, as we were in our rooms moping, Dad cleaned out every store in town of Christmas lights and decorations. He worked for three days out here. The gardener, the housekeeper, everyone chipped in. They still talk about how much fun it was for them that first year—they were keeping it a secret from us. When they were done, they brought us out here in our pajamas and flipped on the lights, like we were in some kind of movie."

"There have never been movie Christmas lights as elegant as these." Her voice was hushed but playful.

"Well, I think Mom drew the line at some of Dad's suggestions. Anyway, you can imagine how much we loved it. Of course they had to do it again the next year, and we got to help."

"Do you still help?"

"Every year."

He'd tried to refuse the year after Aaron died. Aaron, his baby brother, had loved the lights and to put them up without him had seemed like it would dishonor his memory. Adam had been so angry that the car had hit Aaron's side instead of his. So burdened by the guilt that came from knowing that he'd insisted Aaron switch seats with him. He'd been so mad when his dad insisted they all get out there and set up the lights. But somehow stringing the lights had given them a way to talk about Aaron without crying for the first time in months. It had a healing effect none of them had expected and had made the lights even more special than before.

Adam shook away the somber direction his thoughts had taken.

"I'm usually here for the entire setup, but I got busy with this case, so I haven't been here the past few days."

"I'd say you had a good excuse."

Sabrina wandered through the flower beds and bushes, the trees and fountains. In the glow of the twinkling lights, she looked like an angel. After a few minutes, she settled on a bench with a perfect view of the entire garden and Adam joined her.

"Your parents aren't what I was expecting."

"What were you expecting?"

"I guess I thought they'd be more like your aunt Margaret."

"That's understandable."

"When your mom said dinner would be casual, I was expecting at least three courses, but she really did mean casual. When she pulled out the paper plates and the chicken salad . . ."

"Were you disappointed?"

"No. I was delighted. I realize she may have done it on purpose to put me at ease, but I like her even more for it."

"I like her a lot too."

They sat in silence, the water falling through the fountains, the wind rustling the trees, the lights throwing shadows on the ground.

"You're a lot like your dad." There was something in Sabrina's whispered words that rattled Adam. "He's a man of conviction, I think. I'm not good at reading people, but I feel . . ."

Feel? Sabrina didn't talk much about feelings.

"I don't know how to describe it, but I feel something similar around you and your dad. You make me feel safe. And so does he. Like he's the kind of man who wouldn't let you down."

Ah.

"Bri, I would never—"

"I know." She rested her head on his shoulder and if it had been ten degrees warmer, he would have gladly sat there until dawn. But a shiver rippled through her and he knew it was time to go.

"Can we come back?" she asked as they walked toward the gate that would take them to the driveway.

"Any time you want," he said.

He opened the gate for her to go through, but she turned back to him. "I had a lovely evening, Adam. Thank you. And thank you for sharing your lights with me. They're so beautiful."

"I wouldn't want to share them with anyone else."

"Really?"

She looked up and he reached for her face. Her arms slid around his waist and the space between them evaporated as he pressed his lips to hers. Gentle. Soft. Her mouth quivered beneath his for a brief moment before he pulled away.

He'd never been a kiss-on-the-first-date kind of guy.

But then again, he'd never had a first date quite like this one. And never with a woman as extraordinary as Sabrina Fleming.

The reflection of hundreds of twinkling lights shone in her eyes. And something else. Something that scared him more than Lisa Palmer's killers or Barclay Campbell's evil schemes.

Trust.

Her trust was hard-earned and could be far too easily lost.

She stepped onto her toes and kissed him. It was over much too soon. She stepped back but took hold of his hand before walking through the gate, pulling him along with her. There was a chance he'd forgotten how to breathe. Or talk. Or do both at the same time.

Sabrina Fleming had kissed him.

He would never be able to walk through the garden Christmas decorations again without remembering this night.

Father, please let her be the one with me in the years ahead.

15

Wednesday morning was not off to a fabulous start.
Sabrina had spent the night at Leigh's. She'd been so
tired when she and Adam had returned to Leigh's last
night that she hadn't had the energy to do more than take a few
bites of the yummy dessert Leigh had made before she had to tell
everyone good night. She'd expected to see them all at breakfast,
but when she got up this morning Leigh was the only one home.

There was some sort of investigator meeting at seven this morning they all had to attend, so she hadn't seen or spoken to Adam
since last night.

She'd been a bit forward last night. Kissing him like that. She
didn't know why she'd done it.

Well, okay. Maybe she knew why. Kissing Adam Campbell had
the potential to become a favorite pastime. But . . .

"Dr. Fleming, are you okay?"

Sabrina looked up from the monitor. Her favorite grad student,
Chance Lawrence, stood in the door of her office.

"I'm fine, Chance. What can I help you with?"

"There's a cop in the hall. He wouldn't even let me scan myself
in until he'd compared my ID to some list. And then there was

another cop inside who asked me what my business was and how long I intended to stay."

"Oh, yes. I gave them a list of approved students who could enter. Nothing to worry about."

"With all due respect, it doesn't seem like nothing to worry about."

Officer Dave had moved closer to her office door and now stood only a few feet away from Chance. "Dr. Fleming."

Chance jumped.

Dave stared Chance down but spoke to Sabrina. "Everything okay?"

"Completely fine," she said.

Dave's response to her assurance was to step back. Two feet.

Chance turned back to her, eyes wide. "What on earth are you working on, Dr. Fleming? No one will tell us anything. You look like someone beat you up, and you're moving like you're eighty. No offense."

"None taken. And I'm sorry, but I can't talk about it," she said. "I can assure you my injuries are healing nicely, and Dave is harmless to anyone who doesn't try to harm me."

Chance nodded, but the worry didn't leave his face. "Okay. If you won't tell me why we're under lockdown, will you tell me what's up with the flowers? We've got red roses by the door. Purple roses in here. Did you start dating a florist and not tell anyone?"

"I'd forgotten about the red roses. Would you mind getting rid of them?"

"Seriously?"

"Very seriously."

"Okay." Uncertainty dripped from each syllable. "Do you want me to get rid of the purple ones too?"

"No!"

Chance backed up a step and threw both hands in the air. "Sorry."

Dave came all the way to her door this time. "Dr. Fleming?"

Sabrina couldn't stop the frustrated groan that slipped through her lips. "I'm fine." She blew out a long breath. "Dave, I've asked Chance to dispose of the red roses by the door. But if anyone touches the flowers in here, you have my permission to chop off their fingers."

"Very good, Dr. Fleming." Dave stepped away from her office.

"It was a joke," she called out after him. He turned back to her, his face a stone. Then winked.

Whew. At least Dave wouldn't be lopping off phalanges anytime soon.

"Chance, I apologize. I'm a bit tense and I'm working on some critical files right now. But I'm fine. I hope your holidays are lovely and I'm looking forward to your project for the spring."

How many times had she told people she was fine in the last five minutes? Why wouldn't anyone listen?

"Thank you, Dr. Fleming. I'll check back in on you later, okay?"

"Not necessary."

"I want to."

"Fine."

Chance left the room and she checked her watch.

Again.

For the fiftieth time in the past hour.

Get it together, girl. It was one kiss. Well, two. And he's working.

Maybe some caffeine and one of the muffins Leigh had sent with her this morning would help her focus.

She pulled herself out of her chair—her abdomen and rib cage were still tender to the touch, making it difficult for her to maneuver—and popped a salted caramel coffee pod into her single-cup brewer.

The water hissed and a hint of sweetness wafted toward her. She left her coffee to finish and went in search of the muffins.

"Excuse me, Dr. Fleming?"

Oh, for the love. All she wanted was a muffin. And her lab back. This was usually her favorite time of year. She loved her students. Well, most of them. But she relished the few weeks of the year when most of them were gone and the lab was quiet.

Having protective cops dogging her every move was not working for her.

"Yes, Dave?"

"I'm very sorry to bother you, ma'am, but Investigator Campbell is on his way up."

Adam arrived two minutes later. She saw him on the monitors as he spoke to the officer in the hall. He moved with purpose. Intensity. Almost with . . . ferocity?

He was worried. Very worried.

The realization startled her. The emotions of most people were a total mystery to her. But not Adam's. At least not this time.

He walked into the lab and barely spoke to Dave. He came straight to her office and closed the blinds on the windows facing the main part of the lab before he reached for her and she settled into his arms. He buried his face in her hair and for a long moment, all she could hear was the sound of his heart beating.

"I need you to do something." The words were so quiet, they were barely more than breath.

She nodded.

"I need you to do one of your deep dives—like what you did on Leigh's case."

She had the skill set, but it wasn't strictly her area of expertise. More of a hobby she'd picked up over the years as she worked with FreedomForAll. Not everyone with computer forensics skills also had good—for lack of a better term—hacking skills. But she did. "Who?"

She heard him swallow. "Barclay Campbell."

She knew that name. In fact, he'd been on her personal radar for the past year. She'd been involved on a case where they freed three young women being trafficked from a spa. Barclay Campbell owned that establishment, but there'd been no evidence that he'd been aware of the situation. He'd said all the right things and used the right tears at the right time but hadn't convinced her. She suspected that, at the very least, he'd chosen to turn a blind eye.

But she'd never looked into it quite the way Adam was asking her to look. And while her abilities weren't in question, she couldn't help but wonder why Adam wasn't asking the techs from the sheriff's office to do this.

"Why me?"

"Because I know he doesn't have you in his pocket."

The implication being he didn't trust his own forensics team.

This was bad.

This was very, very bad.

"Have you told anyone else?"

"Gabe, Ryan, and Anissa. This morning. No one else. And we've agreed it goes nowhere else."

"Wow. I feel like I've been invited to sit at the cool kids' table."

"You're the coolest person I know." The words were heartfelt, but instead of hugging her tighter, he stepped away from her. She missed the closeness now that it was gone.

"Sorry," he said. "I need to be more professional at work."

"You aren't at work," she said.

He shook his head. "But you are, and technically, I'm here on official business."

"Fine, if you want to be all rational about things." It shouldn't bother her. It was good he was able to do that. She, however, wanted to see what would happen if she—

"You have to stop looking at me that way." Adam backed farther away.

"What way?"

"Like you might be thinking the same thing I'm thinking. One of us has to hold it together, and if you can't do it, then we're in trouble because I'm holding on by a thread over here."

He was? "You don't seem particularly distressed."

"Well, *distressed* isn't the word I would use, but don't let appearances fool you. I've been trying to hold it together around you for two years, and now that I . . . that we . . . that . . ."

"To be honest, I'd rather you didn't hold it together around me."

"Not helping, Bri."

"Not sorry."

That made him laugh. And apparently he was even more distracted by her when he was laughing, because he covered the space between them far faster than she'd been prepared for.

The laughter faded and he held her gaze. "I promise. I'll do everything in my power to be sure you're never sorry."

He caressed her cheek with his thumb but came no closer. "I'll see you tonight?"

She couldn't get any words past her throat, so she settled for nodding.

He reopened her blinds and hurried from her office.

She watched him chat with Dave for a few moments before leaving. Dave resumed his perch in the main lab.

She retrieved her coffee and opened a new window on her computer screen.

Time to dig up some dirt.

16

Dave tapped on her office door. "You about ready to call it a day, Dr. Fleming?"

Sabrina nodded. "I'm sorry, Dave. I hope I'm not keeping you from something wonderful this evening."

"I'm not trying to rush you. And there's not much wonderful waiting on me, ma'am. Just some frozen pizza and TV before I get some sleep and do it all again tomorrow."

"This must be an incredibly boring assignment for you."

"On the contrary. It's fascinating. And quite an honor, if you don't mind me saying so."

"An honor? Why would babysitting me be an honor?"

He smiled. "You're pretty famous. Plus, it's obvious that Adam's crazy about you. Being asked to provide security for someone like you, working on a big case . . . it's a nice vote of confidence. Adam told me he'd asked for me specifically because he knew I could keep my head on straight and I would take good care of you. Makes a guy feel good to hear something like that."

The part about her being famous was ludicrous, of course, but the rest of it made sense. "Thank you for explaining," she said. "And I do feel quite secure with you here, so I'd say Adam chose well."

"Thank you. I appreciate that."

"I need ten more minutes to wrap up what I'm working on, and then I'll be ready to go."

"Are we headed to the sheriff's office or Ms. Weston's home?"

Sabrina's watch read 5:15 p.m. "I'm going to say Leigh's house because I need comfortable clothes and a squishy chair to sit in. Those chairs in the homicide conference room are awful. If they want to talk to me tonight, they'll have to do it at Leigh's."

Dave laughed. "Sounds good, ma'am. You won't mind if I call it in, will you?"

"By call it in, do you mean tell Adam?"

Dave looked everywhere but her.

"It's fine, Dave. Go ahead. Tell him I said not to be late."

"Yes, ma'am." Dave's laughter floated back to her as he returned to his self-assigned station at the front of the lab.

Eight minutes later she'd emailed a copy of her day's work to a secure server. She also had a flash drive in her pocket.

She wished she were going to do what she'd told Dave. Go to Leigh's, curl up in a squishy chair, and relax.

But everything would change tonight.

Because she'd found so much more than dirt.

Adam was late.

Sabrina's brain swirled with the information she'd learned today. She couldn't wander around the kitchen while Leigh cooked anymore. "Do you mind if I walk down to the dock?"

"Go for it," Leigh said. "Just let the deputies know what you're doing."

Right.

She slipped onto the deck and a uniformed deputy whose name she didn't know materialized by her side. "Everything okay, Dr. Fleming?"

"Yes." She started second-guessing herself. She needed solitude. Would she get it? "I'm walking down to the dock. Don't shoot me, okay?"

"Of course, ma'am. I'll be nearby."

Awesome.

She tried to pretend he wasn't there as she settled into a chair and listened to the water lapping on the shore. It was lovely out here. Chilly but not so cold that she was uncomfortable. A mild evening for December.

Father, give me the words. Help me know how to explain what I know and what I suspect. Help Adam to hear it. And for the victims . . .

Even in prayer, she couldn't find the words to express her anguish. So she didn't try. She sat with it, with God, and let him carry it for her. The tension didn't leave, the ache didn't disappear, but there was something else with them. A confidence that God hadn't forgotten. That God hadn't lost control. That even now he was at work. And with that confidence came a peace no scientist would ever be able to measure.

Steps on the dock alerted her that she wasn't alone.

She turned, oh so slowly. After sitting all day, her body ached. But she forgot about that when Adam's form materialized in front of her.

He knelt beside her chair. "You shouldn't be out here. You're too easy a target—"

"Seriously?" She didn't hold back on the sarcasm. "I'm sure someone's been sitting around waiting for me to come onto the dock so they could take me out."

Adam didn't argue the point. His hand was warm as it slid across her arm and his fingers laced through hers. "I missed you today."

"Really?"

He lifted her hand to his lips. "Really."

"Oh." Should she say something like "Me too," or would that

just sound like she was going along with what he was saying? She had no idea how to do this.

"I'm trying, Bri." He kissed her ring finger.

"Trying to do what?"

"To take it slow." He kissed her pinky.

"Oh."

"I thought it would be easier. That knowing that I might get to hold your hand—or maybe even steal a kiss—would somehow make the day shorter."

"How's that working out for you?"

"It isn't working at all." He traced a circle on her hand with his thumb. "It's much worse."

The scraping of a door opening behind them warned her their moment of solitude was coming to an end. She should tell Adam about Barclay while they were alone.

So why was she leaning in for a kiss?

When Adam's mouth met hers, she almost forgot what she had to do tonight. Almost.

She was fairly sure Adam wouldn't resent her for being the messenger, but just in case, she couldn't risk missing out on another kiss.

A throat cleared from several feet behind them. Wow. That guy hadn't been joking when he said he'd be nearby. "Excuse me, Dr. Fleming. But your presence has been requested in the house for dinner."

Adam pressed his forehead to hers. "I know we need to talk," he said. "After dinner?"

"Okay."

Sabrina tried to eat. The food was delicious. Leigh had outdone herself as usual. But the pork tenderloin stuck in her throat. She nibbled at the twice-baked potato—something she usually would have had seconds on. She gave up trying to eat the salad.

She looked up and found five sets of eyes on her.

She was so busted.

Anissa was sitting to her right, and she squeezed Sabrina's hand. "You might as well tell us what you found today."

"Is it that obvious?" Sabrina asked.

Across from her, Leigh nodded. Ryan put his arm around Leigh's shoulders and gave Sabrina a smile that was somehow both encouraging and compassionate. How did he do that?

Gabe was between Ryan and Anissa. He leaned back in his chair, blew out a long sigh, and nodded at her.

They were all ready.

She turned to her left. Adam had his elbows on the table and his face held more sadness than she thought she could bear. She hated to be the one to confirm suspicions.

"Before Sabrina begins," Adam said, "I need you all to know that she hasn't told me what she found yet. But I did some investigating of my own this afternoon and if her findings converge with mine, I'll need to remove myself from the investigation."

"Why?" Gabe asked.

"I'm fairly certain the district attorney would frown on me investigating my own family." Adam shrugged. "She's a stickler about that kind of stuff. Although in this case she would also have to recuse herself since her mother was a Campbell."

"Wait. The DA is a Campbell?" Gabe looked around the room. "Am I the only one who didn't know that?"

"I knew," Ryan said.

"I didn't." Anissa shrugged. "But does it really matter?"

"No. There's no way to avoid some family overlap in a case like this," Ryan said. "Not in Carrington, anyway. The investigation won't be compromised by your presence in it to this point. We'll need to document everything from here on out."

"Agreed," Gabe said.

Sabrina swallowed and looked at the circle of friends around her. "I don't think I can do this without my computer."

It took three seconds, and the entire table erupted in laughter. "What's so funny?" Sabrina looked from face to face. She didn't see any malice. This was what she'd come to know as good-natured teasing from them.

"It isn't funny." Leigh wiped her eyes. "At all. But we were wondering if you'd be able to present any information without a spreadsheet. You just proved we know you well."

"Oh," Sabrina said.

Anissa squeezed her arm. "You know we're only laughing because we love you, right?"

"And because we needed something to break the tension." Ryan stood. "Let's get Sabrina set up and get this investigation moving in whatever direction it has to go."

No one got in a huge rush. Food was put away, dishes were placed in the dishwasher, and coffee was brewed while Sabrina hooked up her computer to Leigh's TV.

Sometimes Adam forgot that Sabrina was a professor. But when the homicide investigators requested their assistance last spring when Leigh's life was in danger, he'd learned Sabrina preferred to present evidence with a spreadsheet or some PowerPoint slides. It helped her think and process the information. And kept her from getting nervous.

Not that she needed to be nervous with this group. Not anymore. Over the past few months, since they'd solved that case, they'd all become friends. Closer than he'd imagined they could ever be.

But her hands trembled as she connected a flash drive to her laptop.

The others were in the kitchen, and he couldn't stand to see her so anxious. He stepped behind her and slid his arms around her waist. He couldn't deny that he loved the way she leaned into his embrace while still working on the computer setup.

"Why are you nervous?"

"Because it's bad."

At her words, the growing unease he'd been experiencing all evening ballooned into full-on dread.

"Hey." He turned her around so she was facing him. "We'll figure this out. We'll get to the bottom of it."

Her eyes shimmered with tears. "We can't fix this. Not completely."

"We never can," he said. "Aren't you the one who told me I can't stress about what I didn't know? But that I have to take responsibility for what I can do moving forward?"

She nodded and a tear dripped from her chin. He tried to wipe the tears from her face, but they wouldn't stop.

Lord, help me. Help her. Help us.

The muscles in her face clenched and she blinked over and over. She took several deep breaths and he found her some tissues from the box on Leigh's coffee table.

"I can do this. I have to do this."

"I know. I'm sorry." He could see the others waiting in the kitchen, giving them some privacy. Giving Sabrina a chance to regain some composure.

A few more breaths, and she gave him a tight smile before taking a position by the TV. "I'm ready."

Gabe came in first. Then Ryan. Then Anissa.

Leigh went straight to Sabrina. "I got called in to work, so I'm heading out. It's probably for the best. I'm not supposed to be here for this part anyway. But I'm praying, and if you need me, just call. I'm lousy cop material, but I'm a great listener."

"Thanks, Leigh."

"You guys make yourselves at home. I'll see some of you in the morning." Leigh kissed Ryan and slipped out the door to the garage.

The rest of them found seats. Except for Sabrina. She remained by the TV, swallowed hard, tapped something on her laptop, and without making eye contact with any of them, began.

"I think we have a major human trafficking ring operating out of Carrington. I need you all to understand that I don't have the kind of proof we would need for an arrest, but I think when I'm done, you'll see where I'm getting this from. As always, if you see flaws in my logic, I want you to point them out to me. I'm not infallible."

"Close enough." Gabe's muttered words generated nods of agreement from Ryan and Anissa.

"I can't begin to tell you how desperately I want to be wrong tonight." Sabrina tapped her computer again and the seven photographs from Lisa Palmer's briefcase appeared on the screen.

"When we saw these photographs, there were any number of ways we could have gone in searching out the common thread. We could have looked at location, ownership, clientele, etcetera. But at Adam's request, I spent today looking at all of these locations to determine how they connect back to Barclay Campbell."

Gabe clicked the top of a pen on his notepad. "How's he related to you, Adam?"

"He's my father's first cousin. His father was my grandfather's brother."

"Sorry for the interruption, Sabrina." Gabe tapped his pen to his temple. "Just trying to get it straight in my head."

"Not a problem. Now, as you all know, the Campbell family is responsible for approximately 30 percent of the business revenue in Carrington County."

"That seems a bit high," Adam said.

"Well, I did a search today, and it's actually a touch low. When you take all the branches of the Campbell family into account, going back to your great-grandfather and his four sons, you have a very large family. And while there have been a lot of sons born into the family, the daughters have also been very astute at business, and there are at least six different surnames that I've been able to determine are, for our purposes, Campbells."

"That's a lot," Ryan said, "but how does that tie in to our case?"

"I'm glad you asked."

Adam caught Ryan's eye and gave him a little nod of appreciation. He didn't think Sabrina even realized Ryan's question had been more for her benefit than anyone else's, but it had been effective.

"When you look at the business ventures of the Campbells, you can see a rather clear line of demarcation that begins with Adam's grandfather and then is even more clear with his father. As Adam has already told us"—she tapped her computer and a new screen popped up—"his branch of the Campbells owns and operates CHG, the Campbell Holding Group, and they own and operate most of the high-end hotels and several of the fancier restaurants in town, including the resort on the lake and all of its properties. They also have multiple other enterprises."

She flipped to another screen. "You can see how the businesses were handed down from Adam's great-grandfather all the way to Adam and Alexander when you trace them through CHG. Everything is transparent. Easy to follow."

Grandmother would die if she saw this. Grandfather wouldn't approve either. This was so not anyone's business.

Sabrina didn't seem to notice how uncomfortable this was making Adam. "But when you try to do the same thing with the other branches of the Campbells' businesses, it gets messy in a hurry. I don't think most of it was done to be shady, although there are a few transactions I think careful examination would show were intended to skirt tax laws."

The screen changed again. "But when you hit the holdings of Barclay Campbell, what was messy devolves into madness."

Anissa raised her hand.

"You guys don't have to raise your hands, but go ahead."

"I thought all the Campbell companies were privately held. How are you getting this information? We don't have warrants for any of this."

"They are privately held, but that doesn't mean everything stays private. If you know where to look, you can find out all sorts of things from public records. And you can find out even more if you know where to look on the internet. This isn't the kind of stuff anyone would stumble onto in a basic search, but it's there if you look hard enough and smart enough."

Adam couldn't take it anymore. "What has Barclay done?"

Sabrina's shoulders drooped. "I need more time. A lot more time. And some trustworthy help. And warrants to get more info than I can find legally on my own. But Mike sent me the files he'd recovered this morning. I looked through those files for anything connected to Barclay Campbell, and I've found some disturbing discrepancies."

Gabe sat up straighter. "Such as?"

"Such as the fact that Barclay has way more money than he should. He has to be laundering it somehow, but I haven't figured out how yet."

"How on earth did you figure that out?" Gabe's question wasn't one of disbelief but of obvious amazement.

"It's the files on the laptop," Sabrina said. "There are accounting records from four of Barclay Campbell's companies. The thing is, all of them are extremely profitable. And all of them involve very cheap labor."

"Which is why you're thinking human trafficking." Anissa leaned forward and put her head in her hands. "I hate these cases. Hate. Them."

"Which businesses?" Adam asked.

"They all have initials. BCC, BCH, BCP, BCF. I'm guessing here, but I'm assuming that stands for Barclay Campbell and then some other aspect. Hotels? Properties? I'm not sure about the others."

"Cleaning." Adam groaned. "BCC is Barclay Campbell Cleaning."

Sabrina blew out a breath. "That makes so much sense."

He held her eyes for a long moment. He wouldn't need the rest of her carefully prepared slides. He knew where this was going.

"Is it a real business?" Anissa asked.

"It's real in that it exists, but I don't know if he's gone through the appropriate legal channels to legitimize it."

"What do you know about it?" Ryan directed his question to Adam but then turned to Sabrina. "I'm sorry. Should we wait to chase this rabbit trail?"

"It isn't a rabbit trail. Adam's got the scent. He can probably get you where I'm going."

Adam stood. He wanted to hit something. Or more to the point, someone. How had they been so blind? "I don't know how we missed it. Heaven help us. I had no idea."

"You haven't done this, Adam. And you may be the only one who can help us bring it to light." Sabrina's soothing words stretched across the space between them. She was right. He needed to man up—even if it meant watching his family's name get dragged through the muck.

"Okay," Adam said. "I don't talk about this much because you guys would hassle me about it and it's none of your business. But my father intends for me to take over the family business someday."

Three faces registered surprise. Sabrina's was not one of them.

"You're going to quit?" Gabe shook his head in disbelief.

"No, I'm not going to quit. But assuming I don't get myself shot or blown up, I'll be eligible to retire when I'm in my forties, and Dad wants me to be prepared to take his place when the time comes."

"Is that what you want?" Anissa frowned in concern.

"Honestly? I don't know. It's hard for me to imagine doing what

213

he does all day. I haven't said yes, but I haven't closed the door on it. Alexander has. He doesn't want it and says he never will. He wants to fix arms and legs, and he's wanted that since he was six. No one was surprised by his choices."

"Bet they were surprised by yours."

Gabe wasn't wrong. "Very. But while the extended family had a duck over it, once my parents realized I wouldn't back down, they were always supportive. Concerned, but supportive. All Dad has asked is that I stay involved in the business so if he had a health issue, I would know what was going on and could step in. At that point I could decide if I wanted it to be permanent or until we could sell things off or transition the business."

"Makes sense." Anissa's expression was still clouded. "But that's a big burden for you to carry."

"Sometimes. But Dad's good about scheduling appointments around my work. We have board meetings at night. He even works around my dive team schedule. I think he's so relieved I'm willing to do it at all that he's happy to accommodate me."

"So how does your business intersect with Barclay's?" Gabe frowned.

"It doesn't. But Barclay wanted it to. About a year ago, he came to Dad with a proposition. Said he was working with DOR, which is the hospitality arm my aunt and uncle own and Darren works for. He pitched an idea to take over all our housekeeping and groundskeeping and maintenance at the hotels and the resorts."

"Do you currently keep that in-house?"

"Yes. Everyone who works on a CHG property works for CHG. We don't have anything outsourced."

"Seems like you could save money by outsourcing it," Anissa said. "I'm not a business expert, but I can see the value in that."

"The monetary value, yes. But the human cost is too high for us. Of course we could make more money, but we make plenty without doing that. And our employees make a very fair wage, have good benefits, and are considered part of the family. I have a cousin who runs that part of the business and she's amazing. Everyone loves her. She runs a tight ship, tolerates no junk, but rewards performance lavishly. Dad's given her a lot of latitude, and she's made that department one of the best in the entire corporation. But that isn't why we turned down Barclay's offer. We turned it down because it didn't make sense on paper. There was no way he could do what he was claiming. We know how many maids, valets, and groundskeepers we have on staff. We know how many it takes to run our hotels properly and we know how much it costs to pay them, provide benefits, everything. Even if he paid everyone minimum wage, the numbers didn't add up."

Father, why didn't we see it a year ago?

"At the time, we told him we preferred to keep everyone as employees of CHG and we weren't interested in making a change. I didn't have much to do with that decision beyond agreeing to it. Dad was the one who ran the numbers. We figured either Barclay didn't know what he was doing or he'd made some bad calculations before he presented it to us. Dad even told him he needed to check his numbers because they didn't match up. Barclay said he would, and it's never come up again."

"But if the employees of BCC were victims of human trafficking—specifically labor trafficking—then would the numbers make sense?" Gabe asked the question like he was dreading the answer.

"Oh yeah." Adam turned to Sabrina. "Can you go back to that slide with the photographs?"

She did.

"I don't know how we'll ever prove it unless Sabrina can find a smoking gun in those files, but I know this is what Lisa Palmer was coming to talk to me about."

He pointed to the yacht. "A yacht like that would have a staff—housekeeping, chef, maybe someone specifically for maintenance—

215

other than the captain. Most yachts like that are designed so you never see the staff."

He pointed to the restaurants. "These are all small, locally owned restaurants. He could have people doing the night cleaning when no one else is there. Or some of the back-of-the-house work like dishwashing. Maybe even bussing tables."

He pointed to the private homes. "My grandparents have six full-time staff members. But Senator Carson? Probably twelve. And with the exception of the butler who opens the doors and maybe the chauffer who drives them around, no one outside of his family ever sees the staff."

He blew out a long breath. "And then we have The Porterhouse. We'd heard they'd outsourced almost everything about a year ago and their profit margins have skyrocketed. They've had enough money to actually do some of the renovations and updates they desperately needed to do to stay competitive. Honestly, I was happy for them. I hate for anyone's business to go under, and during the high season all our properties are at capacity. It's a competitive industry to be sure, but there's room for a place like The Porterhouse to thrive."

"But the staff . . ." Anissa trailed off like she couldn't bear to finish her thought.

"I have no proof, but if you suddenly quit paying your staff, you'd have plenty of money left over for other projects."

"How are they getting away with this?" Anissa rubbed her face in her hands. "How are these people working these jobs and no one realizes they aren't getting paid?"

"Would you like me to explain it?" Sabrina's gentle question reminded Adam that he'd hijacked her slides. Not that she seemed to mind.

"Please." Adam tried to smile at her as he spoke.

He didn't know how he was going to handle this. If his suspicions were correct, Barclay had been running this "business" for at least three years. Maybe longer.

How many of Barclay's so-called employees had been living in fear that long? How many of them had he seen in a restaurant or on the street and had no idea he was looking into the face of a slave?

17

A dam flopped back into his chair and Sabrina skipped through a few slides. "Adam's covered some of these."

He stared at the ceiling. He looked so miserable. She wasn't surprised Adam had understood immediately. If she could get this over with, she could . . . what? She couldn't fix it. Couldn't change it.

A guy should expect his girlfriend—if that's what she was—to be comforting. Right? Not that she had a clue how to do that. She might need to text Leigh for advice. Or maybe Anissa could help her?

She forced herself to focus on the faces of the three homicide investigators, all of whom wore expressions that even she could tell were a mix of horror and fury.

"Anissa, your question is one we get a lot when we talk about modern-day slavery and the rise of human trafficking in this country. Most people assume slavery is a thing of the past, but it isn't. The statistics are terrifying, and unfortunately the Carolinas are known hotspots for human traffickers."

"Why the Carolinas?" Ryan pointed to her slide that showed

huge red circles of human trafficking centers right over their current location.

"We have major transportation arteries from the Gulf to the massive cities of the Northeast, combined with our own midsize cities and large rural areas. It's easy to move people and hide people and make people disappear."

She flipped to a new slide. "The reality is that most of the people caught up in human trafficking entered the country legally. They have passports or visas, but their traffickers take them from them and then use intimidation, abuse, sexual assault, or threats of deportation to force them to work for little or no pay. Because they're away from their own support systems and speak little to no English, they're particularly vulnerable. And they often come from countries where the police are corrupt, so when they see one of you walking down the street, they don't even think to ask you for help."

Sabrina flipped to a new slide. "Now, when most people think of human trafficking, they tend to think sex trafficking. And that's certainly a huge component of it. But many people don't even realize labor trafficking exists. Men, women, and children are coerced into working under inhumane conditions, for ridiculously long hours, and with little or no pay."

She pulled a stack of papers from her bag and handed it to Anissa. "Will you take one and pass it around?"

As Anissa shared the pages, Sabrina explained what they were looking at. "This is a typical scenario for a labor trafficking victim. They're recruited in their home country. Sometimes they're stolen away from their homes and smuggled in, but more often they pay someone to help facilitate their move to America. They have legitimate papers and come into the country with the promise of jobs that will pay enough for them to live here and still have money to send home to help support their families."

"But they get here and nothing is like what they were led to believe," Ryan said. "They have their passports, visas—anything that could be used to identify them and prove that they are here legally—taken away. They're told they owe money for their transport and they have to work it off before they'll be free to go elsewhere." He looked at the others. "This is sickening."

"It's more prevalent than most people realize," Sabrina said. "These are people who came to this country in search of something better. But they don't know American laws or customs, and they don't speak enough English to communicate their concerns. The traffickers will often abuse them in the beginning to get them to comply. After that they may not use physical harm because they don't want to 'scuff up the merchandise,' but they will use threats—often of harm to their families—to be sure they do what they're told and keep their mouths shut."

"I need to hit something." The way Gabe was punching his fist into his palm, Sabrina had no trouble believing him.

"If we go back to our photographs"—Sabrina flipped back to the seven pictures from Lisa Palmer's briefcase—"here are some plausible scenarios. Remember, I have no proof."

Three heads nodded. Adam had shifted from staring at the ceiling and now had his head in his hands.

"The yacht." Anissa dove in. "The entire staff could be slaves."

Ryan pointed to the restaurants. "Any of the staff in those restaurants could be slaves. We don't question it when the busboy doesn't speak English or the girl rolling the silverware in the back doesn't engage in conversation. The servers, hosts, even the chefs may all be legit, but the prep crew, the cleaning crew, the dishwashers all could be victims of trafficking."

Sabrina pointed to the slide again. "We've already discussed the senator's home. And of course, there's The Porterhouse."

Adam's head popped up. "Housekeeping, laundry, groundskeeping, kitchen staff . . . all of them could be victims."

"You all know I work with an organization that is very involved in the hunt for sexual predators and human traffickers," Sabrina said. "I've seen this before, and while I have no proof, I'm confident Barclay Campbell is using trafficked human beings in his business ventures. I doubt he's the brains behind it, and I doubt he's the recruiter. My guess is someone got some leverage on him and then used that leverage to bring him into the business. Once he got in, there was no way out."

Adam shook his head. "Don't give him an out, Bri. We don't need to make excuses for him."

"These aren't excuses. These are observations," Sabrina countered. "Why else would a legitimate businessman get into something as seedy as this? Sure, he can make some good money, but it's impossible to justify this as anything other than being a modern-day slaver."

"Dad says Barclay's always had a mean streak."

"I don't know, man," Gabe said. "Mean streak or not, buying and selling human beings for profit takes things to a whole new level of depravity. You have to be either a coldhearted fish or in deep enough trouble that you are willing to go down a path that there's no return from."

Anissa shifted in her seat. "What kind of money are we talking about?"

"A woman working seventy hours a week could potentially be worth over fifty thousand dollars a year." Sabrina shuddered. "I hate talking about people like they're commodities, but that's how they're viewed. A strong man in a construction job could be worth even more."

"But we have no proof." Adam popped to his feet and paced the area behind the sofa. "We need a friendly judge to give us a warrant to get into Barclay's computer without his knowledge."

"I don't know any of them friendly enough to do it with what we have," Ryan said.

For a few moments, they talked over each other, throwing out different names of judges in the area.

"We can't risk it." Gabe's pronouncement silenced them. "We've got a state senator possibly involved. A prominent businessman who is a member of Carrington's most respected family."

Adam rolled his eyes at that remark, but he didn't say anything to contradict the statement.

Gabe continued. "We don't know who's involved and we can't risk tipping our hand. Not yet. We need more proof."

Sabrina didn't say anything. She wasn't a cop.

"I want to go straight to The Porterhouse and find all their housekeeping staff and interview them," Gabe said. "But if we move too fast, we could spook the traffickers. They could kill these people."

"Or move them." Anissa clenched and unclenched her hands as she spoke. "Put them to work somewhere else. Cut their losses here."

"Sabrina." Ryan's calm and measured voice made Sabrina think of the way a cat purrs . . . right before it pounces. "You do this kind of stuff all the time with those groups you work with. What kind of law enforcement task forces are out there? And I'm not talking about the two investigators in our own department who are assigned to human trafficking. They're good investigators, but even if we bring this to them, they're going to need help and a lot of it. I'm talking about state- and federal-level kind of stuff."

"There are several task forces in the area that are focused on human trafficking. And there are some fine investigators on them too," Sabrina said. "They work on the local, state, and federal levels. One of them has some FBI involvement. Why?"

"He's thinking about how we're going to bring down the whole organization. Not just Barclay Campbell." A tight smile crossed Adam's face. There was no humor, but there was something else. Maybe appreciation? He liked Ryan's idea.

Whatever it was.

"I know we would all like to end these people's suffering tonight." Ryan leaned forward and laced his hands in front of him. "But we don't know what we're dealing with. If we run off half-cocked, we could do more harm than good in the long run. In the short run, we need to start thinking about who we can bring into this investigation without risking anyone getting worried that we're on to them."

He turned to Sabrina. "How much longer do you think you're going to need to go through Lisa Palmer's hard drive?"

"Ideally? Even with Mike helping, it will be at least a couple of weeks. Maybe longer because of the holidays. And I wouldn't recommend trying to get warrants until we've gone through everything we currently have access to."

"But if it's going to take that long to get all the data, why wait on the warrants?" Gabe asked. "Why not ask for them now?"

"I know you want to be doing something, and I realize you may be under some pressure to show that the investigation is moving forward," Sabrina said, "but what if we find evidence that a judge is involved and you've asked that judge for a warrant?"

"That would be bad," Gabe agreed, "but when we have enough evidence, I know exactly which judge I will trust with this."

"I'm glad," Sabrina said, "but I'm still holding out hope for the forensics team searching through Lisa Palmer's house to uncover something. A key to a safe deposit box. A fireproof box. Something."

Gabe scoffed. "Sabrina, the odds—"

"Aren't good. I get that. But so far we've found her laptop and her briefcase. She knew people were watching. She wrote a note to Adam on her body, for crying out loud." Sabrina pointed to the photographs on her computer. "She laminated those photographs. Who does that? And then she threw them in the lake in broad daylight. Why would she do that unless she'd already thought through the fact that they wouldn't be ruined in the water and the investigator she wanted to talk to was on the dive team? She was determined to get this information out, and I'm not convinced she didn't leave more evidence for us to find."

Sabrina had to pause to take a breath. "Before we start trying to tap Barclay Campbell's phone or trace his internet usage, I think we need to keep searching for what Lisa Palmer already put together for us. She died for this information, and regardless of how many bad decisions she made in her life, it looks like she was trying to set things right in the end. I would like to honor that."

No one spoke. Sabrina wasn't sure whether that was a good thing or not. Gabe, Anissa, and Ryan stared at the floor, but Adam caught her eye. The look on his face was indecipherable to her. Was he disappointed? Frustrated? Embarrassed by her little speech?

"You're amazing," he said.

So, not upset.

Gabe cleared his throat. "Anyone else feel like they just got taken to the woodshed?" Four heads bobbed. "Dr. Fleming, when you get all rational and logical and passionate at the same time, you are a force to be reckoned with."

"That she is." The look on Adam's face had shifted to one she was beginning to recognize. It was the look that made her skin tingle.

Ryan rubbed his hands together. "Okay. What's the status of Lisa Palmer's house?"

"Still too hot to handle," Gabe said. "But we may be able to start sifting through tomorrow. Definitely by Friday. I've warned forensics we're going to need to look through everything. I'll be out there when they get started."

"Who's going to be in charge of that work?" Anissa asked.

"Dante," Gabe answered.

"Good. He's the best." Ryan turned to Adam. "What's the status of Lisa Palmer's banking and financial accounts?"

"The banks have been cooperative, but there's no record of her having a safe deposit box, if that's what you're wondering," Adam

224

said. "I sent the forensic accountant all the banking records, and she's looking through them for anything suspicious. She doesn't know anything about the human trafficking angle—she's just tackling it as she would any other potential homicide."

Ryan nodded at Gabe. "It's your case, bro. Anissa and I don't have anything else to add from the dive team aspect. We searched the entire area around the car and came up empty. Forensics has the car itself. Sabrina has the hard drive. And we have no reason to suspect Lisa Palmer threw anything else in the lake." He glanced at Anissa. "I'm not trying to speak for Anissa, but I think I'm safe in saying this. We'll help you any way we can."

"Definitely. Anything." Anissa's agreement came fast and firm.

"Thanks." Gabe cleared his throat. "I don't know what we'll run into in the weeks ahead, but I'm sure I'll be calling on you for something. I just wish we could make it go faster."

"I have one suggestion," Ryan said. "We need to think of ways to get ourselves in proximity to some of these victims. Maybe if we could talk to them, or at least start to get an idea of who they are, get some photographs, start trying to find out how they got here and what their status is, maybe we could get someone to trust us enough to talk to us."

"It's a great idea, but I can't afford to stay at The Porterhouse." Gabe rubbed his thumb and fingers together in the universal sign for money. "Or eat at The Back Door. And the senator sure isn't going to be inviting—"

"The Back Door. That's it." Adam's voice held a mixture of triumph and despair. "I can't believe I missed this too."

"Missed what?" Three voices joined Sabrina's.

"The charity gala on Friday. I could be wrong, but I think there will be a whole bunch of victims present."

Sabrina saw nothing but confusion on everyone's faces.

Ryan found his voice first. "What makes you say that?"

"The Back Door," Adam said again.

225

Gabe had circled around and flopped back onto the sofa beside Anissa. "You aren't making sense, bro."

Adam shook his head like he was trying to clear his thoughts. "The Back Door is providing the food for the gala, and the gala is happening at The Porterhouse."

Anissa slid over to create some space between her and Gabe. "And you think if the workers at The Back Door are being trafficked, then they might be at the gala and it will take all of The Porterhouse staff—who may also be slaves—to accommodate the people for the gala?"

Adam paused before he answered, and when he spoke there was sadness in his voice. "I do."

Gabe rubbed his hands together. "Now we're getting somewhere. I'm going to need you to give me all the dirt you can on this gala."

Anissa elbowed Gabe. "Be nice."

"What did I do?" Gabe rubbed his rib cage. "That hurt."

"Adam's mother started the Christmas Charity Gala years ago. It's kind of a big deal." Anissa spoke in a terse whisper.

Gabe responded with a look of chagrin. "Sorry, man. I didn't know it was your family's thing. I wasn't trying to be rude."

"I know. But Anissa's right. The first Christmas Charity Gala was held thirty years ago." Sabrina was tapping away on her laptop, and Adam tried to ignore her. Not that he ever could. But who knew what kind of rabbit trail she'd taken off down? Best to keep going with the story. "And my mother did start it. But over the years it's taken on a life of its own."

"What do you mean? Your family doesn't run it anymore?" Ryan walked toward the kitchen as he asked the question.

"Not exactly. We're still heavily involved, but when it was started, our family didn't have a specific way in which we supported charities."

"But you do now?" Ryan returned with a two-liter bottle of Coke and a plate of cookies.

Anissa slapped Gabe's hand away as she helped herself to the first cookie. "Do you guys not pay any attention at all?"

"What is that supposed to mean?" Ryan went back toward the kitchen.

"Nothing." Anissa shrugged. "Sorry, Adam. This is your business, and it's your business how much you want to tell."

"Thanks. But now you have me curious. I want to know what you were going to say."

"Are you sure about that?" Anissa asked.

Sounds of ice falling into plastic cups came from the kitchen, and Adam used Ryan's absence to try to gather his thoughts. He didn't want to have this conversation. It had been ingrained in him from childhood—you didn't talk about the family money or family politics with anyone outside of the family.

Ryan returned with his hands full of cups. "I don't see what the big deal is. He's with friends. His secrets are safe with us. We never ratted him out for being in love with Sabrina, did we?"

Gabe laughed so hard he choked on his cookie. Anissa speared Ryan with her most disapproving look.

Sabrina looked up from the laptop and shrugged. "You've already told me it was love at first sight, so this isn't really new information."

Even Anissa laughed at that one.

Adam wanted to be mad at them, but Ryan had made a solid point. What was he trying to protect anyway? Why did he care if they knew? It wasn't anything to be ashamed of, and if anyone would understand, it was this group.

"Fine," he said.

He gave Anissa a nod and she took the lead. "Adam is on the board of TCC—The Campbell Charities. The board manages the distribution of all of The Campbell Holdings Group's charitable contributions. And they're the presenting sponsor for the Christmas Charity Gala each year."

"When do you do all this? You help your dad run the family business and you're on the board of TCC?" Gabe sounded impressed.

"He's been on the board since he turned twenty-one."

How on earth would Anissa know that?

"Okay. Fine, Miss Know-It-All," Gabe said. "I may not know much about high society, but I do know that being on the board of a charitable organization doesn't mean you have access to the details of an event like this. There's usually a special committee for something like that." Gabe poured a Coke and handed it to Anissa, then poured one for himself.

"You're correct that I don't have all the details, but the planning committee had to present their recommendations for this year's event for board approval. And that's how I know The Back Door offered to provide the catering this year. There was some discussion about using them. The food is excellent. No one is disputing that. But the concern was how it would work with the budget. But it turned out that The Back Door had volunteered to cover the costs of their staff. They're providing the food and beverages at cost, and they said they were going to pay their staff and would offer the gala their services free of charge. They're providing the waitstaff, the catering staff, the bartenders, and even the bathroom attendants."

And now he knew how they were able to afford it.

"We typically use our own restaurants and hotels for the event, but they renovated The Porterhouse recently and it was a good chance to drive some business their way. They've struggled for the past few years, and it seemed like a way to be a good neighbor and give the gala a different feel this year. And it would have been crazy to pass up the proposal from The Back Door. I thought it was an extremely generous offer at the time, but it never occurred to me that they might be able to make such an offer because they had no intentions of paying their staff to begin with."

"The Back Door isn't very big." Anissa took a sip of her drink. "Do they have enough staff to cover an event as big as the Christmas Gala?"

Adam considered her question. "Combined with The Porterhouse staff? Yes."

"Okay, let's go back a little," Gabe said. "Because I don't exactly run in high-society kinds of circles and I didn't grow up in Carrington. What's the big deal about this gala?"

"It's the place to be," Anissa said. "The tickets are twenty-five hundred dollars a person, and you have to be invited to be able to purchase them."

"You what?" Gabe turned from Anissa to Adam. "You invite people to this thing and then charge them to come? That's . . ." Gabe's mouth continued to move, but no words came out.

Anissa raised her cup to Adam in a mock salute. "Congratulations, Adam. You've done what I thought was impossible. You've rendered Gabe speechless."

He acknowledged Anissa's remark with a "You're welcome" before responding to Gabe.

"It didn't start out that way," Adam said. "But over the years as the demand grew, we had to start sending invitations and then each year we were able to raise the price. It keeps the event intentionally exclusive and extremely lucrative. Charities make pitches in June to try to be the featured charity for the gala because it's guaranteed money."

"So you don't put the money into your Campbell charity thing. This money all goes to a specific charity?" Gabe asked.

"Not one dime goes into any Campbell account," Adam said. "We're the presenting sponsor, so we're footing the bill for the majority of the event. We've found by contributing in that way, we're actually able to raise far more money for the charities than we could have contributed on our own."

"It's genius." Ryan stifled a yawn. "How do we get our people in?"

Leave it to Ryan to be at least three steps ahead.

"Are you asking me out?" Gabe fanned himself in mock embarrassment.

"Not me," Ryan said. "Leigh's working, and I've already committed to watching my niece and nephew. I'm helping my parents with the kids while my sister is out of town. She's supposed to be home by nine on Friday, but there's no way I can be available before ten."

"So you pay twenty-five hundred dollars to go to this? And then you have to pay another twenty-five hundred to take a date?" Gabe shook his head. "No way we can get the captain to sign off on that requisition."

"Adam's going." Sabrina's quiet observation pulled everyone's attention back to her and the TV screen, where a guest list appeared.

"How did you get that?" Adam asked. "That list is supposed to be confidential."

She smiled. "It wasn't hard to find."

"There's no plus one listed for you," Anissa said. "You aren't taking a date?"

"No." He'd never taken a date.

"Why not? You could take Anissa and we could have ourselves a little investigation." Gabe turned to Anissa. "What do you think?"

"I think you're making a lot of assumptions about my free time. And you missed the part where Adam said he wasn't taking a date. Besides, it would look very suspicious if he took me."

"Why?" Gabe asked. "You're gorgeous. He's the most eligible bachelor in town. What's suspicious about that?"

Anissa punched Gabe's arm. "Maybe because he has a girlfriend, you moron."

"Not that anyone knows about yet." Gabe grabbed her fist before she could hit him again.

Ryan caught Adam's eye. "If you don't stop them, they'll do this all night."

230

He was right. "Would you two hush? I am not taking anyone. If the two of you would like to go, I think I know how I can swing it."

"The two of us?" Gabe asked.

"Why aren't you taking anyone?" Anissa asked at the same time.

Oh, good grief. They were going to make him say it out loud, weren't they? "It's complicated."

He tried to communicate to Anissa to drop it, but she either didn't get the message or she chose to ignore it. "Doesn't seem complicated to me."

"Fine. I need to talk to Sabrina for a few minutes," Adam said.

"There's nothing you can't say in front of us, man. I'm hurt." Gabe pretended to pout.

"There are a million things I wouldn't say in front of you, so stuff it." Adam turned and saw an ocean of pain in Sabrina's eyes. "Please." He led her through the French doors, and she followed him out onto the deck. He couldn't help but notice that she didn't take his hand or touch him in any way. He needed to explain himself. And fast.

He closed the doors as she leaned against the rail of the deck, facing the water. Lake Porter stretched out before them in the inky blackness. The night air was cool on his arms. She had to be chilled, but her stiff posture warned him to keep some distance. He leaned against the rail beside her.

"You don't have to take me to the gala, Adam."

"I want to."

"Doesn't seem like it."

How could he explain without making it worse? "I have a good reason."

"So you don't want to."

"No! I do want to, but I have a good reason for not doing it. Unless you . . ." He stepped away from the railing and ran his hands through his hair.

"You may be making this harder than it needs to be," she said as she continued to look over the lake. "Try telling me the truth."

"I don't think you'll like it."

"Well, I certainly don't like wondering why this is such a big deal, so I'm not sure how you could do much worse."

Awesome.

"Fine. Here's the deal." She turned around. He kind of wished she would have stayed the other way. This was going to be harder to say to her face. "The Christmas Charity Gala is a big deal in my family. It's not the kind of place you take a casual date. Not if you're a Campbell. In fact, the only thing more off-limits than the gala is Sunday lunch."

His grandmother had a strict rule about Sunday lunch. No dates allowed until there was an engagement ring on her finger.

He saw it on Sabrina's face the moment the implications became clear.

"I promised I wouldn't rush you," he said. "I told you I could show you being with a Campbell wasn't such a horrible thing. That it might even be fun. But on Friday night it won't matter if you're there only for this case or not. The reality is, if you come to the gala with me, certain assumptions will be made and there's nothing I can do to stop them."

"You could tell your family why I'm there," she said.

"Theoretically, yes. But under the circumstances, I think it would be best to keep my family as in the dark as possible. And the truth is, I want you there. And it would be okay with me if all the things people will assume are true . . . were actually true about us. But I can't ask you to come with me knowing what kind of gossip you'll be exposing yourself to. Not without warning you."

Sabrina considered his words. He wished he knew what was going on in that brilliant mind of hers. Was she mad? Did she understand why he was so conflicted about this?

232

"So you're saying if I go to this gala with you, all those debutantes and their society mothers will assume you're off the market?"

"That's one way of putting it."

"Then I'm in."

Wait. What?

18

The look on Adam's face was priceless.

"Come on." Sabrina took his hand and pulled him back toward the door. "We need to get a game plan together."

As she pulled him to the door, he pulled her back toward the rail. They collided and he wrapped his arms around her. "Bri." His breath tickled her ear. "You aren't jealous of those debutantes, are you?"

She squirmed in his arms but didn't try too hard to get away. What fun would that be? "No."

"I thought we were going to be honest with each other?"

"Let's go inside and talk about the gala."

"I like talking about this. I'm utterly intrigued."

"And you'll have to stay that way. It's late. And we have a lot of work to do." She ducked out of his arms and opened the door.

"You two get everything worked out? Because we've found something very interesting at the top of the guest list." Gabe pointed at the TV, where the graphic for the charity gala had been blown up.

She didn't love that someone had messed with her computer. It felt a bit like an invasion of privacy. But she couldn't be too aggravated because the graphic for the gala listed the sponsors for the event.

All seven of the photographs from Lisa Palmer's briefcase were represented. What were the odds that this was an accident? Was it possible that FreedomForAll was actually helping the perpetrators and not the victims?

Adam slumped against the doorframe. "You have got to be kidding me. Are we seriously pouring money into a charity that's dirty?" Adam obviously didn't think it was an accident.

Sabrina rubbed his arm. "How do you think I feel? I volunteer for this organization."

"Come on, guys." Anissa patted the sofa. "We're clearly dealing with some devious and deviant individuals. They've done an excellent job of covering their tracks and keeping themselves off the radar. But we're on to them now, and we're going to take them down."

Anissa was right. Of course. Maybe. Hopefully.

"You said you had an idea of how you could get us into the gala." Gabe pointed at the screen. "I think I'd be interested in hearing it."

Adam took Sabrina's hand and walked back to the group. Sabrina grabbed her laptop and settled beside Adam on the love seat.

"We had a meeting last week to discuss security for the gala," Adam said. "It's always tight. Quite a few uniformed personnel outside. Others inside, but always on the perimeter. No one wants heavily armed law enforcement officers in the main ballroom."

"Well, it might detract from the festivities." Gabe rolled his eyes.

"That's the concern. But we've talked about having some plain-clothes deputies. Only in this case they would be black-tie deputies."

"So they can blend in," Gabe said.

"Yes. You and Anissa could go. I could get you in as security so you wouldn't have to pay. You could mix and mingle and dance the night away. And as security, it would give you access to the kitchens and the staff. It would even give you a reason to speak to them."

"What do you think, Bell?" Gabe asked Anissa. "You said you'd do anything."

"I'm regretting my word choice at the moment." Anissa didn't look excited about this idea at all. "And I think if you want me to show up at a party with you, you're going to have to ask me very nicely."

Sabrina had never fully understood the animosity between Anissa and Gabe. Something about Anissa kicking Gabe off the dive team for missing training sessions when he was working undercover and then having to let him back on when he quit working undercover.

Adam had told her those two could barely stand to be in the same boat together for a while, but they'd thawed toward each other quite a bit over the past few months.

Still, even she could see that Anissa didn't want to go to a formal gala with Gabe.

Anissa's entire body was rigid, and while she was sitting beside Gabe, at least a foot of space was between them. He closed the distance and spoke in a whisper none of the rest of them could hear.

As he spoke, Anissa's expression softened. She almost smiled but then sort of pinched her lips together.

Gabe pulled back and Anissa cut her eyes over at him. Whatever was going on between those two was beyond Sabrina's ability to discern, but she could tell when Anissa had made up her mind. "Fine. I'll go." Somehow the terse words didn't match the way Anissa's entire body had relaxed. "But if you stomp on my feet, I'll have you cleaning the boat for a year."

Gabe didn't argue with her but looked at Adam. "Okay. We're in."

"I'm in too." Sabrina grinned at Anissa. "Any suggestions about where I can find a dress at this point?"

"No idea, but we'll ask Leigh tomorrow. She'll know."

Ryan shuddered. "Y'all please have that conversation when I am somewhere else."

"This will be awesome." Gabe leaned toward Sabrina for a fist bump. "A double date."

Anissa smacked his arm. "They will be on a date. We will be working."

"Killjoy."

Everyone laughed at Gabe's sour expression. When the laughter subsided, no one seemed to want to break the silence.

Adam wrapped his arm around Sabrina's shoulders and she didn't complain as he pulled her against him. Her eyes slid closed and she couldn't find the willpower to force them open.

She had no idea how long they sat that way before the sounds of people standing pulled her back to the moment and she opened her eyes. Ryan was gathering cups. Anissa had the now-empty plate of cookies. Gabe tossed a throw pillow back onto the sofa.

"Let's get some sleep," Ryan said. "Leigh will not be happy with me when she finds out how late the three of you were up."

"Okay, Dad." Gabe smirked. "We'd hate for you and Mom to fight."

Everyone said their good nights and promised to touch base Thursday afternoon, if not sooner. Ten minutes later, Sabrina's last conscious thought was a prayer for the men, women, and children held in captivity a few miles away.

Please, Father. You came to set the captives free. Help us find them. Help us get them out.

———

Adam's first call Thursday morning was to his dad.

His dad didn't even say hi. "Everything okay?"

"Not really, but we're hanging in there."

A heavy sigh filtered through the phone. "How can I help?"

"I need to get a security team into the gala."

"I see."

How much did his dad see?

"Who did you have in mind?"

"Gabe and Anissa."

He heard the sound of scratching. Probably his dad writing something down. "Okay. I'll take care of it."

"Thanks, Dad."

"No problem. But I have a question for you."

"Okay."

"Will it be safe for your mother to be there?"

The question made Adam smile. Forty years into their marriage and his dad still looked out for his mom like they were newlyweds. "I don't expect anyone to be in danger, Dad. Just had a few things come up this week that made me think it would be a good idea."

He hoped his dad was reading between the lines. "Sabrina's coming with me, and I wouldn't consider having her or Mom there if I thought they would be in danger."

"Sabrina's coming *with* you? Wow. Then please ask her to save me a dance."

"I will."

"Adam?"

"Yes, sir."

There was a long pause. "I'm proud of you, son. You know that, right?"

"Yeah, Dad. I know."

"Okay. I love you."

"Love you too."

Adam hit the end button and stared at the phone.

"You're moving kinda fast, aren't you?" Gabe leaned over his desk.

"That was my dad."

"Sure it was." Gabe gave him an exaggerated wink. "Can you come by my office when you get a few minutes?"

"Now?"

"If you're free."

Adam followed Gabe to the homicide office and closed the door behind them. "What's up?"

"Who's in charge of security for the gala?"

"The security staff at The Porterhouse has the lead," Adam said. "Not that I currently have much confidence in them, but they've taken care of hiring off-duty officers to provide additional security. Why?"

"Any of our guys?"

"I don't know, but I can find out. In years past, I've seen plenty of deputies from the sheriff's office and officers from the city police department. Why?"

"I want to know who the good guys are. Or at least who they're supposed to be."

"I'll get a list."

"Thanks."

The door opened and Anissa entered.

"Good morning, Anissa," Adam said.

Her only response was a slight dip of her head as she took a sip of coffee.

"Too early, dude," Gabe stage-whispered.

"Ah. Not a morning person. Sorry."

"It's not that I'm not a morning person," Anissa said. "But no one is a four-hours-of-sleep person. I can't even pretend to be perky on anything less than five."

Gabe shook his head. "You had it right the first time, man. Come back after she's had another cup of coffee and she'll be a delight."

"Thanks for the tip." Adam headed for the door.

"Campbell?"

He turned back to Anissa. "Yes?"

"Don't expect to see your girlfriend tonight. We're going dress shopping."

"Thanks for that tip too." As he left the homicide office he heard

239

Gabe badgering Anissa about what kind of dress she was looking for. If those two survived Friday night, it would be a miracle.

Two hours later, Adam wasn't sure if any of them would survive
Friday night. When he saw the head of security for The Porterhouse
on Friday, it was going to take all his self-control not to slug the guy.

He gripped the phone tighter. This man was making him crazy.
"Walt, I need that list."

"I'm not comfortable giving you this information." Walt was a
two-hundred-fifty-pound retired marine and he wasn't comfortable?

"Whyever not?"

"You're a Campbell. How do I know you aren't trying to do
some sort of corporate espionage?"

Adam counted to ten. Slowly. "I'm going to pretend you didn't
say that."

"I'm just doing my job, kid."

"First of all, I'm not your kid. Second, in this situation the
fact that I'm a Campbell is the very reason you will give me the
information I'm requesting. It happens to be my charity sponsor-
ing this event, and in that role, I'm the one following up on the
security. If you're unwilling to provide the information, my next
phone call will be to Sullivan, and I can assure you I will let him
know I plan to make it a point to let all our biggest donors know
the security at The Porterhouse isn't up to snuff."

"Our security is excellent."

"Then what are you afraid of, Walt?"

"I'm not afraid of anything!"

"From where I sit you seem quite defensive. I'm rapidly coming
to the conclusion that you've dropped the ball and don't have the
kind of security we were told to expect."

"How do I know you aren't going to use this to get information
about The Porterhouse?"

240

"What do you think I'm trying to get that I don't already have? I played with Sullivan's kids in elementary school. I've roamed all over that property. I know where the secret door to the kitchen is and how to get into the boathouse from the laundry."

"Well, that's not the—"

"That *is* the point. I know the property, and I know the owners, and in this moment I'm an extremely influential guest. If I found out the head of security at one of my hotels was giving a guest the kind of runaround you're giving me, I'd fire him."

"I'm not giving you the runaround."

"You certainly aren't being accommodating, and you should know the first rule of hospitality is to give the guest what they want. All I'm asking for is the list of officers and the rotation schedule. We have some antsy donors who are requesting we provide additional security. I can't assuage their fears when I'm guessing about your security protocol for the evening."

"I don't know—"

"Okay. I'm done."

He hung up the phone and pulled up the number for Sullivan on his cell. Before he could hit dial, his office phone rang. "Campbell."

"You're a jerk, Campbell." Walt didn't give him a chance to respond. "Check your email."

Click.

Adam couldn't help but chuckle as he set both phones down, checked his email, and opened the attached file.

One security profile glowed on the screen. He hit print but continued to study it while he waited for the hard copy.

It was as complete and thorough as he'd expected it to be. Walt was a curmudgeon, but he knew how to run security for an event. Adam scrolled through the pages. What was here that Walt didn't want him to see?

He pulled the pages off the printer and spread them on his desk. The officers and deputies Walt had hired were solid. And there were an adequate number to cover the parking lot, interior spaces, and building perimeters. The Porterhouse in-house security was taking the property perimeter patrols, which made sense. There was little logic in having officers unfamiliar with the property stumbling around in the dark.

He studied the facility map. The huge house-turned-inn on the lake had long been one of his favorite Carrington landmarks. He'd spent many happy summer hours playing tag in the fields behind the hotel, climbing trees, and riding his bike on the nature trail they'd built for guests. Sean Sullivan had been one of his best friends and they'd explored every inch of . . .

Something was missing.

He compared the map he was looking at with the mental images he was dredging from the far corners of his memory.

Where were the little cabins?

The property map showed a large field at the far edge of the property, but no cabins.

Maybe Sullivan had knocked the cabins down. They'd been old twenty years ago. Or they'd seemed old, anyway.

But . . .

He called his dad again. "I have a quick question."

"Shoot."

"Did Sullivan tear down those little cabins at the back of The Porterhouse property? Or did I dream they were there?" His dad and Sullivan had known each other for decades. Most people thought they were bitter rivals, but that had never been the case. They weren't close, but they had a cordial relationship.

"You didn't dream them, and I'm not aware of Sullivan tearing them down. As far as I know, they're still back there. Why?"

"Um. No real reason." He explained his run-in with Walt and that he was studying the security plan for the gala. "The cabins aren't on the property diagram, but I have this memory of Sean and I playing in them."

"My guess is they use them for storage now. They probably wouldn't want them on a property diagram the guests would have access to."

"True. Thanks, Dad."

"Any time."

"Bye."

"Adam. Wait."

"Yes, sir."

"I told your mother about Sabrina coming."

Oh boy.

"She's ecstatic."

"Okay."

"I need to know if I should rein her joy in a little."

And that answered the question about how much his dad was picking up. "I'm thrilled she's coming. I won't pretend that if circumstances were different I probably wouldn't have asked her this year, but that's only because I'm trying not to rush her."

"Got it. I'll take care of things on this end. You be careful."

"Yes, sir. Thank you."

He hit end on the phone and grabbed a pencil. He traced in the twelve cabins he remembered. They'd been tucked back in the woods at the edge of the property. He thought they'd been approximately twenty-by-twenty feet, with low roofs, but his ten-year-old self might have had a skewed perspective of size. There had been little fire pits at each one. And hammocks. He'd loved the hammocks.

None of them had running water. There'd been two bathhouses, each with a shower and a toilet. He'd used them many times over the years when they'd been too busy playing to go back to the house for a bathroom break.

If Sullivan was using forced labor . . .

He walked to the homicide office and went straight to Gabe's desk. "I might know where some of the victims are being housed."

19

Sabrina didn't want to go dress shopping.

Adam had come by the lab and shared his theory about the victims, but he'd flatly refused to consider her suggestion that they raid the place tonight.

"Bri, we have no proof. We don't even know if the cabins are still there. We'll make up an excuse to look for them on Friday night, but for now we have to stick to the plan."

"Fine. But I'm shopping under duress."

His face crinkled in concern. "You don't have to have a dress. Not for me. I don't care if you come in jeans and a T-shirt if you'll be more comfortable."

He so didn't get it. She had to have the fancy dress, shoes, and hair or she would stick out like the nerd she was and draw even more attention to herself than she was already going to do by showing up on a Campbell's arm. But how could she explain that?

"You don't have to come at all, Bri."

"I want to come."

His expression said he didn't believe her.

"I do. It's . . . complicated."

He traced her cheek with his thumb. "This week has been intense—

emotionally and physically. You still have bruises under your makeup. You probably still have a headache. And I'd bet big money your entire body is hurting."

"I could say the same about you. Well, except for the part about the makeup."

He grinned at her remark, but his smile faded. "I'm worried about you. At some point, this is all going to catch up to you and it's going to be too much. I don't want to be responsible for adding the final straw."

"And you think a dress will be the final straw?"

"I have no idea."

Poor guy. He was meeting himself coming and going.

"I'm tougher than you're giving me credit for."

"You're the strongest woman I know. And I know some of the strongest women in the state." He spoke with a conviction that left no room for argument. He believed what he was saying. "But I've learned a lot from the men who love those women. I know when a strong, determined woman gives her heart to a man, it's his responsibility to cherish and protect it because he's the only one who knows how fragile that heart really is."

He tucked a stray hair behind her ear. "I know you can handle the dress shopping and the gala and the gossip. That isn't the issue. But you're doing important work right now and you've had a difficult week. If this is going to be distracting and stressful, then I'd rather you skip it. I don't ever want you to do anything out of some perceived obligation."

She planted a kiss on him then. One that left both of them surprised by its intensity.

"Thank you," she said when they finally broke apart. "I needed to hear that."

"If I could remember what I said, I would say it again." He did have a bit of a dazed expression, and she quite enjoyed that she had the ability to do that to him.

Four hours later, she was clinging to that kiss to keep herself going. "How many dresses have I tried on?"

Anissa laughed. "Three."

"Feels like thirty." This entire process was one massive torture session. Not only did she have to try on dresses, but Anissa insisted that she come out into the large mirrored space near the entrance to the dressing room and model each one. And she had almost no privacy. There were four individual stalls, but they didn't even have real doors. The only thing between her and any total stranger who also happened to be in the dressing room were two swinging doors with a disturbingly large gap in the middle.

"They've all looked great." Anissa sounded like she meant it, but she might have been lying just to calm her down. Sabrina couldn't tell.

"I can't move in them. I need to be able to move. And breathe. Breathing is important."

"Don't forget the part where you need to make Adam's mouth fall open and those society girls cry over their loss."

"Yeah. That too."

They tried on dresses for another thirty minutes. Nothing was right. One was too tight. One too revealing. One would have been perfect for Adam's grandmother. She'd given up on yet another gown when there was a knock on the dressing room door.

Anissa would want to see it anyway. "I'm coming." She gathered the long skirt of the dress in her arms and backed out of the stall. The little jacket that came with the dress fell to the floor and she bent over to grab it.

A shot rang out.

Too close.

She hit the floor.

Two more shots fired in rapid succession from somewhere behind her. Her ears rang. What was happening?

The air filled with screams. "Sabrina!" Anissa's anguished voice cut through the cacophony.

246

"I'm okay." She was. Wasn't she?

She rolled over.

"Don't look." Anissa stood between her and a large mass on the floor. The dress Anissa had been trying on was covered in what could only be parts of the man she'd shot.

"Is he dead?"

"Very. Are you okay?" Anissa spit the words.

"Fine." Physically, at least.

"Pete!" Anissa called out through the dressing room door. "Get in here." Anissa kicked open each of the other stalls and then returned to Sabrina's side.

Sabrina got to her feet. "Pete's here?"

"Of course he is. You don't think Adam would let us go shopping without extra security, do you? Not after what happened Monday."

The part of Sabrina's brain that wasn't screaming in panic was impressed by Anissa's calm.

"Call Adam." Anissa's terse order didn't leave any room for argument.

Sabrina tried to ignore the trembling of her fingers as she pulled up her most recent calls and hit Adam's number.

"Hi." How did Adam make that one word sound like a caress? "Done shopping already?"

"Not exactly."

"What's wrong?" There was nothing gentle about his tone now.

"Someone took a shot at her." Anissa spoke loud enough for Adam to hear her. Sabrina put the phone on speaker.

"What? Where are you?" Adam's voice had gone from gentle to concerned to full-on panicked.

"We're in the dressing room. Pete's not responding." Anissa's voice was like ice.

"Stay on the line with me. Don't hang up."

"Okay." Sabrina had no plans to disconnect the call.

"Gabe!" Sabrina could picture Adam getting Gabe's attention. "Someone came after them. Get backup over there."

"Are they okay?" Gabe's voice was faint, but Sabrina could hear the worry.

"They're both on the line."

"We're fine, Gabe." Anissa was still spitting her words. "But we're not leaving this dressing room until someone gives me the all clear. I've got one guy dead. No one else is in here with us. Three shots fired. One by him. Two by me."

"Hang tight, Bell. We'll get you." Gabe probably meant his words to be comforting, but even Sabrina could tell how angry he was.

The sound of doors slamming came through the phone. Gabe was talking to someone about backup.

"Bri, are you injured?" Adam asked.

"No."

"He shot at her in the dressing room. I don't know how he missed." Anissa pointed to the bullet now lodged in the wall of the dressing room.

A bullet that should have hit her in the chest. "I dropped the jacket."

"You what?" Anissa looked confused.

"The jacket. I thought it was you knocking on the door. I backed out, but I dropped the jacket, so I bent down to pick it up . . ." The reality of what had happened was sinking in. "I should be dead."

The sound of a revved engine reached Sabrina's ears. "We're at least ten minutes away," Adam said, "but there's a police unit in the parking lot. Gabe's talking to them now. They're on their way in."

"Okay." What else could she say? She was trapped in a dressing room trying very hard not to look at the body of the man who'd tried to kill her.

Why would anyone think she was a threat?

Who would want her dead?

"You, in the dressing room! Put your hands up!" That was not Pete.

Anissa didn't look impressed. "I'm Investigator Anissa Bell. If you come in here with a weapon drawn, I will shoot you and get your identification later." She waved her hand at Sabrina and whispered, "Get as far to the side as you can."

Sabrina complied with her order. She liked Anissa. A lot. But right now she was kind of scary. When she backed into the corner of the stall, she understood what Anissa was doing. She'd effectively gotten Sabrina out of sight of whoever would come into the dressing room.

"No one needs to shoot. I'm mall security. Got a call someone thought shots had been fired."

"That's because they were," Anissa said. "Why don't you stay where you are and make sure no one comes in here?"

"Um . . . I'm going to have to call this in."

"You go right ahead. While you're at it, close the store for the night."

"What's going on over here?" A new voice. Female. Bossy.

The security guard's voice dropped and a hushed conversation happened beyond what Sabrina could hear.

The bossy voice then came over the intercom system. "Ladies and gentlemen, could I have your attention, please? Due to unforeseen circumstances, we've been asked to cooperate with the police department in an investigation, and this requires us to close our doors immediately. We apologize for any inconvenience this may cause you and ask that you proceed to the nearest exit at this time."

The hum of talking outside the dressing room faded as people responded to the request. Then a new voice. Female. Firm.

"I'm Officer Tollison. Got a call from a buddy over at the sheriff's office that you might need some assistance."

"Claire?"

"Anissa?"

"I wouldn't go in there if I were you," the security guard warned. "She threatened to shoot me."

"It's safe to enter," Anissa said.

Sabrina couldn't resist watching through the crack in the stall. A petite blonde in full uniform peeked through the dressing room entrance and then walked all the way in.

"Well, this is great, Anissa. I thought I was getting off for the day, but this paperwork will take me the rest of the night."

"Tell me about it. Thanks for responding so quickly."

"No problem. We were the closest unit to the scene—had just responded to a disturbance across the street when dispatch notified us of the situation here. I'm glad to help. What do you need?"

"I need a perimeter around us so we can get out of here. I need you to look for one of our guys. Plain clothes. Pete Stanfield. He should have been nearby, but we can't reach him."

"On it." Officer Tollison spoke into her radio for a moment and another officer appeared at the entry to the dressing area. They conferred for a few seconds and then he walked away. Officer Tollison gave Anissa a tight smile. "We've got three units on the scene already and more on the way—so we'll have your perimeter set up in no time. And we'll find your missing deputy."

"Thanks," Anissa said. "And, Claire, you might want to give them a heads-up. We have some worried sheriff's investigators en route."

"Yeah. Gabe sounded like he was ready to crawl through the line when dispatch patched him through. I don't think I've ever heard him rattled before."

So that explained it. She was a friend of Gabe's. Or maybe she'd worked with Gabe? But Gabe was sheriff's office and Claire Tollison was city police. Either way, she seemed nice and slightly less scary than Anissa at the moment.

"What a mess, Anissa," she said. "I'm sure you're dying to get out of that dress. Let me get an evidence bag. And some scissors. Because there's no way you want to pull that over your head."

Anissa blew out an exaggerated sigh. "Good point."

Claire disappeared, but her voice carried as she assigned officers to secure the perimeter of the store, clear the building, guard the room, and find her some scissors.

Anissa leaned against the wall. She still had her weapon drawn, but she didn't have it aimed at the door anymore.

"Where are they?" Adam's question broke through the murmurs of the others.

"We're coming in, Bell," Gabe called. "Don't shoot us."

Sabrina stepped out of the corner as Adam rushed through the door. "Bri." He climbed over the dead body without giving it a look. His eyes raked over her. There was nothing suggestive about it. He was clearly looking for injuries. Making sure for himself that she was okay. He took her face in his hands and his lips found hers for just a moment. "I'm so glad you're okay."

All the fear and terror and confusion swept over her afresh and she clung to him. "I don't understand what's happening," she said.

"Me neither. But we'll figure it out."

After the fiasco on Monday, he'd made sure Juan stayed as close as he could get to Sabrina. An effort complicated by the constant presence of police officers.

Juan was an idiot. If he'd been more efficient on Monday, they wouldn't be dealing with this issue.

But Juan had made a friend at the university and that friend had overheard the conversation. Sabrina was going dress shopping.

It had been a hurried plan, but it was a good one. It would work.

And now Juan was inside with orders to finish the job.

He should have left Juan to do the work alone, but he hadn't been able to resist being nearby.

He'd seen her go in. Now he waited for her to come out.

He'd been listening to the police scanner for the last hour. Nothing but the usual midsize city drama.

How he wanted to be away from it all.

Soon.

So soon.

Years of cultivating the right relationships. Hours spent smiling at people across the table when what he really wanted to do was jam a steak knife in their eye.

Not that he ever had. He knew who he was and what he wanted. He had no bloodlust of his own. No desire to watch the life leave an enemy. No compulsion to make anyone suffer.

But if someone wanted to kill and it helped him achieve his goals at the same time? Well, that was fine with him.

The radio chatter picked up. This was it.

He sat straighter in the seat of his car. He could almost feel the tropical breeze on his cheek. The sand under his feet. The chill of the drink in his hand.

Multiple units responding? Shots fired?

Excellent.

He closed his eyes. He could taste the saltwater on his tongue. Smell the coconut oil warming on his skin.

He deserved this. All the years he'd fixed everyone else's messes. Now it was his turn to relax.

His turn to let someone else deal—

The siren jolted him out of his fantasy.

The Carrington Police had responded far more quickly than he'd expected. Kudos to them.

He got out of his car. He couldn't resist the opportunity to hear what was happening up close.

252

He walked along the perimeter of the mall. If anyone noticed him, it would look like he was looking for his car.

"What happened, officer?" a young woman asked from the sidewalk.

"I can't say," he said. "Please go on to your vehicle and leave the premises."

"Do you think the mall will reopen tonight? I needed some earrings."

A woman leaving the mall paused. "Honey, some guy got shot. Tried to kill a girl in the dressing room." Her words were hushed. "No way they'll be reopening tonight. It would be best for you to go on home."

"Is that true?" the young woman asked the officer.

He didn't deny it. "I'd recommend you go home, miss."

How was this possible? Sabrina didn't carry a weapon. And he'd given clear instructions to Juan to be sure the officer with her was out of commission before he tried anything.

He took the long way back to his car. But he no longer could risk her coming out and seeing him.

He was on the interstate before he screamed. "No!"

It was midnight before they finally pulled into Leigh's driveway.

Leigh was working and Ryan was on niece and nephew duty tonight, but Leigh had insisted they stay at her house again.

Gabe and Anissa had ridden in the front seats. "Wait here." Gabe handed the keys to Adam. He and Anissa entered Leigh's home with their weapons drawn.

Sabrina huddled against Adam.

"It's a precaution," he told her. "You're safe."

"If you believed that, you wouldn't be sitting here coiled tight and ready to spring."

253

She might have him there. "I almost lost you tonight. I'm not inclined to take any chances."

"I'm not complaining," she said.

Lights flicked on through the house as Gabe and Anissa checked every room. Gabe reappeared at the door and waved them in. "Let's get inside," he said.

Gabe held the door for them. Anissa waited inside. She walked straight to Sabrina and put her hands on Sabrina's arms. "You need to sleep."

Sabrina shook her head.

"At least go take a shower. That's where I'm headed. Let's wash as much of this night off as we can."

"Okay." Sabrina allowed Anissa to lead her up the stairs. When she disappeared into her room, Gabe turned to him.

"We have a problem."

"Tell me about it."

They walked into the kitchen. Leigh always had a supply of goodies and tonight was no exception. Fresh-baked red velvet cupcakes awaited them along with a note that she'd prepped the coffeepot with decaf and all they had to do was turn it on if they wanted some.

Gabe hit the power button and inhaled a cupcake in three bites.

"Is Anissa okay?" Adam pulled the paper off his cupcake.

"She's ticked."

"Has she ever—?"

"No."

Adam's heart sank. It was a common misconception that police officers shot perpetrators several times a year. The reality was that most of them made it through their entire careers without ever having to fire their weapon at a suspect. Even fewer ever actually killed anyone.

Gabe grabbed the cream from the fridge. "How does Sabrina take her coffee?"

"Black."

"Think we should wait for them?" Gabe helped himself to another cupcake.

"No. My guess is they may be a while. It's gonna take more than one shower to wash that away."

"True."

They waited for the coffee to brew, then poured their own cups and settled at the kitchen counter. "What are you thinking?" Adam had his own thoughts, but he wanted Gabe's insights. Gabe had worked undercover for years, and he had a better understanding of the criminal mind-set than Adam would ever have.

"I think we're missing something. Someone thinks Sabrina is a threat. They have specifically gone after her. Twice. We need to find out who the dead guy is and how he was connected to her."

"You're assuming he wasn't just hired to do a job."

"It's possible he was, but that's the other thing that doesn't make sense. Both attempts were up close and personal."

"What do you mean?"

"The first attempt was hands-on. He got in her path and wrestled with her. And after she was knocked out, he could have used a gun to kill her quickly and still gotten away, but he didn't. It makes me wonder if his first choice was to kill her with his own bare hands."

Adam couldn't stop the shudder that rippled through him. "But he didn't have any trouble using a gun tonight."

"True, but even there, he was going for a close-range shot. And we saw what happened. There's blood and brain all over the place. You can't avoid it."

Adam got the point. "Someone didn't mind the mess."

"Which makes them either a professional, which is unlikely because they would have done a better job if it, or we're dealing with someone who wants some vengeance. For something." Gabe took a sip of his coffee. "Hard to imagine she could make anyone that mad."

"I can't think of any cases she's worked for us that would generate this kind of response, but she works for departments all over the country. I don't know the details of those."

"Tomorrow you need to get the details, and you need to get more intrusive into her personal life." Gabe gave Adam a meaningful look. "She's not going to like it."

"Not going to like what?" Anissa entered the kitchen. Hair wet. Face scrubbed.

Gabe slid a coffee cup toward her. She nodded a thank-you and poured a cup.

"Someone's targeting Sabrina," he said. "We're going to have to get all up in her business."

"Beats the alternative." Anissa reached for a cupcake. "How many of these did you eat?"

Gabe was the picture of innocence.

"Don't look at me." Adam lifted one finger. "I've had one."

She broke off the bottom of her cupcake and crammed it on the top, sandwiching the icing in the middle.

"You're weird." Gabe handed her a napkin.

"Coming from you, I'll take that as a compliment."

"That's how I meant it."

She took a huge bite and Adam gave her a chance to swallow before asking, "How is she?"

"Shaken. Scared. Afraid for you. For all of us. Confused. Questioning. She's reacting exactly the way you'd expect anyone to be in her case. Except for the part where she's smarter than any of us so her mind is spiraling multiple steps out from where we are now. She's got moves and countermoves in her head, but she can't get a handle on what triggered these attacks. She says she has no idea who would be doing this or why."

They sat with their cupcakes and thoughts. Gabe got up and poured everyone another cup of coffee.

Still no Sabrina.

"Should I go check on her?" Adam asked Anissa.

"Give her a few more minutes. She's had a hard night."

"So have you," Gabe said.

Anissa traced the rim of her coffee cup. "I was doing my job. I'm trained for this. She isn't."

"Okay." Gabe didn't seem to want to press her any further tonight, but the look he gave Adam told him he didn't believe her either.

Anissa was officially on administrative leave pending the outcome of both an internal and external investigation into tonight's shooting. The outcome wasn't in question, but it didn't change the fact that she'd had to leave her badge and her weapon at the office. The weapon she had with her now was her personal one. And given the events of the evening, she was unlikely to be without it for a while.

She'd probably be able to return to work by Monday, but she'd be on desk duty for at least six weeks. And she was looking at mandatory psych evals and counseling.

It seemed like a good time to change the subject. "So when did Claire say she'd have something for us?" Adam asked.

"Possibly tomorrow, but it could be Saturday," Gabe answered. "It depends on when they get to the autopsy. But do you think the autopsy is going to tell us anything? We already know how he died."

Anissa flinched at Gabe's remark. Adam was pretty sure Gabe noticed, but he was trying not to let on. "Claire will be using everything else—fingerprints, DNA, personal effects, facial recognition, surveillance cameras—to try to figure out who this guy is."

"I'd like to think we can trust her to keep us in the loop. Can we?" Adam reached for another cupcake.

"Yes," Gabe said. "I worked an undercover case with her— joint task force between the city, county, and state. She's solid. And she's not the type that needs recognition. She just wants to stop the bad guys."

"So tomorrow we find out who our bad guy was, and then—"

"We figure out why he tried to kill me." Sabrina spoke from the edge of the kitchen.

"That's the plan," Gabe said. "Cupcake?"

"I'm not hungry, but thanks."

"Eat a cupcake, Sabrina." Anissa pulled one off the platter and set it on a small paper plate. "Trust me. You'll feel better."

"I'm not sure about that." Sabrina slid onto the barstool beside Adam. Gabe poured a cup of coffee and set it beside her. "Thanks."

She pulled the paper from the cupcake and set it on the plate. Then she tackled it with one of the forks Leigh had left out for them. For someone who wasn't hungry, she made awfully short work of it and reached for another. "How's Pete?" she asked.

Gabe muttered something under his breath and Anissa elbowed him. "It wasn't his fault, Gabe." She turned to Sabrina. "He's fine. Just mad."

"What happened?" Sabrina took another bite of cupcake.

"He's having a hard time piecing it together," Anissa said, "so Claire's going to get the security footage from the store. The last thing he remembers was a teenage boy running straight at him. Pete was in plain clothes, so the kid didn't know he was a cop. He said the kid wasn't that big, so he figured he'd be able to tackle him with no problem. And it wasn't a problem. Except for the part where we found him propped against the wall asleep—and struggled to wake him up. He was drugged somehow. We just aren't sure of the specifics."

"Poor Pete." She wiped her mouth with a napkin and looked up. "I know I stink at reading body language, but you three are about as subtle as a Fourth of July fireworks show. What aren't you telling me?"

Gabe laughed. Anissa smiled. But both of them looked at Adam for the response. "We aren't keeping anything specific from you.

But tomorrow we're going to need to dig into your past. Your parents, your college professors, your students, your cases. Somewhere there's someone who is very unhappy with you."

"Great. I'm sure I'll sleep like the righteous with that to look forward to."

"Sorry," Anissa whispered.

"Don't be." She stood and put her now-empty coffee cup in the dishwasher. "I'm going to bed. You guys can interrogate me in the morning. Good night." She smiled at all of them and hurried out of the kitchen.

"Aren't you going to follow her?" Anissa asked Adam.

"No. I think she needs some space."

"I agree." Gabe dumped his coffee down the drain. "Let's reconvene in the morning. Who knows? Maybe our subconsciouses will make some sense out of things as we sleep."

"Or not."

Two hours later, Adam's phone rang.

"Campbell."

"Sorry to wake you, Adam."

It took Adam's sleep-fogged brain a few seconds to process the voice, but once it did, he jumped to his feet and grabbed his weapon. "Lane, what's wrong?" Lane Edwards was on patrol outside the house tonight. The last thing Adam had done before turning in was to make Lane promise to call him if anything suspicious happened.

"Nothing's wrong, but I thought you might want to know that you are, or were, the only one asleep in the house."

"What do you mean?"

"Dr. Fleming is in the dining room with a laptop. She's been in there for about thirty minutes. And Gabe and Anissa are having a . . . um . . . conversation. On the dock."

Conversation? "What exactly are Gabe and Anissa doing?" Were they—no. They didn't even like each other.

"I don't want to get in the middle of it," Lane said. "Anissa's my dive team captain."

"She's mine too. And Gabe's. So what's going on?"

"I think she might've had a nightmare. She was on the porch, and I think she'd been crying. When I came around on my patrol, she told me she'd be on the dock and to leave her alone. The next time I came around, Gabe was with her. I think he's trying to help her process everything from tonight, but I'm not going close enough to find out, and I don't recommend you do either."

"Good idea."

He hung up the phone and made his way up the stairs, pausing when he caught sight of Sabrina. Her hair was pulled up in its usual messy twist thing. Her glasses were on the end of her nose. She had a bottle of water beside her, but it was unopened. She was sitting at the dining room table and she had three notepads—two on one side of the computer and one on the other.

"I can see you, Adam." She didn't look up. "Go back to sleep."

"Not gonna happen."

"There's no sense in none of us sleeping. At the rate we're going, you may be the only one fit for duty tomorrow."

He stepped into the dining room. "What are you working on?"

She still didn't look up. "I'm making a list of everyone who would want to kill me."

He glanced at the notepads. All but one of them were empty. He couldn't quite read the one word she'd written.

"How's that going?"

"It's not a long list." She shuddered. Was she cold? Or was it the idea of whoever had made it onto the list that frightened her?

He leaned against a chair. "Care to tell me who you've eliminated?"

"Almost everyone I know."

"That's good."

She continued to stare at her monitor with unseeing eyes.

"Are you willing to tell me who made the list?"

260

She blinked several times before turning to focus on him. When she did, the pain and confusion in her eyes pulled him toward her like a black hole. He knelt beside her and put an arm around her. "Bri? What's wrong?"

"I can only think of one person." She tapped the paper.

He slid the notepad toward him and read the one word she'd written.

Mom.

20

I f Adam was shocked, he didn't show it.

"Can you tell me why you put her on the list?"

"A lot of little things. A lot of big things. The main big one is that I suspect that she held a human being as a slave for a decade. That's not something she would want to be publicly known. And of course there's the fact that, other than a few charities, she's the beneficiary of almost everything I have or will have when I turn thirty. If she kills me now, she gets it all."

"Those are strong motives."

"That's why she's on the list and why I'm about to get all up in her business." How she dreaded it. What else might she find?

Adam's forehead wrinkled. "I don't want you to have to dig into her life. I'll do it. First thing tomorrow."

"I can do it." She couldn't shove this off on anyone else.

"I know." He reached for her laptop and gently closed the lid. "But that doesn't mean you should. Anything you find out about her could be considered invalid if we wind up going to trial."

"Not when I'm the expert."

"Exactly. You're the expert. And as the expert, we need you to stay on Lisa Palmer's case. I can't help as much with that. I can help with this."

He took her hand and pulled her to her feet. "You need to sleep."

"I can't. I keep hearing the gun—" She would be hearing that *pop-pop* for the rest of her life. "I can even smell it. Smell him."

"Then I'll stay with you." He led her into the living room and set a pillow on one end of the sofa.

She sat on the edge as he walked to a basket by the fireplace. She would humor him for a few minutes and then she would get back to work.

He returned with a blanket. "Please. At least try."

She rested her head on the pillow and he tucked the blanket around her. He planted a light peck on her forehead. "Go to sleep, Bri. I'll be right here."

She thought he might sit at her feet, but instead he grabbed a pillow, tossed it on the floor near her head, and took a seat.

He must have taken a shower before he went to bed because she could smell his shampoo. Not anything overpowering, but enough that it drove the scent of bullets and death away. She studied the back of his neck, his shoulders. He wasn't leaning back against the sofa, but instead he had his arms draped around his knees.

She wondered why until she caught the outline of the bandage through his T-shirt. "Does your back still hurt?"

"Not too much," he said. "Leigh's probably going to take the bandage off tomorrow. I mostly notice it when I lie down. I'm a side sleeper, so it hasn't been too bad."

"Good." She was losing the battle with consciousness, but she was terrified of what was waiting for her in her sleep.

"Bri, I'm praying for you. Right now. Go to sleep, babe."

And she did.

When she woke Friday morning, he was asleep on the floor beside her. That didn't surprise her, but the sight of Anissa in the recliner and Gabe in the oversized chair did. Maybe she wasn't the only one who'd been having nightmares.

Except . . . she hadn't. At least, she didn't think she had. She checked her watch. Six thirty. The darkness outside was fading.

Motion on the deck caught her eye. She almost reached for Adam but relaxed when she recognized the figure of Lane pacing back and forth. He seemed like a good guy. Young. Eager. Kind.

Father, protect him as he protects me. Protect all of them. Show me what to do. Help me see beyond my fears and insecurities to what is the truth of this situation. Help us free the captives. And help me accept whatever I must face in the days ahead. Help me remember you love the fatherless and the orphans. That even when our parents abandon and desert us, you never will. Help me to be able to forgive as you forgave, because there is no way I'll be able to do that on my own.

Adam stirred on the floor. His eyes fluttered open and found hers. "Hey," he whispered. "How did you sleep?"

"Fine. I think."

His sleepy smile was quite possibly the most attractive thing she had ever seen, and she had to force herself to stay on the sofa. "I fell asleep too. I woke up when Gabe and Anissa came in, but then I crashed."

"Came in?" Where had they gone?

"Long story. I'll explain later."

He rolled into a sitting position and rested his chin on the sofa inches from her. "You're beautiful."

She could feel the blush spreading all over her body. If he thought she was beautiful first thing in the morning, then he was delusional. Not that she minded this type of delusion.

"I'll make us some coffee," he said. "It's going to be a long day."

He wasn't kidding. She'd gotten to her lab by eight thirty, which given the amount of security Adam, Gabe, and Anissa had insisted on, was a small miracle. She still had Dave on the inside, which was quite comforting. But he wasn't alone. He'd been joined by someone named Evan. Outside the lab were two more officers whose names she'd not heard. And then, as if it wasn't crazy enough around there, they'd called Tyler from campus security. He was circling the building every three minutes.

She was not going to be able to live like this. And she had one huge problem.

She still didn't have a dress.

The gala was tonight. Why they held the gala on a Friday night was a mystery to her, although apparently it had been that way forever and no one was willing to change it.

She'd tried to get out of it. She'd volunteered to stay at Leigh's, barricaded behind closed doors with a phalanx of officers patrolling the house, but no one had liked her plan.

"Sabrina, we have tons of security at the gala. You'll be safer there than anywhere else," Gabe said.

"We'll have your back," Anissa said.

Anissa was still going with Gabe. Since they were volunteering their services and weren't technically there on official police business, the captain had agreed to it.

"I would never consider having you there if I thought you'd be in danger," Adam said. "You'll be with me all night. Gabe and Anissa will stay close. We've reviewed the list of officers providing security and they're all great. Plus we're going to add a few others of our own that The Porterhouse staff won't know about."

She still didn't know if it was a good idea.

Her phone buzzed. Leigh. She held on tight because Leigh was going to be a mess. "Hello."

"I have so many things I want to say right now." Leigh's voice quavered. "But Anissa told me to stay focused. You need a dress and I can help you."

"I wouldn't be able to wear anything of yours." Leigh was at least four inches shorter than Sabrina. And probably a size two.

"I'm not talking about my clothes. Don't stress about it. Come to my house at two o'clock. We'll make it happen."

This made absolutely no sense, but Leigh was very hard to argue with. "Fine."

"Sabrina?"

"Yes."

"I'm glad you're okay."

"Thanks."

She heard Leigh sniff as she disconnected the call, but she couldn't dwell on it. The last thing she needed was to start crying.

She poured herself into her methodical search of Lisa Palmer's hard drive. When she found a file that looked promising, she sent it to Mike. Mostly she found a lot of stuff that had zero relevance to this case.

She worked through lunch. There had to be more there. Finally, around one o'clock she pulled up a few files that seemed out of place. Lots of receipts from the same restaurant. There had to be something significant about it. She'd gotten so focused that she jumped when her phone rang.

It was Adam.

"Hey." She filled him in on what she'd found, but he cut her off.

"This sounds like a promising lead and we can talk about it more tomorrow, but don't you have somewhere to be?"

She looked at her watch. It read 1:45.

"Yikes!" She put the phone on speaker as she raced around her office making sure everything was secure before she left. "Adam?"

"Yes?"

"If Leigh can't find me a dress . . ."

"I told you I didn't care if you wear jeans and a T-shirt."

"I'm not wearing jeans." She hadn't meant to snap at him, but she kind of had.

"Okay." He was backpedaling fast. "But I know you own some lovely dresses. You could wear something you've worn to a fundraiser. It doesn't have to come to the floor or be something you've never worn before."

He had a point. Although she'd rather hear the assurance from a girl. Guys didn't pay attention to anything like that.

"Sabrina, you're going to be the most beautiful woman there just by walking in the door. Please don't stress about the window dressing. I certainly won't be."

"I wish I had your confidence."

"If you don't have it for yourself, then have it in me. I would never put you in a situation that would embarrass you."

He was worried about embarrassing *her*? That was crazy. She was worried about embarrassing *him*.

"You'll be fine. More than fine. You'll be great."

"Okay."

"Sabrina?"

"Yes?"

"I'll pick you up at six."

This was crazy. Completely and utterly crazy.

Adam had spent most of the past two days working with the captain, Ryan, Gabe, and the two human trafficking investigators they had on staff. No one else was being brought in. No warrants had been requested, although everyone was in agreement about which judge they would ask.

They'd come up with a dozen different scenarios for what they would do if they found any evidence of victims on the property at The Porterhouse. The human trafficking investigators had been added to the security detail and assigned to the kitchen. The hope was that they would be able to spot any signs that the workers were victims of labor trafficking, and in a best-case scenario they might be able to talk to a few of them and find out where they lived, where they were from, and where their families were. The kinds of questions it would be natural to bring up in conversation but that could be vital to their investigation.

It was already midafternoon on Friday before Adam had a chance to dive into the life of Sabrina's mother, Yvonne Fleming.

Yvonne Fleming wasn't a nice person. He'd found posts on social media from irate employees—former employees—all of them claiming she expected perfection from mere mortals. That no one could live up to the high standards she set. One hypothesized that she was an alien. Another that she was the world's only living survivor of a heartectomy.

Bottom line—she was hard to work for and a lot of people hated her for it.

But YTT Healthcare was a publicly owned health-care system, and the stockholders loved her. She ran a tight ship. She expected the best of her employees and anyone who contracted to do work for YTT. She'd successfully sued at least three different companies for breach of contract when they failed to meet her requirements.

Bottom line—she was hard to work for and a lot of people loved her for it.

Just like hundreds of other executives all over the country.

There had never been a hint of impropriety. And it wasn't because people hadn't looked for it. They just couldn't find it. Her taxes were paid in full and on time. YTT had a reputation for meeting and exceeding regulations. In fact, one sure way to get fired was to have your department fail an inspection.

She had a zero-tolerance policy for mistakes.

Adam tried to imagine how Sabrina had come from a woman like this. He'd seen Sabrina with her students. She was demanding and firm, but she tempered that with grace and kindness. She made her students clean their lab so the cleaning crew wouldn't have much to do. The one time he'd heard her get upset with a group of students was when they left a mess and made the comment that the janitors would take care of it. Her wrath had been somewhat beautiful to behold. And those kids had learned a good lesson. But she hadn't kicked them out of her program.

She picked up trash off the street.

She bussed her own table at restaurants.

She overtipped for everything.

Sabrina was as unlike Yvonne as it was possible for her to be.

But Adam couldn't find anything that would cause Yvonne to want to kill Sabrina. And Yvonne had been on a tour of YTT facilities over the past three weeks. She'd been in a different location every few days. Lots of flights. Lots of hotel rooms.

For someone who liked everything done efficiently and tolerated no error, she didn't seem to be managing this "kill Sabrina" mission well at all.

Which made him wonder if she had anything to do with it.

Yvonne had a new boyfriend. A lawyer named Ezekiel Kemp. Did Sabrina know anything about him?

Somehow he doubted it, but he wasn't going to mention it tonight. It could wait until tomorrow.

"You ready for tonight?" Gabe leaned against Adam's desk.

"Ready as we'll ever be. Ryan checked with his sister about babysitting her kids. Rebecca promised she'd be home no later than ten. He'll come straight here and be available for whatever we need."

"Good. I have a feeling we'll need him. I'll feel better knowing he's got our back."

Gabe's remark struck a nerve. "Are we doing the right thing, Gabe? Should we try to build a huge team and work it from every angle?"

Gabe didn't respond with some glib remark. He stared out the windows and chewed on his lip. "I'm all for cutting off the head," he said. "But this isn't drug trafficking or money laundering. This is slavery. If we can free them tonight? This weekend? Versus the months of posturing and planning we'd be dealing with if we waited on a task force, then I'm all for getting whatever limb we can reach now. Some of these traffickers are weak. They aren't hardened criminals. They're evil, but they're marshmallows. We squeeze hard enough, and they'll be fighting each other for who can be the first to turn on the rest of the organization."

He slapped the desk. "So chop-chop, pretty boy. Time to get fancy and go catch the bad guys."

At six o'clock, Adam Campbell was sweating.

He rubbed his hands on the pants of his tuxedo and knocked on Leigh's door. Anissa opened the door and she was . . . stunning. "Wow."

She smiled. "Thank you. But you ain't seen nothing yet." She stepped to the side and he entered the house. "She'll be down in a second."

Gabe was standing in the living room and Anissa went to him. "Quit complaining," she said as she helped him adjust the holster that would hold his weapon at his side. "I can assure you this is more comfortable than the one I'm wearing."

Adam tried not to think about where that might be. Her black dress had a high collar, no sleeves, and fit tight to the waist. No way she had a weapon concealed in that area. The dress flowed from her waist and was a little bit shorter in the front than in the back. Not that he had personal experience, but it seemed like the perfect dress for someone who might need to be able to go into "cop mode" in a hurry.

She helped Gabe put his jacket on, then turned him around to face Adam. "Can you tell we're armed to the teeth?"

"You both look fabulous. You'll blend in beautifully. Thank you."

Gabe's eyes were fixed on the stairs. "She, however, will not

270

blend in at all." He winked at Adam and offered his arm to Anissa. "Let's give them a moment, shall we?"

Adam turned to the stairs. And tried to remember how to breathe.

Sabrina descended and came all the way to him before he regained his ability to speak. Even then, all he managed was "You . . ."

"It's not too much?"

He shook his head. "Definitely not."

Her gown was green. That much he was sure of. And it fit her perfectly. He thought it might be satin. Or silk? It went to the floor. And had a top that kind of wrapped around her shoulders.

She had on high heels. He couldn't see them, but her face didn't usually come this close to his when they talked.

Her hair was up, but little curls framed her face in a most alluring way.

"Leigh found it. It's about fifty years old. You don't think it will matter? That it isn't new?"

Was she seriously concerned about this? "There's nothing to worry about there. I may refuse to let anyone else dance with you for fear they will attempt to steal you away."

She laughed. "There's nothing to worry about there. I'm not available for stealing. And neither, might I add, are you." Her eyes held his and he couldn't help but wonder what she saw. He barely even knew what he was feeling. Joy. Desire. Those were the only two he could articulate, but there was a vast sea of emotion he didn't know how to access right now.

He leaned forward to claim her lips. He released her far sooner than he wanted to. "Ready?"

"Not even a little bit." She rubbed his lips with her thumb. He hadn't thought about the damage he might do to her lipstick.

"Sorry," he whispered.

"Don't be."

Leigh came down the stairs in her scrubs. "Thank you," he said.

She grinned with obvious delight. "I've had so much fun. I know you'll have a blast. I hope you catch the bad guys while you're at it. But I don't want to see any of you until tomorrow. Got it?"

Anissa and Gabe reentered the room.

"That goes double for Gabe," she said. "Be safe tonight."

"Yes, Mom," Gabe said with a laugh.

They said their goodbyes, and Adam ushered Sabrina to the waiting limousine. Gabe and Anissa climbed into Adam's Audi. "You'd better be careful, Chavez."

Adam slid into the seat of the limousine beside Sabrina. "I usually despise limos," he said. "But I'm beginning to see their advantages." He made sure the window between them and the driver was up. "Are you okay about tonight? Have everything you need?"

Even in the dim light of the back seat he could see the look of barely suppressed terror on her face.

Maybe if he could get her distracted she wouldn't be so nervous. "I want to hear all about this afternoon," he said. "Leigh must have been in her element, getting to play real-life dress up."

Sabrina's eyes widened. "She was like a kid with a new set of dolls. And Anissa—I didn't know she was such a whiz with hair. She's a pro. Although she did tell me if that got out it would ruin her reputation so to please not tell anyone. But I assumed she didn't mean you."

She seemed more relaxed and they talked the rest of the way to The Porterhouse, but as the limousine rolled to a stop by the long red carpet out front, he could almost feel the stress enveloping Sabrina like a fog.

"Hey." Adam rubbed her hand with his. "First, because I'm on the board, we're some of the earliest to arrive, so you don't have to worry about walking through a throng of people. And second, Gabe and Anissa will be coming in right behind us, so you'll have familiar faces from the beginning."

She blew out a breath like she was trying to cool off a hot chocolate.

Her eyes met his. "Do not leave me alone."

"Never."

He climbed from the limo, then reached for her. She slid out beside him and he got a good look at the heels she was wearing. Good grief. Those things were deadly weapons of their own. Would she still be able to walk in them by the end of the evening?

"Nice shoes," he whispered as they walked inside.

"Thanks. They're equipped with GPS tracking and an emergency flare. I think they technically belong to the sheriff's office. Anissa brought them to me and told me not to ask questions."

She grinned at him as the doors opened and they walked inside. He had no idea what sort of stunned expression was on his face when his mother's voice broke through his shock.

"Adam. Sabrina. How lovely to see you both. Come."

The next thirty minutes were a whirl of activity. And it had been far easier than he'd expected to keep his promise not to leave Sabrina alone. She'd introduced him to her friend Martine and others who had volunteered countless hours to this event. Then he'd introduced her to each of the other board members and to the gala committee members. Sabrina stood by his side, smiling and nodding, occasionally chiming in or making a kind observation about someone's dress or a particular decoration.

If she'd been trying to run for "woman most likely to impress his mother," she was doing a great job. But she wasn't. She was just being herself, and he adored her all the more for it.

Gabe and Anissa had made a round of the location and had spoken to the security personnel—hopefully there wouldn't be any tension between them. And Leigh had unexpectedly shown up outside with all of their heavy coats in her car. Bless her.

He wasn't surprised he'd forgotten the coats after he'd seen Sabrina. He'd forgotten how to speak. The only reason he'd kept breathing was because his brain kept all that stuff going for him without conscious thought.

The guests began to arrive—first in a slow trickle, then a steady stream. He made it a point to speak to everyone he could and introduced Sabrina to all of them.

As the evening progressed, her mental acuity floored him. She forgot no one. Not a single name or occupation. She nodded, smiled, and spoke to people in lines and on the dance floor.

"She's amazing." Adam's mom tugged on his elbow. "But I'm not going to give up my dance."

On cue, Adam's father emerged from the crowd. "Dr. Fleming, would you do me the honor of sharing this dance with me?"

Her eyes sought Adam's. She was nervous, but pleased.

"If you take my girl, then I'm taking yours."

His dad laughed. "Fair enough."

His mom was laughing as he spun her onto the dance floor. "You've been the talk of the room tonight." She smiled at him. "I've been accosted by no less than five irate mothers wanting to know where she came from."

"I think you're enjoying this a little too much."

"I think I'm enjoying it exactly the right amount." She winked at him. "You two make a striking couple. Where on earth did she find that exquisite dress on such short notice?"

"Leigh found it."

"It's perfect. A little vintage—nothing like anything off the rack. No one around here is wearing anything like it. And the green is a stroke of genius. It's the perfect color for her skin tone and her eyes. But I have to tell you, I'm more impressed with her poise. If she's nervous, it isn't showing."

"She is."

"Then you need to get her out of here."

"You just said she was doing great. Why—"

"To give her a break."

274

Oh.

"She could probably use some fresh air. Grab those coats Leigh brought for you and go for a walk along the promenade by the lake. Give her a few minutes to let down her guard. Steal a kiss or three."

"Mom!"

She squeezed his arms tight. "I love seeing you happy, dear. I can't help it."

"Thanks." He pecked his mom's cheek. "You're the best."

He scanned the crowd. His father and Sabrina were easy to spot. They appeared to be deep in conversation. He danced his mom in their direction. "Adam?" His mom's voice had lost all its earlier jollity. "I know what you're up to. Be careful tonight."

"We will."

21

A rt Campbell was an excellent dancer.

"I taught Adam everything he knows." He paused. "Except for the law enforcement stuff. I didn't teach him any of that."

A couple brushed against them and Sabrina made eye contact with the woman. "Art, do you know those people?"

He rolled his eyes. "You mean the woman who's been trying to murder you with her glares for the past hour?"

"Has it been that long?"

"Yes, but I'm glad you hadn't noticed."

"Well, I have now."

"Her name is Tasha. Her family and ours have been friends for a long time, and I'm afraid she's always had designs on Adam."

"Huh."

"But Adam never liked her. When they were seven, she accused Alexander of doing something both boys insisted Alex was innocent of. I think if she'd blamed Adam, he would have handled it better, but he couldn't tolerate her trying to get his brother in trouble. He's always had a protective streak. Always been a warrior. We tried to offer him other options, but none of them

276

stuck. For a long time he talked about going into the military, but I think he's always been most interested in protecting those close to home."

"It must be hard for you," she said.

"It is. I pray. A lot. We never took church attendance seriously when the boys were younger. We went, but it was more about social propriety. Keeping my mother happy. But after we lost our Aaron . . ." He gave her a grim smile. "A lot of things changed. Adam changed. He's more serious about God than any of the rest of us these days."

"His faith is important to him."

"It is. And I respect that. But I can't lie to you. If his mother loses another child, I'm not sure there's enough faith in any of us to survive it."

"Obviously I don't want you to ever have to find out," Sabrina said, "but in my experience, it's not about how big our faith is. What matters is how big our God is."

He cocked his head and seemed to be considering her words. "I'm not sure that isn't just semantics."

"And I'm sure it's about so much more than semantics. If you're worried about having enough faith, then you're putting faith in yourself and of course you can fail. But when you keep the focus on the God you believe in, then everything changes. He's big enough for all our doubts, fears, and questions. He's big enough for our anger and our pain."

"But sometimes he allows awful things."

"He does." Sabrina glanced around the room. Servers were everywhere. Were they having this conversation in a room where evil was on display? "But that's when we have to remember that he's bigger than we are. His thoughts are above our thoughts. His ways are above our ways. And if he has allowed something awful, there's a purpose that's beyond anything we can imagine."

"Do you really believe that?"

"Not every day." She might as well be honest. "I'm very intelligent. I often start thinking I know the best plan because I've
evaluated the plans on the table and chosen the one that makes
the most sense. Then when God doesn't do what I expected, or
what I think is best, I get mad."

"Sounds familiar."

"But when I do that, I'm proving I still think I know best. And
the truth is, it's entirely possible that I'd chosen the best scenario
of the three or four available to me. But God is infinite. He's eter-
nal. He looks at a situation and doesn't see three or four possible
paths to a solution. He sees thousands. And he can see that solution number five hundred eighty-two is best, and because he loves
me, he chooses not to allow me to have the solution I chose. Not
because I chose poorly, but because he's chosen the best."

Art shook his head. "I'm going to be chewing over this conversation for a while. I may have some more questions for you later."

"I'd love to hear them," she said. "An untested and unchallenged
faith is unproven. And the scientist in me likes to see things proven."

Art nodded at someone over his shoulder. "Adam and Abby
are heading this way. So I hope you'll forgive my abrupt change
of subject."

"Of course."

"You and Adam need to take a walk. Take Gabe and Anissa
with you. Go see if those cabins are still out there."

"Sir?"

"I've been watching the staff come and go tonight. I have a
suspicion and I don't like it. But if I go out there it will draw too
much attention. Two young couples in love out wandering the
property? You'd be able to get much farther than I."

"Art, I know Adam wouldn't want you to take that kind of risk.
Let him handle it."

"I will. You'll tell him?"

"Of course."

278

Adam and Abby danced beside them for the last few bars. As the song faded, they all clapped and Adam reclaimed her while Art pulled Abby toward him. "I was telling Sabrina they needed to get outside and enjoy this lovely evening," he told Abby.

"A fabulous idea," she said. "You kids go have fun. You can't make the tongues wag any more than they already are. Might as well make the most of it." She grabbed Adam's sleeve. "If you can get a photographer to catch you and Sabrina kissing, that will be the cherry on top of the evening."

"Mom!"

Art and Abby glided away.

"You okay?" Adam asked.

"Yes, but I need to talk to you. Outside?"

"Let's go."

She should have known it wouldn't be that easy. It took forty-five minutes for them to make their way to the coat check. She slid her arms into her jacket and walked with Adam out the side doors. "Your dad said we need to go around back and look for the cabins."

"What?"

"I know, but that's what he said. He said we should take Gabe and Anissa and—"

"And what?"

"Well, he didn't come right out and say it, but I believe he was thinking if we acted like we were trying to find a place to be alone we'd be able to get by with just about anything."

Adam didn't like it. She could tell by the way his mouth had pinched into a flat line. But he was considering it.

"Leave it to Dad to make a suggestion like this one," he said. He pulled his phone from his pocket and dialed. "Gabe, can you and Anissa come outside and stay close but not too close? I'll explain later."

A few nods and a couple of grunts and he slid the phone into his pocket. "They're on their way. Let's walk to the back fountain. Nothing about that will raise suspicions."

"You really know your way around this property, don't you?"

"Yeah. Sean Sullivan and I were good friends. We played all over this place. I've always had a soft spot for it."

"Why?"

"Maybe because it was one of the few places my family had no say over. Sean and I loved that people were surprised by our friendship. They assumed the Campbells and the Sullivans were like the Hatfields and McCoys, but we weren't. Our moms were good friends. Our dads got along. It was fun."

When they reached the fountain behind the hotel, Adam made a show of pointing out the various features farther and farther away. "Gabe and Anissa are back there," he said in a low voice.

"Now what?"

He pulled her into his arms and anyone watching would have assumed they were kissing. Instead he whispered, "If we follow along the far edge of this courtyard, there's a small door in the wall. If they're using it, it won't be hard to find or open. When we go through it, we'll need to stay close to the wall as long as possible. Are you up for it?"

"Of course."

"In those shoes?"

"I forgot to tell you the best part about these babies." She slipped out of her shoes and with a quick twist, removed the heels. She put her now-flat—and much more comfortable— sandals back on her feet and slid the heels into her pocket. "Now I'm ready."

He did kiss her then. Long enough that she almost forgot why they were out here.

Almost. But not quite.

When he grabbed her hand and took off toward the wall, she followed him without hesitation.

In the darkness, Adam went more by memory than sight.

It had been a couple of decades since he'd been back there, but it hadn't changed much.

And that bothered him. It should have changed. A lot.

No hotel stayed in business if they left things the same for twenty years.

He hoped anyone watching would assume he was looking for a place to be alone with Sabrina and would, out of courtesy, leave them alone.

They crept along the wall behind the bushes and there it was. The door was not only still there, but it also had new hardware and new hinges. But it wasn't locked.

He heard something coming from the other side and ducked down behind a bush, pulling Sabrina with him.

The door opened and two young Hispanic women emerged, both dressed in maid's uniforms. They were speaking in Spanish.

One of them asked the other how she was feeling. The other replied that she felt horrible and hoped someone got sick from being around her since the boss wouldn't let her stay in bed.

"Did you get all that?" Sabrina mouthed the question to him.

He nodded. He hadn't learned Spanish from infancy the way she had, but his parents had insisted he know how to communicate with everyone who worked for them. They'd also insisted he learn Latin and some Greek. Surprisingly enough, he'd used all of them since joining the sheriff's office.

His mother was rather smug about that.

Adam waited until the two women were completely out of sight before he approached the door again. If someone was on the other side, he and Sabrina would have to pretend they were looking for some privacy.

He opened the door and stepped through. Sabrina was right on his heels. He paused to get his bearings and then stepped behind a tree a few feet off the path. More voices floated toward them. As they watched, eight more people, six women and two men, emerged from the trees at the end of the field, walked up the path, and passed through the door and onto the hotel grounds.

Adam tried to determine if any security cameras were out there. Although . . . what you don't record can't be used against you later. Maybe they weren't worried about their employees—if that's what they were—leaving. And they'd probably never needed to worry about someone trying to break into this area.

At least not until tonight.

When it had been clear for several minutes, Adam found the path he'd used as a child. This path was inside the tree line and not as well marked as the one the workers had been using. But it did the job.

He kept walking. It didn't take long before the outline of the first cabin came into view. It didn't appear anyone was inside, but he could hear voices from farther down the path.

He and Sabrina slipped past the first cabin and the second appeared a few moments later. As he remembered them, they'd been out of sight of each other. Far enough apart for the illusion of privacy, but not so far apart that it was annoying for the staff when they were making the rounds between them.

A dim light glowed around the door frame. No lights showed in the windows. Were they blacked out?

It took them fifteen minutes to make the loop, and from what he could tell, people were living in at least eight of the twelve cabins. But there were still just the two bathhouses.

And they stank.

"We need to get back," he said. "People will get suspicious."

"But we haven't found anything," Sabrina said.

"We know those employees had to have come from here. And we know people are back here right now. And staying here often enough to wreck those bathhouses."

But she was right. They hadn't seen anyone enter or leave the houses.

A door opened and a young woman emerged. Alone. She glanced around and darted to one side of the house.

This was interesting.

While he was trying to come up with a plan, another figure darted past them, going in the same direction as the first. Over the next ten minutes, three more people emerged and went in the same direction.

Adam had texted Gabe after the second person, and he and Anissa had eyes on the small group.

Gabe texted Adam that it appeared they were all assembled and whatever meeting they were planning had begun. Gabe was going to get closer so he could try to listen in. Anissa had eyes on Gabe. Adam and Sabrina moved until Adam had eyes on Anissa.

It felt like an eternity, but it was only a few minutes before a text lit up his screen. "They're being trafficked. Lisa was going to help them. They're terrified. Trying to decide what to do."

Gabe moved back toward Anissa's position, and Adam and Sabrina met them there.

"Do we dare let them know they have friends?" Gabe asked.

"Maybe," Adam said. "But will they panic if we show ourselves?"

"Let me go." Sabrina was insistent. "I'm not a cop, so they may be willing to listen to me."

"What do you think?" Gabe directed the question to Anissa.

"Maybe if I go with her? My Spanish isn't as good as yours, but I'll be able to keep up."

Gabe considered it. "You don't look threatening, at the moment."

"I'm not threatening to them regardless," Anissa said.

"But they don't know that." Gabe had a good point.

"I don't know." Adam couldn't imagine sending Sabrina in there. Would these poor people believe them when they told them they could help? Or would they react in fear?

Sabrina grabbed Anissa's arm and walked in the direction of the group. She didn't try to be discreet or subtle. Instead, she went for the big reveal. She threw her head back and laughed.

Anissa didn't hesitate. She joined right in. "Can you believe it?" She practically screamed the words.

The clandestine group froze, then one of them stepped forward. "Excuse me," he said with a heavy accent. He pointed toward the main hotel. "Please," he said.

"Oh." Sabrina looked around in apparent astonishment. "My goodness. How did we get so far away?"

"*Por favor*," a young woman said. "*Por favor.*"

Those poor people were terrified. But now Anissa and Sabrina were right in the middle of them.

Sabrina leaned toward one of the young women and spoke in Spanish. "My name is Sabrina. I can help you."

The small group froze.

"We believe you're being held against your will. That you've been lied to. Mistreated. We can help you."

"Sweetheart," a young man spoke in English. "The last person who tried to help us is dead. She went to the cops and wound up in the lake."

"Lisa Palmer died before she could tell the police anything," Sabrina replied in Spanish. "I'm not a police officer, but I have Lisa's computer. I have her photographs. I've been trying to put together a case. That's how we found you tonight. And we can help you."

"They have our families," a young man said. "They aren't here. If we talk to you, they'll kill them. Or worse."

This was a wrinkle. If they freed these people tonight, would they be sentencing their loved ones to death?

"Do you have any idea where they are?" Sabrina asked.

"We've figured it out," one of the men said. "There's a rotation. They didn't realize when they put us all here that we'd be able to put it together. They think we're stupid."

284

"Can you tell me where the others are?"

Silence was the only answer Sabrina got this time.

"What if I make a few suggestions? Could you tell me if I am right?" Anissa asked.

No answer.

Anissa started with the big one. "Senator Carson."

Nothing at first, then slow nods.

"We've already got The Porterhouse and The Back Door."

More nods.

Anissa named the remaining locations from the photographs. "That's all we know," she said. "Are there more?"

This time they shook their heads no.

"If we could get search warrants. Tonight. For all of these places at once. Would you be willing to help us?"

The same young man who'd been worried about his family glared at Sabrina and Anissa. "I thought you said you weren't police."

"I'm not," Sabrina said, saving Anissa from answering. "But my friends are. They want to help. This"—she pointed around them—"is wrong. This isn't what America is about. This isn't what humanity is about."

"What do you need to know?" a woman asked.

Anissa took a small step toward her. "How many of you are there?"

"We don't know, but we guess around two hundred."

"Do they have your passports, your visas?" Anissa asked.

"They take our papers when we come. Make us work to pay off our debt." The young woman who spoke had a fire in her eyes. She was ready.

"Has anyone ever paid off their debt?" Sabrina's question seemed to surprise them.

Multiple people responded. "No."

The hardest thing Adam had ever done was walk away from

those people. Anissa had produced a burner phone from some mysterious pocket in her dress and they'd left it with the group, along with the promise that they would return.

They hurried back toward the hotel. Gabe called Ryan, whose babysitting duties had ended thirty minutes earlier.

Ryan went straight to the one judge they felt they could trust.

And Adam and Sabrina danced.

"Are we doing the right thing?" she whispered in his ear. After they'd made it back inside, they'd gone straight to the dance floor and blended in with the dancers. It felt like they'd been gone hours, but in fact it had been only one. The party was still in full swing. The senator was still there, chatting with Barclay Campbell. Surprise, surprise.

The owners of The Back Door had had a bit too much to drink and were singing along with the orchestra.

The owners of the spa were chatting with the owners of the cleaning company.

He'd never noticed how chummy they all were.

Adam made eye contact with his dad. One quick nod. He hoped his dad understood.

They danced number after number. They chatted and munched on canapés and tiny portions of shrimp and grits, and they tried not to let on how much their stomachs were churning. They smiled, nodded, and posed for photographs.

And still there was no phone call. No word. They switched partners with Gabe and Anissa so they could safely exchange information.

The knot in Adam's gut continued to grow. What if they'd made a mistake? What if the captain was in on it? What if the judge was in on it? What if it was about to end with all of them as fish food?

"Gabe says to tell you to relax. Ryan would have warned us if anything wasn't going as planned," Anissa said.

He twirled her away from him, then back to him. "I don't have his confidence."

"You don't have his experience. He says this judge is a crusader. The type that will take what we have and run with it."

"I hope he's right. Lives are quite literally at stake."

22

abe was fun to dance with, but Sabrina couldn't enjoy the experience. She waited until he'd pulled her close to his chest to continue grilling him. "But what if someone decides they want some task force to try to take down the big people at the top? We can't leave the ones we know are in slavery to suffer. I can't do that."

"I know."

"I talked to them, Gabe. I looked into their eyes. And in every one of them I saw Rosita. I wish someone had helped her. What if someone knew and did nothing because they wanted a bigger fish?"

"Judge Yates won't want a bigger fish." He seemed confident.

"How do you know?"

"Because sometimes the bigger fish isn't the most satisfying catch. And Judge Yates has one fish he's been after for a long time."

"And we're giving him that fish?"

"On a shiny, silver, too-many-years-of-jail-time-to-count platter."

That did seem like good motivation. "We're doing our part right now," he said. "This is as important as getting the warrants and running the raids. We've been planning this for two days, which isn't a long time, but it's long enough. Ryan knows what he's doing and I'm not going to lie—I'd love to be with him right now. But the longer we dance, the longer we keep the guilty parties partying, the better the odds of success. We don't want to lose lives because we wanted to be part of the action."

He was right. Annoyingly right.

"Look," he said. "Adam and Anissa are chatting it up with the man of the hour."

Sure enough, Adam and Anissa were deep in conversation with Barclay Campbell. She studied them as they talked. The way Anissa smiled. The way Adam nodded. Even knowing what she knew, she couldn't see any sign that they were faking it. They seemed to be enjoying the conversation.

"How do they do that?"

"Lots of practice." Gabe had been undercover for years.

"How did you do it?"

Gabe frowned.

"I'm sorry. That was an inappropriate question, wasn't it? I should've known." Dumb. Would she ever learn?

"It's fine," he said. "It's hard to explain. Usually it involves becoming another person. Like being a character actor. It wasn't me anymore. It was someone else."

He nodded toward Adam and Anissa. "In their case, it's about remembering the long-term goal. You remember you don't want the short-term satisfaction that would come from slugging him more than the long-term satisfaction of seeing him go to jail for what he's done."

"Is that enough?"

"Not for long, but it will get you by until you can get away from the creep."

That made her laugh.

She felt the vibration of a phone in Gabe's tux pocket. He winked at her and reached for the phone without missing a step.

"Chavez."

There was a pause. A smile flitted across his face. "Okay."

He put the phone back into his pocket. "Get ready, *señorita*. Things are about to get very interesting."

He danced them toward Adam and Anissa, who were back on the floor. They met in the middle, and in one fluid motion she found herself back in Adam's arms.

"Gabe says soon. Someone called him."

"Yes," he said. "Have you noticed the servers aren't coming back from the kitchen?"

She hadn't, but now that he mentioned it . . . where there had been ten or fifteen black-clad servers milling around at all times with platters of champagne and trays of finger foods, she didn't see one anywhere.

Oh, Father, please let them be safe. Let them all be safe.

Adam's phone buzzed. He glanced at it, then pulled her close so she could read it.

Rescues made from:

The kitchens and the shacks behind The Porterhouse - the staff there is helping us make sure everyone is accounted for.

Senator Carson's house

Gus Johnson's yacht

The Back Door was empty, but the staff is at The Porterhouse and all are accounted for.

The cleaning crews were at three different offices downtown. We have them all.

The h/t investigators have support staff coming from Raleigh.

The captain should be there any moment.

If everything went as planned, the Carrington County Sheriff's Office would be called in to seal the exterior doors. No one would be able to leave the gala tonight until they'd been cleared. And the big fish would be arrested on the spot.

Sabrina leaned against Adam. His arms tightened around her. "It's okay, Bri. They're free and they have advocates who will fight for them to be sure they're treated fairly. Why are you crying?"

Was she?

He pulled a handkerchief from his pocket and dabbed her face. She had to get control of her emotions. This was ridiculous.

But when the captain appeared at the edge of the dance floor, flanked by a handful of deputies on each side, and marched through the crowd straight to Senator Carson and Barclay Campbell, she couldn't stop a few more rogue tears from escaping.

There was no sleep for any of them that night.

Anissa couldn't do anything in an official capacity, but she stayed with Sabrina. Adam went to the sheriff's office with the others. Of course everyone who had been arrested lawyered up immediately, but the evidence was overwhelming. There were real, live people who'd been informed of their rights and who were more than happy to testify against their captors.

Some of the victims were so traumatized they wouldn't speak to anyone, but some of them had been ready for this for a while. They'd known it was wrong. They'd known there should be a way out, but they hadn't been able to figure out how to get out without endangering the others.

So they'd stayed.

Sabrina would never get over the level of sacrificial love on display in the face of depravity and inhumanity.

Art and Abby opened their own hotels—currently in the low season so not at capacity—to house the victims. Families were reunited. Husbands with wives. Mothers with sons. Fathers with daughters.

There were tears and laughter and rage and anger.

Because not everyone was enjoying the reunions. Ten women—three of whom didn't appear to be over sixteen years old—had been taken to the hospital for treatment. They'd been found in a basement room at the Van Storbers' spa, and the officers who'd found them would probably need therapy after what they'd seen. The women would need counseling and treatment for a long time.

Sabrina walked among the newly freed in one of the huge Campbell hotel ballrooms. She smiled and answered questions and held a couple of babies and listened to the stories. Each one different. Each one the same.

They'd saved and borrowed to come to America. But when they'd arrived, they'd been told they would have to work off their debt first. Families were divided and shuffled from one place to the other. No one stayed in any location for more than a few months before their captors moved them to a different one. No one knew where their families were—until someone messed up and put some cousins together at The Back Door.

That had been the first mistake, but it hadn't been the fatal blow. Lisa Palmer had been.

She'd found the group at The Porterhouse. Gotten names and descriptions of loved ones and found them at The Back Door and at the Van Storbers' spa. She'd told them what was going on. She'd given them hope. They'd made a plan.

Then she'd died and they'd been sure it was all over. That someone would come and kill them all. Now, they wanted to let their families back home know they were alive.

Sabrina made a few phone calls, and a deputy arrived thirty minutes later with her laptop and another for Anissa. Abby provided them with the hotel's Wi-Fi password and they went to work.

Sabrina and Anissa asked each family for their names and if

292

there was someone they wanted to contact. They looked up phone numbers and emails and even managed to get a few people on the phone in the dead of night.

The work of restoring these families would take months. Years. But it had begun.

23

Adam poured another cup of coffee. He'd lost count of how many he'd had. He probably wouldn't be able to sleep for another twenty-four hours.

The press had gotten wind of Friday night's events and descended overnight on the sheriff's office in far greater numbers than was typical.

But no one was talking.

The sheriff hadn't been thrilled he'd been left out of the loop until the warrants were already being served, but he understood the need to run the operation as tightly as possible. And to his credit, he'd put a gag order on everyone associated with the case.

"No one's going to benefit from these people's suffering," he said. "I will tolerate no grandstanding or political posturing. That this went on as long as it did—right under our noses—is a tragedy. A stain on our county and on our law enforcement community. We'll have plenty of time in the weeks ahead to discuss how this happened, where we dropped the ball, and what we can do to ensure nothing like this ever happens again, but for now our focus is undivided. We'll see that the victims are protected and given everything they need to start their lives fresh. And we'll see that the men and women who perpetrated these heinous crimes pay for their actions." The sheriff then threatened to fire anyone caught talking to the press and told them to get back to work.

At five in the morning, Adam was in the observation room watching the captain and Gabe interview Barclay Campbell. Barclay's lawyer had arrived at the sheriff's office before Barclay did. Barclay had been processed first and even though his lawyer was demanding he be sent home immediately, Barclay had the look of a man who knew he was going down.

He wasn't going to make it easy on them, but he knew.

A deputy peered into the room. "Investigator Campbell?"

"Yes?"

"I'm sorry, sir, but there's a woman downstairs who says she wants to speak to you and only you."

"Who is she?"

"It's Mrs. Van Storber."

Five minutes later, Adam sat across the table from Mrs. Van Storber. She'd been at the gala and was a person of interest, but there was no proof she knew what was going on.

"You wanted to speak to me, ma'am?"

"You were at the gala tonight."

"Yes."

"You knew this was going to happen." She didn't say it as a question.

"I'm not at liberty to discuss the specifics of the investigation," he said. The truth was, he hadn't known at all. If they hadn't found those shacks occupied and the people ready to talk, none of this would have happened.

"Well, I'm here to tell you that you haven't looked far enough. Not yet. You've only scratched the surface."

"Are you telling me you knew about the women in the basement of your spa?"

She twitched in her seat. "There was nothing I could do."

"You could have come to the police. You could have made an anonymous phone call."

Her eyes widened at his words.

"It was you," he said. "You're the source of the tip about the girls at Barclay's spa last year."

She didn't confirm it, but she didn't deny it either.

"Why would you try to get those girls free and not the ones on your own property?"

She snorted. "It isn't *my* property."

"You're his wife."

"He bought me."

Adam's mouth went dry. *Oh, Father. No.*

"We have children. Four of them. They are my life. I couldn't risk it. He would've had me killed, and then he would've raised my sons to be just like him. No." She shook her head. "I couldn't take that chance."

"Mrs. Van Storber—"

"Please. Call me Greta."

Somehow he got the feeling this was more about her wanting to avoid hearing Van Storber's name than about her trying to achieve any sort of familiarity.

"Greta, you're going to need an attorney. A good one. Because unless you have proof . . ."

She stood and turned her back to him. She reached behind her and lifted her shirt.

Bile rose in Adam's throat. Her back was covered in scars . . . and fresh stripes.

She lowered her shirt and turned around. "I have proof."

Adam still couldn't speak. How could he tell her the physical beating—while horrific—wouldn't stand up in court unless she could somehow prove her husband had done it.

"Mr. Campbell, Lisa Palmer trusted you. She'd done her research. She said you were the one who would be able to see this through. She told me if anything happened to her, you were the one I should talk to."

She removed her watch and slid it across the table to Adam. "It's in there."

Adam studied the timepiece. The hands weren't moving. He turned it over and opened the back.

One microSD card rested where the watch gears had been.

"I need to leave before my husband finds out I was here," she said. "I trust you won't tell him where you found this."

"Of course," he said. "But, Greta, take your children and leave. Now. Don't stay there another hour."

She stood. "You make it sound easy. There's nothing easy about this. Even from a jail cell, he still owns me. I'm not here for my own freedom. I'm here for theirs. Take care of that, Mr. Campbell. People died to get it to you."

"Wait."

She paused at Adam's word.

"Do you know who killed Lisa?"

"Some men who work for my husband, but I don't know their names. But I know they didn't mean to kill her. At least not right away. They didn't know she was sick. They waterboarded her . . . and she died."

That explained the drowning.

"The men who were torturing her panicked when she died before she gave them what they needed. They tried to make it look like a suicide and hoped it would just go away. One of them drove the car into the lake and put her behind the wheel and swam out. Then they went to her house and took her computers. They went back to the lake Sunday morning and realized the car was visible, so they pulled her out of the water." A small sob escaped Mrs. Van Storber, but she pressed on. "They pulled her out and one of the men pretended to be a hero."

"How do you know all this?" Adam asked.

"My husband was furious when he found out. There was a lot of yelling. It wasn't hard to put it all together." She shrugged. "If they had told him what they'd done, he would have disposed of her body himself. But he was out of town, and by the time he found out, her body had been discovered and the police were already searching her house. That's when he decided to blow up her house. He didn't know she'd left the insurance policy with me. If he ever finds out, I'll be next."

She walked out the door and he let her go. He couldn't hold her, and he feared if he tried to and her husband got wind of it, he'd have one of his men beat her. Or worse.

He called Sabrina.

"Hey." Her voice was filled with fatigue.

"Any chance you could come here or I could meet you at your lab?"

"What's going on?"

"New evidence. A microSD card."

"Have you looked at it yet?"

"Are you kidding me?" He knew better than that. "I haven't even touched it yet."

She laughed. "Good. Can you meet me at my lab around six thirty?"

"Yes. And Sabrina, make sure someone comes with you. I don't want you driving alone."

"Why? We got them."

"I know. Humor me?"

"Fine. I'm sure Anissa won't mind."

By 7:00 a.m., Sabrina had made a copy of the memory card and gone to work. It took her no time at all to find the files. None of them were encrypted. Lisa Palmer had laid it all out there for them.

Most of it they'd already figured out. Mr. Van Storber had been the ringleader. He had the connections with the recruiters who actually took the money and got the people to the States.

Barclay Campbell had gotten involved after some late-night poker games went south a few too many times. But once he was in, he was all in. He'd gone from a reluctant participant to a full-fledged supporter. He'd been influential in bringing in Senator Carson. They'd been friends for a long time. He'd convinced him it would be an easy way to save hundreds of thousands of dollars per year. Of course, it also meant they now had him over a barrel.

Lisa's notes told them things they hadn't known. That the Sullivans owed so much money that they were about to go under and the senator had made the connections that brought The Porterhouse into the mix.

That FreedomForAll wasn't a dirty charity after all, but that the traffickers had been intentional about volunteering with the organization so they would be able to deflect suspicion away from the worst offenders.

That Mrs. Johnson had no idea her yacht staff were slaves.

The group had stuck with labor trafficking until last year, when they'd ventured into sex trafficking. The women who had been sex trafficked had been kept separate from the other victims and had either died or been sold to their abusers, who had then taken them out of state.

The information went on and on. Some of it wouldn't hold up in court, but it was more than enough to get all the search warrants they could handle. Assets were frozen. Homes and offices and everything in them were sealed.

As Mrs. Van Storber had said, it was far bigger than they'd realized. They would be working this case for months. Maybe years. It was complicated and messy and the kind of thing that left Adam wishing he could somehow bleach his brain and get all the evil images out of it.

Adam's phone rang. It was Gabe. "What's going on?"

"You're not going to believe what they found in the Dumpster at Barclay Campbell's office."

"You sound happy, so I'm going to assume it wasn't a body."

"Nope. Sabrina's phone."

"Hang on. I'm going to put this on speaker so Sabrina can hear." He tapped the button and set the phone on the desk. "Say that again, Gabe."

"We found Sabrina's phone in the Dumpster behind Barclay Campbell's office."

"You're kidding." Sabrina shook her head in disbelief.

"Nope. He's not talking to anybody about anything. Refuses to answer any questions at all. But the phone was in his Dumpster. And it was last emptied on Saturday, so the timing works."

"Yeah." The timing worked, but Adam couldn't make it make sense.

"Guess what else we found in there." Gabe was clearly enjoying dragging out his story.

"What?" Sabrina still looked stunned.

"A piece of an RPG launcher."

"A piece?" Something was very off about this whole situation, but Adam couldn't put his finger on why he felt that way.

"Yeah. Just one. I'm guessing they disassembled it and dumped it in different places around town."

Adam didn't understand enough about RPG launchers to know, but he had to ask. "Is there any way to know if it was from the one used on us?"

"Unlikely. But forensics will check for prints and all that good stuff."

"Certainly does seem to tie them to all the attacks. But I can't wait to find out why they were determined to take out Sabrina."

"Maybe they knew how big of an advocate she is for human trafficking victims. Maybe that made it personal to them."

"Maybe." Sabrina didn't sound convinced. Neither was Adam.

"Although, I have one other theory, but I don't think either of you will like it," Gabe said.

"Let's hear it," Sabrina said.

"They knew Lisa Palmer had gone to Adam. That's why they killed her."

"We already know that," Adam said.

"True, but if that's the case, what better way to derail you than by taking Sabrina out?"

Adam met Sabrina's eyes. If she'd died last Monday, or Thursday, what would he be doing now? Grieving. Planning a funeral. The very idea sent chills down his spine.

But would he be working this case?

Not likely.

"But we weren't, you know . . ." Sabrina frowned.

Gabe laughed. "You weren't together? Technically not. I'll grant you that. But anyone with half a brain knew how Adam felt about you."

"I didn't," she said.

"That's because you're an overthinker. That massive brain of yours was a hindrance to you, my dear."

Sabrina actually looked flattered rather than offended.

"Regardless," Gabe continued, "the captain wants to pull back on the security detail. We need every deputy we can spare working this case."

"I don't like it." Adam couldn't shake the sense that they were missing something.

"I think it's wise," Sabrina said. "I don't need babysitters, and if it frees up people to help the victims and bring the perpetrators to justice, then I'm all in favor."

"I still think you need to use caution," Gabe said. "We don't yet have proof of what was going on. We don't know if our guy in the morgue is the same one who fired the RPG or even for sure if he's the one who attacked you Monday morning. So don't do anything crazy. Make sure Adam knows where you are."

"I will."

Adam disconnected the call. Sabrina walked to her office window and stared out into the parking lot. "Someone's going to need to tell Tyler to stand down."

Adam joined her. Tyler was making a circuit around the building. "Would it be wrong for me to forget to tell him? Maybe for another couple of weeks?"

Sabrina smiled, but there was a sadness in her eyes.

"What's on your mind?"

She sighed and bit her lip. "My mom."

24

abrina couldn't meet Adam's eyes. She crossed her arms and stared, unseeing, out the window.

"What about your mom?" Adam's gentle question should've been easy to answer. But it wasn't.

"I can't live this way anymore. I need answers. I really thought it was possible she could've hired someone to kill me. Who thinks that about their own mother? It's sick."

Adam wrapped his arm around her shoulders and pulled her toward him. She didn't fight him, but she didn't uncross her arms. "First, it isn't sick. It's what we do. We look at all the possibilities. Family members aren't excluded. And your mother was a valid suspect."

"You would never suspect your mother of doing that."

"No. I wouldn't. But my relationship with my mother is quite different from yours. And I would treat my mother as a suspect if circumstances warranted it. I wouldn't believe it and I would be certain she would be exonerated, but I wouldn't avoid considering it."

"I need to talk to her," Sabrina said. "Confront her."

303

"Okay. I hear you. And I'm not saying I disagree. But are you prepared to deal with the repercussions of that conversation?"

"It's not like our relationship could get any worse. We don't see each other often as it is. We talk once a month. It's not like I'm going to accuse her of trying to have me killed."

"No."

"Just of having a slave." Because that was so much better? She pulled away from Adam. "She's going to hate me."

"Or," Adam said, "she may be relieved to get it out in the open. If you're right, then she's been living with this guilt for at least three decades. If you're wrong, then you can learn to deal with your mother without that huge issue always between you."

"True."

"You know I'll support you no matter what you decide."

"Thanks."

"But can I make a suggestion?"

Uh-oh. "Of course."

"Sleep on it first."

"Sleep?" She yawned. "What's that?"

Adam yawned too. "I hear it's this thing where you close your eyes and when you open them, you have energy. I'm sure I've experienced it in the past . . . I just can't remember when."

"I'll sleep eventually."

The adrenaline from last night's raids and all the events that had followed them had definitely worn off. No matter how much work she had to do, sleep was going to take precedence. And soon.

"How much longer do you need to send these files over to Gabe?" Adam asked.

"They're ready. Gabe needs to see them. I assume he's still running point on this since we don't know who actually killed Lisa Palmer yet?"

"He is. But they're already putting together a joint task force between the city police, county sheriff, state bureau of investigation, and possibly some immigration control officers to work the rest of it. The captain's trying to figure out who's interested and capable, and who actually has time to devote to it."

"I wouldn't want to be him right now," Sabrina said.

"Me neither."

They both yawned again.

"Okay, tell me what you think of this plan. I'll drive you first to Leigh's to pick up your stuff and then take you home. I'll even stop by the grocery store if you want so you can restock your fridge. And then you'll sleep and we'll discuss everything tomorrow."

"I like that plan. When are you going to get some sleep?"

He smiled. "Soon. I talked the captain into stationing one deputy in your driveway for tonight. So once he gets there, I'll go back to the office and see how everyone's doing and then I'll crash. The captain's already said he wants everyone who was up all night to go home by six tonight. Says the last thing he needs right now is one of his deputies falling asleep behind the wheel and causing a wreck."

"That doesn't sound very nice," Sabrina said.

Adam laughed. "He's not being mean. That's his way of saying he wants us all to get some rest without sounding like he's being a mother hen."

"Oh." She could see that. "Because y'all are so tough."

Adam laughed harder. "Exactly. Now let's get out of here."

He scanned the supplies in front of him.

Two guns.

Two canisters of tear gas.

Rope.

Gloves.

Bleach.

Plastic bags.

He couldn't believe it had come to this.

What was the point of keeping everyone's secrets—their dirtiest, darkest, most depraved secrets—if you wound up losing everything?

He wasn't asking for more than he deserved. He wanted enough money to live out his life in peace. Without constantly looking over his shoulder.

He'd seen his opportunity three years earlier when Martin Fleming had looked him up. He hadn't heard from or seen the man in seventeen years and there he was, sitting across from him in a deli telling him his life was ending. Soon. And not only that, but also that the early onset dementia would mean he would forget who he was and who the people around him were before his soul departed from his body.

Martin said he was the only person he could trust because he'd kept his secret for almost thirty years.

Well, Martin had been right about that last part anyway. He had kept the secret. And it was a whopper.

And with Martin's mind slipping away, he'd set the plan into motion that would give him both his wealth and his freedom.

Because while he knew a lot of secrets, they'd always been a double-edged sword. If he ever told—if the truth ever got out—he would be on the run for the rest of his life.

But Martin was dead. And with Juan dead, too, the secret would die with Martin's daughter.

And he would finally be free.

There was one huge downside to living in a tiny house.

She couldn't pace.

Not that she spent a lot of time pacing, but tonight she wanted to. She'd picked up her phone—and returned it to the coffee table—at least eight times in the past fifteen minutes.

This was ridiculous. It was only seven thirty, but she was exhausted, and she wasn't going to call her mom until after she slept, so she might as well get started sleeping. She turned off the lights and climbed the ladder to her loft bedroom.

Ah. Bliss.

Her own bed. Her own space. She'd missed it.

But something had changed.

The quiet was a little too quiet.

The serenity was a little too serene.

If she didn't know better, she might think she was lonely.

No. Not Sabrina Fleming. She didn't do lonely. She did fine on her own.

Her phone buzzed and she snatched it from the shelf over her bed.

The text was from Leigh.

My house is too quiet tonight. Miss you. You're probably already asleep and I hope you are. But call me in the morning, okay?

Before she could reply, the phone buzzed again. This text was from Anissa.

Hey. Just checking on you. Call me if you need anything.

This was what it was like to have friends. Real ones.

She shot quick replies back to both of them and returned the phone to the shelf. As she snuggled back under her covers, her heart was full.

Thank you, Father. Thank you for giving me more than I even knew to ask for. Please help me to trust that you know what I need before I ask, that you know how best to handle the situation with my mother. Give me the wisdom I need.

She didn't know when she'd fallen asleep, but the ringing of her phone woke her. She answered it without opening her eyes.

"Hello."

"Hello, Sabrina. Did I catch you at a bad time? You sound terrible."

She was awake now.

"Sorry, Mom. I was working all night last night, so I crashed early."

"Oh, I woke you. Then my apologies."

She didn't sound sorry. She sounded annoyed.

"It's okay. What do you need?" Her mother never called unless she needed something, and this call wouldn't be any different.

"I'm going to be in the area tomorrow. Since I'll be in Colorado over the holidays, I thought I might stop by and say hello."

"Sure. What time? Where would you like to meet?"

"I thought I'd come to your place. See this tiny house you're living in. Check on your father's place."

"Mom, there's nothing to see here."

"Be that as it may, it will ease my mind."

Part of Sabrina wanted to tell her to stay away, but hadn't she just asked God to give her wisdom? And now her mother would be coming to her house. Maybe she would be able to ask about Rosita without destroying their relationship.

"Okay. What time?"

"I'll be in Raleigh for a breakfast meeting with one of our smaller medical groups." Only her mother would schedule a meeting during the breakfast hour on a Sunday in December. Those poor people who worked for her must hate her. "So let's say eleven? Will you be home from church?"

"I wasn't planning to go tomorrow, so that will be fine."

"Oh? Well, then that's excellent. See you then. Goodbye."

Sabrina checked the time. Nine thirty. So not an unreasonable time for her mother to call. Except for the fact that she wanted them to meet in a little over twelve hours. Maybe she'd been hoping Sabrina wouldn't be available. She'd seemed a bit shocked that Sabrina wasn't planning to go to church.

Sabrina hadn't felt the need to explain that she'd intended to sleep until nature awakened her and not a minute before. Mainly because she was exhausted but also because a tiny part of her wondered if she was still a target, and the thought of drawing danger to a place of worship terrified her to her core.

She would go next week, when Adam could come with her.

She typed a few words of a text to Adam but stopped. He should be asleep by now and there was no need to wake him. Not over this.

She would email him. He'd see the message tomorrow.

25

Adam shuffled into the office at nine forty-five. Church would be starting soon, but he wouldn't be there. He'd have to watch the service later. For now, he needed coffee.

Gabe was filling a thermos with coffee. "We've got to stop meeting like this." Gabe looked awful.

Adam poured himself a cup. "Have you even been home?"

"No. But I'm headed there as soon as the meeting's over. Captain's orders."

"His orders were to go home last night."

"I know, but this case is so big . . ." Gabe rubbed his free hand over his face. "I can't make any mistakes."

"Then go get some sleep." Adam splashed some cream into his cup. "You're going to make mistakes if you don't."

"You're sounding like Ryan now." Gabe grumbled as he walked toward his office.

"Not sorry," Adam called after him.

"Meeting's at ten," Gabe called back. "Don't be late."

Adam went to his desk and tried to make sense of what he'd been working on Saturday afternoon. If his own chicken scratch and random piling system were any indication, he should have gone home hours before he had. He could barely follow his train of thought on anything in front of him.

He glanced at his phone. He hadn't tried to call or text Sabrina for fear of waking her. She'd been exhausted when he left her at her place. He was hoping she would sleep until noon.

He turned on his computer, but it was still starting up when he went to the first meeting of the newly formed Carrington County Human Trafficking Task Force.

Sabrina stepped outside when she heard the car in the driveway. The policeman who'd been on guard all night had been replaced with an hourly patrol. Adam wouldn't be happy about that, but at least for the moment she wasn't sorry to have one less thing to have to explain to her mother.

Her mother wore a disgruntled expression as she stepped out of the shiny black Suburban. "I asked for a Prius. A Prius. And this"—she waved a dismissive hand toward the SUV—"this monstrosity is what they gave me. Most backward rental agency I've ever seen. Said they only had one Prius and it had been picked up earlier today. This would never happen in Virginia."

No hello. No good to see you. Just straight to the criticisms of Sabrina's new home state.

Sabrina didn't bother with a reply.

Her mother cast her gaze on Sabrina's house. The land around it. The red MINI Cooper sitting in her carport.

"Well, are you going to invite me in or leave me standing out here in the cold?"

Sabrina pointed to the door. "Make yourself at home, Mother."

Her mother took one step inside and stopped. Sabrina had to catch herself to keep from slamming into her mother's back.

"How do you live like this?"

"I like it, Mother." She tried—so hard—to keep her voice neutral. "I have everything I need."

Her mother stepped the rest of the way inside and moved toward the sofa. Sabrina followed her and closed the door behind them. "Can I get you some water?"

"No. Thank you. I'm quite full from breakfast."

Sabrina perched on the edge of one of her chairs at her table. *Now, Lord?*

Her mother set her purse on the floor. "I need to discuss something with you."

So maybe not now. "Okay."

"I'm getting married."

Getting married? Sabrina couldn't have heard that correctly. Could she?

"I realize this may have come as a bit of a shock, given that I haven't mentioned him before."

"Well, yes."

"It all happened so quickly. I had no idea he was even thinking marriage. And then . . . he proposed."

"And you said yes?"

"Of course."

"Just because someone asks doesn't mean you have to say yes, Mother."

"I'm clear on how this works. And you of all people should know that I have no problem saying no."

That was for sure. "So that's why you're here? To tell me you're getting married?"

"Yes, and to check on your father's estate."

"Why do you care about Dad's estate?" Something was very weird here.

"To be honest, there are a few things he took with him when he moved out. If they're in that house, I'd like them back."

"What kinds of things?"

"A few books. A picture. Nothing of great value. I'm not trying to take anything that doesn't, technically, belong to me anyway. But I doubt I'll be in this area again anytime soon, and it would help if I could look through the house to see if there are things I want before you sell them off at some auction."

Her mother made *auction* sound like a dirty word. But her request, while annoying, was valid. It was entirely possible that her father had absconded with a few of her mother's things.

He would have done it for spite if for no other reason.

And there was nothing in the house Sabrina wanted, so if the items meant that much to her mother, she could have them.

"Fine." Sabrina retrieved the keys to the house. The doors had electronic keypads, but she'd rather not show her mother the code. "Do you want to drive or walk?"

"Walk. Definitely. I will not foul the air any more than necessary."

"Excellent." Sabrina pointed to the door. "You first."

26

Adam struggled to keep his eyes open during the new task force meeting. Many of the people present were hearing the information being presented for the first time, and their outrage at the travesties being committed against the men and women in their own community was palpable.

But none of this was new information for him. Nothing earth-shattering had been discovered during the night.

No one confessed in return for a plea deal, although to be fair, it didn't sound like the prosecutor was offering anything.

And with the evidence from the microSD card, there would be no difficulty getting warrants for files, documents, computers, and records. The forensic accountants would be busier than they'd ever been before.

The meeting lasted two hours.

Gabe had even nodded off once.

The captain hadn't been pleased that Sabrina hadn't been in attendance, but no one had told Adam to ask her, and after sitting through it, he was glad. She hadn't missed anything.

Claire Tollison waved him over. "Hey," he said. "I'm glad you're on this. You'll be a great fit."

"Thanks. I'm so excited." She grinned, then frowned. "I mean, it's awful. Of course."

"But it's a fabulous opportunity for you," Adam said. "That's nothing to be ashamed of."

She nodded. "Thanks for understanding."

"No problem. Any news on our dead guy?" He'd been hoping for some sort of identification. Tox screen. Anything.

Claire shook her head. "Sorry. I can send you the report if you'd like. There's not much to see. He wasn't high. Wasn't drunk. His prints aren't in the system. We're running DNA to see if there are any matches, but you know how long that can take."

Weeks if they were lucky. Months was the more likely time frame.

"He had a couple of pictures, a Breeze transit card, and sixty bucks in his wallet. No change in his pockets. No keys either." Her frustration was evident. "I've reached out to a buddy in Atlanta who is trying to use the Breeze card to see if he can track down where this guy has been in Atlanta. But it's not like you can use Atlanta's rail system to get to Carrington. It's like he just appeared in the dressing room and opened fire." Her expression lifted a little. "I did get the video from the mall that night. Finally. They sent it over late yesterday, so I'm going to try to find him coming into the mall and see if we can figure out where he came from."

Solid police work. Sometimes that was all it took.

"Sounds good. Let me know if I can help."

"Will do."

Thirty minutes later, Adam finally made it back to his desk.

How was it possible to have over eighty emails in his inbox when he'd cleared it yesterday before going home?

He scanned the list. Most of them could wait. A few from family members or friends who wanted to see if he could give them an inside scoop on the scandal rocking Carrington today.

315

Nope.

Ah. Sabrina had sent him an email last night. He opened it and read her brief message.

"You don't look happy." Anissa stood beside his desk.

"Neither do you."

"I'm not, but you go first."

"Okay. I have an email from Sabrina. Her mother was going to stop by for a visit this morning."

"This would be the same mother we considered to be a suspect in the attempts on Sabrina's life?"

"The same."

"I don't like it."

"Neither do I. Now it's your turn." He kept scanning his inbox while he waited. Anissa wasn't one to overshare. Maybe if he didn't make eye contact she would spill whatever had her shorts in a twist this morning.

"Ugh. I'm fine. Just tired. I came in to beg the captain to let me help, but he says I'm still on administrative leave."

"You know his hands are tied. It will only take another couple of days to get you cleared enough to come back to desk duty. Go home and get some more sleep."

"I will, but the captain told me to take Gabe with me and Gabe won't leave."

And there was the problem. He kept scanning through his email, but Anissa was still standing there. What was she expecting him to do? "Where's Ryan? Between the two of you, I think you should be able to force him to leave. He's so tired he's barely functioning as it is."

He clicked on the email from Claire Tollison. She'd included the autopsy report and the photographs of the contents of their dead guy's wallet.

That picture . . .

He clicked on the picture.

Opened it to full screen.

Fatigue fled.

He grabbed his phone and dialed Sabrina's number.

"What are you doing?" Anissa asked.

He held up one hand. "Come on, come on. Pick it up."

Nothing.

"Adam"—Anissa leaned over and got in his face—"what's going on?"

He showed Anissa the photograph. "This was in the guy's wallet."

"The guy I shot?"

"Yes."

"So?"

"I've seen this picture before."

"Where?"

"In Sabrina's living room."

27

He watched Sabrina and her mom walk out of Sabrina's house. The cops never found this spot in the fence. They'd looked everywhere for how Juan had gotten into the gated property to attack Sabrina, but they still hadn't figured it out.

And how would they?

Unless they took the time to touch every single bar in the fence, they would never notice the one place where two of the iron bars had been replaced with plastic. They wouldn't be able to see how they twisted right off. They would never know how easy it was to remove them and step through. They would never realize how this spot was out of sight of the security cameras.

This had been one of the first projects he'd taken on when he'd hatched his grand escape plan. He hadn't known then if he would need it, but he'd been determined to cover all his bases, and making sure he could access Martin's property had been a high priority.

And thank goodness. He'd thought Juan would be able to take care of that little brat, but Juan was dead and he was freezing his toes off contemplating the best way to make sure everything continued on as planned.

Sabrina and Yvonne paused at the Suburban and Yvonne got her coat. Then they walked toward Martin's house.

He wasn't close enough to be sure, but it didn't look like they were talking. So what were they doing? They could barely stand to be in the same room with each other and now they were going on a winter's morning stroll?

He stifled a yawn and jammed his fingers deeper into his coat pockets. The only thing keeping him going was the thought of white beaches and hammocks. He could almost feel the rope etching patterns on his back, the sweat on his brow, the weight of his eyelids closing for an afternoon snooze.

But the only way that would happen was if he took matters into his own hands, even though he didn't want to. It would be messy.

But then it would be over.

Today.

28

They walked to the house in silence.

Sabrina wouldn't characterize it as companionable silence. More like the silence that falls between total strangers sitting together on an airplane who've given up trying to keep the conversation going but can't get away from each other for two more hours.

She kept a steady stream of silent prayer going. *Now? Should I say something?* But no nudge forward came.

When the house came into view, her mother paused. "Figures." She kept walking.

"You know I have no idea what you're talking about, don't you?" Sabrina didn't even try to keep the frustration out of her voice. "If you want to say something about the house, please say it. Otherwise, I'd appreciate it if you would keep your remarks to yourself."

Her mother looked at her in surprise. "My, my, haven't we grown sassy."

"I've always been sassy, Mother."

"Perhaps. Maybe I should say you've grown more vocal in your sassiness."

Perhaps.

"What do you want to know, Sabrina? Your father was a complicated man. My relationship with him was complex. But you're his daughter and you're not my therapist. I know I've handled most of our"—she pointed between her and Sabrina—"relationship badly, but I don't feel bad about the things I've tried to spare you from. There are things that once you know them, they cannot be unknown. You don't get to go back to the way things were."

Was it possible her mother would divulge the information she had been seeking? "I would rather know," Sabrina said. "What I don't know is driving me crazy."

"Just remember, you asked for this." Her mom pointed to the path that wound around the house. "Does this go all the way around?"

"It does."

"Then let's keep walking."

Sabrina had no complaints and they turned to the right, their feet crunching on the tiny white gravel path.

"I loved your father at one time, Sabrina. Truly. I thought if I could get pregnant, then everything would be okay. And I did. And things seemed to be better during the pregnancy. But I went into premature labor and we lost the baby. I hemorrhaged so much they had to do a hysterectomy to save my life."

"But . . ."

Her mom looked at her then. "We adopted you, Sabrina. You were a week old when we picked you up at an agency. Your mother was single and unable to take care of you."

"How is that possible?" Sabrina stared into the eyes of the woman she'd called *Mother* for almost thirty years. "I've seen the records. Your medical records. My own."

"Your father had a lawyer who said he could make it so there was absolutely no evidence that you weren't actually ours. People knew I was pregnant and that I'd had a hard time during delivery. We'd requested no one—not even family—come to the hospital.

And back then they kept us in the hospital a lot longer than they do now."

She gave Sabrina a sad smile. "I don't know where your dad got the idea. But he came to my hospital room and told me he knew about a baby girl. That she was gorgeous. She needed a family. That no one needed to ever know that our baby had died. We would have this baby girl and everyone would assume . . ."

Sabrina was speechless. Her mother didn't try to explain anymore. They made it back to the front of the house before she could corral her swirling thoughts enough to ask any questions. "But why would it have been so bad to grieve your own baby?"

"It was a different time, and I was so shattered and exhausted, I wasn't thinking clearly. By the time I was in a more stable frame of mind, you were already ours. It was done. So for the past thirty years, I've told people I had one baby and I never mention the one I lost."

Her mother hadn't been kidding when she said this was complicated.

"But what about my eyes and my hair. I look just like dad. Everyone says so."

"Yes, you do."

29

A dam looked from Anissa back to the photo on his screen. "How on earth would this guy have gotten this picture? And why? It's not like it's a current photo to help him know who he was looking for. In fact, you have to look closely to even realize it's Sabrina. She was a little girl . . ." Adam didn't like the direction his thoughts were going.

"I'm calling Claire."

Anissa pushed the speaker button on his phone and paced in a circle around his desk while he dialed.

He didn't bother with any pleasantries when Claire answered. "The photograph of the young girl and the woman you found in the guy's pocket. Was there anything on it? Any writing? Any notes on the back?"

"Uh, hello to you too. Hang on a second. Let me look."

Adam counted to twenty before Claire responded. "There's something written in Spanish. *Mamá y hermana.*"

Mom and sister? Was it possible?

"Adam? What's going on?" Claire asked.

Adam looked at Anissa while he answered Claire. "I think our killer may have been Sabrina's brother."

Anissa dropped her head into her hands. "I killed her brother! Are you kidding me? She's going to hate me."

Adam pulled her hands away from her face. "You killed the man trying to kill her. If she struggles with this, it won't be because you killed him. It will be because she's trying to figure out why on earth he was trying to kill her. I don't think she even knew he existed."

He leaned toward the phone. "Hey, Claire, I'm going to need to know anything and everything you can give me on our guy. Anything identifying about him. Tattoos, birthmark. An estimate of age. Nothing is too inconsequential. And I need it yesterday."

"Got it. I'll call when I have something."

After he disconnected the call with Claire, he redialed Sabrina.

"What are you doing?" Anissa asked.

"Trying to call Sabrina again."

"You can't tell her something like this over the phone." Anissa was not handling this well. She looked like she was going to cry.

"I'm not going to tell her anything over the phone. I'm going to tell her I need to talk to her about the case and ask her if she'll come here. Or offer to go there."

"Oh. Right." The fight dissipated from Anissa and she leaned against his desk. "Good idea. Sorry."

The phone rang.

He put his hand over the speaker. "It's okay. And you'll be okay. She won't hold it against you."

Anissa huffed. "I hope you're right, but you'll forgive me if I don't hold my breath. People get really funny when you kill their siblings."

Gabe and Ryan walked up in time to hear Anissa's final hissed words. Gabe leaned in close and whispered. "Whose sibling was killed?"

"Sabrina's." Adam and Anissa answered at the same time.

"She has a sibling?" Ryan shook his head. "What have we missed?"

"*Had* a sibling," Anissa corrected him. "A brother. Who tried to kill her, and I shot him."

"Her brother tried to kill her?" Gabe turned to Ryan. "We've missed a lot."

When his call went to voicemail, Adam disconnected the call and grabbed his cell phone.

Anissa was filling Gabe and Ryan in on the photograph, but Adam wasn't paying attention. When Sabrina had set up her new phone earlier in the week, they'd both turned on the "find my friends" locator app. She could find him—and he could find her—or least find her phone.

"She's not answering, but her phone is at her house."

"Maybe she turned it off so she could sleep. She's basically been awake for the past week." Gabe took a sip of coffee.

Anissa took the coffee from Gabe and turned to Ryan. "Why are you letting him drink coffee? He needs to sleep."

"He won't listen to me," Ryan said. "You talk some sense into him."

Adam was done trying to be nice. He called dispatch. "Can you get me the deputy who is at Dr. Sabrina Fleming's house?"

He listened in shock as the dispatcher told him there was no one there. "Guys!" The three investigators ended their side conversation. "The captain pulled the deputy who was stationed outside Sabrina's house. She's out there alone. I've got to get over there." Adam grabbed his coat and looked for his keys.

"Go," Anissa said. "We'll see who is in the area who can drive by. And we'll get some units headed that way—no sirens, low key, just in case." Anissa handed Gabe his coffee. "I'm not supposed to be working, so you're coming with me, because when I say *we*, I really mean *you*."

"Yes, ma'am."

Adam found the keys. In his coat pocket, right where he'd left them. Man, he was still not firing on all cylinders. Ryan was the only one still standing by his desk.

"Pray I'm overreacting," Adam said.

"I will, but I'm going with you." Ryan followed him as they race-walked to the elevators.

"Why?"

"In case you aren't."

30

S abrina opened the front door. The house smelled stale. She needed to come back later this week and air it out.

Taking care of this place had been a low priority for the past week.

She paused in the foyer as her mother—the woman she'd always known to be her mother—walked around and looked at the place for the first time. Sabrina let her take the lead and followed her as she wandered through the rooms.

"So," she said, "you think the fact that I look like Dad is just one of those things that happens in a lot of adoptive families?"

Her mother ran a hand over a brass elephant that Sabrina could remember from her youngest days. "I did."

The implications of those two words were more than Sabrina's mind wanted to deal with. She sat on the edge of a love seat. She was done. Done being nice. Done playing games. She waited until she had a good view of her mother's face and then she spoke. "Tell me about Rosita."

Her mother closed her eyes, almost in slow motion. She pinched her lips together. She took a deep breath and blew it out. But she still didn't look in Sabrina's direction. "I hated her."

"Why?" Sabrina was almost certain she knew, but she didn't want to guess. She was tired of wondering. "She was wonderful to me. I adored her. Why did you hate her? Why did you send her away?"

That got her an unexpected reaction. "How did you know I was the one who sent her away?"

"Dad was out of town and he knew how much I loved her. He would have at least let me say goodbye. And I heard you fighting later. I didn't hear every word, but I knew he was angry."

"He was angry." Her mother said the words under her breath. "Yes, he was. But he knew I was right. He never should have brought her into our home. And there was no way I was going to sit by while she gave him another child."

"Another . . . ?"

"She was pregnant."

"I have a sibling?"

"Theoretically, yes."

Sabrina tried to process everything she'd heard. She wasn't used to feeling overwhelmed by information, but this time she was. Images from her childhood—her father talking to Rosita in the hall, her mother, well, her adoptive mother, berating her over her clothes, Rosita snuggling with her when she was afraid of a thunderstorm. She scanned through moment after moment, and all of them looked different in light of this new information.

A fresh ache engulfed her as she thought about all the anger she'd felt toward Rosita after she left. She'd been so hurt. So upset.

So wrong about everything.

Not that it was her fault, but had she missed some clues? Probably. But apparently even as an adult it was easier for her to suspect her parents of keeping Rosita as a slave than to imagine a completely different scenario.

Her heart hurt. Her mind whirled. And a sibling? She might have a brother or sister somewhere out there? What would that be like? Would she ever find them?

If she did, would they want to know her?

Maybe. Maybe not. Because she still hadn't gotten to the one question she'd always wanted the answer to.

Sabrina looked out the window and for the first time in forever felt peace that now was the time to ask. "For the past decade, I've suspected you and Dad kept Rosita as a slave."

Her mother laced her fingers in front of her and sighed. "I guess in a manner of speaking we did."

She was admitting it?

"I still don't know how your father met Rosita. And I don't have proof, nor did he ever admit it to me, but it is my belief that he got her pregnant around the same time I got pregnant. I have no idea what he intended to do had our daughter lived, but when we lost her, he must have seen it as an opportunity to keep you in his life. And of course he would hire your own mother to take care of you."

"*He* hired Rosita?"

"He did everything. I was so weak from blood loss and grief. He was the one who set up the adoption and hired Rosita. He said he was trying to make it as easy as possible for me. I actually believed him at the time."

"This is messed up," Sabrina said.

"It is," her mother agreed. "Because as far as I know, my adoption of you was completely legal. I saw the paperwork where your birth mother signed over her parental rights to me. Assuming I'm correct in my theory of events, your father was technically your father twice. By birth and by adoption."

Sabrina's mind scrambled to pull together the threads of this crazy story and make them make sense.

"So Rosita signed over her parental rights to you, allowed you to adopt me, then came to work for you to take care of me?"

"Yes. And I don't know what sort of pressure she was under that enticed her to do that. But once it was done, she was effectively a slave in our home. Because I'm certain she would never have willingly left you. Not when you were a baby."

"But she left me when I was ten."

Her mother dropped her head. "I didn't give her much choice."

"What do you mean?"

"I threatened to have her deported. But since you were legally mine, you would have stayed with me no matter what. I knew she would have done anything to stay in the States. Even if it meant leaving you for a time. To be honest, I never expected her to go far. I figured your father would set her up somewhere, and when you turned eighteen she would come back into your life and the whole thing would be out in the open."

"But she never came back."

"No, she didn't."

"Do you know where she is?" Sabrina held her breath.

"No. I haven't seen her since the day she walked out the door. And if your father knew where she was or what happened to her, he took it to the grave."

"Did you ever ask him?"

Her mother sat on the sofa across from her. "No. I didn't. I threw myself into my work and tried to pretend none of it had ever happened. And I know you won't believe this, but I am . . . sorry, Sabrina. Truly I am. I know this is a shock, and I know it's a lot to come to terms with. I've had decades to deal with it and it still sometimes shakes me to my core."

Sabrina couldn't sit still any longer. "I need some air." She ran out the door and into the yard. If she'd had anything of substance to eat this morning, she would have hurled it into the bushes. As it was, she paced around the front yard.

Rosita was her mother.

Her father was her father.

Her mother wasn't her mother.

She may have a sibling.

Rosita left her.

And she never came back.

31

W hy don't you let me drive?" Ryan grabbed Adam's arm and pulled him toward his own vehicle.

"I can drive."

"You can, but you shouldn't. You're tired and distracted and worried. All understandable under the circumstances. But all good reasons to let me drive. It doesn't do you any good to try to swoop in and save the day if you wreck the car on the way."

It annoyed Adam that Ryan was right. "Fine." They climbed into Ryan's truck. "While you drive, help me think this through. What are we dealing with here? Is she still in danger? Because if the guy from the dressing room was her brother—a brother she didn't know had existed—and if he's the one who tried to kill her at her house on Monday, then the attacks had nothing to do with our case. And Anissa killed the guy who was trying to kill Sabrina. So it's possible the danger has passed."

"True," Ryan said, "but we don't know why he was trying to kill her. So maybe the danger is still very real."

"Drive faster."

Sabrina lived twenty minutes away, and a lot could happen in twenty minutes.

A lot of very bad things.

He'd snuck around to the back of the house and come in through the kitchen in time to hear everything.

He'd always wondered how much Yvonne knew. Martin thought she'd been clueless.

Guess this proved how clueless Martin had been.

He'd been waiting for ten minutes for Sabrina to come back inside. Yvonne hadn't moved from the sofa. She looked beaten. And weary.

Not surprising really.

The door opened and from his spot he saw Sabrina return to the den, where Yvonne was waiting.

"I'm going to need some time to process all of this," she said to Yvonne.

Funny how she didn't seem angry. She seemed sad.

He'd expected more rage.

Oh well.

"I left my phone at the house. Do you want to stay here and see if there's anything you want, or do you want to come with me?"

What? No. She couldn't go back to the house. He needed her to stay here.

"If I stay, will you come back?" Why did Yvonne even care?

"Yes." Sabrina spoke in a measured voice. Like she was determined not to lose her temper or start crying. "I'm sure I'll have more questions."

He stepped into the den, gun drawn. "I'm sure you do," he said. "But I'm afraid you won't be going anywhere. Have a seat."

"Mr. Kemp?"

"Ezekiel?"

Both women spoke with the same confused tone.

Sabrina turned to Yvonne. "How do you know Mr. Kemp?"

Yvonne glared at him. "Ezekiel is my fiancé."

"You're going to marry Dad's lawyer?"

The shock on Yvonne's face was worth the annoyance of letting these two thorns in his side chitchat. Way better than taking them out with the tear gas before shooting them. "His . . . what?"

"Mr. Kemp is Dad's lawyer. The one he hired after he was diagnosed with dementia. The one who rewrote the wills and is the executor of my trust." Sabrina was furious, and she turned on him now. "Dad trusted you."

"Your father no more trusted me than he trusted Yvonne here to be fair to you after he died. I've known him since before you were born, and he never trusted anyone."

"Before I was born? I thought he hired you a few years ago."

"He hired me for the second time a few years ago."

Yvonne's hand was at her throat. "You handled the adoption."

"Very good. I would clap, but my hands are full. Now, Sabrina, I've asked you to sit. Side by side on the sofa. That's nice."

She sat, But Sabrina—typical Sabrina—had more questions. "You handled the adoption? Then you knew Rosita. You knew the whole story. Was she really my mother? What happened to her?"

He should have shot her by now, but he was kind of enjoying the way their faces registered their surprise and then the moment when they understood. It was fascinating.

"Of course she was your mother. Yvonne's no idiot. And yes, she was pregnant when Yvonne here kicked her out. She left out the part where she'd made Rosita believe she would hurt you"—he pointed at Sabrina—"if she didn't leave. It was a very effective strategy. If Rosita took you with her, the police would eventually arrest her for kidnapping and no one was going to believe an illegal immigrant when she claimed you were her biological daughter.

"But if she stayed with you, Yvonne here promised her you would be a very sick child—a little something in your breakfast smoothie to make you vomit. A little shove down the stairs. Maybe a loose wheel on that bicycle you loved so much. Rosita couldn't risk having you harmed."

Sabrina looked at Yvonne with fresh shock. "How could you do that?"

Yvonne defended herself. Typical. "I would never have harmed you. It was a threat. And it worked."

"Oh, it worked all right. She was terrified. Left town and never looked back." Ezekiel was enjoying this far more than he'd expected.

"Do you know what happened to her?" Sabrina's eyes darted around the room. He needed to speed this up before the little brainiac figured a way out of there.

"She moved to Wisconsin. Got a job working in housekeeping. Had the boy. His name was Juan."

"Was?"

She didn't know. This would be fun.

"Juan has been looking for you for the past five years," he told Sabrina. "His mother told him everything—on her deathbed."

"She died?"

He'd expected more emotion from Sabrina. Maybe she needed a few more details. "Cancer. No money for health care. I mean, you have to appreciate the irony. Your birth mother dies from a cancer people survive all the time when they go to the hospitals your adoptive mother manages. It's sad, really."

Sabrina didn't acknowledge him. She barely seemed to be paying attention to him at all. Yvonne was paying attention though. "Why did it take Rosita's son five years to find Sabrina?"

"It's possible he got some misinformation that led him in the wrong direction."

"You lied to the boy?"

"I was protecting my client from spurious claims."

Yvonne was tracking with him. "You were protecting Martin's money."

"Of course I was."

"And that's what this is all about."

"Of course it is."

"So what's your plan? Kill us? That won't help you."

"You'd think that, wouldn't you? But if you both die, the trust in Sabrina's name remains under my execution. My plan was to let Juan do my dirty work for me with this one"—he pointed to Sabrina—"and then once I was married to you, my dear, well, what's yours would be mine. And when you died, tragically, in a few months, well, it would all be mine."

"You'd kill us over a few thousand dollars?" Sabrina still wasn't looking at him, but she must have been listening more than he'd realized.

"No. Of course not. But I would kill you over several million."

"Million?" Yvonne shook her head. "Martin never had millions."

"Not when he was with you. But years ago Martin's father sold some land to the town they lived in. And he was smart about it. He sold the center of the property but kept acres around the perimeter. The area has grown and that property is worth a fortune now. Martin negotiated the sale of a huge chunk of property before he lost his mind. The money is in a trust for Sabrina and Juan. Of course, now that Sabrina's friend took care of her brother, I won't have to worry about divvying up any of that cash."

"My friend did what?" Sabrina asked.

"Your friend. The girl cop. She killed your brother."

"He was my brother?"

Oh yes. The expressions on both of their faces. He would never forget them. So worth telling them.

"What? Wait. Was he the same one who attacked me?"

"Now you're putting it together. He wanted to take care of you himself, and I was fine with that, but then he panicked at the first sound of a siren and didn't finish the job. It made things much more complicated."

"But why was he trying to kill me? What had I ever done to him?"

"The version he heard was that you knew about him and wanted nothing to do with him, and you'd convinced your father to cut him from his will. The only way he would be able to get anything from your father's estate was to take you out of the picture."

"That's ridiculous," Sabrina said. "If he'd come to me and told me he was my brother, even if I didn't believe him, it wouldn't have taken more than a simple blood test to prove paternity. And I had no interest in Dad's money. I wouldn't have minded sharing it."

"True, but he didn't know that. He blamed you for his mother's death and his own poverty. You were the favored child and he was the castoff. He was more than willing to take you out."

32

Ryan and Adam arrived at Sabrina's home thirteen minutes later.

"That was some great driving," Adam said. "Thanks."

They parked beside the Suburban. "I guess this is what her mom's driving," Adam said. "Nice."

Ryan pointed to the house. "I'll take the back."

Adam waited until Ryan was behind the house and knocked on Sabrina's door.

No answer.

He knocked again.

Still no answer.

He tried the door. Locked.

He pulled his key ring from his pocket.

Ryan emerged from the other side. "Dude, you have a key to her place? That's moving awfully fast."

"It's not like that." He slid the key into the lock and braced himself for what he might find. He opened the door and entered quickly. Ryan was on his heels.

Adam went right. "Clear."

Ryan went left. "Clear."

Sabrina's phone was on the counter beside her laptop.
But where was she?

The whole time Mr. Kemp was talking, Sabrina was pressing down her panic and shoving aside the pain and confusion. There would be time for emotions later. But only if she could get them out of this—and the only way she could do that was to outsmart this guy. He was wearing gloves and was draped in plastic. She suspected he had a plan to stage a murder-suicide. Or maybe a double homicide with the mysterious assailant remaining at large.

She studied the room, looking for a way out. Something that would help her. The problem was that there wasn't anything she could use as a weapon. There were lots of books and knickknacks but nothing sharp.

The caregivers had hidden everything that could be considered dangerous to protect Dad and themselves.

What she wouldn't give for an antique letter opener right about now.

"So you think by killing us, you'll get access to the money?" Her mom seemed skeptical.

"I know I will. I've been working on this plan for over three years. It's solid."

"And where did proposing to me fit into this solid plan of yours? Why not just kill me?" Her mom really did seem sad.

"I'm thorough," he said. "It's what has kept me in business all these years. I don't leave loose ends. I think of every contingency. Keeping you close gave me access to your files, passwords, and records. And helped me be absolutely certain that you had no idea what my role in your life had been."

He sighed. "And now it's time for that to come to an end."

Her mother gripped her hand. "I'm truly sorry, Sabrina."

33

t had taken Adam and Ryan ten seconds to decide to call in the cavalry. Sabrina never went anywhere without a phone or a computer.

"It's possible they went for a walk," Ryan said.

"It is."

"I'll take the heat if we're wrong."

They opened the gate to the drive so it would be accessible when their backup arrived and drove as far as they could, leaving Ryan's truck on the side of the driveway, hidden in the trees.

"I've never been in the house," Adam said.

"Well, lucky for you, I have. Come on." Ryan took off through the woods.

"Where are we going?"

"Around back. There's a back entrance the caregivers used—it has a keypad. Sabrina gave me the code when we were checking the house last week."

"Great."

It took them five agonizing minutes to get to the back door, and there was no way to know if they'd been seen. Or for that matter if there was anyone to see.

339

"Will the door set off a chime when we open it?" Adam scanned the area as Ryan punched in the code.

"I don't remember. We should assume that it will. Ready?"

Sabrina couldn't believe any of this was happening.

From the very beginning of her existence, this man—Mr. Kemp, if that was even his real name—had been an unseen force for evil and now he was going to end her life before she could live it. She wasn't afraid to die. But she wasn't sure if her mother—adoptive mother—was ready for eternity. She wanted to have the opportunity to show her what forgiveness and grace looked like. Assuming she could manage to give it.

She would figure out what to do with the ugliness and lies later. Right now, she just wanted to live long enough to feel the pain of the loss and sort through the hard truths of her life.

Lord, help me. Help us.

He raised his arm and pointed the gun at Sabrina. "Sorry, but it has to be you first."

"No!" Yvonne lunged at him as he fired.

"Ready!"

Ryan opened the door and Adam followed him in.

The sound of a gunshot rang out and he didn't even hear the chime.

He followed Ryan as they moved through the house. Quickly but cautiously. They had no idea who the bad guys were, how many of them there were, or what they were running into.

Sirens filled the air around them as deputies arrived. But were they too late?

Another shot rang out and Adam ran past Ryan and into the den.

Mr. Kemp's first shot hit her mother, but her mother's momentum carried her into him and he stumbled. Sabrina reached behind her and grabbed the only thing she'd been able to see that could be a weapon. The brass elephant from the sofa table. It weighed a good fifteen pounds. She stood and heaved it at Mr. Kemp as he fired again.

Pain sliced through her leg and she couldn't stay on her feet. She fell to the floor.

Another shot, but this one sounded different.

"Don't move!"

Adam? She couldn't see him, but that was definitely Adam's voice. What was he doing there? How had he found her?

"Don't do it!"

Another shot rang out. This one was so close her ears rang. But there was no impact—no new pain. Had he shot her mother again? Was she alive? Why was everything blurry around the edges?

Adam's face appeared in her fading vision.

"Sabrina!"

34

S abrina!"
   She wasn't responding.
   Blood was everywhere.
Adam pressed down hard on her leg. He'd rather hurt her than lose her. "Come on, Bri. Hang in there."

Ryan was working on Sabrina's mother. A huge red circle was spreading on her abdomen. She was gasping for air.

The paramedics raced in and took over. Adam recognized their voices before he remembered their faces. Clark's deep register would be in his mind forever. He was with Ryan.

"Oh, Dr. Fleming. Not you again." Dorothy knelt beside him. "Keep the pressure on there."

"Is she going to be okay?"

Dorothy didn't answer, and her silence terrified him more than anything he'd seen in the last few minutes.

Dorothy was a tiny little thing and young, but she took over in a way that both impressed and frightened him. In less than a minute, Sabrina was on a stretcher and the paramedics were running out of the house with her. He was right behind them.

"I don't have room for you in the back, sir." Dorothy fixed him with a firm look. "We're headed to Carrington Memorial. You know the way."

And with that, the driver slammed the doors and flew down the driveway.

The second ambulance followed moments later.

Ryan grabbed his arm. "I'll drive."

35

Sabrina had survived so much in the last few weeks. Adam had been her rock. He'd been put on administrative leave for killing Kemp, and even though he'd been under investigation, he'd refused to leave her side while she recovered. She'd lost a lot of blood, but the wound itself had been quite minor. If Adam hadn't been there to apply pressure, the outcome could have been quite different. But with a few transfusions and some quick surgery, she'd recovered quickly.

But then the truly hard things began. He'd been with her when they took her mother—she would always think of her as her mother—off life support the day after Christmas. He'd been by her side when she'd agreed to allow the hospital to use her mother's body as a tissue donor. It had been her mother's wish and she saw no reason to disagree.

Even after he'd been cleared to go back to work, he'd sat with her through hours of interviews with the sheriff's office as they tried to sort out what had happened.

He'd taken care of getting her dad's house cleaned up. He'd held her when she cried but couldn't tell him why she was crying.

She'd leaned on him at the graveside service on New Year's Eve.

Two graves.

Two lives separated yet connected.

She'd insisted they bury her brother beside their father. Her mother went on the other side. She didn't think they would mind.

The service had been brief and somber. When it was over, Adam had stood by her side as people came by. Abby Campbell was first. She reached for her hand and squeezed. "We're here, Sabrina. Whatever you need."

"Thank you."

Art stepped toward her and kissed her cheek. "You aren't alone, Sabrina. I hope you know that."

All she could do was nod.

Grandfather Campbell put one hand on her left shoulder and one hand on Adam's right. "We're so sorry for your losses, dear." He looked at Adam. "You take good care of her." He winked at Sabrina. "If he messes up, you let me know. I'll sort him out."

"Yes, sir."

He squeezed her arm and stepped away.

Grandmother Campbell stood across from her, and even in that setting she was an imposing figure. Perfectly coiffed hair. A handkerchief in one hand. Her purse clutched in the other. Sabrina was shocked to see her. After all the details of her family's sordid story had gone public, she'd rather expected Grandmother Campbell to refuse to acknowledge her in any way.

Adam had tensed as she took a step closer and patted Sabrina's hand. "It is right and appropriate to grieve for them. No matter what they've done. No matter how many mistakes they made. It's complicated and messy, but that's what families are." She made a little tsk noise. "I expect to see you at Sunday lunch in January. If you're well enough to stand out here in this freezing cold, you can certainly sit at the table, so don't try to make excuses."

Sabrina was so stunned that she couldn't think of anything to say other than "Yes, ma'am."

Grandmother Campbell patted Adam's cheek and winked at him. Then stepped away.

Leigh and Ryan were next, with hugs and reminders of food and fellowship waiting for them later.

Then Gabe, who shoved Anissa in front of him. Anissa had been conspicuously absent over the last few weeks, but Adam had said he'd seen her at their mandatory sessions with other law enforcement officers who'd been involved in shootings and Sabrina understood why she'd stayed away.

"I'm so sorry," Anissa whispered and turned away. Sabrina grabbed her and wrapped her in a hug. "You saved my life. He was confused and wrong, and he would have kept going until he'd succeeded in killing me. The only person who deserves the blame for his death is Kemp. Not you. Please don't take on a guilt you don't deserve."

Anissa had hugged her for a long time. No one had seemed to feel there was a need to rush. Gabe's usual fast-paced approach to life had been missing as he stood there. When Anissa stepped back, he produced a handkerchief, which she took with a grateful nod. He'd nodded at both Sabrina and Adam and followed her to where she was being hugged by Leigh.

The captain and the sheriff had come. Her new buddy Dave. Even the paramedics, Clark and Dorothy.

Someone had told her once that funerals weren't for the dead, but for the living. And for someone who'd done most of her living alone, the outpouring of affection and compassion had been humbling and eye-opening.

She'd never been more alone in her life—her father's entire family was dead and her mother's family had refused to come to the funeral to avoid being associated with any form of scandal—but somehow she knew Art was right. She wasn't truly alone.

Adam picked her up on Sunday and they went to the early service at church. It was a surprisingly mild January day, and when they left church he told her he had a little surprise.

"But we have to be at lunch—" Not that she wasn't completely terrified about that prospect.

"We have plenty of time."

Adam drove them to Leigh's house, but instead of going in the house, he led her down the path that led from the driveway to the lake. "Come on. I got permission." They walked to the dock and Adam climbed aboard Leigh's boat.

"We're going out on the lake? Now?"

"Why not?" Adam grinned at her.

"Okay." What was he up to? She climbed aboard and settled herself on the wide seat at the back.

Adam skillfully maneuvered the boat into deep water and cruised up the lake for a few minutes before cutting the engine in an isolated cove. He let the boat bob on the water as he climbed into the back with her.

"I love you, Sabrina Fleming." He planted feather-light kisses on her eyelids.

"I love you too." All the doubts she'd felt before were gone. He was hers. She was his.

It was ridiculous that it had taken such harsh circumstances for her to be so sure, but as his kisses moved from her eyelids to her cheeks, she couldn't remember why she'd ever doubted they would work as a couple. "You're just doing this to try to convince me that lunch with your family is a good idea. Not that I'm complaining." She reached for his face and pulled his lips to hers.

He kissed her so completely that she wasn't sure where she was anymore. The boat could have floated onto the shore and she wouldn't have noticed. When he pulled away, he didn't go far but pressed his forehead to hers. "Let's skip lunch."

"Very funny."

"I'm not joking. My family is important, but not more important than you. You come first. Always and forever. Know that."

"I do."

"Hmm. I'd love to hear you say those words again, in a slightly more formal setting." He slid from the seat and knelt before her. In his hand was a ring so stunning it nearly took her breath. A large brilliant-cut diamond was nestled in a collar of smaller diamonds and set in a classic platinum band. "I know this may seem sudden, but it isn't. I've loved you for two years. I was an idiot not to tell you that the first time I saw you, but I'm not going to waste any more time. I want to be with you and no one but you, for better or worse, forever. Will you marry me?"

He asked the question like he wasn't sure of her answer. Did he really think she would say anything other than yes?

She put her arms around his neck. "I love you." She couldn't resist kissing the lips that would be hers forever.

He returned the kiss but after a ridiculously short amount of time, he pushed her back. His eyes were full of love and laughter when he said, "Is that a yes? Because if that's a no, I'm really confused."

"Yes. Always yes."

He slid the ring onto her finger. "Now, where were we?"

They were late for lunch.

Lynn H. Blackburn is the author of *Beneath the Surface*, *Hidden Legacy*, and *Covert Justice*, winner of the 2016 Selah Award for Mystery and Suspense and the 2016 Carol Award for Short Novel. Blackburn believes in the power of stories, especially those that remind us that true love exists, a gift from the Truest Love. She's passionate about CrossFit, coffee, and chocolate (don't make her choose) and experimenting with recipes that feed both body and soul. She lives in South Carolina with her true love, Brian, and their three children.

"LEIGH'S ABILITY TO RESCUE HERSELF, RYAN'S
RESPECT AND SUPPORT, AND A TERRIFIC CAST OF
LAW-ENFORCEMENT AND HOSPITAL PERSONNEL MAKE
THIS VIVID START OF **BLACKBURN'S DIVE TEAM
INVESTIGATIONS** SERIES A REAL PAGE-TURNER."

—Booklist

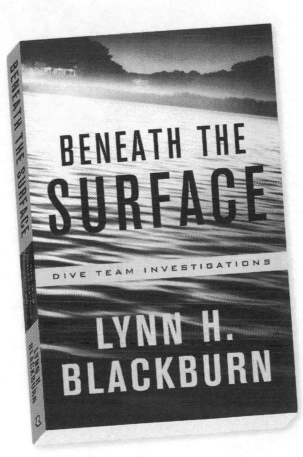